YOU'RE ALWAYS WITH ME

D1585624

ANDY MASLEN

TYTON PRESS

ALSO BY ANDY MASLEN

Torpedo

Three Kingdoms

Ivory Nation

Crooked Shadow

Brass Vows (coming soon)

Other Fiction

Blood Loss – A Vampire Story

Purity Kills

For Dan Meron,
who helped me discover the truth.

'A first visit to a madhouse is always a shock.'
Anna Freud

PART I

DREAMS AND
NIGHTMARES

1

Mel

It's my last therapy session of the day.

I'm tired, and the smell of the psych ward — disinfectant and unwashed bodies — has taken up residence in my sinuses.

But I paste a welcoming smile on one last time. It's important.

The puffy-eyed woman who sits down opposite me has the doughy complexion and suddenly gained weight of the heavily medicated.

This is our first session together. I experience the same thrill I feel whenever I have someone new to work with. It's an intoxicating mixture of anticipation and, if I'm honest, nervousness. I am hired by the psychiatrists who run this place to work with their patients and make them well. Failure, I tell myself, is not an option. Though this adds unnecessary pressure to what is already a pretty stressful job.

Don't get me wrong. I love my work. I know, I know, it's such a cliché to say it, but I do genuinely believe I was put on this Earth to help people.

I introduce myself, as I always do, with a simple sentence followed by an even simpler question. A rudimentary social exchange that even very young children manage to work out for themselves.

'Hello, my name's Mel. What's yours?'

I know her name, of course. But giving clients an easy way in to what can be a long and troubling conversation is vital to the therapeutic process.

'Em,' she says.

I smile. 'Hi, Em. Is that short for something?'

She bites her lip, then nods.

'Emaline. But I hate that name.'

Em it is then.

'Tell me why you're here, Em,' I say.

And we're off.

An hour later, Em leaves and so do I. Though while she returns to the rounded corners and locked doors of the psychiatric ward, I drive to my consulting rooms at the Lavender Therapy Centre in Hammersmith.

Altogether, there are six of us. There's me, with my specialisation in the emotional and psychological problems that can affect new or soon-to-be mothers. Alan Ogilvy, a psychotherapist specialising in PTSD. Charmian Bernbach, German, as her name suggests, who's a Reiki healer and naturopath. Suzannah Saatchi, aromatherapy massage. Henry Abbott, a lovely old Irishman who offers Jungian psychoanalysis. And Alicia Trott, a hypnotherapist.

We see each other in the mornings and evenings as we arrive and leave after the last of our clients has departed.

Occasionally a free hour will coincide and one or two of us will meet for a coffee and a sandwich in a nearby cafe. But on the whole, it's a fairly solitary life.

Solitary! I know, that sounds strange, right? How could it be solitary when every hour is spent in the company of another human being? One who really needs us to be there for them?

Of course, it isn't solitary in the physical sense. Although, sometimes, I do find myself wishing, just for a moment or two, that I could have some space.

What I mean is, each of us, me, Alan, Suzannah, Charmian, Henry and Alicia, we exist in our own parallel worlds within the centre's four walls, each listening, massaging, questioning, healing but never truly in company. We're with our clients but they're not really with *us*, if you know what I mean? They're with themselves, or, more usually, with the person or persons whose words and actions caused them such pain and trauma that they've beaten a path to our door.

2

_____

Mel

I have been seeing Em once a week for two months now. Dr Silverman has adjusted her medication and outwardly, at least, she's regained a little humanity. With her hair washed and brushed, and a little makeup, she is an attractive brunette. She has darting, intelligent eyes and a quick temper.

Leaving aside the psychiatric diagnosis that led to her being sectioned, she is very like me. In fact, she's similar to a lot of the women I have worked and socialised with over the years. She is a married, middle-class, professional woman. She is articulate. And she presents as perfectly normal.

Our initial sessions were long silences, punctuated by bouts of crying and agitation. Twice I had to call for an orderly to restrain her. Once, during a particularly bad piece of acting out, Dr Silverman had to come and administer a sedative.

But gradually, I think she learned to trust me, and therefore to relax. As she did so, she began to tell me about herself.

Sometimes, as I probe the stories she tells me, she lashes out, not physically, but with a sharp tongue. Asks me what gives me the right to rootle – her word – around in her psyche like an old woman scrabbling through the bargain bedlinen in the Harrods sale.

And I tell her, patiently, about my qualifications; the diploma that hangs in a black frame on the wall of my consulting room. I explain that our weekly sessions are under the supervision of her psychiatrist, Dr Silverman, and he would hardly hire me if he didn't trust me.

And what a tale she tells me.

She says she was abused as a child. By her stepfather. It left her with a conflicted attitude to sex. On the one hand she finds it terrifying, because it stirs up all those awful, traumatising memories of the abuse. On the other hand, she craves it because, for her, it symbolises affection and is bound up with her ideas of self-worth and self-esteem.

Em tells me that her husband is controlling. Within a month of the wedding he had, and I quote, 'got me pregnant'. She says he saw it as a triumph. Vindication of his manhood, which, needless to say, is what we in the psychotherapeutic world classify as toxic.

After her baby was born, she succumbed to deep post-natal depression. Her husband tried everything, up to and including a private GP, who prescribed a range of medication, but to no avail. Finally, feeling he had no option if he was to save her and protect his child, he had her sectioned.

Or at least, this is her story. Dr Silverman has explained to me that, in fact, it's all inside her head.

We covered it during my training. It's a variation of Munchausen's Syndrome. In the classic presentation, patients make themselves physically ill, or at least claim to be, so they can receive medical treatment. It's a cry for help, really, a way of becoming the centre of attention when normally they're ignored, unseen, invisible.

In the psycho-emotional presentation, patients, though we call them clients, present with a range of psychological symptoms – anxiety, depression, feelings of hopelessness or paranoia. They engage a therapist and, for an hour a week, or more if they can afford it, they become the centre of the therapist's universe. But it's all false. A fake. A con. Saddest of all is that the people they're really fooling are themselves.

I don't think this describes Em. I think she really does have a range of interconnected, deep-rooted problems. Of which her delusions are a part.

I also believe that with my help she can work through them and discover her true self.

In time.

3

Mel

I have just finished a large glass of wine.

Drinking after work isn't something I generally resort to. But something about today's session with Em left me on edge, a feeling I couldn't shake even after a call with my mentor.

On the drive home from the hospital, I'd decided to discuss it with Jonathan, my husband, but he texted me to say he had a client dinner. He's a banker. One of those mysterious people who make money by making money, if you know what I mean. Extremely well paid, incredibly stressed and, just at the moment, almost never around.

Which is a shame, because I could really do with a shoulder to cry on.

Why was I drinking Pinot Grigio at the kitchen table, and flicking through my Facebook feed when I should have been doing yoga or going for a walk? Because Em was in a combative mood today.

I'd asked her about her baby. Given that the child is a total fabrication, part of the delusional architecture, as we call it, that both hampers her recovery and reinforces what she believes to be her sanity, I wanted to find a way to explore the issues that led her to 'give birth' to him.

'Tell me about him,' I said.

She glared at me, those bright eyes not darting around the room for once but fixing me like a butterfly under a collector's pin.

'Do you have any children of your own, Doctor?'

I smile my reassuring smile. 'You know I'm not a doctor. You can call me Mel.'

She cocks her head on one side and asks again.

'Well? Do you?'

I shake my head. It's actually a bit of a sore point. I'd quite like to try for a baby, but Jonathan simply doesn't have the time, he says, or, frankly, the energy.

'It's not a good time, darling,' he says when I suggest it again. 'Amélie's set us these impossible targets. She's riding us like bloody racehorses. Maybe next month, yes?'

Amélie's his boss. French, as her name suggests. And by all accounts, a pedigree bitch.

I look at Em, holding her gaze but keeping my own friendly, non-confrontational.

'One day I hope to.'

'Why not now?'

'It's not a good time.'

She snorts. 'It's never a good time. You should have it all out,' she spits, gesturing at her own abdomen. 'Make sure you can't – ever.'

This isn't helpful. I try to move the conversation along.

'How is your husband coping with childcare?'

She rolls her eyes.

'How should I know? I'm not sure if you've noticed, but I can't actually see my house from here.'

This is one of those locked doors in her psyche that we need to open. You see, the reason she doesn't know how her husband is coping is because there's no child to care for, is there?

Then a tear wells at the inner corner of her left eye, rolls over the lid and tracks down over her cheek before plopping onto her shoulder. Something about the way she doesn't even attempt to brush it away, despite the fact that it must tickle, bothers me.

'I do know, Mel,' she says, sniffing. 'And I'm sorry for being rude just now.'

Is this it, I wonder? Have we reached a turning point?

'Go on,' I say quietly. 'Tell me.'

'Justin doesn't need to worry about childcare because…'

She stops, sniffs and then a second tear begins its snail-like progress down her cheek. The right one this time, as though, like Shirley Temple was apparently able to, she can control which eye she cries out of.

Should I prompt her or remain silent and let her resume when she's ready? Laypeople always assume we therapists are bottomless wells of compassion, able to sit in Trappist silence for hours on end while we wait for our patients to divulge this titbit or that. But in reality? No, sometimes we get impatient.

'Because…'

'I killed him,' she whispers, looking down at her lap, where she is unpicking the stitching on a battered old teddy bear.

I maintain a professional calm. Inside, I am rejoicing. This is a breakthrough! Obviously, she hasn't murdered anyone. I think we'd have heard from the police by now. But it's a dramatic shift in her narrative. And that marks progress.

'Justin?' I ask.

She shakes her head.

'Harry.'

I admit, I was not expecting her to claim she had murdered her own baby. It's so profound, this admission of the worst crime a mother can commit, that even though the entire episode is fantasy, it shakes me.

That was three hours ago. She was my last appointment at the hospital and I returned to my treatment rooms at the Lavender Therapy Centre in Hammersmith. Fortunately I had no private clients either and could catch up with paperwork.

I look at my empty glass. Then at the bottle. It's one third empty. These modern glasses are deceptive. *Just one*, we say to ourselves, but that single glass is enough to start us down the slippery path to oblivion. I, though, am not a drunk. My relationship with alcohol is perfectly normal. I just happen, this particular evening, to need another glass.

If Jonathan were here, he'd share the bottle with me as he told me about his day. But he's in Dubai. There's a lot of what he calls 'high-end M&A action' out there at the moment.

4

Dr Nathan Silverman FRSPsych

My patient, whom I will call F, is pleasant, intelligent and, outwardly, perfectly sane. No raving or wild-eyed lashing out at the staff.

F was admitted to the residential psychiatric unit I manage two and a half years ago in the grip of a severe psychotic illness.

Since then, I have been treating her with a multi-modal regime of drug and talking therapies, complemented with the sort of strict routine that can often engender a feeling of security in the most disturbed patients. A good diet, regular exercise and structured days including a mixture of solitary and group activities.

We have stabilised her moods with lithium, and the mixture of anti-psychotics, anti-depressants and anti-anxiety drugs have mitigated the worst of her symptoms, though with the expected range of sadly unavoidable side effects.

The talking therapies are best described as a work-in-progress, but here is the crucial point. At the moment, I believe F would present a danger to herself, and possibly members of the public, if she were to be discharged from my care. For that reason, she continues to stay with us as a resident, under the terms of her sectioning.

This may all sound rather bleak. It isn't meant to. Just honest. And there are glimmers of hope. Of light among the shadows.

As F has progressed away from most of her psychotic symptoms, though the delusions still hold her in their grip, I have linked up with a local psychotherapist to complement my own work with her. The psychotherapist specialises in emotional disorders surrounding pregnancy and motherhood. After an interview to assess her suitability and taking up her references, I decided she'd be perfect.

The psychotherapist sees F once a week and I am hopeful that, combined with my own work, the group therapy and the drugs I am prescribing, we may eventually be able to return her to the community. Eventually. It's a long road.

My office shares a wall with the common room. I have blinds that I can lower to shut myself in when I need to reduce the amount of visual stimulation – some of the patients can be frankly a little *too* visual at times. Right now the blinds are up, admitting the white light from the large rectangular space that serves as sitting room, TV room, games and rec room for the patients, of whom we currently have eighteen.

Today, F is sitting curled up in an armchair beside a radiator. There is a window above her right shoulder. It looks out onto the hospital car park. It's not ideal, but needs must in the NHS. Parkland with a winding stream and forests drawing the eye to distant hills would be preferable, but hard to arrange in urban Hammersmith.

She is talking animatedly to D, another patient. D is silent. Hardly surprising. She has Cotard's Syndrome. It's an extremely rare condition, fewer than 200 cases worldwide at the time of writing. Sufferers believe themselves to be dead, or to not even exist.

F leans forward and cocks her head to one side as if to catch what D is saying. She nods and touches her finger to the point of her chin. Good point, she mouths. (I have, over the years, become adept at lip-reading. You'd be surprised at how useful a skill it is for a psychiatrist.)

I am leaving for a conference in the US tomorrow and will resume these notes on my return.

5

Mel

I am exploring with Em, on a weekly basis now, the new story she has constructed. Like a lot of delusions, its internal architecture is amazingly consistent.

She tells me all about the nursery she found. The brand of organic baby food her baby prefers. The parks they used to visit. Even the precise shade of his bowel movements. Turmeric, if you're interested.

On the night when she says she killed him, she claims to have been found by her husband sitting beside a bath full of water, holding her baby under the surface.

But the problem for Em is that she is childless. Like me. So every time we have a conversation about her supposed infanticide, I am contributing to her delusion. And, though I shouldn't say this, I do find it hard to indulge this woman as she stares, red-eyed, at me and insists that, yes, she did kill her own child.

Somehow, talking to her every Thursday has brought my own childlessness into sharp focus. And I *would* like a baby of my own. I have resolved to talk to Jonathan about it again when he's back. I know what he'll say. 'It's not a good time.' It's what he always says. But here's my question. When *is* a good time?

I mean, it's not as if we don't have the money. That's the excuse a lot of my girlfriends used to put forwards. 'We'd love to get pregnant, but we just can't afford it,' they'd say.

And by the way? Ugh, to that whole 'we' business. Last time I checked, it was the woman who got pregnant, complete with varicose veins, backache, morning sickness and a bladder the size of a walnut. I can do without these sympathetic-looking blokes with their puppy dog eyes and turned-down mouths. *You're fine!* I want to scream. *You're not the one whose vagina is going to have to emit a bowling ball, now, is it?*

Except, neither is mine, is it?

We need to move Em on from simply discussing her fantasies. There must be some way to shake her out of the grip of this delusion. Dr Silverman hired me to work with her because of my expertise in treating women with postpartum depression and psychosis. But the trouble is, that presupposes there was a *partum* in the first place. Treating *imaginary* ailments is pushing me right to the edge of my comfort zone.

I've tried to talk to him about Em, but he seems reluctant to get involved. He is responsible for her medication, he says, and the 'overall parameters of her therapy', as he rather pompously calls it, but it is down to me to work out how to bring her to an understanding that it's all – please don't laugh – in her mind. Only then can we begin the next phase of her treatment: recovery.

I did manage to arrange a meeting between the three of us a day or so ago, at the end of our regular session. Nothing formal, just a casual chat in the lounge. I made some coffee and even brought in a cake. Dr Silverman was due in five minutes and I had to go to the loo. I told Em to wait and hurried away.

But when I got back, Dr Silverman was sitting in one of the armchairs, legs crossed ankle over knee, looking at me with an all-too-easy-to-read expression. *Well. Where is she?*

She'd left.

I found her in her room after Dr Silverman had retreated to his office and asked her why she'd vanished.

She shrugged.

'It wouldn't have helped. Besides, I don't trust him.'

'Why?'

'He looks at me like I'm nothing. Like I don't even exist.'

'Of course he doesn't!' I said, forgetting professional calm for a moment and reverting to the sort of basic thing a layperson would say.

'No? I'm just a chart to him. Meds? Check. Docile? Check. Still yakking to my therapist every Thursday? Check. Fine, she's all good.'

I could see that she was descending into one of her depressive episodes. And we were already out of time. I reassured her as best as I was able and left her in her room, picking at a loose thread on a knitted rabbit she keeps as a memento of her 'baby'.

I've dropped an email to Dr Silverman. I think we need to find a new way of working through her delusions. Because I'm starting to doubt myself. I feel anxious for the whole of the day before our meetings and it's starting to interfere with the work I'm doing with my other clients.

There must be something we haven't tried yet.

6

Nathan

My mind, as they say, has been well and truly – and literally – blown! Although I am within touching distance of my sixtieth birthday, I would like to think I am still capable of learning.

I believe, as a psychiatrist, it's essential. I have seen too many colleagues become wedded to this outdated doctrine or that fashionable explanation for mental illness, only to see their faith shattered by a new discovery from a field outside their own, narrow specialisation. (Or shall we call it back alley?)

To explain. Five days ago I flew from London to Portland, Oregon, for a conference. The meeting was titled 'New Perspectives: Mental Health and the Healing Applications of Psychedelics.'

We've known for years that psychedelic drugs alter perception and consciousness in ways we don't fully understand. The hippies were onto it in the sixties, and they were only discovering wisdoms that ancient peoples had known, and treasured, for millennia.

But not just hippies. There have been perfectly respectable academics and clinicians who have attempted to push open the doors of perception. Timothy Leary was the pioneer, with LSD. Who can forget his (in)famous slogan, 'Tune in, turn on, drop out'?

Then came John Folger with MDMA, now better known as Ecstasy. Elaine Godspeed followed with ketamine. And now, the bête noire of the political-pharmaceutical complex, Dr Flick Barber with psilocybin aka magic mushrooms.

All these visionaries have pushed for greater funding of research into the psychotherapeutic uses of so-called 'illegal' drugs. All have been vilified by politicians, insurance companies and big pharma with their entrenched suspicion of anything they can't tax, profit from or control.

The conference, then, was an attempt to bring the debate into the twenty-first century. To engage advocates, activists, clinicians, journalists and politicians in a rational, patient-centred conversation about the way forward.

To a certain extent, I think we're pushing at an open door. The recent trend towards legalising not just medical but recreational marijuana in the US has not resulted in the States filling with spaced-out zombies too stoned to pursue the American Dream.

Quite the contrary! One of the speakers was the CEO of a cannabis production company or, as he styled himself, much to the audience's amusement, a 'weedpreneur'.

But the highlight of my time in Portland was Flick Barber's keynote address, and the events to which it led. In forty-five minutes of riveting, evidence-based advocacy, she laid out a strategy for the treatment and cure of PTSD-sufferers using psilocybin.

I was fortunate enough to be seated to Flick's left at the close-of-conference dinner. Flick is short for Felicity. I suspect she'd not have to fight quite so hard if she used her full name in her dealings with regulators. She's as engaging and passionate up close as she is with a cheek mic and a laser pointer on a stage before thousands.

I asked her whether she had any associates in the UK in the psychiatric profession. Her answer, delivered in a sun-drenched Californian accent that reminded me of my time in San Francisco in the late eighties, delighted me.

'Why, Doc, you offering?'

It seems she's been looking for support on this side of the Atlantic. Although at the governmental level in the States the idea of socialised medicine is anathema, the NHS is regarded with a great deal of appreciation as one draws closer to the front line of medical science.

I suggested that if she were amenable, and able to help me design a protocol, I would be willing to lobby for a clinical trial of her psilocybin-based treatment at my own unit.

She looked at me over the rim of her martini glass.

'You ever hear that drug-world slogan, Doc?' she said, taking a sip and smacking her lips. 'Never get high on your own supply?'

I conceded that I had.

'It's bullshit!' she said, before popping the stuffed olive into her mouth. 'You can't lobby for it if you've never tried it.'

I smiled at her. 'How do you know I've never tried it?'

'Oho!' she said, before draining her glass. 'What do we have here? A respectable psychiatrist with a secret history eating shrooms at Burning Man? Or was it Glastonbury?'

Glass-don-beary.

'Knebworth, actually. Eighty-nine. I saw Cliff Richard and the Shadows.'

'Kudos,' she deadpanned. 'Seriously, though, Nate. What I and my team have formulated is about as far away from a mushroom omelette, or however you took it, as an aspirin is from willow bark.'

'Or tamoxifen is from yew tree needles?'

She nodded. 'My room. Half an hour. Don't be late.'

I wasn't. Perhaps some part of my sad, middle-aged man's ego had thought Flick might make a pass at me, and how I'd have to explain to her that I was happily married. In fact, she was all business.

The alcohol had seemingly had no effect on her and as she prepped a little infusion of clear liquid, she spoke as clearly and as articulately as she had from the lectern earlier in the day.

Flick explained that I'd need a guided trip. It was how the few experimental programmes permitted in the US had allayed the concerns of regulators and hospital ethics boards.

In my preparations for her talk, I'd done some background reading.

'So, you'll be my shaman?' I asked.

'That's about it,' she replied. 'Some folks just fly off and have a totally blissed-out time. Others have a kind of bumpy take-off. It can be a little disorienting and the guide is there to hold their hand, literally, and guide them through the clear-air turbulence into the upper atmosphere. Ready?'

I was. And in what seemed like moments later, I was flying. I don't know whether Flick's aviation-inspired language had been planned all along, but I entered the most transcendent state of wellbeing I have ever experienced.

I felt I was an eagle, or at least a man with an eagle's sensory acuity and weightlessness, soaring high above the Earth. Everything made sense to me and somehow I could see the answers to all the problems facing me in my professional and clinical career.

Chief among them was F's treatment-resistant psychosis.

* * *

The aroma of freshly brewed coffee woke me. I opened my eyes, blinking in a thin sliver of sunlight entering the hotel room between the deep-golden curtains.

Flick was kneeling beside me, fully dressed, holding a white mug under my nose.

I straightened. I was lying on the couch in her hotel room, beneath the throw she'd taken from the bed. I still wore my shirt and underwear from the day before. My suit trousers and jacket were hanging on the outside of the wardrobe door and my shoes were nestled side by side underneath an armchair like newlyweds.

I gestured at the clothes on the wardrobe door.

'Did you…'

She shook her head and smiled that wide, eye-crinkling smile she's famous for. The one that gets her on the covers of otherwise boring pharmaceutical and psychiatric journals. 'Alternative Pharma's Answer to Farrah Fawcett on the Magic of Mushrooms', one gushing, if culturally dated, headline had it.

'*You* did. I combined the sillo with a little light hypnosis, just to smooth off the rough edges. You got a little antsy at one point, said you wanted to go home to Rebecca. That's your wife, right?'

'Of thirty-five years, next Tuesday.'

'*Mazel tov!*'

She had to catch an early flight back to San Diego, but we agreed to correspond via email to set up the trial, assuming I could secure the necessary approval.

7

Mel

I'm so excited. It seems my email did some good, after all.

Em has been selected to undergo a revolutionary new drug treatment. As her therapist, I'm to accompany her on what I, and her doctors, all hope will be the start of a one-way journey to wellness.

She's lying on a couch. I'm sitting at her head, ready to hold her hand if she needs comfort.

We make a strange quartet. Dr Silverman looks exactly like what he is, an NHS consultant psychiatrist in a tweed jacket and well-worn 501s, his blue lanyard and ID lying against his chest. His associate from America is something else entirely.

Dr Barber looks entirely too glamorous to be a clinician. Or a scientist, for that matter. The most amazing thing about her is her hair. It's sun-bleached and tousled, and it reaches halfway down her back. She has glittering blue eyes, like sun sparkling off the sea. I may have a faint girl-crush on her, though I think I am doing a decent job of hiding it.

'How are you doing?' I ask Em in a whisper.

She looks up at me and nods. Smiles. I see a faint tremor in the muscle beneath the fine line extending from her nose to the corner of her mouth.

'OK. A bit nervous.'

'That's perfectly all right,' I say, in as comforting a voice as I can manage.

'Sure it is, honey,' Dr Barber says. 'I always get a little,' she waggles her head, setting her hair swinging, 'wobbly before I fly anywhere on a trip, and this is a big one. That's why I'm here. I'll guide you and deliver you back to earth all safe and sound.'

I look down at Em. She seemed reassured by Dr Barber's words, even if they are delivered in this sort of drawling surfer accent that makes me think of *Baywatch*.

It's time for Em to take the drug. I must show my surprise because Dr Barber laughs, softly. 'What, you weren't expecting me to give her a handful of raw mushrooms, were ya?'

I shrug. 'Sorry, Dr Barber. I'm not sure what I was expecting to be honest.'

Her sea-blue eyes widen. 'Hey! Enough with the "Doctor Barber" already. Only my mom calls me that. Call me Flick or get the hell out!'

I start to apologise again, and this time her laughter is louder. It's infectious, too. Dr Silverman and then Em join in, and soon we're all laughing. I wonder if we're about to engage in some sort of group hysteria. But Flick snaps us back to the present. And the business at hand.

'OK, honey. You ready to walk free again?' Em nods.

Flick hands her the tiny glass vial of clear liquid. 'Like it says in *Alice in Wonderland*, "Drink me".'

I watch her bring the vial to her lips, hesitate, just for a second, then tip her head back, empty the liquid into her mouth, and swallow.

She lies back against the cushions and closes her eyes. Dr Silverman is recording everything, on video and on a separate audio app on his phone. I find I'm holding my breath and let it out in a controlled hiss.

Em stretches out her hand, seeking mine. We interlace fingers and she squeezes lightly, just once, then relaxes. I close my eyes, too, trying to imagine what she must be experiencing. What she's seeing.

'Do you know why you're here?' Flick asks, in a soft voice, a couple of tones deeper than her usual speaking voice.

Em answers in a matching, deep tone.

'I killed my baby. I couldn't handle it. I lost my mind.'

'Do you know when?'

So Flick's approach is to allow Em to believe in her delusion. At least for a while longer.

'It was last month. January the twenty-sixth.'

'Which year?'

'This year.'

'Are you sure?'

'Of course I'm sure. I wouldn't forget something like that, would I?'

'Honey, it was 2019. You got the date right, but not the year.'

'Oh. OK. Yes, you're right.'

'I want you to picture him, can you do that?'

'Of course I can! Can I pick him up?'

'Go ahead, he's your baby.'

Em speaks in a different voice now. Higher-pitched,

31

cooing, as if she's speaking to a baby. Her mouth's so close it seems her voice is echoing inside my head. I don't want to open my eyes in case somehow I break the spell. She's accessing deep-seated memories of the most traumatic day of her life.

'Hey, little one, hey,' she says. 'Let's get you up. We'll go to the park and look at the ducks.'

She continues to talk to him, sometimes little more than babbling, and I imagine her looking down at her infant son, getting him ready for a trip to the park, poking chubby hands into the sleeves of a snow suit, maybe tickling him under his chin.

Flick's voice breaks in.

'Can you look at him closely?'

'Mm-hmm.'

'Now, you're going to notice something about him, but when you do, you will not panic, you will stay incredibly focused on him and your surroundings.

'You're going to take it all in, every incredible detail. Every stitch in the thread lining his clothes, every fine hair on his cheek, the tiny pink cuticles on his fingernails, each individual eyelash. You're going to feel such love for your son.

'But you're going to understand something about him and you're going to understand something about yourself at exactly the same time. Yes, you did kill him. But you were very, very ill at the time. The sleeplessness. An abnormal hormonal imbalance in your system. The postpartum depression. They dropped you all the way down into the abyss. He's dead, but you can hold him in your heart and you can go on living. Look now.'

This isn't how I thought Flick would play this at all. I thought we'd show Em that her memories are all false. There never *was* a baby. Alive *or* dead. But she knows what she's doing. And this is very much her show. I must be patient.

I'm holding my breath. Looking down as Emelina must be. I see a baby. *My* baby. So beautiful. In his burnt-orange and teal snowsuit we paid such a ridiculous lot of money for online. His eyes are closed. I know he's dead. And just like Em, under Flick's guidance, I realise that I can move on. I don't have to stay locked into that moment of bottomless grief.

Em and I scream together.

I feel her hand tighten on mine. So hard I fear she'll crack the bones.

I realise I've lost all track of time. How long has Em been gone on her trip? I hope they had enough space on the hard drive to capture it all.

I open my eyes. To find I'm looking at the ceiling. I must have fainted at some point. I'm on my back on Dr Silverman's couch. He's sitting a few feet from me. Flick is by his side, and they're both looking down at me, with what I would describe as hopeful smiles.

I raise myself onto my elbows. There's no sign of Em. She must have run out. The shock of it.

'Hey,' Flick, says to me. 'How are you feeling?'

'I'm fine,' I hear myself saying. 'Did I faint? It is quite hot in here.'

She smiles. 'No, honey, you didn't faint.'

I frown. I look at Dr Silverman. He's smiling too, though there's something else going on in that expression. Something I'm groping towards.

'Hello, Mel,' he says. 'How was your trip?'

8

Mel

The next day, and each day for three more after that, I go to meet with Dr Silverman in his office. I feel as if I've been acting in a play that lasted for two and a half years.

Little by little, he explains what happened to me. How the post-natal depression I suffered deepened into full-blown psychosis. And as the memories flood back, I look back fondly on the agony of giving birth. It was the last time I felt fully human. You see, Harry didn't sleep.

If it was just the daytime naps, I think I'd have coped. But Harry didn't sleep at night, either. I mean, obviously, he slept. Sometimes for as long as two hours at a time. I'd eventually get him down at around 11.30 p.m. and just collapse into bed. Between then and 5.00 a.m., Harry would wake up three or four times a night, crying, and then screaming.

I drifted through my days like a zombie. Jonathan was

back at work after taking a week's paternity leave. Jonathan works for a French bank in Canary Wharf. He deals with clients. Wining and dining the high rollers to bring in business.

The post-natal depression didn't kick in straight away. Not like some poor women who are plunged into the depths as soon as they come round from the pain relief.

No. My black ghost crept into the house while I staggered from one mug of coffee to the next. Stealthy as creeping mould in an unventilated bathroom, it wrapped its tendrils about me and threaded them into my brain. By the time I realised what was happening to me, it was too late.

Jonathan was sympathetic. But he was incredibly busy with work. He had client dinners two or three times a week. Sometimes more. He had to go. The bank pays him a lot: they expect him to work whenever he's needed, which is all the time.

In the end, he took me to the doctor. We have a private GP. Jonathan says we're actually doing everyone who uses the NHS a favour by opting out. He says someone more deserving can have our place in the queue. 'And we still pay our taxes so it's double-bubble for them,' he says.

I found it hard, at first. The private medicine thing, I mean. We come from such different backgrounds, Jonathan and I. My parents were hard-working, respectable working class. Dad was a welder at a factory down the road and Mum cleaned offices. But Jonathan's folks, well, if they're not actually upper class then they're within spitting distance. Not that Angela and Gordon would ever do anything as vulgar as spit.

Jonathan had to come in with me. At that point, I was practically catatonic. The doctor wrote me out a prescription for anti-depressants.

The tablets did work. In a way. The blackness faded to a sort of grey. And I managed to deal with Harry. I fed him, changed him, took him to the park. But I felt as if someone had wrapped me in a veil. Light and sound could get through but nothing else. No feelings. No sense of joy that I saw on all the other mums' faces. I just functioned. Like a robot. A mumbot.

But Harry still woke constantly in the night. I got so desperate I even asked Jonathan if we could have a night nanny. At the start I'd have looked down my nose at any woman who couldn't manage her own child. But after three months, I was ready to hire anyone who promised me a single night of unbroken sleep.

Jonathan said no. It wasn't the money, he said. It was the principle. I'd been the one who wanted a baby after all. He said if I couldn't look after my own baby what was the point? Really? Why not just give it up for adoption? He was right, as always. So I persevered.

Then, one night, or, technically I suppose it was morning, Jonathan came out of the spare room where he'd taken to sleeping, and found me in the bathroom. He told me what happened. I drowned Harry in his bath. It happened exactly the way I'd projected onto Em.

They sectioned me that same night. Poor Jonathan was out of his mind with grief. He lost his son and his wife at the same time.

I feel hollowed out. The grief for Harry is there, but it's like a weight on my back. I can feel the drag of it, slowing me down as I try to climb out of the hole I've been living in. But I can't really see it. I can't reach it.

At night, while I lie awake, I say his name, over and over again, trying to bring him back to me as vividly as he appeared during the magic mushroom trip. But he's just a faint image, an *idea* of a baby.

I try to force myself to cry. But when tears do, eventually, come they feel fake, like a Hollywood method actor thinking about a tragedy to make themselves cry on demand.

Despite what's happened, despite *everything* that's happened, knowing I killed my own child, knowing I was sectioned by my own husband, I feel back in myself. I feel *me* again. Everything I experienced was a delusion. The retraining, the therapy centre, all of it. It was here.

Dr Silverman tells me that sometimes I 'counsel' my fellow patients. He says I've been particularly attracted to a poor girl called April. She has a terrible illness where she thinks she's dead. She sits and listens to me for hours on end apparently. I suspect she was 'Em'.

And he shows me how clever my delusional self has been. He writes out my name in big block capitals on a whiteboard.

MELANIE

And then, beneath them, he writes out another name:

EMALINE

'Do you notice anything about your name and Emaline's?' he asks me in a gentle voice that makes me want to cry.

I stare and stare. And then, I see. I stand up, cross over to stand beside him at the whiteboard and, silently, hold out my hand for the marker, with its pungent acetone smell.

I place the tip of the pen on the first letter of my name, and I draw a slightly wobbly line down and sloping to the right until it runs into the second letter of Emaline's. I repeat the process six more times and then I hand back the pear-drop-smelling marker and resume my seat.

Dr Silverman joins me.

'You've been calling yourself Emaline since you arrived,' he says. 'It's not uncommon in people living with dissociative personality disorders. Even as their self fractures into multiples personalities, some trace of control often remains. It's as if there's someone trying to resolve everything, giving the new selves the same initials as them, or using anagrams, as you did. Claire/Carlie, perhaps, or Warren/Warner. The fact you called her Em makes it even more obvious.'

I ask him what happens now. Am I free to go? To leave this place and go home? He explains that there's a certain amount of work to do first, not least assessing the extent to which the psilocybin has 'fixed' me. He goes on to explain how in the US soldiers with debilitating PTSD have been cured in just a single trip, so he is very hopeful.

'What about Jonathan?' I blurt out. I realise I haven't even thought of him. 'Has he been visiting? I have no memory of his coming here.'

Then I stop myself. Of course I haven't! I have no memory of even *being* here. For the last couple of years, I've been inhabiting an entirely fictional world where I'm a successful psychotherapist.

The reality is, I was an account manager for an advertising agency. I think back to my former 'colleagues' at the Lavender Therapy Centre. And their surnames. Ogilvy, Bernbach, Saatchi, Abbott and Trott. Famous admen, every one of them. I gather from my conversations with Dr Silverman that the agency terminated my contract some time back. I can't blame them.

'Jonathan came every week for the first few months, but you became first upset, then angry and, I'm afraid, eventually violent,' Dr Silverman says. 'We agreed his visits were counterproductive. I've been sending him regular reports and we speak on the phone every month or so.'

'Does he still love me?' I ask, suddenly desperate to believe that though I have lost everything, including myself, for two and a half years, my husband, at least, still holds me in his heart.

Dr Silverman smiles, sadly, I think. 'That's a little above my pay grade, I'm afraid. But let's fix up a meeting. You can start to explore your feelings for each other again.'

'He doesn't know?' I ask, shocked. 'I thought you'd have told him straight away.'

'I wanted to give you a few days to settle down. I'll be honest with you, Mel, this is the first time I've ever worked with psilocybin. The ethics committee at the hospital is, as you can imagine, desperately concerned to ensure that we have the strictest protocols in place. I didn't inform Jonathan because I didn't want to raise false hopes before we'd thoroughly tested you and documented the entire process.'

It makes sense, I think to myself. Dr Silverman tells me he's putting me through an intensive round of individual and group therapy, to explore the traumas that led to my being sectioned. It makes sense. Though I am dreading it.

9

Jonathan

Harry completed our little family.

But we had a rocky couple of months after he was born. For a big lad, he didn't seem to need much sleep. Mel took it pretty hard. At first I thought it was just a touch of the baby blues.

I did what I could, getting up to do the night feeds with the breast milk she expressed with that dreadful little pump. But Mel's depression got worse. I had to pretty much take over looking after Harry full time. I took extended paternity leave from the bank, about which, believe me, they were *not* happy. Amélie Aubert, *la grande* boss, called me from the Mothership in Avenue Kléber.

'Jonathan, how do you expect me to hit our quarterly targets without you?'

I did my best to explain the situation, but her contempt was practically squirting out of my ear bud.

'Do you not have nannies in England?'

I tried again. Explained how, despite everything, Mel still felt it should be her, as Harry's mother, who looked after him. We just needed some time to get her back on her feet and I'd be back at my desk.

'Please, Amélie,' I said. 'I'll make it up to you. I promise. First thing when I'm back, I'll call Ibrahim Al-Janabi at the National Investment Commission of Iraq and restart our relationship.' I adopted a jokey old-time American accent and said, 'There's gold in them thar hills.'

My charm worked. She laughed in that way she has. The one that has the middle-aged old farts from the Financial Conduct Authority eating out of her soft-skinned palm.

'Fine,' she said. 'Go play at Happy Families with your lovely Melanie. But as soon as she is better, I want you at your desk. On the phone. Making money for Lemaire et Monceau.'

I knew she'd give in. What choice did she have? Firing me for wanting a little extra pat leave would have been like cutting her arm off because she had a touch of tennis elbow.

I'm not ashamed to admit that I struggled at first. I suppose I'm not what you'd call a natural father. Don't get me wrong, I loved the little guy. But at that age, well, it's pretty much an unbroken stream, and I use that word advisedly, of piss, shit, snot and vomit.

I'd spend ages getting him dressed and looking his best, zipping him into his snow suit, strapping him into his buggy, a very expensive one, by the way, constructed from aviation-grade aluminium and Kevlar with run-flat tyres, the works. And he'd get this furious, concentrating look on his face, cheeks darkening to a sort of cherry red, eyes bulging and watery, and then he'd relax and smile up at me, and I'd know he'd just filled his nappy.

I got used to it. I even made a kind of sport of it. How fast could I get him cycled through from front door to the changing table in the nursery, cleaned up, re-nappied, dressed and out again? Record time, four minutes, seventeen.

Anyway, shit happens, right? Joke.

Then I'd take him up to Richmond Park in the Range Rover. That was the bit I did enjoy. Harry did, too. I'd push him around looking at the deer, or people on horseback. We'd go to the cafe and I'd grab a coffee and a Florentine, read the *FT* on my phone, while he gummed his way through a banana.

Amazing the number of yummy-mummies who eye up a guy on his own with a baby. It's the ultimate irony. The one accessory that makes you sexually desirable to practically every woman on the planet renders you unavailable.

I'd smile back, maybe exchange a few words about our respective charges. Share parenting tips, stuff we'd read in a magazine or online. Then it would be time for someone to change a nappy or calm a screaming infant and the whole merry circus would start up all over again.

Just as I was starting to find my feet, regaining my routine after those early crazy weeks of minimum sleep, maximum chaos, I had the worst night of my entire life.

I woke up and thought I heard the bath filling. I checked the time: it was three in the morning. I got out of bed and went into the bathroom, imagining for some weird reason, that Mel had decided to have a bubble bath.

The sight that confronted me will live with me for ever. Mel was leaning over the edge of the bath, and she was holding Harry under the water. I think I screamed.

Anyway, I pulled her away and dragged Harry out but even then I knew it was hopeless.

I confess, I lost it. I threw her against the wall. I think she might have knocked herself out on the taps. Then I called the police.

Later, I had to make the heartbreaking decision to have Mel sectioned. I had no choice. Losing them both in one, awful night? It broke me.

10

Mel

I find the group therapy sessions painful at first. All that sharing doesn't come naturally to me. But, little by little, I realise I have nothing to lose by opening up. Especially when I see how much worse everybody else has had it.

I start by telling them about how Jonathan and I met. We got engaged six months to the day after our first date. It felt like a genuine meeting of minds. Well, souls, really.

Having children together seemed like the most natural thing in the world. I'd never really thought of myself as a mother until I met Jonathan. I had my career and that seemed like the way I wanted to live my life. It helped, I suppose, that a lot of my friends were also childless – child-free, we used to correct each other.

But with Jonathan, everything felt, I don't know, right, somehow. Shortly after our honeymoon, he said he knew I wanted to wait before trying for a baby, but as we loved each other so much and it felt so right, why didn't we start straightaway instead?

Jonathan and I were lucky, I suppose. That or, as he liked to say, 'just incredibly fertile'. We'd just made love for the third time that day – it was right in the sweet spot of my cycle and he'd told me he'd booked a day off work specially.

It can be so mechanical, trying to conceive, all those positions the online forums say are the best for conception. We tried a couple of times, me with my legs up towards the ceiling, but I got the giggles and Jonathan got caught up in it and lost his erection. After that we went back to the way he liked to do it and – ta-da! – it worked anyway.

I more or less breezed through my pregnancy. Yes, I had a little bit of morning sickness in my first trimester, but mostly it was just mild nausea I could breathe through or dispel with a full English breakfast, which, though I'd never enjoyed before, I found myself cooking up every morning for a month.

Jonathan took such good care of me as well. He made sure I didn't experience any stress, carefully managed my social life so it didn't put any strain on me. And even though all the research I'd done suggested that the odd little glass of red wine really wouldn't do the foetus any harm, when he suggested it would be better if I just stopped drinking altogether, I was happy enough to comply.

He even gave up himself, 'in solidarity, darling', he said as he locked the drinks cupboard and ceremonially put the little silver key on a high shelf where I couldn't reach it.

11

Jonathan

Mel's psychiatrist calls me one evening. I'm watching the rugby. Thompson has just run a try from the halfway line. I'm actually cheering when my phone rings.

'Jonathan, it's Nate Silverman. At Hammersmith Hospital. Is now a good time?'

'Go ahead, Nate,' I say, pausing the TV.

All I need to do is make sure I don't see the result online before I finish watching the match.

'It's about Melanie,' he says.

I start. 'What about her? Has she attacked one of the other patients?'

It's all I can think of.

'No, no, nothing like that. She's better,' he says.

'Better than what? Better than she has been? Better than another patient? What?'

He laughs. 'Sorry, it's been a long and stressful day. I mean, she's better. As in recovered.'

'I *beg* your pardon?'

Of all the meanings his words could have conveyed, I did not imagine – for one second – he meant this.

'Melanie has recovered.'

I am in a state of shock, I realise. I am struggling to take in his words as anything other than sound. I try again.

'How?' I ask. 'You told me her condition was intractable. That you foresaw no possibility of it ever going into remission.'

'I know, I know,' he says. He sounds like he's been drinking. 'I can't give you all the details yet, but, suffice it to say, we were able to get her onto a trial of a revolutionary new therapy and it worked.'

He invites me in to come and see Mel for myself. To witness her transformation with my own eyes, he says, in a slightly overblown phrase.

We agree I'll come in the following afternoon.

I clear the line then call a woman I first met thirty months ago.

'She's better,' I say.

'That's excellent news. Thank you.'

I unpause the match, but my heart isn't in it anymore. How could they even *think* of letting her out? After what she did?

12

Mel

On the fifth day, when I knock gently on Dr Silverman's door, there's a change in his voice as he asks me to come in. I hear it at once. He's tense. The normally soft edges of his voice, like those worn-in tweed jackets he wears, are gone. In their place a sharp crease.

I go in and smile at him.

'Have a seat, Melanie,' he says, looking up at me from the papers on his desk.

Which is unusual, because normally his desk is clear when we talk. I peer at the topmost sheet and catch a glimpse of what looks like some sort of government crest at the top of the paper.

'That sounds ominous,' I say.

I go for a jokey tone, though my stomach is already knotting with fear. Is he not letting me out after all? Did

49

the ethics committee put the boot in? Am I about to learn that this will be my home for ever?

He offers a tight-lipped smile, more of a grimace, really, in return. He sighs, and it sounds as though he has the cares of the world on his shoulders.

'Melanie, do you remember when you first arrived here?'

'Kind of,' I say. 'It's all a bit blurry.'

'Of course,' he says. 'Well, do you remember *why* you were brought here?'

I nod, swallow down the lump that swells in my throat like a fast-growing tumour.

'Harry drowned in the bath.' I catch a questioning look in his eye. 'By which I mean that *I* drowned him. I know that. I'm not in denial. But I was ill. *Very* ill. It wasn't my fault. Not in the legal sense. You know that,' I add, hearing panic in my voice and not liking it. 'You told me.'

I expect Dr Silverman to concur, to say comforting words like oh, yes, of course, in a *legal* sense it wasn't your fault. But in a moral sense, in a very personal, *psychodynamic* sense, this is something you'll have to carry with you for the rest of your life. You're just at the start of a long and painful journey, but with appropriate support I'm sure you'll…

'I'm afraid that's not strictly true.'

I feel lightheaded, dizzy. My fingers tingle and little silvery-white sparks dance crazily like flies around the edges of my vision.

'What do you mean, not *strictly* true?'

'The police have been in contact. They want to interview you in connection with Harry's death.'

I'm hyperventilating, and I can't stop.

'What do you mean, *interview* me?'

'I'm sorry, Melanie, but when you were sectioned, it

brought all legal proceedings to a halt. You were judged not to have, in the medico-legal jargon, "capacity". That means —'

'I know what it means,' I snap. A couple of my older girlfriends have parents with dementia. The lawyers are always talking about capacity. 'It means I wasn't capable of making rational decisions for myself.'

He smiles and it looks so smug I have this sudden flash of anger and I think I might launch myself across the desk and give him a good slap just to wipe it off his face. I think he catches my intent because he draws back from me.

'It's a little more complicated than that,' he says. 'But yes, if you like. You were judged not fit to plead to the charges.' He steeples his fingers under his chin and looks at me over his glasses, which have slipped down his nose. 'The problem is, now you are.'

I am struggling to understand this. He's just told me in the space of a few days, that I was not, in fact, a successful psychotherapist, but actually locked up in a secure psychiatric unit suffering from a particularly severe form of a psychotic illness. And that I drowned my own child while in the grip of said psychotic illness. Now, he's telling me the police want to speak to me? To *interview* me?

I open my mouth, though to be brutally honest I have no idea what's going to come out, when there's a knock at the door. Dr Silverman looks at me and his expression is that of a guilty child caught with his hand in the biscuit tin.

'Come in,' he says loudly.

I twist round in my chair to see who's interrupting my therapy session.

The door opens. A woman walks in, followed by a man. She's mid-thirties, overweight but she hides it well with a nicely tailored suit. He's younger. Slim. Very dark skin. Hair cut into a really stylish crop with mini-dreads standing up on his head.

'Thanks for calling me, Dr Silverman,' she says. She has a Welsh accent. Lilting, musical. With a hard edge. A harp with steel strings.

Her eyes flit around the office, alighting on each object like bees sipping nectar. Finally she looks at me. Her stare is sharp, questing. I feel like she's X-raying my soul. She pulls a black leather wallet out of her inside pocket and opens it in front of my face. It's a police ID. What do they call them? Warrant cards?

'Melanie Walker?' she asks.

'Yes,' I say. I'm barely able to breathe at this point and my voice sounds like it's underwater.

'I'm DC Ffion Parry, Metropolitan Police. This is DC Kent. I am arresting you on suspicion of the murder of Harry Walker. You do not have to say anything. But, it may harm your defence if you do not mention when questioned something which you later rely on in court. Anything you do say may be given in evidence.'

13

Mel

I just sit there, mouth flapping open and shut like a goldfish. The male officer puts a hand out and cups my elbow in a weirdly intimate gesture. I levitate to my feet as if he has enough strength in his hand to lift me bodily just using the upwards pressure on the joint.

'Turn around, please, Melanie,' he says in a soft voice.

Zombie-like, I do what I'm asked. It's like when I first started taking the tablets our GP prescribed. The young cop could have asked me to strip naked and I probably would have gone along with it.

The image produces a sudden urge to laugh. I barely suppress it. I feel the hard, cold edges of a pair of handcuffs bite painfully into the delicate skin on the insides of my wrists. That kills the incipient giggles stone-dead.

I let the cop lead me out of Dr Silverman's office, casting a look over my shoulder at my former psychiatrist as we leave. He shrugs. And it's as eloquent a gesture as I have seen anybody make, ever. Sorrow. Guilt. Compassion. Helplessness in the face of officialdom. Fatalism. Jesus! He should be an actor; he's wasted as a shrink.

They march me out of the hospital, into the carpark and the back seat of a silver Vauxhall Insignia with black cloth upholstery that smells, faintly, of sick.

'What about my stuff?' I ask the female cop.

'It'll be transferred to our station, to the evidence locker,' she says, turning round in her seat to look at me between the tall headrests. 'Don't worry, it'll all be taken care of.'

'There's been a mistake,' I say. 'There must've been. I didn't murder Harry. I was mentally unwell. *Really* unwell,' I add, for emphasis, in case the fact that they've just collected me from a secure psychiatric unit hasn't made a sufficient impression on them.

'Let's save it for the formal interview, shall we, Melanie?' Then she turns to the male cop, who's in the driver's seat. 'Fancy a beer after work, Rob? My shout?'

He turns and nods as he releases the handbrake and pulls out of the neatly demarcated parking space. 'We should get a picture for the station Twitter account. You know, "Police newsflash: DC Parry buys a round".'

'Cheeky sod,' she says with a grin. Then he accelerates and the hospital recedes until it is lost to view.

* * *

If I thought being arrested in Dr Silverman's office was bad, I soon realise there's a whole hierarchy of shame, embarrassment and humiliation available to the police. It exists out of sight of law-abiding members of the public, just waiting to enfold them in its grip if they should transgress.

No, wait, that's not right. If they should be *suspected* of transgressing. I have nothing to fear. I didn't murder him. Harry. I didn't murder Harry.

My journey begins in the custody suite at Hammersmith Police Station. It's underground, so there are no windows. I suppose they design them this way so prisoners can't smash them and escape. Instead of natural light, the people who work here are bathed in the depressing blue-white of neon tubes. It makes everyone look sick.

DC Parry marches me up to a booth at the desk. It's at chest height on my side, which means I have to look up at the custody sergeant. It makes me feel like I'm eight years old. I suppose the floor is higher on that side. Anyway, he looks down at me over half-moon glasses. I try to smile at him, but my mouth trembles and I have to clamp my lips to stop myself sobbing.

He looks a little like my Uncle Ian. Thin, with prominent cheekbones laced with thread veins. He regards me with curiosity. No hostility, or none that I can see. No boredom, either. Rather, the gaze of a collector being brought another specimen by a researcher, their unspoken question, *Is this good? Have I done well? Will you keep it?*

'Who do we have here?' he asks, still looking at me over the thin gold wire of his glasses.

I'm not sure whether he expects me to answer. It sounds like the sort of patronising question officials like to use.

'My name—'

'Prisoner is Melanie Ruth Walker,' DC Parry says.

'Charge?'

'Murder.'

My legs have been trembling since I arrived in front of the cop who looks like my Uncle Ian. Now my knees give way spectacularly. I fall sideways and lurch against DC Parry.

I reach out, trying to break my fall and my hand makes contact with her right breast. I have just enough time to think to myself that it's surprisingly firm for a woman who looks on the soft side when she whirls round and punches me in a spot in the angle between my neck and my collarbone.

The pain makes me cry out. She steps back, banging against the Perspex screen on the left-hand side of the booth and I crumple to the floor. Electricity is shooting from my neck down to my fingertips.

She squats down beside me, her right thigh huge in my collapsing field of vision.

'Try that again and I'll add assaulting a police officer to the charges.' She leans closer and murmurs in my ear. 'Not that it'll make much difference considering you killed your own baby, you sick bitch.'

Then she hauls me to my feet and shoves me forwards so I collide with the lip of the counter.

The custody sergeant's expression hasn't changed. Although perhaps now he's thinking that here, after all, is a specimen that's definitely worth further consideration.

He leans forward slowly. Not like DC Parry did, not a snake-strike. I notice he's cut himself shaving this morning. Just below his left nostril on that little fleshy bump before the lip begins, there are two parallel cuts, maybe a millimetre or two apart and about three millimetres long. A twin-blade razor, I think. Which is odd, because don't most men use triple-bladed razors these days? Or five, even? I try to think of the slogan from the ads. My brain's mushy.

'You'll find life in here is a lot easier if you don't cause trouble, Melanie,' he says. 'You won't be with us for very long, so why not sit it out, do what you're told and try not to get too stressed, OK?'

His voice, which I interpret as kind, makes me cry.

'Oh, for Christ's sake,' DC Parry says.

'Number seven,' the sergeant says.

'Thanks, Sarge.'

She takes me by the left elbow and walks me away from the booth to a narrow corridor lined with doors. Everything here is white. I expected, I don't know, brickwork, dingy institutional green paint. But this feels more like a hospital.

We're joined by a hard-faced woman in black chinos and a navy blue jumper. Her hair is cut very short; her lips are a thin line. She regards me with a look I imagine she bestows on dog turds she avoids in public parks. She pulls a bunch of keys out from her thick waist on a retractable wire and unlocks a door. It has the number '7' stencilled on it in shiny black paint.

I imagine they'll simply slam the door closed on me and leave me to stew in my own guilt. But I said there was a hierarchy of humiliation. It ratchets up.

'Strip,' DC Parry says. Beside her, the hard-faced woman smirks.

'What?'

She looks at me as if I'm stupid.

'Take your clothes off.'

Even though I'm fully dressed, my hands go to my chest and the front of my jeans.

'Why?'

'You're a suicide risk,' she says. 'Can't have you hanging yourself, now can we?'

I look down at my feet. I'm wearing trainers. 'I thought you just took people's shoelaces away.'

'We do. And we will. But you could fashion a noose from your bra. Or,' she glances at the front of my shirt in an appraising way I find uncomfortable, 'pull out an underwire and stab yourself with it.'

I look at her, consider pleading that it's really unnecessary. That at this point in my life the very last thing I would do is kill myself. But there's something implacable in her gaze that suggests I'd be wasting my breath.

I almost turn away, then find some reserve of pride. If she's going to make me undress in front of her, I'm not going to hide. I lock eyes with her and take my clothes off. The cell is warm and I'm relieved not to shiver. I don't want them to see it and mistake it for fear. (Although I am, to be frank, absolutely terrified at this point.)

As I hook my thumbs in the waistband of my knickers, she says, 'That's enough. You can keep those on.'

Then the hard-faced woman, the warder or whatever they're called, hands me a pile of cleanish grey sweats. I retreat a couple of feet to get dressed while she scoops up my clothes. She holds my bra up in front of her like it's some sort of object she's never seen before. It's the last of my decent ones. Midnight blue with bronze lace trim.

'Nice,' she says. 'Wish I could afford stuff like this on my pay.'

'Have you got a lawyer?' DC Parry asks me.

I want to say of course I haven't! I've been locked up in a secure psychiatric unit for the last two and a half years. But instead, I say, 'No, sorry.'

I immediately regret that 'sorry'. It sounds pathetic. And why should I have a lawyer? It always baffles me on those TV shows where Americans always have a personal attorney. Do they really do that? Even truck drivers or waitresses?

'We can arrange legal representation for you,' she says. 'It's free,' she adds.

I find a shred of defiance. Of the old me, who ran advertising accounts and took clients to lunch.

'No. I have money. I want to call my husband. I believe I'm entitled to a phone call.'

DC Parry smiles at me. She appears to be enjoying herself.

'That's what you *believe*, is it?' she says in a nasty tone of voice. 'And you formed that impression where? Off the telly, was it?'

I realise that this is exactly where I 'formed that impression'. But she's not done and I realise here is another level of humiliation she's probably been waiting for me to reach.

'You're not *entitled* to a call. It's at my discretion, and,' she holds up a hand in my face as I open my mouth, 'I will get round to it. I promise.'

'Thank you,' I say as calmly as I can manage. 'When you do, I would like to call my husband. He can find me a lawyer.'

'Fine by me,' she says.

Then she steps back and nods at the warder, who steps forward and slams the door shut.

And I am alone.

I turn a complete circle. The cell seems to have been fabricated out of a single piece of plastic. There's a low bench that runs the entire length of one wall. On it lies a thin pad with some sort of wipe-clean cover in navy blue. There's a stainless-steel toilet. No seat. And a washbasin like you get on trains. A round-cornered aperture with engraved symbols on its upper edge for soap, water and dryer. A single button, set flush to the steel.

And that's it. God knows why she was worried about

my hanging myself. I'd like to know how, given there isn't a single hook, shelf or pipe you could tie a noose around.

I sit on the bench. The anxiety that has been simmering just below the surface ever since she arrested me in Dr Silverman's office suddenly comes to the boil.

My palms feel sweaty and I rub them on my thighs. My breath is coming in short, quick gasps and little white sparks are shooting around the edges of my vision. I feel frightened.

The panicky feeling intensifies and I feel that I might start screaming and then not be able to stop. So I do the only thing I can think of.

I slap myself. Hard, across the cheek. It stings but it doesn't feel enough. I do it again, the other side this time. Harder. It hurts enough that tears spring to my eyes. But the panic has subsided.

I lean back against the wall and close my eyes. I steady myself with the thought that as soon as I speak to Jonathan, we can start clearing this mess up. He'll know a good lawyer. Probably through the bank. From one of the big City firms. And we can afford it. Well, technically, Jonathan can afford it.

When they walk me into whatever smelly interview room they use to frighten innocent people, my hotshot City lawyer will lay the law down, literally, and get me out of here.

The thought calms me down. Tiredness, like a great black wave, engulfs me. It's the stress, I suppose. Plus Dr Silverman did say the change to my drug regime would have side effects that could include lethargy. Which is another problem. What about my prescription? I'm supposed to get it filled so I can start taking them tonight.

Despite the worry this produces, I can't keep my eyes open. I lie down on the thin, hard pad and try to relax. I have enough of whatever he was giving me in the hospital to keep me levelled out at least until tomorrow. Then I can ask about getting my prescription. My lawyer won't let them get away with denying me medical treatment.

Finally, I sleep. And I dream about Harry.

14

DC Ffion Parry

Ffion walked away from the cell door feeling proud of herself. Firstly for arresting a child-killer. Secondly, for not knocking the silly bitch unconscious when she made a grab for her tit. She'd had a fair run in the medical system with her oh-so-convenient mental health diagnosis, but now it was over. Dr Silverman had obligingly declared Walker to be cured. And that was that.

She called Jonathan. After he'd called her the other night, she'd gone back over all her files for the night of the murder. And she'd recalled how utterly devastated he'd been in the days and weeks afterwards. He seemed to shut down emotionally, as if displaying even a shred of grief might open a floodgate that would see him drown in his own tears.

After arresting Mel on the night of Harry's death, Ffion had been assigned as his family liaison officer. There wasn't really any detective work left to do, but she was there to support him and keep him posted on the development of the case against his wife.

He was good-looking, in a posh-boy sort of way. Always immaculately groomed, even though his son had just been murdered. His aftershave smelled like it cost more than Ffion earned in a shift. And as for his suits, a month wouldn't be enough.

There'd been a moment or two when, sitting over a bottle of wine with him late at night, she could have sworn he was making a pass at her. But she'd dismissed it. She was happily married and the poor guy was emotionally shattered.

Jonathan answered the way he always did.

'Walker.'

Not even 'Jonathan Walker'. She found that interesting. As if he thought there was only one Walker interesting enough to figure on anyone else's radar. Or was she overthinking it? After all, she had just called his phone.

'Jonathan, it's Ffion. We've just taken your wife into custody.'

'Oh, thank God! I was worried her shrink would somehow wangle it so she got off scot-free.'

Ffion smiled at his strangely archaic language.

'Not a chance. Thanks to you, we were there this morning.'

'Did she give you any trouble?'

Ffion thought back to the attempted assault at the custody desk.

'Nothing we couldn't handle. Listen, I want to thank you again,' Ffion said. 'We'll be interviewing her tomorrow morning. In the meantime, she said she wanted to talk to you about arranging a lawyer.'

'Did she now? Probably thought I'd just rush off to one

of the big City firms and hire their best guy. Or girl,' he added hastily, making Ffion smile. *Good boy*, she thought. *Picked yourself up just in time.*

'Do you want to speak to her?'

'No. I don't. The next time I see my wife I want it to be in a courtroom.'

'You're sure? Sorry, I have to be belt-and-braces about this. We don't want her lawyer – whoever she eventually gets – picking us up on procedural issues.'

'I understand. It's fine, Ffion. Really. And to answer your question, yes. I'm sure,' he said. 'Now, you'll have to excuse me, but I've got to jump on another call. Japan.'

Ffion pulled up the case files. She had a lot of reading to do to get back up to speed on the case. As she paged through the original crime report and the witness statements, a picture emerged of a cold-blooded killer who'd somehow managed to convince a judge, a jury and a member of the medical profession that she wasn't bad, just mad.

Melanie Walker had been found by her husband kneeling on the bathroom floor, holding her baby son under the bathwater. He'd struggled with her and in the ensuing scuffle she'd fallen into the bath and knocked herself out.

The police surgeon confirmed that the wound to the back of her head was consistent with having fallen against the mixer tap. She'd found bruises on Melanie's upper arms consistent with Jonathan having to hold her off.

Melanie had also had traces of baby lotion under her fingernails that matched the one found on Harry's skin.

And Jonathan had confirmed that over the preceding months, ever since Harry had been born, she'd made repeated threats to kill him, citing his unwillingness to go down for naps and inability to sleep through as reasons.

Jonathan had initially thought these were symptoms of post-natal depression and had, at her insistence, taken her to see a private GP. The doctor had prescribed anti-depressants and sleeping pills, which had, in Jonathan's words, 'taken the edge off her feelings', enabling him to stop worrying she intended to harm the baby.

Then he'd woken to find his wife had murdered their child. Christ! How he hadn't killed her himself, Ffion would never know. But instead he'd done the responsible thing and called the police and an ambulance. Given the details calmly and clearly to the operator at the call centre and then waited with his now catatonic-acting wife.

From then on, one at a time, the wheels had well and truly come off the case. At least as far as Ffion and her colleagues were concerned. For a start, Melanie had been sectioned under the Mental Health Act 1983.

In a preliminary hearing before a judge, Melanie Walker's brief, with the help of the all-too-plausible Dr Silverman from Hammersmith Hospital, had argued that her client was unfit even to stand trial, by reason of her severe psychotic illness.

'Your Honour, you have heard from a distinguished psychiatrist, Dr Nathan Silverman, of Hammersmith Hospital,' the lawyer said. 'Dr Silverman diagnosed my client as suffering, at the time of the alleged attack, and ever since, from a severe mental illness, namely puerperal, or, postpartum, psychosis.

'My client's illness, which, if anything, has worsened, means she will be unable to meet any of the criteria laid down in the Criminal Law (Insanity) Act 2006 for a trial to go ahead,' the lawyer said, in a clipped Home Counties accent. 'She does not understand the charge, nor is she able to instruct counsel, challenge jurors or follow evidence. I request that she be declared unfit for trial.'

The judge had listened patiently while the CPS lawyer, buttressed by a Home Office-approved forensic psychiatrist, did his best to present Melanie Walker as mentally competent to face the rigours of a murder trial.

The judge retired to her chambers for an hour, then returned. As she sat, she looked straight at Melanie Walker and smiled sadly.

Ffion turned to Rob.

'We're screwed,' she whispered, earning herself a frown from the judge.

Which they were.

'I find that the defendant does indeed meet the conditions detailed in the Criminal Law (Insanity) Act 2006 as to be unfit for trial. She is to be held in a secure psychiatric unit until such time as she is deemed by her doctors to have recovered from her illness. However,' she paused and stared at Ffion before continuing, 'I do *not* find that there is a reasonable doubt that Mrs Walker committed the alleged crime. Therefore, at such time as her doctors do declare her fit to stand trial, she will be brought before the court again to stand trial for murder.'

Ffion had apologised personally to Jonathan afterwards. And she'd made him a promise.

'If you ever need me, Jonathan, call, OK? Just call. And if – when – she gets let out, I will be there, waiting.'

He'd taken her hand in both of his, a curiously intimate gesture and smiled, sadly.

'Thanks, Ffion. I know you did your best. I'll just have to try and move on with my life.'

* * *

Ffion's first thought on waking beside the snoring form of her husband was, *that was then. This is now.*

She arrived at the nick early. She re-read the key pieces of evidence, even though she'd taken copies home and studied them until 2.00 a.m. The front desk called her at 9.00 a.m. to say that Melanie Walker's lawyer had arrived.

She allowed herself a small smile of satisfaction. So the alpha bitch with her fancy job in advertising thought she'd be meeting with some five-hundred-an-hour legal eagle, did she? Well, she was about to meet reality coming the other way at high speed. More like a fifty-quid an hour legal aid muppet without the smarts to get a decent job.

'Send him up.'

Five minutes later, the doors to the CID general office swung open and a man carrying a burgundy leather briefcase with gold latches strode in.

In his decent-looking navy suit, Ffion thought he looked a cut above the usual duty solicitors they got around Hammersmith nick.

Then she noticed he was carrying a shiny yellow cycle helmet in his other hand and immediately revised her opinion downwards. Another right-on, tree-hugging human rights lawyer, was her damning judgement.

Pasting a smile on her face, she moved to intercept him before he could start wandering around snooping over people's shoulders. From the grey flecks in his full head of wavy black hair she put his age at forty, though he had a boyish look about him, including a dimple in his left cheek.

'I'm DC Parry. Are you Melanie Walker's solicitor?'

'That's right,' he said, smiling easily. He transferred the bike helmet to his left hand and held out his right. 'Rufus Goddard. I don't think we've met. Sorry, I'm new. I transferred down from Leeds last month.'

Rufus? There was a name to conjure with! But he was open, friendly and, up close, nicely attractive.

She shook hands, noting the warm, dry skin and

exactly the right amount of pressure in his grip: not the dreaded dead fish, but not the macho bone-crusher, either.

'I've booked a room for you to meet with your client,' Ffion said. 'We've scheduled the interview for nine thirty.'

* * *

At 9.31 a.m., Ffion turned to her left and nodded at Rob. He switched on the digital interview recorder, whose high-pitched bleep lasted for seven seconds, setting her teeth on edge.

Facing them across the table were Melanie Walker and her bicycling lawyer. Rufus.

After each person had stated their name, Ffion rounded it out with details of the interview and charge. She repeated the official caution, then opened the folder in front of her and looked down at the top sheet.

'Why did you kill him, Melanie?'

Immediately, the lawyer leaned to his right and murmured into Melanie's ear. Ffion held her breath. He'd be advising her to go 'no comment'. They always did. The smart ones, anyway. Make the cops do the work. Don't give them anything. It's their job to make the case against you, not yours to pull it down. And the smart clients listened. The question was, what kind of a client was Melanie Walker?

The disobedient kind, it turned it out.

'I don't know. I was out of my mind from lack of sleep,' she said. 'Have you got children of your own? Do you know what it's like to be sleep-deprived for month after month after month?'

Ffion did have children of her own. Two, as it happened. And she knew a little about motherhood and the trials it brought. But unlike the woman in the faded grey sweats opposite her, she'd not resorted to murdering them just to get a bit of shuteye.

'You're going to stand trial for murder, you know that. And now you've been certified sane by your doctor, you've got nowhere to hide.' Ffion held up a hand as the lawyer opened his mouth to protest. 'So my question is, Melanie, why don't you confess now, get it off your chest and save everybody the heartache of a long and emotionally draining legal ordeal at the end of which you're going to be found guilty?'

Melanie scratched the back of her neck, and began pulling at the hairs there. The action bothered Ffion. There was a feverishness to it she didn't like.

'I didn't murder Harry,' Melanie said, finally. 'How could I? He was my baby. I loved him.'

'You killed him. Funny kind of love.'

Tears rolled from the inner corners of Melanie's eyes, around the hollows in her gaunt cheeks and into the neckline of her sweatshirt, which soaked up the liquid and turned from pale to dark grey.

'Do you have any more questions for my client, DC Parry?' the lawyer asked.

Ffion nodded. She leaned forwards and dropped her voice. Offered a small, apologetic smile.

'Melanie, look, I'm sorry for my remarks just now, OK? That was bang out of order,' she said. 'But the evidence is clear. You were found by your husband holding your baby under the water. You do remember that, right?'

Melanie tilted her back, looked upwards and frowned. Her head rolled forwards again until she was looking at Ffion. Something had changed in her expression in that brief period when she'd apparently been consulting the suspended ceiling tiles.

'No. I don't remember that. I know that's what you're

telling me. And I know that's what Jonathan told you. But I can't remember it at all.'

Ffion pursed her lips.

'Harry drowned, Melanie. *You* drowned him. That's why I think it would be better if you confessed now, you see.'

'I can't confess! I don't remember.'

'No jury's going to believe you if you stick to that story. They'll just think you're lying. And, like I said, given you're fit to plead, they'll convict you and you'll go to prison. Probably for a very long time.'

The lawyer interrupted.

'DC Parry, my client has already indicated that she doesn't wish to confess. If there's nothing else?'

Ffion shook her head and sighed. It had been worth a shot. But without a confession, the lawyer was right. It would have to go to trial. And then, who knew what would happen? Juries got all kinds of funny ideas.

PART II

TRIAL AND ERROR

15

Mel

My trial is at Kingston-Upon-Thames Crown Court.

They've let me wear my own clothes. Rufus insisted. He also spoke to the police about my medication. I'm so thankful I have a good lawyer. I am still struggling to understand why Jonathan wouldn't hire a lawyer for me. But for a legal aid solicitor, Rufus is all right.

Actually, no, that's unfair. He's very good. I asked him about barristers. When he explained how much a good QC would cost, I nearly fainted: £500 an hour. And up.

I have some savings, but, from what Rufus says, even a two-week trial would bankrupt me. I'll get a state-funded lawyer instead. Not ideal. But Rufus said he'd see if he could track down a good one for me.

The lawyer he finds is called Alfie Weir. He's a pupil barrister at a modest set of chambers in Kingston. Qualified, but still finding his feet. Rufus assures me Alfie is very good. But that name. Alfie. I have – had – friends who named their little boys Alfie.

He looks about twenty, though I suppose he must be older to be a qualified barrister. He gives off this sort of electric energy. I wonder, uncharitably, if he's handled many Crown Court murder trials before.

We meet before the trial begins in a windowless wooden conference room under the court. Alfie says he is going to follow a three-pronged strategy. One, demonstrate that I am of good character. Two, establish that at the time of Harry's death, I was suffering from psychosis and therefore not legally culpable for my actions. Three, offer an alternative narrative that might actually exonerate me altogether. He intends to suggest that Jonathan murdered Harry.

I tell him this is plain wrong. Jonathan *loved* Harry. But he smiles and tells me to trust him as my barrister. Frankly, I am so frazzled from anxiety, insomnia and lack of daylight and peace and quiet that it's all I can do to stay upright and awake.

I ask him if he thought I should go makeup-free, but he says no. Jurors, especially the female ones, would see that for what it was, a transparent attempt to make myself look ill – or like a victim. They don't like that sort of thing, apparently. Instead he suggested going for a minimalist approach, so I have just a whisper of eye-shadow and a little natural lip-gloss.

I'm wearing a charcoal-grey jacket over a cream blouse and a pair of simple black trousers. Black low-heeled shoes. Rufus said to avoid anything that jurors might feel jealous of: expensive jewellery, for example, or obviously designer label stuff. Chance would be a fine thing.

* * *

It's just after 10.00 a.m. I am led up from the cells beneath the court by a guy in his late forties or early fifties in a G4S uniform. The guard doesn't talk to me. Doesn't look at me, either. He walks half a step behind me, which is very disconcerting. I can't see him; I can just feel him there. Presumably ready to cosh me to the ground if I run.

We enter the courtroom; a dreary, functional, fifties' era space with an excess of mid-brown wood. He leads me to the dock and opens a little gate so I can enter. It's a tiny space and it's made even more claustrophobic by the scratched Plexiglas screen that surrounds it.

We sit down on two hard chairs. He's so close I can smell him. A warm, off-putting aroma like school dinners. Overcooked mince. Boiled cabbage. I think it must be prison food: it's the exact same smell as the grey ready meals they've been bringing to my cell.

We rise for the judge. It's a different one from my original trial. A man this time. He looks to be about seventy, although under the long grey curly wig it's hard to be sure. He has a bulbous nose, drooping jowls and looks unwell. He sits and we all follow suit.

The jury are sworn in by the jury usher.

The judge eyeballs me.

'Melanie Walker, to the first charge, of murder, how do you plead?'

'Not guilty by reason of insanity, Your Honour.'

'To the second charge, of infanticide, how do you plead?'

My right leg is wobbling, and I press my right palm against my thigh to steady it.

'Not guilty by reason of insanity, Your Honour.'

He makes a note.

After that, he makes some introductory remarks then

looks over at the prosecution lawyer and smiles. 'Ms Toombs?'

The prosecution barrister is a QC, a Queen's Counsel. Rufus explained that put her several rungs above Alfie on the ladder of legal firepower. She reminds me of the head girl at my grammar school. Or rather, what I imagine Fenella Wilding would have turned into.

She's about fifty. Beneath her scruffy grey wig, a perfect, oval face, which, unlike mine, is devoid of makeup. She speaks clearly. Her voice is neither loud, nor strident, yet it carries a kind of understated authority. She strolls over to the jury and stands before them, favouring each with a half-smile.

'Ladies and gentlemen of the jury. This case concerns the deliberate killing of a six-month-old baby.' She pauses. 'His name was Harry Walker. I want you to remember that name, because over the coming days and weeks, there will be a great deal of legal argument to which you must pay attention. But I want you, in fact, I *plead* with you, to remember that at the heart of this case is an innocent child. A baby. And his name was – is – Harry.

'Harry was found dead by drowning in the bathroom of the family home on Richmond Hill. The prosecution will present evidence to you that will prove that the defendant, Mrs Melanie Walker, Harry's mother, murdered him.

'At the end of the trial, you will see that the case against Mrs Walker is proven beyond reasonable doubt and I am confident you will therefore bring in a unanimous verdict of guilty. Thank you.'

She resumes her seat with a flourish of her black robe.

The judge looks over at Alfie.

'Does the defence wish to make an opening speech?'

Alfie stands. 'No, Your Honour.'

He's told me in advance this is normal and I shouldn't worry.

I worry.

'Very well. Ms Toombs, you may begin the prosecution case.'

'The prosecution calls Detective Constable Ffion Parry.'

DC Parry is fetched by an usher. She marches into court and steps into the witness box. As if on autopilot, she places her hand on the Bible and holds her right aloft. In a rapid-fire but clear voice she gives the oath.

'I swear by Almighty God that the evidence I give shall be the truth the whole truth and nothing but the truth.' The last half of the sentence comes out as *truthwholetruth-nothingbuttruth*. She turns to the judge. 'I am Detective Constable Ffion Parry. My collar number is 7845.'

Ms Toombs strides over to the witness box.

'DC Parry, please tell the court what happened on the night of Wednesday the twelfth of May 2019.'

DC Parry looks at the judge. 'Your Honour, I request the court's permission to consult my pocketbook as it contains a contemporaneous record of the events of that night.'

'Go ahead, DC Parry,' he says.

They both act as though this is a mini-drama they've played hundreds of times before. Perhaps they have.

She pulls out a black notebook and opens it at a marked page. She brings the court with her from receiving the call to attend a crime scene by the control room at Hammersmith police station, then kicks up a gear.

'I entered the bathroom. Mr Walker was on his knees beside the bath, holding his dead son in his arms. They were both soaking wet. Mrs Walker was also soaking wet and was on the floor beside them.'

'Kneeling?' Ms Toombs asks. 'Or was she lying?' She puts a nasty emphasis on the last word.

'She was lying,' DC Parry repeats, looking, briefly, at me. 'She was in some sort of trance.'

Alfie is on his feet. 'Objection! Your Honour, DC Parry is not qualified to pronounce on my client's psychological state at the time of the incident.'

The judge sighs. 'Thank you, Mr Weir. Sustained. Ms Toombs?'

'Yes, Your Honour. Thank you. Would you rephrase your last remark, please, DC Parry?'

She nods. 'Mrs Walker was lying on her back. Her eyes were wide open and staring. She was not moving. She was breathing shallowly to judge from the rise and fall of her chest. She was unresponsive.'

'Thank you.'

Ms Toombs elicits from DC Parry a series of facts that paint a detailed portrait of the scene with me as the guilty party. I can't fault her. Especially because the basic facts aren't really in dispute. She finishes with DC Parry and sits down.

The judge asks Alfie if he wishes to cross-examine the witness. Alfie gets to his feet and crosses the courtroom to the witness box.

'DC Parry, this is your first murder case, I believe?' he asks in a confident tone.

'No, sir. I have assisted, or been the lead investigator, on thirteen murders since I joined the MIT.'

There's a ripple of noise through the courtroom. The judge calls for silence. Alfie looks down at his notes. Then he drops a sheet of paper. He stoops to pick it up.

He's blushing when he straightens. This is a terrible start. Maybe I should have taken out a loan and hired a

QC after all. But it's too late for that. We'll just have to make the best of it.

'Have you ever dealt with a case of infanticide before?'

'No.'

'You say my client appeared unresponsive. Not that you're qualified to make this assessment, but you said she was in a trance.'

'Yes.'

He wrinkles his nose. I think he's going for a look of puzzlement, but it comes off as stagy. Like he's in a sixth-form play.

'Did that strike you as odd?'

'No.'

'No? You've discovered a terrible scene. A drowned baby, a distraught father, and the mother is lying there, catatonic.'

'Catatonic, sir? I didn't think I was qualified to pronounce on the defendant's mental state?'

'DC Parry, show proper respect to the court, please,' the judge interjects. But he's smiling. And I see a couple of jury members grinning.

Alfie consults his notes again. He clears his throat.

'You say you've investigated thirteen murders. Were any of the people you arrested in a catatonic state after committing their crimes?'

'No.'

'Yet here is a woman who, according to her husband, has just drowned her own child. Yet she wasn't crying, screaming, tearing her clothes. Wide awake but unresponsive?'

'Yes, sir. Sometimes murderers go into shock afterwards.'

Alfie's set a trap and walked into it himself. She's just

got away with suggesting I'm a murderer when that's supposed to be the jury's decision.

He looks down at his notes. 'No further questions.'

The prosecution asks the judge if DC Parry can be released. He nods and she leaves the witness box to join a couple of detectives sitting towards the back. One, an older guy, pats her on the shoulder. I lip read, *'Well done'*.

Ms Toombs calls Jonathan next. He looks over at me from the witness box and smiles sadly. If it was in an ad, the headline would be, 'More in sorrow than in anger'.

Today is the first time I've seen him in what feels like a lifetime, but, in reality, is only two and a half years. Maybe a little longer to account for time between getting out of hospital and the trial.

Ms Toombs leads him through 'the awful events of that night'.

He answers clearly, but in a voice that trembles from time to time. She must have coached him because whenever he answers one of her questions, he looks at the jury.

I see what they're trying to do. Her questions elicit answers that paint me as a dangerously out-of-control mother whose irrational, demanding, yet still totally sane behaviour was more than her patient, long-suffering but ultimately overwhelmed husband could cope with.

— How had Harry's sleeplessness affected Jonathan?

— Well it was difficult at first. He hadn't realised just how much love and care a little boy needed.

Understanding nods and smiles from the more maternal-looking members of the jury.

— Had Jonathan ever experienced any feelings of hostility towards Harry?

— Of course not. Just frustration that he wasn't able to

split himself in two so he could care for his baby son and his wife.

— Did he regret not being able to save his baby son?

— Of course! But with both bathroom and bedroom doors closed, he hadn't heard anything until it was too late.

A younger woman on the jury, mid-thirties maybe, looks like she'd like to jump Jonathan's bones right here in the courtroom.

By the end of his testimony, Jonathan has twice broken down and the judge has actually asked him if he needed a moment to collect himself. But Jonathan offered the judge a brave-boy smile and said no he was fine and sorry for wasting the court's time.

A couple of the women in the jury box have been looking at me as if they'd like to string me up from the rafters right here in the courtroom. I don't blame them. Going on what Ms Toombs has just teased out of Jonathan's mouth, I come across as a self-obsessed, whining bitch who used her own dubious claims of mental health problems as a smokescreen for the cold-blooded murder of her child.

Ms Toombs proceeds to call more witnesses, including a paramedic and a CSI.

Alfie declines the opportunity to cross-examine all of them except the CSI. He's bald. Black glasses. A real egg-head.

'Mr Buckman, we've heard that you were part of the team that investigated the crime scene at 159 Richmond Hill,' Alfie begins, 'and that you surveyed the spare bedroom. Can you tell the court what your general impression was of the room? For example, was it being used on the night of Harry's death?'

'It was, yes.'

'How did you reach this conclusion?'

'The duvet was thrown back, the pillows were dented and there were male items on the bedside table.'

'Sorry, Mr Buckman, "male items"?'

'An Omega Seamaster watch. Gold cufflinks set with what appeared to be emeralds. A black leather wallet, which included a driving licence and an ID card for a merchant bank in the City of London. Lemaire et Monceau. They're French. The driving licence and the ID were both in the name of Jonathan Walker.'

'Thank you. Tell me, Mr Buckman, did you receive anything from the forensic pathologist who conducted the second post-mortem for the defence?'

'Yes. A feather. Six-point-five millimetres long.'

'What did you do with this feather?'

'I submitted the feather to an ornithologist at the Zoological Society of London. After performing a DNA analysis on the feather, he confirmed that it came from a goose. Specifically, a Hungarian Frizzle Feathered goose.'

'Did you examine the spare room for signs of goose feathers?'

'I did, yes.'

'What did you find?'

'The pillows – there were four on the double bed – were filled with goose-down.'

'Goose-down,' Alfie echoes. 'Did you send a sample to your expert witness?'

'Yes I did.'

'And what did they tell you?'

'They came from the same breed.'

'The Hungarian Frizzle Feathered goose?'

'That's right, yes.'

'So we have a feather found in the victim's throat that matches those found inside the pillows where Mr Walker was sleeping that night.'

'Objection!' Ms Toombs is on her feet. 'The witness merely identified the presence of what he calls "male items", but they in themselves do not constitute proof that Mr Walker was using the bedroom on the night his son was murdered.'

Alfie punches straight back. 'Your Honour, my next question will elicit an answer that I hope will satisfy the court.'

'Very well, Mr Weir. I'll allow it. Overruled.'

'Mr Buckman, did you, during the course of your investigation of the spare room, analyse the sheets on the bed?'

'Yes.'

'Did you discover anything that led you to believe that Mr Walker had occupied the bed for at least part of that night?'

'I did.'

'What did you find, please?'

'Semen.'

Alfie frowns. 'Old?'

'Fresh.' He looks at the jury. 'It was wet.'

'Who did this semen belong to?'

'We conducted a DNA test and compared it to the sample provided by Mr Walker. The profiles were an identical match.'

'Did you reach a conclusion to how Mr Walker's semen ended up on the sheets that night?'

'I assume he deposited it there during an act of masturbation.'

'Thank you. No further questions.'

The judge asks Ms Toombs if she wishes to re-examine the witness.

She stands and shakes her head. 'No, Your Honour. Does Your Honour have any questions for the witness?' she asks in a solicitous tone of voice.

'No thank you, Ms Toombs.'

'Then I request that the court release Michael Buckman.'

The judge nods and Michael Buckman leaves the witness box.

Ms Toombs strides over to the jury.

'Ladies and gentlemen of the jury, that concludes the case for the prosecution.'

16

Mel

'Mrs Walker?'

I start. The judge is looking at me.

'I'm sorry, Your Honour. What?'

His thick black eyebrows elevate so they're disappearing under the front of his wig.

'The usher is waiting for you to swear.'

For a moment I struggle to process this sentence. Then I look down. My left hand is resting on a black book. The Bible. And my right hand is held up as if in a greeting.

Yes. Of course. Alfie just called me as a witness in my own defence. I must have left the dock and crossed the courtroom and mounted the steps to the witness box. I have no memory of doing it.

The usher, a young woman with sandy hair caught up in a neat little tortoiseshell clip, is holding up a small white card in front of me.

I read the words aloud.

'I swear by Almighty God that the evidence I give shall be the truth the whole truth and nothing but the truth.'

When he was preparing me for the trial, Rufus asked me whether I was a Christian. I told him the truth. I said I was brought up Church of England, but that was more because that's what everybody did. None of us was exactly religious. We went to church at Christmas and Easter, but apart from weddings, christening and funerals, that was it.

I said I wanted to affirm, but Rufus advised against it. He said that although increasing numbers of witnesses did affirm, juries, especially older members, still mistrusted witnesses who opted not to swear before God. I said I thought that was old fashioned. Rufus said maybe so, but my fate rested in the laps not of the gods, but of twelve old-fashioned people. So if I could manage to swallow my secular pride, God would go down better with the jury. So I swore.

The usher takes the Bible away.

'State your name, please,' the judge says.

'Melanie Walker.'

He nods. 'Thank you.'

Alfie comes over to the witness box.

'Mrs Walker, can you describe to the court your feelings when you discovered you were pregnant with Harry?'

'I was elated. Delighted. Thrilled. All of the positive emotions you'd expect.'

'Did these feelings change in any way as your pregnancy progressed?'

'No. If anything they intensified. I couldn't wait to hold my baby in my arms.'

'Have you ever been in trouble with the police before this?'

'Never.'

'Not even a speeding ticket?'

'No.'

'You used to work in advertising as an account manager.'

'Yes, that's right.'

'A stressful job, I imagine.'

'It had its moments. Long nights, early starts, working through the weekend.'

'A lot of people working in those sorts of jobs turn to illegal drugs or alcohol to ease the pressure. Did you?'

'No.'

'Did your employer require its employees, including you, to submit to random drug tests?'

'Yes.'

'Did you ever fail one?'

'No.'

'Outside of work, did you perform any volunteer work?'

'Yes. I was a school governor.'

'That must have brought you into contact with children.'

'Occasionally, yes.'

'Were you ever accused of, investigated for, or charged with, inappropriate behaviour around the children?'

'No.'

'And you had a clean bill of health as far as your DBS application form went?'

The judge leans forward.

'Mr Weir, could you clarify? DBS?'

'Apologies, Your Honour. DBS stands for Disclosure and Barring Service. It replaces the old CRB,' he hesitates, 'again, my apologies, Your Honour. Criminal Records

Bureau check for applicants' suitability to work with children.'

'Thank you, Mr Weir, please continue.'

'Mrs Walker, can you please tell the court what happened in the days and weeks after Harry was born?'

'I was OK for a few days, then I began to feel depressed. Harry wasn't sleeping well, which meant I was permanently exhausted. The black feelings persisted, then deepened and eventually my husband took me to a GP. He prescribed sleeping pills and also a course of antidepressants.'

'Did they help?'

'A little. I felt numb. The sleeping pills meant I was getting a few hours' sleep every night but the depression got worse. I wasn't functioning well at all.'

'And after the terrible events of the night when Harry died, what happened to you?'

'I was declared unfit to stand trial by a judge and sectioned.'

'Sectioned meaning?'

'I was taken to a secure psychiatric unit at Hammersmith Hospital where I was diagnosed with postpartum psychosis.'

'How long did you stay at the hospital? A few weeks? A few months?'

'Two and a half years.'

'That must have been terrible for you.'

'Not really. I was delusional. For most of the time I believed that I had retrained as a psychotherapist and I had a practice room at the hospital. The people I believed I was treating were actually my fellow patients.'

'But you're better now?'

'Yes. The psychosis was eventually cured by my doctors.'

'Let's move on to the night Harry died,' he says. I feel a hard lump forming in my throat. I know what's coming. 'Can you tell the court what you remember?'

I told Alfie before that I didn't have a proper answer to this question. My memory is incomplete. There are chunks missing, like a second-hand book where the last few pages have fallen out and you only realise right at the end. He said not to worry and to answer as truthfully as I could manage.

I inhale. My future rests on what I say next.

'I remember giving Harry his last feed.'

'What time would that have been?'

'It was 11.37 p.m. I remember because we have a rainbow clock in the nursery and I always checked the time when Harry woke up.'

'Then what?'

'Then I lay him down, face up, snuggled him in with his teddy and went back to bed.'

'With your husband?'

'No. Jonathan was sleeping in the spare room by then.'

'Why?'

'He said he needed his sleep and it disturbed him when I had to get up in the night. It happened a lot. Harry wasn't a great sleeper.'

'What do you remember next?'

I shudder involuntarily. I feel cold all of a sudden.

'I was sitting in the bath, fully dressed. It was freezing cold. And I was holding Harry in my arms.'

I pause and, suddenly, I am crying. I fish a tissue out of my sleeve and blot the tears. I sniff and then blow my nose. In seconds, the tissue is sodden.

'I know this is difficult for you, Mrs Walker,' Alfie says, 'but please, continue if you can.'

I nod.

'I thought Harry was alive. I remember him screaming from the nursery. It woke me up. I think it was about 2.00 a.m. I stumbled next door and picked him up and then my mind is a blank until I'm in the bath with him.'

'When you recall that moment, you sitting in a bath of cold water with Harry in your arms, was he alive at the time?'

I nod. 'He was screaming even louder.'

'I should think he was, if he'd been dunked up to his neck in cold water. And then what?'

'Then Jonathan came into the bathroom and started shouting at me. I think he grabbed me.'

'And what did he do next?'

'I can't remember. Everything from that moment on is a blank. I'm sorry.'

'Thank you. No further questions, Your Honour.'

I'm surprised Ms Toombs didn't raise any objections during my testimony. The judge asks her if she wishes to cross-examine me. She does. Of course she does. Then I discover why she was content to let me talk uninterrupted.

'Mrs Walker,' she says to me, while looking at the jury, an effect I find disconcerting. 'Thank you for sharing that story. Now, at the time of poor little Harry's death, it's been established that you were suffering from puerperal, or postpartum, psychosis.'

'Yes,' I say, grateful she hasn't called my diagnosis into question.

'Are you still suffering from puerperal psychosis?'

'No.'

'No. In fact, as you have just testified, you're cured.'

'Yes.' Then I realise my one-word answers might sound defensive to the jury. I notice a couple of the women are observing me closely, one of them actually scowling. 'I am. Thanks to Dr Silverman.'

Dr Silverman's in the public gallery and I look up at him and smile. He looks straight back at me. I think he smiles back. It's hard to tell.

'Ah, yes, the good Dr Silverman. Please tell the court how Dr Silverman cured you of this terrifying mental condition?'

Alfie's on his feet. 'Objection! It's already been established that my client is fit to stand trial. I see no relevance in pursuing this line of questioning.'

The judge looks at the prosecution barrister.

'Ms Toombs?'

'Your Honour, the Crown intends to show that there are aspects of the defendant's treatment that call into question, not her fitness to stand trial, but the veracity of her recollections.'

'Overruled,' he says, firmly. 'Continue, Ms Toombs.'

She nods graciously. 'Thank you, Your Honour.'

Then she turns to me briefly before resuming her address to the jury. They seem impressed with her so far. One of the men smiles at her, which she ignores.

'Your cure, Mrs Walker? How was it effected?'

'Well, I was on a regime of drugs and a lot of talking therapy, of course.'

'Of course,' she says smoothly. 'And that was all?'

Damn her! She knows, of course she does. What do they say about good lawyers? They never ask questions they don't already know the answer to. It's a bit like the advertising business. When you write 'Would you like younger-looking skin?' it's not because you think the woman reading the ad might say, 'Don't be daft! Why would I want that?' It's because you've done your research. You know she's going to say, 'Are you kidding? Of course I would!'

'No,' I say quietly, as if by whispering the jury won't hear me and I can avoid what I know is coming next.

Rufus and I discussed it. He said the only way I could avoid answering questions was not to testify in my own defence. But there were risks associated with that choice, too. Back to the bloody jury again.

He told me they often interpreted a defendant's refusal to testify as evidence they had something to hide. And I don't. So we agree it's best, on balance, that I do go into the witness box.

But now I'm here, it doesn't seem such a good choice. Too late, Mel, too late.

'No?' she repeats, sliding up to the witness box and eyeballing me from two feet away. 'What else did Dr Silverman prescribe? Exercise, perhaps?' She turns to the jury. 'Yoga?'

The smiling man puts his hand up to cover his mouth.

'No,' I say.

'Well, what then?'

'A new treatment. From the US,' I say, laying out the story the way Rufus and Alfie made me learn it.

I wanted to say a revolutionary new treatment, but Rufus said that was a terrible choice of word. It conjured up two connotations, both negative. Either anarchists daubing statues with graffiti and chucking petrol bombs at police cars, or something bordering on fringe medicine that the prosecution could dismiss as quackery.

But why would they want to do that? I asked him. *They need to portray me as sane.* Rufus said they'd try to destroy my credibility as a witness. Having been declared fit to stand trial, they could do what they liked without risking the judge abandoning the trial for a second time.

But still I find it impossible to volunteer information. I simply can't do it. My heart is pounding in my chest and

I'm sure the jury must be able to see the sweat beading on my top lip. It's taking all my willpower not to wipe it away.

Ms Toombs has no problem with my reticence. She turns to me and offers a smile that reveals perfect white teeth. Veneers, I think. Mother Nature is never that kind to the English.

'What was it?' she barks.

'Pardon?' I ask, startled by the abruptness of her question and the sharpness of her delivery.

'What was this revolutionary new treatment from America that cured you of the psychosis you claim you were suffering from when you murdered your baby boy?'

'Objection!' Archie yelps, rising to his feet as if propelled by a spring.

'Sustained,' the judge says. He turns to the jury. 'The jury will disregard the prosecution's last question.'

'I'm sorry, Your Honour,' Ms Toombs says.

She doesn't look it, though. As she turns away from him and back to me, she smirks. I can read the expression all too well. *He told them to ignore it but they can't.*

'Isn't it in fact the case that your cure consisted of your taking magic mushrooms?' She turns to the jury. 'Magic mushrooms are a Class A drug in the same category as LSD, cocaine and heroin.'

I see the jury paying really close attention to me now. They look like the kind of people who buy the whole 'war on drugs' line from the government.

'No,' I say. 'You've got it wrong.'

She widens her eyes and turns to the jury, spreading her hands wide as if to say, *goodness me, how could I have been so silly?*

'Have I?' she asks, in a sing-song voice. 'Then perhaps you'd be kind enough to tell the court precisely *how* I've got it wrong?' She makes air quotes around the last three words.

'I didn't take magic mushrooms. I took a carefully prepared dose of pharmaceutical-grade psilocybin,' I say. 'Under strictly controlled conditions and in the presence of Dr Silverman.'

'Forgive me,' she says smoothly. 'I'm afraid I only got a C in my chemistry GCSE,' she offers a self-deprecating smile to the jury. Smiling man laughs openly, to be instantly admonished by the judge. 'Where precisely does one get this pharmaceutical-grade,' she frowns, 'silo-bin, was it?'

She mispronounces it on purpose, I think. Like George 'Dubya' Bush used to say 'nucular' instead of 'nuclear'. The man went to Yale, for God's sake!

'Psilocybin,' I say. 'Well, it's derived from a few different species of fungus and—'

'Fungus,' she says over me. 'Like mushrooms?'

'Yes,' I say.

'Magic,' she says, and I swear I see her wink at Smiling Man.

It's like taking a walk through a tropical jungle with a guide who points out all the traps and then you still walk straight into them. I can feel myself on the verge of tears.

'Very well,' she says, all business now, no more cat-playing-with-half-a-mouse business to entertain the jury. 'So we've established that you took an illegal drug derived from a fungus commonly called magic mushrooms. And as a result, you now have perfect recall of the night you mur...' she pauses, just long enough for the jury to remember her previous question, '...your husband found you holding Harry under the bathwater?'

I picture myself sitting in the bath, holding Harry. But I'm holding him up. And the detective said I was on the floor when she arrived, not in the bath at all. Maybe I blacked out. It's quite possible. Should I say something? No. It wouldn't alter the facts. And I'm exhausted. Suddenly I want very badly to go back to my cell.

'Yes,' I say.

'No further questions,' she says.

I am released and walk back to the dock and my school-dinner-smelling guard.

'The defence calls Dr Felicity Barber,' Alfie says.

17

Mel

Alfie asks Flick a series of questions that allow her to lay out her extensive credentials as a psychiatrist. She's won all kinds of prizes and honorary doctorates. Though, after a while, I notice the jury aren't paying attention anymore. One yawns. Another checks his watch.

When Alfie gives her the chance, she portrays me as a loving mother brought low by a cruel and debilitating illness.

His next question brings tears to my eyes, because I remember vividly that particular conversation.

'Dr Barber, how did Mrs Walker express her feelings about Harry's death to you?'

'She said she regretted it bitterly. She said that she realised what she had done was to rob him not only of the life he had, but of the life he might have gone on to enjoy.'

'Do you believe she murdered her son?'

'No. In fact, I don't even believe she was capable of it.'

'Thank you. No further questions.'

Ms Toombs rises to her feet and crosses the courtroom to address Flick face to face.

'Dr Barber, we've all listened with, I think I can speak for the whole court, astonishment at your long list of professional achievements,' she says, looking at the jury as if for agreement. A few of them nod. 'All those degrees and prizes. And, am I correct in thinking that none other than the *British Medical Journal* described you as a "a pioneer in new treatments for psychotic illnesses"?'

'In one,' Flick says, smiling at the lawyer.

The judge clears his throat. 'Doctor Barber, please answer the prosecution's questions in more conventional English.'

'I'm sorry, My Lord,' she says.

He smiles at her and the expression takes ten years off him. 'It's "Your Honour", actually. But apology accepted. Ms Toombs?'

'Thank you, Your Honour. Dr Barber, if memory serves, you've also been referred to in glowing terms by the *International Journal of...*' Ms Toombs hesitates, but it's one of her trademark theatrical pauses. I can see straight through it and I hope the jury can, too. 'Forgive me if I mispronounce this next word, *Psychopharmacological Research*?'

Flick nods as if accepting being questioned by a lesser being.

'You pronounced it beautifully. And yes, they have been kind enough to praise my work.'

Flick's Californian accent sounded so cool in the hospital. But now, in the wood-panelled courtroom, it sounds out of place, flippant somehow. Like she arrived wearing a bikini and holding a newly waxed surfboard under her arm.

'They called you a revolutionary, is that right?'

'Yup. Said I'd done more to drag the treatment of mental illness out of the dark ages than anyone since Sigmund Freud.'

Ms Toombs frowned and put her finger to the point of her chin.

'Sigmund Freud, the father of psychoanalysis, correct?'

'Correct.'

'Author of *The Interpretation of Dreams*, yes?'

'Two for two,' Flick drawls.

The judge rolls his eyes, but doesn't hold up proceedings.

'And a cocaine addict, yes?'

Fick's eyes widen. She glances at me. Then back at the lawyer.

'Well, you have to remember that in Vienna—'

'We're not in Vienna, Dr Barber. We're in London. Yes or no, Freud was a cocaine addict?'

Flick tosses her hair.

'Yes. Old Siggy was a right old coke-head, don't you know,' she says in a parodic *Lahndahn* accent she must have learned off one of those dreadful American TV shows.

Titters rustle through the public gallery.

'Dr Barber, I'd ask you, again, to show respect for the court,' the judge says.

She dips her head.

'Sorry, Your Honour.'

'We were talking about your press,' Ms Toombs says. '*The British Medical Journal. The International Journal of Psychopharmacological Research*. They like you, don't they?'

'They see the value in the work I do, certainly.'

'But it hasn't all been so uncritical, has it?'

A cloud flits across Flick's high, unlined brow.

'Sorry?'

'Are you familiar with the *New England Journal of Medicine*?'

'Well, yeah, obviously.'

'Dr Barber,' the judge growls.

'Sorry, Your Honour. Yes, I am familiar with the *NEJM*.'

'According to their website, the *NEJM* is the most widely-read, cited and influential general medical periodical in the world. Would you agree?'

'If that's what it says on their site, I guess it must be.'

'You have your reservations?'

'They're a little, let's say, reluctant to engage with cutting-edge research like mine.'

'I see. So when, in the January 17 2019 issue, it referred to you as, and I quote,' she says, lifting a sheet of paper, '"an ill-disciplined adventurer in psychopharmacology who uses the human psyche the way a surfer uses a big wave, more for her own gratification than for exploring the high seas", that's the *New England Journal of Medicine* – by your own admission the most influential medical publication in the world – being *reluctant* to engage with your work, is it?'

'They're the establishment, baby! The patriarchy!' Flick throws her arms wide. 'I mean, have you even *met* their editorial advisory board? Jesus, they make your House of Lords look like a Goddamn festival of diversity!'

'Dr Barber!' the judge roars. 'One more outburst like that and I will find you in contempt of court and you will be taken to a cell.'

Flick's chest is heaving. She's flushed a rosy pink. I can see it creeping up from her throat.

'I'm sorry, Your Honour, truly I am. But the NEJM is —'

'Please keep your opinions to yourself unless and until asked for them by the prosecution,' he says. 'Ms Toombs?'

'Thank you, Your Honour,' she says smoothly, looking as though nothing has happened. 'Psilocybin has been used quite successfully in the US to treat victims of Post-Traumatic Stress Disorder, commonly known as PTSD. That's right, isn't it, Dr Barber?'

Flick frowns. She looks puzzled by Ms Toombs's sudden swerve from hostile to interested. I want to scream, '*It's a trap!*'

'Yes, it is. Has been, I mean. Sorry.'

She sounds rattled. She glances over to Archie. Then me.

'But like all psychoactive substances used in the treatment of mental illness, it does have side effects, doesn't it?'

Flick doesn't answer straight away. Then she brings her hand up to her face and begins chewing a fingernail.

'Dr Barber?' the judge prompts.

'In rare cases, psilocybin does have a few mild and easily treated side effects, yes,' she says. 'But all drugs carry a degree of risk. The contraceptive pill. Anti-depressants. Statins. Even paracetamol.'

'But you weren't prescribing paracetamol to the defendant, were you? You were administering psilocybin, which is, just to remind the court, a Class A drug.'

'Yes, but Dr Silverman had a licence from the government – the *British* government – to conduct the trial. It was all, like, totally legal.'

My heart is sinking faster than the *Titanic*. The way Flick says, 'like, totally legal' makes her sound like some teenaged pothead arguing with a cop.

Ms Toombs smiles. 'Whether the treatment you and Dr Silverman cooked up between you was, *like*, legal or otherwise—'

'Objection!' Archie says, barely making it out of his chair. It sounds half-hearted.

'Sustained. Rephrase if you would, Ms Toombs.'

'Sorry, Your Honour.' She turns back to Flick, who is now gnawing on her fingernail like she hasn't eaten for a week. 'Let's talk about the side effects. Would I be right in saying that the side effects you choose to call "rare", "mild" and "easily treated" include hallucinations that persist for up to a week after the dose is given?'

'Occasionally.'

'A sense of disconnection from reality?'

Flick shrugs. 'It's been reported.'

'Problems with memory?'

Now I see where this is going. Flick doesn't. She looks like a punch-drunk boxer on the ropes. Maybe she thought she'd come into this *Briddish* courtroom and play it like a bloody violin, with her blonde hair and her damned freshly scrubbed beauty. And then, Wham! I fought the law and guess what? The law won.

'A couple of cases. Three, maybe? I can't remember.'

Ms Toombs turns to the jury and favours them with a dumb show of disappointment. Head shaking. Lips turned down.

'Perhaps you've been dabbling in your own treatment then, but let me refresh your memory for you. Isn't it true, Dr Barber, that there have been, in fact, nineteen cases of people whom you or your colleagues have treated who have reported significant memory impairment as a direct result of your treating them with psilocybin?'

'The causal link has never been proven.'

'Were you and your university sued by a Mr Derrick Fogerty of Fort Wayne, Indiana in March of last year?'

'It sounds like you know we were.'

Ms Toombs nods, as if Flick has just offered a compliment.

'What was the substance of his claim?'

'Mr Fogerty accused us, well, me, really, of causing irreversible brain damage.'

I hear a noise. It's as if the whole court, at that moment, becomes a single person and gasps.

'Silence in court!' the judge barks.

'Did you?' Ms Toombs asks again.

'The case was settled out of court.'

'In his deposition, the unfortunate Mr Fogerty said his memory impairment was so severe that,' Ms Toombs reaches for another sheet of paper, '"I can't tell if my memories are real or fantasy anymore". Would you describe that side effect as,' a beat, 'mild?'

Flick shrugs.

My heart drops into my belly. With that single offhand gesture, she's just tossed away the last shreds of her credibility. I see the smiling juryman shaking his head and making a note.

'It was never proved.'

'That's not an answer.'

'No, and I can't give you one, because the terms of the settlement included an NDA for all parties.'

Ms Toombs swivels to the jury and smiles.

'For the benefit of the jury, who may not be familiar with your legal jargon, NDA stands for?'

'Non-disclosure agreement.'

'Oh, I see,' Ms Toombs says. Of course she sees, she's a bloody lawyer for God's sake. 'Like keeping a secret?'

'Like doing what the lawyers told us to.'

Ms Toombs thanks Flick and returns to her table.

Alfie does what he can to repair the damage to Flick's credibility but it's too little, too late. The prosecution have established that Flick's treatment, far from being cutting-edge or even, God help us, revolutionary, is actually risky, disavowed by the world's premier medical journal and capable of screwing up people's memories.

* * *

'The defence calls Dr Ruxandra Begu,' Alfie says.

The woman who takes the stand is in her early forties. She's slight, no more than five feet tall. Yet in the short walk through the courtroom to the witness box, she radiates confidence. Her dark eyes dart this way and that, settling on me for a moment before flitting away again.

'Dr Begu, would you state for the court your job title,' Alfie says.

'I am Senior Forensic Pathologist at Hammersmith Hospital.'

'And that word, "forensic". Could you explain to us what that means?'

'Certainly,' she says with a brief smile. She turns to the jury box. 'The word "forensic" means "relating to the court". As well as being a fully qualified pathologist, I am also accredited by the Home Office to investigate unexplained deaths, conduct forensic autopsies, or post-mortems, and to present evidence in court.'

'Thank you, Dr Begu. Can you tell the court what happened on Tuesday eighteenth May 2019?'

'I was asked by the defence counsel for Mrs Walker,' she glances in my direction, 'to conduct a second post-mortem on Harry Walker. The Crown Prosecution Service had already ordered an initial PM, which was conducted at another hospital.'

'Was your post-mortem report ever used in court?'

'No, because the trial of Mrs Walker was postponed by the judge. My report was sealed until the trial was restarted. In case it should be needed,' she added.

'Thank you. I'd like to take you back to the day you conducted the post-mortem on Harry Walker, if I may. Can you tell the court what your conclusion was as to manner of death?'

'I concluded that the manner of death was homicide.'

'So he was killed deliberately?'

'Yes. That is what I mean.'

'I see. And the cause of death?'

'Harry Walker was asphyxiated.'

Alfie pauses before asking another question. He frowns at the jury. The lines that groove his forehead make him look older, although not by much.

'Sorry, Dr Begu. Asphyxiated. Could you explain that word for us?'

'The word "asphyxia" comes from the Greek: *a*-meaning "without" and *sphyxis*, meaning "squeeze", as in the throb of the heart,' she says in a clear, warm voice, looking at each member of the jury as she speaks. I see a couple of them nodding and smiling. 'What it means in practice is that the body does not receive enough oxygen, and dies. This is called hypoxia.'

'I see. Can you tell us what causes asphyxia?'

She nods. I begin to revise my opinion of Alfie. The way he is walking this clearly highly qualified doctor through her evidence is drawing the jury in. Most are leaning forward, staring intently at Dr Begu, occasionally checking on Alfie to see how he reacts to her answers, perhaps searching for cues as to how they should respond in their turn.

'There are a number of causes. They range from carbon monoxide poisoning to drug overdoses.'

Ms Toombs is on her feet.

'Objection. Your Honour, where is this going?'

The judge, frowning, looks over at Alfie. 'Mr Weir?'

'Yes, Your Honour. I'm getting to that.'

'Please do, then.'

Alfie nods and turns back to Dr Begu. He catches my eye as he does so and his right eyelid droops, just for a moment. Did he just wink at me? My pulse jerks upwards. Is this the moment where the star lawyer, underrated by his client, the prosecution, the judge, jury, press, public and court officials pulls the rabbit out of the hat?

'Drowning?' he asks.

My heart, so flighty just a moment earlier, crashes down to Earth. *No*!

'Yes. Drowning is one of the most common causes of asphyxia,' she says in a loud, clear voice. 'The lungs fill with water, preventing oxygen from reaching the bloodstream and causing generalised hypoxia and death.'

'As happened in the case of Harry Walker?' he says sadly.

The jury are leaning back. They've heard all they need to. Christ! Just when I thought Alfie had a card up his sleeve, he—

'No.'

I hear indrawn breaths. Up in the public gallery, the journalists are all writing frantically in their notepads.

Alfie's youthful features perform a complicated series of movements. His eyes narrow, his brow creases further. His mouth quirks to one side. He reaches up and adjusts his wig.

'I'm sorry, Dr Begu, did you just tell the court that Harry Walker did not drown?'

'That's correct.'

His frown deepens as if he suspects his own expert witness, for reasons unknown, is trying to hoodwink him.

'Then, and forgive me, Dr Begu for pushing you on this, how on earth *did* he die?'

'I believe Harry Walker was smothered.'

I blink and look left at the G4S guard, seeking reassurance that I did, actually, hear what Dr Begu said. He stares straight ahead.

18

Mel

Alfie walks a little distance away from Dr Begu to stand in front of the jury. He sweeps his gaze along the bench.

'Smothered,' he repeats, as if hearing this word for the first time. 'How would a person smother another person?'

'There are lots of ways. As long as the airways leading to the lungs from the mouth and nose are obstructed, you have smothering.'

'Could you give us an example?'

'Yes. A person could push a pillow over their victim's face, hard, and hold it there until the victim was dead.'

I see it then. A look that flashes along the two rows of jurors, like a wave. Disbelief, followed by a realisation that this calmly spoken, highly qualified doctor is telling them a new story. A story that the prosecution and the police have been avoiding all along. This is the third prong of Alfie's strategy.

'But the little boy was found in the bath, according to his father's testimony,' Alfie says. 'Why do you say he didn't drown?'

'It's very simple. I did find a small amount of water in Harry's mouth and trachea,' she turns to the jury, 'that's his windpipe.' A couple of them smile and nod their thanks to her. 'But there was no water in his lungs. Harry Walker did not drown.'

'You mentioned smothering just now, Dr Begu. And you gave the example of a pillow being held over the victim's face. Is that what happened to Harry?'

'I believe it did, yes,' she says.

This time, Dr Begu looks at the judge, rather than the jury. And, miracle of miracles, I see that he is paying just as much attention to her narrative as they are. More, perhaps.

'Do you have any evidence to back up that assertion?' Alfie asks now.

And I realise, all at once, that of course she does. Otherwise he wouldn't have asked the question.

'Yes. I do have evidence.'

'Please explain.'

Dr Begu stands straighter, though she is so short that it has barely any effect. It doesn't seem to matter, though. The court is utterly silent.

'I found a small feather in Harry's trachea.'

'How could a feather find its way into a little boy's windpipe?'

'He must have inhaled it.'

'In your professional opinion, Dr Begu, could Harry have inhaled this feather in normal breathing? Say, while lying on the bed used by his father?'

'No. It is extremely unlikely. In fact, I would say it is impossible.'

'Why are you so sure?'

'The air pressure generated by a baby's breathing in normal circumstances is insufficient to draw a foreign object so deeply into the trachea. In fact, it's much more likely that he or she would sneeze it out again,' she says. 'But I found the feather in the bifurcation of the trachea.' She turned to the jury again. 'Imagine an upside-down capital "Y". The two descending arms lead to the left and right lungs. I found the feather a centimetre before this junction.'

'Then what *would* have caused enough pressure to pull it that far down?'

Dr Begu nodded. 'When we struggle for breath – even very tiny babies – the muscles trying to draw air into our lungs are working two to three times harder than normal. This greatly increases the pressure pulling air – and any foreign objects – inwards.'

'So you're saying Harry was struggling to breathe and this produced enough air pressure to suck the little feather deep into his windpipe?'

'Yes.'

'Dr Begu, you have been shown the crime scene photos, is that right?'

'Yes.'

'Were there any feathers in the Walkers' bathroom?'

'None that I could see, no.'

'Thank you. No further questions.'

It's the prosecution's turn to cross-examine our witness. Ms Toombs rises from her seat. If she's rattled, she's far too much a professional to show it. She lifts her head and sniffs, like a big cat scenting prey.

She smiles at Dr Begu. Prowls across the eight feet of floor between the prosecution table and the witness box. The image of a predator grows stronger in my mind. Not something large and muscular, like a lion or a tiger. More slinky, more deadly, somehow: her legal robe makes me think of a black panther.

'You're extremely well qualified, aren't you, Dr Begu?'

Dr Begu nods. 'I completed a medical degree before specialising in Pathology. After completing the required studies in Anatomical and Histological pathology, I trained for three years in Forensic Pathology at the University of Dundee.'

'Goodness me! Anything else?'

'After gaining my diploma in Forensic Pathology, I took the unusual step of also gaining a diploma in Medical Jurisprudence. I am Home Office-accredited and passed out top of my class in the Expert Witness Training Course run by the Forensic Science Service.'

'And was it stressful, all that studying? All that pressure?'

'Objection!' Alfie says. 'Your Honour, the witness's stress levels during training can hardly be considered relevant.'

The judge purses his lips. 'Ms Toombs?'

'Your honour, it is entirely relevant to the case, as I will show immediately, if Your Honour permits.'

'Very well. I'll allow it. Overruled.'

She nods graciously, the cat bowing before a bigger beast. 'People react to stress in lots of ways, don't they, Dr Begu?'

'I suppose so, yes.'

'Some become addicted to running, for example. The so-called adrenaline buzz. Others to cigarettes, or binge eating. Some people meditate, or do yoga. And others, sadly, turn to alcohol.' She pauses. 'Dr Begu, do you have a drink problem?'

Dr Begu blinks. For the first time since she took the

stand, her composure falters. I see a gazelle drinking at a waterhole, head down, nose to the cool liquid, startled by the realisation she has been joined by something that means to eat her.

'I am teetotal.'

'I'm sure you are. But that's not my question,' Ms Toombs says, sounding as though she merely wants to help the witness better understand what's required of her. 'Let me rephrase it. Are you an alcoholic? I'd remind you, you are under oath.'

The silence stretches out. Five seconds. Ten. The jurors are all staring at the diminutive woman on the witness stand.

'Dr Begu?' the judge prompts.

Dr Begu lifts her head and stares back at Ms Toombs.

'Yes.'

I feel the floor shift beneath me. I imagine Dr Begu is experiencing something similar, but more profound.

'And has your illness ever led to any negative incidents in your professional life?'

'Yes, it has.'

'Could you elaborate for the court?'

My hopes, so recently rising like a helium balloon let slip by an inattentive child, crash to earth, the thin membrane holding the precious gas inside punctured by this one barbed question.

'I was suspended from my post for a month in 2015.'

'Why?'

'I mishandled a forensic post-mortem.'

'Mishandled?'

'I was drunk. I contaminated the body.' Perhaps realising that Ms Toombs would only keep biting down harder if she prevaricated, Dr Begu continued. 'I failed to follow the stipulated hygiene protocol and introduced foreign material into the body cavity.'

'Foreign material? Can you be more specific?'

'A hair. One of my own.'

'Did this,' Ms Toombs pauses, '*failure* have any consequences for the police investigation? It was a murder, I believe? Of a child?'

'The case collapsed.'

'And the murderer walked free.'

'We don't know—'

'What sort of bedding do you have in your house, Dr Begu?'

'Pardon?'

'It's a simple enough question. Your bedding. Duvet, sheets,' she pauses, 'pillows'.

'We have all kinds.'

'Nylon?'

'No, cotton.'

'So, not *all* kinds, then. How about the fillings? Polyester?'

'No.'

'Memory foam? It's very popular these days.'

'No. Down.'

'What type?'

I see what's coming. It's unbelievable. How do these lawyers know all this stuff? Then I chide myself. It's their job, dummy!

'Goose.'

Ms Toombs pauses for a long moment, just to make sure the jury get the point.

'Goose,' she says. 'Not Hungarian, by any chance?'

'I'm not sure,' Dr Begu murmurs.

'I'm afraid I didn't catch that. Could you repeat your answer?'

'I'm not sure. It could be. I'd have to check.'

Ms Toombs smiles sweetly at the pathologist.

'No need, Dr Begu.' She turns to the judge. 'Your Honour, I'd like to introduce into court a sworn affidavit by a Mr Trevor Gough.'

There is a moment of activity as a court official, or possibly a junior member of the prosecution team, I'm not sure, produces a transparent plastic evidence bag and shows it to the defence and the judge.

Alfie tries to argue that this should have been given up in disclosure. Ms Toombs says that the evidence only came to light during the trial itself. The judge retreats to his chambers with both lawyers for ten minutes and the court is cleared.

When we are brought back, Ms Toombs wears a feline smile – the cat that got the cream, or possibly the antelope. Alfie is downcast. He doesn't meet my eye.

'The court allows the introduction of the affidavit,' the judge says.

'Thank you, Your Honour,' Ms Toombs says. She turns to the jury. 'Trevor Gough is the sales manager at Northwood Beds in Guildford, Surrey. In his sworn affidavit he says that his company sold a set of goose-down pillows to Dr Begu on March 1st 2017 through its website. The down in question came from a Hungarian goose.'

Ms Toombs swivels towards Dr Begu, who looks stricken. 'I put it to you, Dr Begu, that given your *questionable* professional history of, in your own words, "contaminating" a body with one of your own hairs, the feather you found in Harry Walker's trachea was, in fact, conveyed there – I am sure quite accidentally – by you.'

'No. I am sure of it. The accident before was a one-off. I have been sober ever since.'

'I'm sure you have been. But tell me, are you saying

that it is a *one hundred percent impossibility*, under *any* circumstances, for a single, *minuscule* feather from your own bedding to have found its way into Harry Walker's windpipe, even by accident. Think very carefully before you answer.'

Dr Begu is red-faced. I can see the shame burning her from the inside. She swallows.

'No.'

'It is possible, then.'

'Yes. But there are strict protocols. I took every precaution—'

'No further questions, Your Honour,' Ms Toombs says, crisply.

I look across at Alfie. He is staring at the table in front of him. He looks like a child whose favourite toy has been broken by bullies. The judge consults his watch.

'Do you wish to re-examine the witness, Mr Weir?'

'No, Your Honour.'

'Then, as it's ten to twelve, we'll break for lunch here. Court will resume at two.'

The usher steps forward. 'All rise.'

Two hours pass in a haze. The warder brings me a sandwich and a can of something sweet and fizzy to drink, but I barely register it. My head is filled with so many conflicting thoughts. After finally regaining my sanity and learning I'd drowned my own child in the bath, it now looks like nothing happened the way I thought it had. What's even worse is that my own legal team is suggesting that it was Jonathan who murdered Harry.

Because that means not only is he a monster, but he then arranged things so it looked like I killed Harry and he was the devastated husband and father who bravely held it together.

19

Mel

It's 2.00 p.m. and we're back in the courtroom. There is a different energy in here now. People thought they were here to hear one story and now it looks as though there's a completely different one unfolding right before their eyes. I imagine the journalists in the press gallery rewriting headlines, altering the angles of their reports. No more, 'Sick mother murders own baby'. Instead, 'Tragic Mel gaslit by murderous husband'.

Alfie stands.

'The defence calls Amélie Aubert.'

After a few minutes, the doors open and in walks the most stylish, beautiful woman I have ever seen. A low murmur ripples round the courtroom until the judge calls for silence.

She is tall and slender. Not skinny, though. She has a fantastic figure. And she's chosen an extremely expensive-looking, above-the-knee dress in a fine-ribbed grey jersey that really accentuates it. Her pinned-back hair is a deep auburn; it flashes with russet overtones under the courtroom lights. Where Ms Toombs prowls around the courtroom, this woman stalks, as if she owns it, and everyone in it.

When the clerk of the court swears her in, she sounds like a ham actor 'doing' a French accent. I'm sure she says, 'nossing' instead of 'nothing'.

Once she's been relieved of the Bible and the card by a clearly distracted clerk, she rests bony hands on the rail of the witness box and waits.

'Ms Aubert, thank you for attending this trial all the way from Paris,' Alfie begins.

She nods as if his gratitude is no more than her due.

'The law matters, no? Especially in a case of such seriousness.'

'Could you tell the court what you do for a living?'

'I am Managing Director of Lemaire et Monceau. We are a small but very successful merchant bank founded in 1743.'

'What is your relationship with Jonathan Walker, the husband of the accused?'

'He is one of my employees.'

'Has he worked for you for long?'

'*Oui.*' She blushes prettily and smiles at the judge, who offers her a nod of forgiveness. 'Sorry, I mean, yes. For eight years and four months.'

'On October 17th 2019, you attended a business dinner at a Michelin-starred restaurant in Paris called La Fête du Pauvre. You were celebrating the conclusion of a successful deal between two major energy companies to build a solar energy field in the Saudi Arabian desert.'

She nods. 'The food was delicious. But the service was

quite terrible. We had to complain,' she says, looking at the jury with a smile as if she imagines they too eat out in Michelin-starred restaurants all the time.

'Was Jonathan Walker present at this dinner?'

I wonder where he's going with this. Clearly he knows the answer.

'Yes, he was. He was instrumental in making the deal happen.'

'And did you have a conversation with Mr Walker towards the end of the evening where you discussed his family life?'

'Yes, we did.'

'I believe Mr Walker made a remark to you about not getting much sleep. Do you remember that?'

'Objection,' Ms Toombs cries. 'Leading the witness, Your Honour.'

'My apologies, Your Honour, I'll rephrase,' Alfie says with a smile. 'Ms Aubert, did Mr Walker say anything to you about his mental health or his general state of mind?'

'Yes, he said he was not getting any sleep because poor little Harry would not sleep through. He said it was driving him crazy. Wait,' she looks skywards, then back at Alfie. 'He actually said "It's driving me up the fucking wall".'

A hiss of disapproval at the swear word – even in her deliciously over-the-top French accent – pierces the silence in which the court has been listening to her testimony. Although in her cultured, super-sophisticated Paris accent, she manages to make even this blunt-edged Anglo-Saxon word sound sexy and chic.

'Did he say anything else about his son?'

She hesitates, and for the first time I see a crack in the facade of casual glamour. 'Yes.'

'Can you tell the court exactly what he said to you? I would remind you, Ms Aubert, you are under oath.'

'He said, "I'd like to strangle the little fucker".'

The gasps turn into mutters and the judge calls for silence. I realise I have tears running down my cheeks. I look across at the chairs occupied by the police. The DC, Ffion her name is, looks like someone just shot her. She's actually wincing. Beside her, the male DC is shaking his head.

'Thank you. No further questions.'

It's the turn of the prosecution. How is Ms Toombs going to catch out this woman who is, at the very least, her equal in power and status? Not by word games, I think. So it will have to be some form of character assassination, like she tried on Dr Begu.

'A celebratory dinner at a Michelin-starred restaurant. You said the food was good. But the service less so?'

'That's right, yes. It was so out of character, I spoke to Patrice personally. She's the *chef patron*,' she added.

'How was the wine?'

And now I see it. Ms Toombs played the alcohol card with Dr Begu and won the trick. She's found a tactic she likes and is using it for a second time.

'Excellent. The cellar at La Fête du Pauvre is the best in Paris.'

'And I imagine there were cocktails before dinner?'

'Oh, yes. A great many. Everyone was in a very good mood. Elated, you might say.'

Ms Toombs smiles and nods in agreement. The big cat is bunching her haunches, ready to pounce.

'And you?'

'Me?'

'Yes, were you…elated?'

She smiles. 'Of course I was! The bank had just made a commission of one hundred and seventy-eight million euros.'

'Such a lot of money,' Ms Toombs muses, looking at the jury as if to say, *So much more than ordinary folks like us could even visualise.* They nod, even though she must earn more than all twelve of them put together. 'How many of these cocktails did *you* have, Ms Aubert?'

The banker smiles. It's like watching a crocodile shrugging off its Wildebeeste disguise and fronting up to the panther.

'None.'

Ms Toombs blinks. She consults her notes.

'None?'

'No.'

'What about the wine, then? How much did you drink in your elation at this extraordinary payday?'

'None. I drank only water.' She turns to the jury. 'Fizzy.'

Smiling Man grins.

Ms Toombs sounds indignant.

'Really, Ms Aubert. You've told the court that your bank had just made a commission of almost two hundred million euros and everyone in your party was elated and drinking heavily. Yet you expect us to believe you drank only water. Why?'

'Oh, it is very simple. I am not proud of this.' She turns to the jury. 'For many, many years I used alcohol to self-medicate. I was under enormous stress as the first female managing director of the bank.' Her accent is thickening. It sounds as though she's putting it on. But maybe it's just because she's let the mask slip a little. 'Then, one day, I wake up in a hotel room and I have no recollection of how I get here. I look in the mirror and I see a very sad woman. That day I stop drinking. I have not taken a drink since then.'

As if she senses where Ms Toombs was attempting to take her, she stares at her.

'My recollection of that night is perfect,' she says in a clear, piercing tone that seems to carry right to the back of the courtroom.

'But when Mr Walker made this remark to you, he was drinking, yes?'

'He was. Heavily.'

'So it could just have been the alcohol talking. A stressed out, sleep-deprived new father, as you said yourself, letting his hair down. He didn't mean it literally, did he?'

'Objection,' Alfie says, rising. 'Leading the witness.'

'Sustained. The jury will ignore that last question.'

'I beg Your Honour's pardon,' Ms Toombs says smoothly, though she's biting her lip.

She doesn't get a chance to rephrase it because Aubert beats her to it.

'I am French,' she turns momentarily to the jury, 'as you can probably tell.' They oblige her with genuine smiles this time. I sense they like her despite or perhaps because of her uncompromising Frenchness. 'But if you will allow it, I would like to quote a line from Shakespeare to you. "The wine cup is the little silver well, where truth, if truth there be, doth dwell." I think Mr Walker was telling the truth *because* he was drunk.'

'No further questions, Your Honour,' Ms Toombs says, then plods back to her table.

'Any more witnesses, Mr Weir?' the judge asks.

'No, Your Honour. That concludes the defence.'

The judge adjourns the trial for the day, explaining we will reconvene at 10.00 a.m. tomorrow morning for the closing speeches. I am led back to my cell. I am beginning to think Alfie is going to pull my chestnuts out of the fire.

20

Mel

Overnight, Ms Toombs seems to have rediscovered a little fire of her own. She marches over to the jury box and rests her left hand on the rail before pointing at me.

'During this trial, the defence has told you all kinds of stories,' she says, leaning heavily on the final word. 'You might have imagined, when this trial began, that their strategy would have been to persuade you that although Melanie Walker, Harry's mother, did indeed kill her infant son, she did so while the balance of her mind was disturbed.

'But no. Instead, they seek to persuade you that, from being mentally unwell, she was, in fact, perfectly *compos mentis*. Their argument? "It weren't me, guv. It was me rotten old man wot dun it".'

She adopts a rough accent for this little line that I suppose she imagines is genuine cockney. But the jury lap it up. Smiling Man laughs aloud before, wide-eyed with shock at his indiscretion, covering his mouth with his hand.

'The defence has seized upon a six-and-a-half-millimetre-long goose feather as evidence that the accused did not in fact drown her son in the bath. Yet the pathologist appointed by the defence to conduct a second post-mortem on Harry Walker admitted, under oath, that it was possible that very same feather came, not from the spare bed in the Walkers' house, but from her own bed. In her own house.

'This same pathologist, an alcoholic whose professional incompetence while drunk had already torpedoed a different child murder case, also suggested to you that Harry didn't drown because his lungs were not filled with water.

'But you will remember, I hope, the evidence of the Crown's own pathologist. He explained to us, in such hard-to-listen-to detail, that in very young babies, even the presence of a small amount of water in a baby's throat, the amount he mentioned was "an eggcup full", could be enough to induce asphyxia and therefore death. Dr Begu agreed that she found water in Harry's mouth and trachea.

'Finally, we have the accused's treatment for her psychosis at the hands of Dr Silverman and Dr Barber. Now, Dr Silverman is a highly respected consultant psychiatrist working in the NHS. But what do we know of Dr Barber, really?

'Well, she wouldn't look out of place in an episode of *Baywatch*, but apart from that, she is an academic who likes to paint herself as a revolutionary. Smashing the patriarchal medical establishment with her brand of tune-in, turn-on, drop-out therapies. Therapies, I would remind you, that rely for their alleged efficacy on illegal drugs classed by our own government as Category A. In other words, as dangerous as cocaine, LSD and heroin.

'Dr Barber was keen to impress us with her qualifications and her glowing press coverage. But remember how reluctant she was to recall the damning judgment of the *New England Journal of Medicine*.

'Leaving aside the opinion of the journal even Dr Flick agreed was the most influential such publication *in the world*, she herself admitted that the side effects of the magic mushrooms she feeds to her experimental subjects include hallucinations, out-of-body experiences and severe memory loss.

'Given that the accused herself underwent this highly controversial, borderline illegal therapy, how can we trust a word the poor woman says? Isn't it, actually, far more likely that she murdered Harry not while insane, but while in the grip of sleep-deprivation-induced rage? That, aided and abetted by two compliant psychiatrists keener on advancing their own careers than patient care, she has assembled this fantasy of her poor husband being the killer?

'There is an old legal concept called Occam's Razor. It means, very simply, that the explanation that involves the fewest assumptions must be preferred to all others.

'In this tragic story of the death of a six-month-old baby named Harry Anthony Walker, I ask you to accept the explanation that meets William of Occam's conditions. He was murdered by his mother. He was murdered by Melanie Walker. I know it. Deep down, I suspect Mrs Walker knows it. And I think, once you have considered the evidence, you will know it too and therefore return a guilty verdict.'

It's Alfie's turn.

During the trial he seems to have grown older. He has

adopted a certain world-weariness in his manner that belies his age. The jury have responded to him before. I hope they do now.

'Ladies and gentlemen of the jury,' he begins, 'infanticide – the murder of a baby – is one of the most horrific crimes any society can contemplate. Why? Because it transgresses against every taboo we have laid down to protect ourselves. But it's doubly horrific when the perpetrator is the child's own mother.'

This sounds like he's summing up for the prosecution, not the defence. I try to keep my face immobile. I mustn't show the jury that his opening words have sent a pulse of alarm thrumming along every nerve in my body.

'You have heard a great deal of evidence that shows how Mrs Walker – Melanie – was suffering a severe mental illness in the months after Harry's birth and in the years that followed his death. But what you have not heard is a great deal of evidence to prove – beyond reasonable doubt – that she was guilty of his murder. Let us remind ourselves that this heinous crime requires not just the act but also the guilty mind, the *mens rea* as well as the *actus reus*.

'The prosecution's evidence amounts to the witness testimony of her husband, Jonathan Walker, whom I note is not in court today, and traces of baby lotion found on Melanie's hands. But isn't it more likely that the baby lotion was there for a far simpler reason? Perhaps, as my learned friend suggests, a reason William of Occam would approve of? That reason being that she had massaged it into his skin after giving him his bath earlier that evening?

'In contrast, we have heard evidence from Dr Begu, a highly qualified Home Office-accredited pathologist. She testified that not only were Harry's lungs free of any water at all, but also that she found a goose feather in his windpipe. A feather that was an exact match to the type found in the pillow Jonathan Walker's head had been resting on that very same night.

'We also heard from Mr Walker's boss, Ms Aubert. She told us that he said to her, "I'd like to smother the little" – and then he used that harsh, revolting word to describe his own son.

'Now, I must remind you that Mr Walker is not on trial here today. You do not have to consider whether the evidence against Mr Walker is strong enough to convict him. All you have to consider, and I believe that when you look at the evidence it will be plain to you, is whether there is reasonable doubt that *Melanie* is guilty. If you think that there *is* doubt, and that doubt is *reasonable*, then you must acquit her of murder.

'That leaves the second charge of infanticide.' He pauses. It stretches out to five seconds. 'I want you to imagine yourself in Melanie Walker's shoes. A first-time mother, out of your mind with sleeplessness and struggling in the grip of a deepening psychosis. There but for the grace of God, you might think, go I. And you would be entirely, morally, right to think that.

'Both before and during her trial, Melanie has expressed deep contrition and remorse for her actions. She understands that by her actions she has taken everything from her infant son: his life, his future, every opportunity to experience what it means to be a human being. She considers, and has stated, that she believes this will haunt her for the rest of her life.

'As you consider the second count of infanticide, you must be sure that Melanie was not only fully *aware* of what she was doing, but that she knew her actions, if indeed they *were* her actions, were *wrong*.

'You have also heard from two highly qualified psychiatrists, Dr Silverman and Dr Barber, that at the time of Harry's death, Melanie Walker was very far from well and, in fact, was suffering from psychosis so severe it had caused her to lose touch with reality. In everyday language, she was insane. Therefore, on that basis, you should find her not guilty by reason of insanity. Thank you.'

The judge makes a short speech to the jury about how he is the arbiter of the law, but they are the arbiters of the facts.

'Owing to the serious nature of the charges in this case, and the consequences for the defendant if found guilty, I am only prepared to accept unanimous verdicts on both counts.'

Then he sends them out to consider their verdict.

I am led downstairs to the cells. It is cool down here. I can't stop shivering. The warder ushers me inside the dank, tiled space and locks me in. I collapse onto the bench and hide my face in my hands. Did Jonathan really murder our baby? I can't believe it. In my mind, I still see myself sitting in that bath full of cold water, holding Harry in my arms and handing him out to Jonathan.

Of course I want the jury to find me innocent. And I know that's what my legal team have been working so hard to bring about. I don't want to go to prison, even if I did kill Harry. It's just, there's this gap in my heart where Harry should be and no amount of clever legal argument is ever going to bring him back to me.

Day turns into night. The jury have been sent home. I try to get comfortable beneath the rip-proof blanket, and I wedge the thin pillow in half beneath my head. I close my eyes.

It seems like it's only a second or two later that I open them again. It's morning. I passed the night in a deep, dreamless sleep. Which is odd, I think. Wouldn't I have spent the entire night in the grip of feverish nightmares of drowning babies and gin-swilling pathologists?

The warder brings me a mean breakfast: two slices of white bread with some red jam thinly spread on it and a plastic mug of weak tea. She leads me to a bathroom and watches me shower and wash and clean my teeth. I am, apparently, still a suicide risk. At least as far as the courts are concerned.

She leads me back to my cell. As she shuts the door, she speaks for the first time.

'I hope they find you guilty, you murdering bitch,' she says, her face expressionless. 'It's just a shame they abolished hanging.'

Then she slams the door and I listen to the scrape of the key in the lock.

Hours pass. I don't have a watch so I don't know how many. Three, maybe? Four? The door opens.

It's the same warder as before. The one who'd like to watch me drop through a trapdoor.

'Come on, you.'

She grabs me just above my right elbow and jerks me towards her, spinning me round so I end up facing away from her. She frogmarches me up the echoing stone stairwell, maintaining painful pressure on the nerves that run into my elbow joint.

The room falls silent as I enter. Everyone looks at me. I see my best friend, Disha, my best, truest friend. She catches my eye and smiles. It's a small sign that not everyone here believes I'm a murderer.

21

Ffion

Ffion scrutinised the twelve members of the jury as they came back into the courtroom and resumed their seats.

Some of her colleagues claimed they could tell how a jury had voted by looking at their faces as they came back into court. If they looked at the defendant it meant they were going with 'Not guilty'. No guilt of their own for sending somebody away, was the point, so they were able to look the defendant in the eye.

But if they avoided making eye contact with the defendant, they were going with 'Guilty'.

This was, in Ffion's considered opinion, bollocks. In the trials she'd attended, which admittedly weren't as many as some of the guys with their thirties on the horizon, where juries looked was about as good a predictor of their verdict as which of two raindrops made it to the windowsill first if it was pissing down outside.

Despite herself, she looked at the jurors as they took their seats. Two or three glanced at Melanie Walker. The rest avoided looking in her direction. Ffion sighed. Could that be a good sign? Then a fourth juror looked over at Melanie and actually smiled. Ffion shook her head in disgust. That was the case down the can, then, wasn't it? Who smiled at somebody they were about to convict of murder?

The judge looked over at the jury foreman.

'On the charge of murder, have you reached a verdict upon which you all agree?'

'Yes, Your Honour.'

Ffion held her breath. It wasn't an unconscious thing. She always did it. A sort of plea to some higher power to nudge the spinning roulette wheel in her favour. After all those hours spent on the case, patiently assembling evidence, all those days when she sat with Jonathan, talking to him as he worked his way down bottle after bottle of expensive single malt, she felt she was owed this one.

'What is your verdict? Please answer only guilty or not guilty.'

Ffion felt her pulse throbbing behind her eyeballs.

22

Mel

The jury foreman glances at me before delivering the verdict on the murder charge. I try to read his expression. I give up. It could mean anything. He saves me the trouble.

'Not guilty.'

My knees buckle and I grab onto the rail in front of me to stop myself falling. I hear one or two cries from the public gallery. I can't believe it – I'm free. I suddenly realise how frightened I've been of going to prison.

The judge asks him for the verdict on the infanticide charge. The foreman looks at me again. And this time I see it. A hardness behind his eyes. Such a vivid shade of blue.

'Guilty.'

But that's wrong, I want to shout. It was supposed to be not guilty by reason of insanity. Were you even *listening* to my psychiatrists?

The judge looks at me. It's not an unkind look, I think. He looks sad.

'Melanie Walker, you have been found guilty of the terrible crime of infanticide: the killing of a child under twelve months old. Indeed, to give it its correct legal name, you have been found guilty of *maternal filicide*: the killing of your own child.'

He sounds as if he is speaking from the bottom of a well. His voice is muffled and echoey and his words bounce around inside my skull as if I am that well.

The judge looks around the courtroom, at the defence and prosecution teams, the jury, the public gallery and the seats occupied by the police officers.

I am crying. The tears are flowing like rivers down my cheeks. I don't even try to mop them with a tissue. They begin plopping into my lap. For a moment I think: what if they flood the courtroom and we all end up swimming for our lives through my tears? Then I shake my head violently. No! That's starting to feel a little too like my bad times at the hospital. I won't let myself go anywhere near that state of mind ever again.

The judge looks at me.

'In deciding how to deal with your case, I have considered very carefully a mass of evidence,' he says, 'including extremely helpful submissions from both the defence and prosecution lawyers, for which I thank them.'

He nods in their direction and I watch as they bow their heads briefly in recognition of this moment of praise. Then he fixes me with that gaze again and I feel my pulse skittering. My vision telescopes until all I can see is that bulbous nose of his and his eyes above it.

'I do not consider that justice would be served by sending you to prison. Under the terms of the Infanticide Act 1938, I am sentencing you to three years' probation and such treatment as Dr Silverman deems necessary to ensure you are fully recovered from your psychosis. You will comply with the terms both of your probation and your doctor's treatment regimen. Failure to do so,' he eyes me beadily, 'will result in an immediate custodial sentence.'

And that's that. After some closing remarks during which the judge thanks prosecuting and defence counsels once more, plus the police, the jury and the witnesses, the courtroom empties.

* * *

I stand outside the courtroom, stunned into immobility, while Alfie crosses the tiled corridor to shake hands with Ms Toombs. They're laughing together and I suddenly realise that this is just another day at the office for them. You win some, you lose some.

Rufus comes up to me.

'I'm sorry, Mel,' he says.

'How could they convict me of infanticide?' I demand. 'The cause of death wasn't conclusive. There was reasonable doubt!'

He holds his hands wide. 'Not for the jury. They believed the prosecution.'

I see a scrum of reporters coming my way and look around in a panic. And see Disha rushing over. She's crying but smiling too and she grabs me by the arm.

'Come on,' she says. 'My car's round the back.'

Disha looks like the sweet-natured, small-boned Indian doctor that she is. But when roused, she can swear like a navvy on payday as my mum used to say.

The first journalist to shove an iPhone at me gets a mouthful that has him reeling back.

'Get away from my friend, you rodent!' she shouts into the startled young guy's face.

Then, leading with her left shoulder, she literally barges through them all, dispensing a few more ripe combinations of Anglo-Saxon and Hindi swear-words.

She leads me at a run to her car, shoves me into the passenger seat, slams the door then jumps in beside me, starts the engine and puts her foot down. The little hatchback lurches forwards and we scatter the few journalists who've kept up with us so far.

'Yeah, that's right,' she yells at them through the window. 'Get lost! *Bakavaas karana*!'

A space opens up and she puts her foot down. The car's little engine screams and we are out.

23

Ffion

As the judge thanked the prosecution and defence teams, witnesses, jury and police, Ffion looked over at the CPS lawyer. Ms Toombs was good. She had a pretty decent strike rate. Just not today. Ms Toombs caught Ffion's glance and rolled her eyes.

Outside the court, Ffion called Rob.

'The Walker case just ended.'

'And?'

'Not guilty of murder, guilty of infanticide.'

'That's a result, then, isn't it? I mean, the CPS said murder was a long shot.'

'Oh, listen to you, Mr Pollyanna. She got probation and a treatment order. That's it.'

'She was ill, Feef. You have to remember that.'

'Yeah, I know. It's just in all the back and forth about what precisely was the nature of her mental health, nobody seemed to be remembering that this was about a dead little boy, yeah? Six months old, Rob! That's all Harry Walker was when he was killed.'

Rob nodded. 'How about a beer tonight? We can put it to bed over a couple of pints.'

* * *

Four hours after Ffion called Rob, they were occupying a wooden table at the back of a riverside pub. The Dove's sheltered terrace overlooked the Thames and the green towers of Hammersmith Bridge shimmered through a light mist rising off the river. Rob had just returned from the bar with two pints of London Pride bitter and a packet of cheese and onion crisps.

'Thanks, mate,' Ffion said, taking a sip of her beer.

'No problemo!' Rob said, doing a passable Bart Simpson impression. 'Listen, while you were in court, the guv asked me to work on that warehouse burglary in Acton. She said we'd done a decent job on Harry Walker, but it was time to let it go and move on to other cases.'

Ffion took another swig of her beer before speaking.

'Fair enough. Can't stand in the way of progress, can we?'

Rob frowned and put his pint down.

'You all right, Feef?'

She hesitated. Because 'all right' was about as far from an accurate description of her state of mind as it was possible to get. Rob was a nice guy, and during the three years they'd been working together, they'd struck up a pretty decent working relationship. Heavy on the banter, light on the mansplaining. Shared confidences over chicken jalfrezis at the Rajpoot on Hammersmith Grove. And gratifyingly free of clumsy attempts to ask her out.

But did she know him *that* well? Well enough to share the secret that had driven her, from the age of six, into a career in the police? She looked at him. He had an open face. Not exactly handsome. But attractive. Widely spaced eyes that always looked as though there was a proper brain behind them.

Maybe he'd understand. She sighed.

'No, mate. I'm not all right. It's the case.'

'I'd got that far on my own,' he said with a smile. 'It's affected you differently to the others. Even when we lost that bank blag last year, you bounced back straight away. What's up? Did it make you think of Mia and Elspeth?'

She shook her head.

'Not my daughters, my sister.'

Rob frowned. 'I didn't think you had a sister. I thought you were an only child?'

'I know, Rob. Because that's what I tell people.'

Rob looked back at Ffion. She saw it, in his intelligent eyes. Understanding dawning. Maybe she'd not have to spell it out for him.

'You had a sister, but she died,' he said quietly. 'When she was a baby.'

She nodded. Wondered whether, after all this time, the memory of Lowri's funeral would reduce her to tears.

'She was eighteen months old. I was five. My mum was fine with me, her health, I mean. But after Lowri was born she went into this massive depression.' She sniffed and took a sip of the beer to moisten her throat, which had suddenly dried. 'She drowned her in her little baby bath. Pale-blue plastic with three ducks on the side.'

'God, mate, I'm really sorry.'

'There was a trial, just like for Melanie Walker. They found her not guilty by reason of insanity. After that, she was sectioned. My dad couldn't cope. He left us,' Ffion said. 'I went to live with my auntie and uncle. They brought me up as one of their own. They had five other kids. My auntie said one more wouldn't make any difference. I call her Mam and Uncle Rhys, Da.'

'What about your mum? Is she still alive? Do you see her?'

'She lives in sheltered accommodation. She never really got better.'

'I wish you'd said something when we were investigating. I could have, I don't know, been more sympathetic or something.'

She smiled then, sniffed again. Reached into her pocket and fished out a tissue to blow her nose.

'Mate, if you were any more sympathetic I'd probably have to slap you.'

'Hey! I could report you to HR for that.'

She finished her pint and gestured at his with her empty glass. 'Same again?'

'Go on, then.'

When she returned with the drinks, she asked Rob the question that had been plaguing her since leaving court that morning. It was so repellent, after all the time she'd spent comforting him, that she could hardly bear to voice it. But there had been something about the young defence barrister's closing speech that had wormed its way into her mind and taken up residence like a parasite.

'Do you think it could have been Jonathan Walker after all?'

'What, who murdered Harry, you mean?'

'Yeah. Do you think he could have smothered him like the defence made out? Then staged the whole thing to put the blame on Melanie?'

Rob took a pull on his beer.

'Did he have the means?' he asked.

'Yes. We know the pillows in the spare room were filled with goose-down.'

'What about a motive? In his testimony he came across as a doting father. When you were his FLO you always said he was completely devastated by it.'

'Yeah, but what about what his boss at the bank said? "I could cheerfully strangle the little fucker". Something like that, anyway.'

Ron waggled his head. 'On the face of it, yes that sounds bad. But he was pissed. I mean, I don't have kids of my own, but I know enough blokes who do. A couple of my mates have said similar things.'

Ffion's eyes flash-bulbed. 'Really?'

'Maybe not exactly like that. But, say, they've had one too many sleepless nights and it all gets a bit much and they just say something like,' Rob ruffled his hair, 'I don't know, "I'd like to lock him in the shed where I can't hear him".'

'I think there's a world of difference between that and what Jonathan said.'

'Fine. And, for the record, I agree with you. So let's say he had motive, too. Sleep deprivation. It's basically the same motive he was implying his wife had. That leaves opportunity.'

'Which is obviously a massive yes. His wife's doped up to the eyeballs on antidepressants,' Ffion said. 'The doctor said he'd given her sleeping pills as well, like a just-in-case option. So, what if Jonathan smothered Harry, put him in the bath, then went and got Melanie and somehow manoeuvred her into the position he said he found her in.'

'That might put the injury to the back of her head in a different light. Maybe she's awake enough to realise what he's doing—'

'Or has just done.'

Rob nodded, 'Or has just done, and fights him off. He pushes her, she goes over the edge of the bath and whacks her head on the taps.'

'Then he's got a perfect story to tell the first responders.'

Rob frowned. 'This is all very well, as far as it goes, but you're not asking the obvious question.'

'Go on then, oh sage one. Enlighten this poor stupid DC from the valleys. What did I miss?'

'Are we really saying a normal bloke would murder his own baby just to get a decent night's kip? Plus, he's put his wife in the frame, so he's going to lose both of them.'

'That's a very good question, mate,' she said. 'But you're wrong. I *have* asked it.'

Since seeing Jonathan's performance in court, she'd been wondering about him.

He'd mounted the steps to the witness box as if he were about to give a presentation at a sales conference instead of testimony in a Crown Court. The way he walked, Ffion remembered, was almost a swagger. He'd looked around the courtroom, lingering on the jury.

He'd smiled at them. It was a good smile. Reassuring, open. A smile that said, *'You can trust me. I'm good with money, I'm good with people'*. Then, as if realising the role he was playing, he'd drooped his lips into an expression of sadness and looked away.

Throughout his testimony, he'd remained perfectly calm. Even when the formidable Ms Toombs had asked him to describe to the court *'the terrible scene that met your eyes'*.

First he nodded at Ms Toombs, then he turned to the jury and explained, at length, exactly what he'd seen, what he'd said and what he'd done. How his wife had reacted. *'She screamed at me like she thought I was the Devil or something.'* How they'd struggled over the limp body of their son before he'd wrested the dead infant from his mother and in the process pushed her backwards, so she fell into the bath and bashed her head against the taps.

But the funny thing was, that during his entire retelling of the story, his voice hadn't wobbled once. His chin remained resolute, his lips firm, his gaze direct. Even when he'd broken down, it had looked staged to her. And when he'd removed his hands from his face, his eyes were clear, his cheeks dry.

Ffion had investigated the deaths of children before. It was by a long way her least favourite part of a job that she otherwise loved. And, without exception, the parents were in bits. Even if one of them turned out to be the killer. Which, depressingly, was more than ninety percent of the time.

Until they were confronted with undeniable evidence of the crime they'd committed, they put on a pretty convincing show of genuine grief.

Jonathan Walker was different. The defence counsel had even tried to pick him up on it. The judge reprimanded him before Ms Toombs was out of her chair to object. And, at the time, Ffion had been glad for the judge's intervention.

'Mr Weir!' he thundered. 'How a man manages his emotions in the wake of the severest pain any parent can experience is neither your business, nor that of this court.'

Alfie Weir, a decent barrister with bright future ahead of him no doubt, had bowed humbly and apologised.

But now, sitting here enjoying a drink with Rob as the evening sun dipped below the horizon and turned the river to molten gold, Ffion started to wonder.

'What if he's *not* a normal bloke, Rob?' she asked.

Rob put his pint down.

'What do you mean?'

Ffion frowned. She could feel the suggestion forming in her head and wasn't sure whether she should express it at all. Once she gave it oxygen, and light, it would demand a life of its own. To be taken seriously. To be *considered*.

'I'm going to say this out loud and I want you to wait until I've finished, before you say anything, right? And if, after that, you think I'm talking bollocks, well, you go right ahead and say it.'

Rob grinned. Though there was an edge to the expression that Ffion recognised. It was the look her partner got when, between them, they saw a case turn a corner.

'Go on, then,' he said. And he stuck his fingers behind his ears and flapped them out sideways. 'I'm listening.'

She took a quick breath. Here it came. The suggestion that might change the way she spent the next few weeks. Or months.

'What if…' Then chided herself mentally. *Come on, girl. This is no time to be backing out.* 'What if Jonathan Walker is a psychopath?'

There. She'd said it. She watched Rob, looking for a reaction. Was she so far off the reservation she'd need to get a cab back, or was she following a righteous trail that would lead somewhere very interesting indeed?

Rob's eyebrows, curved down at their outer edges like boomerangs, drew together. A deep crease appeared between them extending down to the bridge of his nose. He wasn't laughing, thank Christ for that. Then he tapped the tip of his nose with his index finger three times. It was one of the gestures Ffion had long ago grouped under the heading: *What Rob does when he's really thinking hard.*

She wanted to chivvy him along. To tell him to spit it out. To ask him whether he agreed it could even be a possibility. But she held her tongue. No leading *this* witness.

The eyebrows relaxed.

'If he is, then it changes everything,' he said finally.

She was so relieved he hadn't ridiculed her suggestion. It meant at the very least she could work through her feelings about the case without having to skirt this massive boulder blocking the path to the next case.

Ffion pictured Jonathan Walker in the witness box. Had a grief-stricken new father buried his emotions so deeply he had nothing left to express? Or, if you excavated to the very core of his being, would you find nothing at all? No grief. No love. No happiness, sadness, disgust. Nothing. Just an echoing vault of self-centred desire.

Had she been looking into the eyes of a psychopath all along?

PART III

TRUTH AND LIES

24

Ffion

After finishing their drinks at The Dove, Ffion and Rob had gone on to the Rajpoot and consumed a bottle of house red along with their lamb dhansak and chicken jalfrezi. The next day, nursing a vicious hangover, Ffion went to see her guv'nor, DI Russ Palfreyman.

He looked up from his screen and smiled.

'Hey, Feef, not a bad result on the Harry Walker case yesterday,' he said. 'Murder was always going be a long shot. Good work.'

She sat in the visitor's chair opposite him, rubbing her left temple. Her stomach was jumping and she thought for a moment she might have to make a dash for the Ladies. She took a calming breath.

'About that, guv.'

He frowned. 'What?'

There was a lot packed into that one-syllable question. Are you about to tell me you made a mistake with evidence? Did we not release something helpful to the defence in disclosure? Did you pressure a witness? Fix some dodgy forensics to tell a straighter story? Mislay a statement? Please God, don't tell me you destroyed anything before the trial?

'I want to do some digging into Jonathan Walker.'

'The husband? Why? The case is over, Feef. You and Rob brought the killer to justice. She was convicted and sentenced. Job done,' he said, tapping the desk lightly with his finger.

'I know, boss. I just can't shake this feeling that…' And here it came. The moment she made a confession of her own to her DI. He could go ballistic, justifiably.

Too late, Feef. You're in it up to your waist.

'That what?'

'That we arrested the wrong parent.'

Russ leaned back in his chair so far the back of his head hit the wall with an audible clonk. He rocked forwards again, rubbing the sore spot.

'Jesus, Feef, are you out of your mind?'

'No, boss. That's the trouble. The defence lawyer, right? When he was doing his closing speech, he said that Jonathan wasn't on trial so they didn't need to consider whether he was guilty,' she said. 'They just needed to decide whether there was reasonable doubt that Mel did it.'

'Exactly! Doubt on the murder charge, none on the infanticide,' Russ said. 'Like I said, job done. Pat on the back for my two hardest-working DCs. Onwards and upwards.'

Now she'd committed to this course of action, Ffion felt herself relax. She counted points off on her fingers.

'One, the pathologist said Harry didn't drown. She said she thought he'd been smothered. Two, she found a feather in his windpipe that matched those in Jonathan's bedroom. Three, the only real evidence against Mel was his testimony. But if he's a—' She caught herself just in time. Now was most definitely not the time to start bandying terms like psychopath around. Russ would have her out of his office faster than a Welsh winger running for the English try-line at Cardiff Arms Park.

Russ looked at her with narrowed eyes.

'If he's a what?'

'I'm just saying if it *was* him, then laying the blame on his mentally ill wife would be a smart move. Calculating,' she couldn't help adding.

Russ puffed out his cheeks. 'Where are we going with this, Feef?'

'I want to do some digging, boss. On Jonathan Walker.'

'No. I need you clearing some of this mountain of unsolveds I've got to report on at the end of the month.'

'I know. And I will. I promise. But what if I work it on my own time?'

Russ raised his eyes to the ceiling and blew out through flapping lips. And she knew she'd won.

He looked back at her.

'On your own, *unpaid*, time, what you do is your affair. But if I think, or if I even *wonder* if I think, that it's affecting your work, then you stop the moment I tell you, yes?'

'Yes, guv. Thanks.'

Russ rolled his eyes. 'Right. Now get lost before I change my mind.'

* * *

Over the next three weeks, Ffion worked as hard as she'd ever done on her active cases. She didn't want to give Russ even a *sniff* of a *suspicion* that he *wondered* if he *thought* she was slacking. In fact, he came to see her at the halfway point to thank her for her clearing a manslaughter case only two days after it had been committed. But early in the morning, when David and the girls were still sleeping, and late at night when they'd all gone to bed, she worked on.

David had complained about it one night in bed. She'd mollified him by letting him do the sex thing that turned him on so much but which she could take or leave, then returned to the kitchen table twenty minutes later, and her files.

Embarking on her research, Ffion had been half-hoping she'd find Jonathan Walker had a criminal record stuffed with incidents of cruelty and violence. Even though she knew that kind of luck rarely fell into hopeful coppers' laps. Apart from a handful of speeding tickets, the man was a clean skin. She was about to close the enquiry form on the PNC when a note brought her up short.

A traffic officer who'd issued a speeding ticket when Jonathan had been clocked doing ninety-three on the M5 had added a note to his citation.

Driver initially claimed his speedometer was one hundred percent accurate and he had only been doing 73 mph. When I showed him onboard cam footage he then claimed he was a surgeon rushing to operate on a child. I asked for his NHS ID and he claimed he'd left it at the hospital. I suspected he was lying and told him he could just accept his ticket and we could both get on with our days.

That was interesting. Ffion searched through her files for the notes she'd typed up during the Hendon course on serial offenders. Yes, here it was. DCI Cole had talked about how psychopaths lied easily because deep down they didn't care about the truth. To them, it had no meaning beyond what they wanted it to mean. Whereas regular offenders – 'normal' offenders – *cared* about the truth, they just didn't want to admit it.

Textbooks used the word 'glib' to describe the way psychopaths lied. Ffion had a vague idea that glib meant superficial, but then remembered Da's words whenever she'd wondered about a word as a young girl.

'If you don't know what it means, Ffion, there's a good book over there. Not the Bible, the dictionary. Use it!'

The thought of his lilting Valleys accent made her smile as she got up from the table and went into the sitting room to the book case where they kept the *Times Atlas of the World* and the *Oxford Dictionary*.

She flicked to G and found 'glib'. Yes, she'd been right. But as she read the numbered definitions, one caught her eye. 'Shallow. Insincere.' She put the heavy book back in its place and closed the glass-fronted door.

During her research, Ffion had contacted the HR departments of all the banks that Jonathan Walker had worked for. There were five in total, which she wondered about. He hadn't spent more than two years at any one place. Was that normal for a merchant banker? She realised she didn't have the faintest idea. Ask her how long the average villain spent with a particular OCG, or following a particular MO, and she'd recite the data like a schoolgirl at a spelling bee. But the world of high finance was as remote to her as the moon.

Three of the people she'd spoken to had immediately gone on the defensive, citing GDPR. The data protection law was every copper's nightmare. It sounded so great in principle – protecting people's privacy. But in practice it meant every organisation, from a village cricket club to a large company, could refuse to help the police find out even basic information about their members or employees.

Happily, two of the HR managers had been more accommodating. Maybe because after three knock-backs, Ffion had explained she was investigating the murder of a baby boy. It was true, in its way. Although Russ would probably have had a fit if he'd overheard her given the murder in question had already been solved, and prosecuted successfully. Well, according to him, anyway.

The two 'human asset profiles', which Ffion supposed meant personnel files, drew her into a world of thousand-pound lunches – for two – entertainment expenses including trips to Grands Prix by private jet, six-figure salaries and even bigger bonuses.

But once she'd overcome her shock at the obscene amounts of cash being trousered by, as far as she could see, wide boys with five-hundred-quid haircuts and 'glib' lines with banking clients, she began to see a pattern emerging in Jonathan Walker's own MO.

Banks, she realised, were a little like organised crime groups. Especially those run by families. OCGs and PLCs alike preferred to wash their dirty laundry in private.

Drug dealer getting a little greedy and skimming more than his fair share off the profits? A family member would be despatched to offer some friendly advice. Or, if previous advice had been disregarded, a couple of nine-millimetre rounds through the kneecaps.

A banker threatening to castrate a member of a rival team in front of witnesses? A discreet payment to the injured party and a company-mandated anger-management course for the would-be gelder.

She found seven incidents of threats and/or actual use of violence in Jonathan Walker's employment record. The most serious was a fight outside a nightclub on a jolly to

Dubai. Walker had in the words of the Lemaire et Monceau HR report, 'engaged in a physical altercation with three local men that led, unfortunately, to two of them needing medical assistance'.

If the Dubai police had taken any action, it wasn't mentioned in the report. But there was a reference to 'Disc. Pmnt DP' that Ffion interpreted as 'discretionary payment (to) Dubai Police' and a number: 3,000 AED.

Ffion Googled 'Dubai currency'. AED stood for the UAE Dirham. At that day's exchange rate, the 3,000 equated to £626.13. Not a fortune, certainly not for a bank happy to authorise almost twice that for lunch for two, but still a tidy amount. She could easily imagine an underpaid, overworked Gulf copper looking the other way for that kind of money.

Ffion really wanted to track down the men injured in the fracas. She emailed a request to Interpol: a database search for violent incidents involving foreigners in Dubai for the date mentioned in the HR report.

Next, she searched for Dubai A&E departments and found there were only three. It was 11.30 p.m. by her kitchen clock, which meant it was 3.30 a.m. in Dubai. But A&Es operated round the clock. Maybe she'd be lucky and find a bored and willing admin clerk who'd do a search for her.

The A&E receptionist at King's College Hospital was friendly, spoke perfect English, and stonewalled Ffion when she asked about two men who might have been admitted for treatment after a fight some four years earlier.

'I'm sorry Detective Parry, without the appropriate paperwork, I can't help you.'

Ffion thanked him and moved on to Medeor 24x7. This time she was luckier.

'Please hold,' the receptionist said, once Ffion had

explained what she wanted, adding this time that she didn't require any personal data, just details of injuries and the reason for admission.

Ffion watched the red sweep-second hand of the clock on the wall make three complete revolutions. In her ear, a rapid-fire clicking created a visual image. Plum-coloured nails tapping on a pristine white computer keyboard.

'Hello? DC Parry, are you there?'

'Yes, yes, I'm here.'

'OK, well there were two admissions on that night involving foreigners where the patients had been assaulted.' Ffion's pulse hiccupped and she pressed the phone tighter to her ear. 'One was a young woman, French, who was sexually assaulted. The other was a local businessman who was apparently involved in a fight with a Dutch engineer. Is that helpful?'

Ffion swallowed her disappointment. 'Yes. Thank you. You've been really helpful. Have a good night.'

That only left one more hospital.

With a sinking heart, Ffion dialled the number. It went to an answer machine.

'This is the emergency room at Emirates Specialty Hospital. All our staff are busy helping other patients. Please leave a message and we will get back to you as soon as we can. Thank you.' The message then repeated in Arabic.

Ffion left a short message explaining who she was and asking someone to please call her back.

She put her phone down.

'Well that's never going to happen, is it?' she asked the empty kitchen as she snapped the laptop shut.

David was snoring so loudly she could hear him from the bottom of the stairs. Shaking her head, she went into

Mia's room and cuddled up around her daughter's sleeping form. She could still hear David through the wall, but it was dull enough that she could ignore it. With Mia's snuffling breathing making her smile, she fell asleep.

25

Mel

Jonathan sent me a text this morning. It was very short.

Don't come back to the house. I want a divorce.

I can't deal with this right now. There's a little more wine in the bottle. And I know Gav has a nice bottle of brandy in the cupboard beside the fireplace.

I haven't felt able to go back to our house since the trial. I don't think I could face Jonathan. For his part, he's made no attempt to contact me. Instead I'm staying with Disha and Gavin in Ealing. Her practice is there; Gavin works nearby as a science teacher.

The terms of my probation have been explained to me. They're not harsh, though once again I find myself in tears as the implications of the simply worded sentences sink in.

My offender manager gives me a document with them

all laid out in neatly numbered paragraphs. I try to read along as she's talking, but the words refuse to yield their meaning and blur anyway as my eyes overflow.

'You must report to see me at my office in the council building every Wednesday at 10.00 a.m,' she says, poking her little round glasses back onto the bridge of her nose. 'You may not be in the presence of a child under the age of two unless accompanied by a court-appointed person. You may not be in the presence of a child under the age of six unless accompanied by one or both parents, guardians or carers. You may not undertake any work, paid or unpaid, that brings you into contact with children. This includes, but is not limited to, playgroups, nurseries and pre-school activity clubs; acting as a classroom assistant or helping with extra activities such as hearing children read or helping with school trips; Cubs, Brownies, Scouts and Guides.'

There are a few more conditions, but they're administrative. Letting Val – that's her name – know if I'm too ill to attend a meeting. That sort of thing. And at least they don't make me feel like a child-killer who might attack an unsupervised toddler unless under the watchful eye of my offender manager.

I've also met with Dr Silverman to discuss my treatment programme.

It's too much to take in. I can't talk to Disha about any of it, not yet. I'm staying in their loft conversion. It has its own bathroom. Mostly I stay up here, staring out of the window at the back gardens. There's a blackbird that sits on the windowsill and sings its little heart out. I watch it watching me: the yellow ring around its eye is the colour of egg yolk.

I am a convicted child-killer. It sounds so awful. Like one of those horrible men people on social media talk about wanting to castrate or hang, or torture to death in the middle of Trafalgar Square. But all I am is an ordinary woman. A mother.

Something went wrong in my head. I know I did a terrible thing, and I can't even imagine a time when I'll be able to forgive myself, but that 'Guilty'… I can't get it out of my mind. It's like tinnitus, only instead of a ringing it's the jury foreman's voice going round and round like a tape-loop.

'Guilty.'

'Guilty.'

'Guilty.'

'Guilty.'

'Guilty.'

'Guilty.'

'Guilty.'

I batter my palms against the sides of my head trying to make it stop. I lie on the bed and crunch the pillow up against my ears.

It doesn't work.

26

Ffion

Ffion glanced up at the kitchen clock: 7.48 a.m. She was in full-on Mummy-mode as David liked to call it. Munching on a piece of toast spread thinly with Marmite, she fetched cereal boxes out of the cupboard and dumped them on the table, asked both girls if they'd done their homework the previous night – 'Yes, Mum!' – flicked a speck of dandruff off David's shoulder and reminded him he had to buy a birthday present for his mum.

Then it was into the car and a fifteen-minute drive to work. She'd barely sat down and logged in to the system when her phone rang. The display said No Caller ID. Not particularly strange in her line of work; she handed out that many business cards to people.

'DC Parry,' she said, nodding a 'hi' to Rob who grinned at her from the other side of the pushed-together block of desks.

'This is Sarah Jenkins. I'm the A&E receptionist at Emirates Specialty Hospital? You left a message yesterday. Well, earlier today, really.'

The woman had an accent Ffion could place with pinpoint accuracy. Merthyr Tydfil. The town that had branded itself as 'Heart of the Valleys' lay about twenty miles southwest of Ffion's hometown.

'Oh, Sarah, thank you so much for calling back,' Ffion said, letting rip with her accent, like she did when visiting home.

'Sounds like you're a Valley girl, too,' Sarah said and Ffion could hear the smile in her voice.

'Neath, for my sins.'

'Oh well. Can't be helped. How can I help you, DC Parry?'

'Well, for a start, please call me Ffion,' she said. 'I was really hoping you'd be able to help me with identifying a couple of men who were hurt in a fight about four years ago.'

She plunged ahead before the receptionist could cite whatever local rules about data privacy or patient confidentiality applied in Dubai.

'You, see, Sarah, the thing is, I'm working on the tragic murder of a little baby boy. One of my lines of enquiry has brought me to your door,' she said. 'We believe that a person we're looking at might have committed an assault in Dubai about four years ago. We also think that the victims needed medical attention. I was really hoping you'd be able to tell me if they arrived at your department.'

'Of course,' Sarah said. 'Give me the date and I'll run a search for you.'

Punching the air, Ffion gave her the date and then waited. Rob made a T with his two index fingers, raising his eyebrows in mute enquiry. She nodded and mouthed 'yes please'.

A minute passed, then Sarah came back on the line.

'I can't give you their names, but yes, two local men were admitted that night,' she said. She sounded shocked. 'To be honest, reading the reports, it was pretty bad, actually. I wasn't working here then, but imagine Merthyr on a Friday night, at its worst.'

'Doing that,' Ffion said, picturing bloody scraps outside the clubs at chucking-out time.

'Now times that by ten.'

'What happened to them?'

'One had a broken cheekbone and three fractured teeth.'

'Sounds brutal.'

'Yes, but he was the lucky one. The second man had to have his left eye surgically removed. It was so badly damaged they couldn't save it.'

'Is there anything in the report about their attacker?'

'Hold on. I've got to go into a new screen,' Sarah said. 'Right, yes, here we go. Apparently, he was British. Smartly dressed, that's all it says.'

'Were the police involved?'

'They were brought in by paramedics, that's all I can tell you.'

'Thank you, Sarah. I can't tell you how helpful this is.'

'No probs. Tell you what, if you're ever in Dubai, look me up. We can go for a drink together.'

'I will. That's a promise.'

'Of course, I expect I'll be buying.' A beat. 'You know how tight Neath people are.'

Ffion laughed. 'Right. When it happens, I'm going to get you pissed on my credit card. No arguments.'

And with that, she ended the call, smiling at Rob as he placed a mug of tea in front of her.

'Result?' he asked.

'Oh, yes.'

The bureaucratic gods were smiling on Ffion that week. Just after midday on the Friday, her PC pinged with an incoming email. She took one look at the 'From' line – an Interpol email address – and clicked her mouse so fast she accidentally opened the next message down, a scintillating missive from facilities about remembering to turn off lights.

When she got the right email open she scanned it, looking for the relevant information.

Assault reported

Location: outside Boudoir club, Dubai Marine Beach Resort & Spa – Jumeirah St.

Two men assaulted by white male.

Victims required emergency hospital treatment.

Attacker identified by victims as white British, dressed in smart suit. Alleged to be part of group of banking executives. (French?)

Local police investigated.

Case closed for lack of evidence.

Ffion huffed out a breath. This could be it. Damning evidence that Jonathan Walker was capable of, and had in fact committed, an act of shocking violence. Or it could be nothing. Without names, it was meaningless. But it didn't *feel* meaningless.

* * *

That night, she re-read the Interpol email. She needed something more. Just one piece of evidence that would link Jonathan Walker to the assaults on the two Arab men in Dubai.

She realised where she could get it from. Not the bank's HR department. They were jobsworths who'd stonewalled her once already. But what about the lady at the top? Amélie Aubert? She'd seemed quite willing to dish the dirt on one of her own employees at the trial. Maybe she knew more about her star salesman than she'd revealed under Alfie Weir's questioning.

She called Alfie. He was putting his young children to bed, but said he'd call her back in half an hour or so. When he returned her call, she asked him if he had a contact number for the French banker.

'I do, but it would be a breach of client privilege to share that with you, Ffion, you know that.'

'I know that, Alfie, I really do. Look, I'll be able to get it one way or another. But this is the Harry Walker case. I can't afford to hang about.'

'What do you mean? Melanie Walker just got convicted of his infanticide.'

Ffion took a deep breath. Asking a lawyer to bend his rules meant maybe she had to bend her own.

'Alfie, I think there's been a miscarriage of justice. I'm looking at Jonathan Walker. For Harry's murder.'

'Really?'

'Really. And I shouldn't have just told you that,' she said, hoping the concept of privilege extended to overworked detective constables. 'So, if there's any way at all you could maybe let me have Amélie Aubert's number, I'd really appreciate it. I won't tell her where I got it, I promise.'

He sighed. 'Hold on. I'm going to have to put you on speaker.'

The sound changed, picking up an echoey quality.

'Ready?'

'Yep.'

He read out a mobile number.

'You owe me.'

'Of course.'

She opened a browser on her laptop and found Amélie Aubert's photo on her bank's website. The photographer's lights and careful composition had managed to suggest a faint halo around the Frenchwoman's sleek haircut. She was looking straight out of the webpage at Ffion, just a hint of a smile as if to say, we could make lots of money together, you and I, and even have a little fun along the way.

She rang the number Alfie had given her.

'Hello. This is Amélie.'

The accent was broader than it had been in court. *Allo. Zis is Amélie*. Just as Ffion's had been when she was speaking to a fellow girl from the Valleys.

'Ms Aubert, this is DC Parry, from Hammersmith CID. I was—'

' – the lead investigator on the Harry Walker murder. Of course, I remember. How can I help you, DC Parry?'

'I wonder whether I could ask you a few background questions?'

'About what?'

Ffion inhaled. Nothing ventured…

'About Jonathan Walker.'

'I see.'

Ffion heard a sound she thought might be a heavy-bottomed tumbler being put down on a glass-topped table.

Pictured the elegant Frenchwoman sipping sparkling mineral water, leaning back in some fabulously expensive leather recliner and staring out of a penthouse window at a lit-up Parisian skyline. She saw the Eiffel Tower, red, white and blue lights creeping all the way up its slender-gridded legs to the tip.

'Yes,' Ffion said, when it became apparent Amélie wasn't going to say more without a prompt. 'I'd like to ask about his…'

She hesitated, tiptoeing up to the point, wary of saying something that would close the conversation down with the finality of a cell door slamming.

'His what?'

'His conduct.'

Ffion heard the other woman's breathing down the line.

'His conduct?'

It wasn't a no. That was progress as far as Ffion was concerned. She took another tentative step.

'You said in the witness box that Jonathan had worked for you for eight years and four months,' Ffion said. 'Was he ever involved in any…incidents…where there might've been disciplinary proceedings?'

'Why do I get the feeling, you already know the answer to that question, DC Parry?'

The woman was sharp. Then Ffion reproached herself. Of course she was sharp! Presumably you didn't get to be the alpha bitch in a merchant bank by having a B-minus brain. *Or even an A-minus*.

Ffion decided she had to go all in and trust the woman. It was either that or risk losing the momentum she'd built up.

'Ms Aubert—'

'Amélie, please.'

Ffion felt it then. The sense a door was about to open instead of slam shut in her face.

'Amélie, I believe there is a strong possibility that Melanie Walker did not kill Harry at all.'

'And you think Jonathan did?'

Deep breath. Try to ignore the racing pulse.

'I do, yes.'

In the pause before Amélie answered, Ffion heard the sound of the tumbler clinking off the glass-topped table and the whisper of the Frenchwoman's sip of its contents.

'I could believe that. I have been thinking about Jonathan's behaviour a lot since the trial. Let me explain to you a little about my world, if you have time?'

'Of course. Go ahead, please.'

'*Merci.* So, you have the expression dog-eat-dog. In France, we say *l'homme est un loup pour l'homme.*'

'Man is a wolf for man,' Ffion said.

'You speak French?'

'I learned at school.'

'*Très bien.* Anyway, it is extremely competitive, as you can imagine. There are huge sums of money at stake. For our clients, billions of euros,' she said. 'For the bank, divide that by ten. And for the people who bring home the bacon, six- or even seven-figure bonuses.'

'That's a lot of money,' Ffion said, imagining how Da, a lifelong Labour voter who dismissed Tony Blair as a 'Red Tory', would have fulminated about '*bloody parasites, Ffion, leeching off the working classes*'. The memory made her smile.

'Yes, and banks need the people who keep it flowing in the right direction. We call them rainmakers.'

'And sometimes the rainmakers bring down thunder and lightning, too?'

'Just so. Jonathan is one of those people. Very charming with clients, very, we say *plausible.*'

'It's the same in English.'

'Of course. But with his colleagues? *Non*. He, he doesn't care. He can be dismissive, he will lie about things and, yes, he can be aggressive.'

Ffion's pulse kicked up a notch.

'Physically?'

'*Oui*. But this is what I mean about my world. You have someone like Jonathan, you do everything you can to hold onto him.'

'Like paying off foreign police officers?'

This time, the pause stretched out so long, Ffion could actually hear Amélie refilling her glass. Some sort of expensive sparkling water, she imagined.

'This is off the record, yes? I will not testify to this in court, if it gets that far.'

It was a blow, but Ffion had no choice.

'It's just for background, Amélie. I'll find other ways to gather evidence.'

'*D'accord*.' A brief pause. 'Yes.'

'The Dubai police?'

It was the most dangerous question Ffion had asked. Dangerous for Jonathan Walker if Amélie answered in the affirmative. Dangerous for her if Amélie asked how she knew.

'I wonder whether I am again telling you something you already know, but, yes.'

Amélie sighed. Ffion heard the sound of a woman finally shrugging off a burden that had been digging into her shoulders for far too long.

'What happened?'

'Jonathan was entertaining clients in Dubai. They were at a nightclub. A horrible-sounding place called Boudoir. So tacky, *non*? When they were leaving, Jonathan became involved in an argument with some men. I don't know how it happened. All I do know is, according to our client, Jonathan lost his mind. He beat two of them up. Badly.'

'Then he called you and asked you to hush it up.'

'*Exactement.*'

Ffion noticed how Amélie's accent and use of her native language had both increased as the conversation had gone on.

'Amélie, as we're talking honestly with each other, I might say *femme à femme*, can I ask you a very direct question?'

'It seems we are beyond being *diplomatique*. Why not? Ask away.'

'Why now?'

'What do you mean?'

'I mean why are you opening up like this? Jonathan is a star salesman. A rainmaker, as you put it. Why give me all this information now?'

'OK, one, you are a police officer. It does not do to lie to *les flics*. Two, well, do you have children, DC Parry?'

'Yes, two girls.'

'My son, Alexis, is three years and four months. The case, it *touched* me, you know? I am not sure I can have a man like Jonathan Walker working for me any longer.'

'You're going to fire him?'

'Oh, nothing so dramatic. In banking, there are ways of indicating it is time to move on.'

'I understand. You have been more than helpful. *Merci Beaucoup*, Amélie.'

'*De rien*. It was the least I could do. But before you go, I would like to offer you some advice. If you are willing to listen?'

'Of course.'

'Be very, very careful around Jonathan. I don't believe

he sees the world the way others do. The way normal human beings do.'

'I will. And thank you. Again.'

'*Bon nuit*, DC Parry.' A beat. '*Et de beaux rêves.*'

Ffion put her phone down on the kitchen table and blew out her cheeks. She realised she was sweating and wiped her top lip. She might manage a good night. But sweet dreams were out of the question. The picture Amélie had painted of Jonathan Walker was of an ambitious young man who had entered the cut-throat world of corporate banking and treated it like a shark treats a beach full of surfers.

The image, which had emerged unbidden in her mind, brought her back to Dr Flick Barber, the Californian shrink peddling magic mushrooms to anyone who'd get her a licence to experiment. What would she make of Jonathan Walker? Ffion made a note to get in touch. Ditto Dr Silverman.

27

Ffion

Ffion was in early. Correction, she thought to herself as she checked her watch – 7.30 a.m. – earlier. She headed down to the exhibits room.

Peter Muncie was on duty. The long-limbed Trinidadian, his close-cropped curly hair now grey at the temples, had been exhibits room manager forever. Rumour had it Peter could find any piece of evidence just from a description and the bare bones of the case. No reference number needed.

Ffion had no need to put it to the test: she had the case file under her arm.

'Morning, Peter,' she said.

'And a very good morning to you, DC Parry. And what can I do for the Lamb of the Valleys at this ungodly hour in the morning?'

'I'm looking for a pillow. From the Harry Walker case.' She consulted her file. 'Case number...'

'No need,' he said, smiling. 'Case that recent? Hardly a test of old Peter's superpowers, now is it? Wait there.'

She watched as Peter strode off between the wire-racked shelves. He returned a few minutes later with a large brown paper bag under his arm.

'Just put your signature in me little autograph book,' he said, spinning a ledger round for her to sign, 'and it's all yours.'

'Thanks,' she said as she signed and dated the evidence log.

He frowned at her.

'You still investigating that thing? I thought it was all done and dusted.'

'You shouldn't believe everything you read in the papers,' she said, grinning.

'Don't worry, my girl. I don't believe nothing unless I see it with me own eyes.'

Ffion took the pillow up to Forensics. Mike Buckman wasn't in yet so she left the brown bag on his desk and stuck a yellow Post-It to it.

Mike,

Can you do a thorough workup on this for me? Body fluids, epithelials, the works. Compare any DNA with Harry and Jonathan Walker.

Cheers!

Ffion

It took two days before Mike Buckman called her.

'Hi, Mike,' she said, feeling a buzz of adrenaline in the pit of her stomach.

'I just finished my preliminary exam of the pillow. Sorry it's taken so long, we're a bit short-staffed just now.'

'That's OK. I know I was queue-jumping. Please tell me you found something.'

'Ffion, I found something,' he said, the humour evident in his voice, just below the serious tone. 'Specifically, mucus. And what appears to be very milky vomit on the same side. I picked up breast milk and a very weak solution of digestive enzymes, hydrochloric acid and bicarbonate. I also found some epithelial cells on the reverse side.'

'Have you sent any of it off to the DNA lab yet?'

'No, I thought I'd call you first. We had the bean counters in last month. They forbade us to send anything outside without at least a DI's signature on the order.'

'OK, thanks, Mike. That's brilliant work. I'll go and have a word with Russ.'

She ended the call and went to find her guvnor. He'd just emerged from the kitchen with a mug of coffee, so she quickened her pace and reached his office door just before he did.

'Guv, can I have a quick word, please?'

He checked his watch. 'I'm a bit pushed, Feef. Can it wait?'

She shook her head. 'Not really, guv. Five minutes. Please?'

He sighed and swept his arm in a semicircle. 'Be my guest.'

Facing him across his paper-crowded desk, Ffion jumped straight in. Russ liked straight talking.

'I had Forensics take a more detailed look at the pillow from the spare room at the Walkers' house. Mike Buckman found mucus and baby sick, guv. Plus skin cells. You know what this means, right?'

He frowned, took a sip of his coffee, winced.

'It means Jonathan Walker gave his son a bottle at bedtime and the little lad sicked up a bit on the pillow.'

'No! Guv, come on. The pathologist found a goose feather in Harry's windpipe. A feather that matched those in the dad's pillow,' she said, hurrying towards her request. 'Now *we* find mucus and vomit on the same pillow. I think the defence were right. I think Jonathan Walker smothered Harry. The poor soul must have vomited as he struggled to breathe. I want to get it fast-tracked with the DNA lab. If we can prove the mucus and/or sick came from Harry and we get Jonathan's DNA off the epithelials, we can charge him with murder.'

Russ had started shaking his head before Ffion had reached the halfway point.

'No, we can't. For a start, the prosecution did a pretty thorough job on Dr Begu, didn't they? She as good as admitted she could have transferred a feather from her own pillow into Harry Walker's trachea,' Russ said. 'As for the body fluids, I see where you're going with this, but how does it support your version of events more than mine?'

Ffion opened her mouth to reply, then shut it again. *Clop.*

Because the guv'nor was right, wasn't he? Jonathan Walker could just say he was giving Harry his bottle – Melanie's breastmilk from the fridge, don't you know, very *bourgie* – and he must've taken it a little too fast and brought some of it back up.

'Look, guv, I get it, OK. I really do,' she said, unwilling to give in just yet. 'The case went our way. But what if we're wrong? What if Jonathan Walker is a psychopath who murdered his own son and then pinned it on his mentally ill wife? Could you live with yourself if that was the case? Because I know I couldn't. Just let me have two tests. Not even twenty-four-hour. I'd settle for forty-eight.'

Russ rubbed a hand over his face. She saw he hadn't shaved that morning. In fact, since his own baby had been born, Russ had missed more shaves than he'd taken. He looked at her. His eyes were red. Not just from the rubbing. Here was another new father not getting a lot of sleep. She offered a small prayer to whichever gods looked after desperate DCs.

'Two. One forty-eight, one normal.'

Ffion opened her mouth to protest. He held up a hand to forestall her. 'It's the best I can do. There's nothing in the budget for closed cases, Ffion. Zilch. Christ, there's barely enough for the live ones.'

She cut her losses.

'Thanks, guv.'

Back at her own desk, she rang Mike Buckman.

'Can you send everything you found on the pillow to the lab?'

'What about turnaround?'

'Which of the two fluids do you reckon would give the best chance of a DNA profile?'

'Probably the mucus.'

'OK, forty-eight on that, please. The rest'll have to fly economy.'

'Who's going to sign it off?'

'DI Palfreyman.'

* * *

When the DNA results from the mucus arrived on her desk in a much re-used internal envelope, Ffion nodded grimly to herself. It belonged to Harry Walker.

Later that week, she visited a contact at the CPS.

Jack Belkin was the same age as her and, she thought, held similar political views. And while that shouldn't have counted for anything, Ffion felt he'd be sympathetic.

Having explained the background, she got to the crunch point.

'Although Melanie Walker was convicted, I now believe she was wrongly convicted. I think it was the husband.'

'And you want to interview her as a witness?'

'At some point, yes.'

Jack frowned, pulling his lips to one side.

'Strictly speaking, you should go through the Court of Appeal. She needs to be acquitted by the courts, not by a lowly DC with a hunch. No offence,' he added with a boyish grin.

'None taken,' she said. 'But that could take months. Years, even. I need to get this moving.'

'Yes, but if this goes as far as an arrest, his defence could drive a tank through your procedure,' Jack said. 'Relying on the testimony of a convicted felon, specifically a mother who killed her own child, to convict her husband of the same crime? It looks shakier than a Shakydog milkshake that's just been shaken. To put it into legal language.'

'Yes, but what if I just went to see the husband and treated him as a witness not as a suspect?' she asked. 'Then I could just say to any future judge, well, I was just concerned about a couple of bits of evidence. Nothing to do with him as a suspect.'

Jack smiled. 'Nice try. Look, you're a cop, I'm a lawyer. All I can do is offer you legal advice. The courts are there for a reason. If you think Mrs Walker has been wrongly convicted, use them.'

'But if I decided to go down this route, would I be the first?'

He shook his head. 'Sadly no.'

They exchanged a few more words, then Ffion got up to leave and thanked him. But she wasn't feeling much gratitude.

* * *

It took another eight days before the rest of the lab results came back. The sick was also Harry Walker's, and the epithelial cells belonged to Jonathan Walker.

She leaned back in her chair and closed her eyes. She pictured a horrific scene. Jonathan Walker, no doubt as calm as he had been in court, holding a goose-down-filled pillow over his son's nose and mouth. The child asphyxiating, but not before bringing up some of his last feed as he struggled for breath.

She rocked forward. Time to pay a visit to the London office of Lemaire et Monceau.

28

Ffion

Setting off from the station car park, Ffion could picture the whole of the next few months as a speeded-up film in her head. The arrest, the interviews, the trial, the conviction, the celebratory drinks in the pub. The claps on the back, high-fives and then, a few weeks later, the promotion to DS.

But as she left West India Dock Road and turned into Canary Wharf's glass-and-stone citadel of capitalism, the doubts that had been seeping through the glittering movie show in her mind's eye had crystallised into something less encouraging.

What if Jonathan wasn't a psychopath at all? What if he was just a shell-shocked husband numbed by grief? She'd spent enough time with him as his FLO, hadn't she? She'd sat with him, talking late into the night. And then her copper's judgement and her woman's intuition had been in complete agreement. Jonathan was devastated. What if there was a perfectly innocent explanation for the DNA on the pillow? After all, it wasn't hard to imagine plenty of ways it could have happened.

She was already out on a limb, given what the CPS lawyer had advised. She resolved to tread carefully around Jonathan.

She parked on the third floor of an NCP and walked half a block to the salmon-pink granite tower on Cabot Square where Lemaire et Monceau had its London offices. While she'd been driving, the cloud that had been blanketing London for days lifted as if swept aside by a giant broom. Now the sun glinted and glittered off the thousands of plate-glass windows that stretched high above her on every side.

Dodging between two Ubers and earning a comically unaggressive toot from the rearmost Prius, she entered the office block's air-conditioned reception area. Full-sized trees grew, apparently sprouting through cracks in the marble floor. A trick pulled by a clever architect, she imagined.

She glanced at the name board occupying one wall of the vaulted space. Lemaire et Monceau occupied seven floors: 15–21. They shared the building with a government department and a publisher of financial data.

She approached the rough-cast concrete reception desk and realised up close it was waxed, or polished somehow, so that it gave off a satiny sheen.

An immaculately groomed female receptionist looked up and smiled.

'Yes, Madam,' she said in a brisk, accentless voice.

Ffion held out her warrant card.

'I'm here to see someone at Lemaire et Monceau.'

'Right. I'll need their name.'

Ffion shook her head. 'No, you won't. Just buzz me through, please.'

The woman glanced right at her colleague. He nodded.

'The Old Bill are different,' he said, smiling at Ffion, who returned one of her own.

'He's right,' she said. 'We are. The gate, please?'

The woman pressed a button and a thick glass security gate swivelled open on silent hinges.

'Their reception's on the seventeenth floor.'

'Thank you,' Ffion said breezily.

A black security guard in a sharp dove-grey suit nodded to her as she walked through the narrow gap.

She emerged from the lift into an opulent, hushed room, thickly carpeted, furnished with soft-looking leather couches and smelling deliciously of freshly brewed coffee. It looked more like the sort of place she could imagine art buyers waiting to be shown rare paintings than a bank's reception area.

At the desk, swirling varnished wood this time, she showed her warrant card.

'I'm looking for Jonathan Walker.'

'Will he know what it's about?' the woman behind the desk asked.

'Is he in this afternoon?'

The woman blinked, her eyes huge behind thick-lensed spectacles.

'Well, yes, but—'

'Perhaps you could just point me in his general direction. I'll find my own way, thanks.'

'Bank executives are very busy. People normally make appointments,' she said. 'This is very irregular.'

The woman was fighting gamely for protocol, Ffion gave her that. What she wanted to say was that when it came to irregular, nothing came close to murdering your infant son. What she actually said was,

'This is police business,' she said. 'It *tends* to be irregular. Now, where is Jonathan Walker? Please.'

The receptionist turned and pointed to a glass door behind and to her left.

'In the general office. Go down the aisle between the desks, past the coffee station, then International Corporate Sales are all grouped in the far corner overlooking the yacht basin.'

Yeah, they would be, Ffion thought, imagining Da's reaction.

'Thank you,' she said. She pushed through the door and into a room the size of a football pitch filled with men and women, but mainly men, yammering into phones, hunched over keyboards, standing in clusters waving their arms about as they argued and generally created industrial-strength hubbub. *Like Hammersmith nick*, she thought as she walked through the noise.

She reached the halfway point and looked to her left into a small, white-painted room in which a couple of young men were chatting while they stuck pods into chromed coffee machines.

'Excuse me,' she said. 'I'm looking for Jonathan Walker. I don't suppose you could point his desk out to me, could you?'

One of the men looked her up and down, quite openly. The other smiled.

'What's Johnno doing now? Investing in sheep farming?'

The other man laughed then muttered to his friend.

'Hey, what's the definition of a Welsh virgin?'

Ffion had had enough. She whipped her warrant card out and stuck it in the joker's smooth-cheeked face.

'Ooh, go on, then. What is it? I love a good joke, I do,' she said, dropping into a broad Merthyr accent. 'You know, when I'm not down the pit, like? Or working on the daffodil harvest?'

The guy blushed.

'Sorry. Bad taste. You want Johnno, yeah?'

'Yeah. I want Johnno.'

He had the decency to blush. *Probably not a psychopath, then*, Ffion thought.

'Right. Follow me, please.'

She let him lead her through the ranks of identical workstations, each bristling with phones and screens and festooned with Post-Its.

He stopped about twenty feet from the floor-to-ceiling windows that gave onto a vista she could imagine stretching all the way down into Essex and the English Channel.

'ICS – I mean International Corporate Sales – are all over there,' the young banker said. 'Johnno's the guy standing by the window.'

'Yes, I see him. Thank you.'

Ffion strode over to where Jonathan Walker was looking out over a basin currently hosting a couple of monstrous yachts gleaming white against the jade-green water.

He was speaking rapidly in French. Ffion managed to translate a few disjointed phrases.

…biggest deal…unfair…other banks…to have me…

She wondered if he was discovering how banks had ways of edging rainmakers towards the exit without doing anything as vulgar as firing them.

29

Ffion

Ffion waited while Jonathan finished the call. He slid the phone back into his pocket and turned away from the window.

'Bitch!' he said, his teeth bared in a feral snarl.

Then seeing Ffion, he smiled, and it was as if that animalistic person had simply vanished.

'Sorry, can I help you?'

He didn't recognise her. Odd.

'Jonathan, I'm DC Parry.' She showed him her warrant card. 'I was the investigating officer on your son's murder. Your family liaison officer, remember?'

'DC Parry, of course!' He ran a hand over his immaculately cut hair, though not a strand was out of place. 'Sorry, I didn't recognise you. The trial was so stressful.' He looked around, frowning. 'We're actually a bit short on meeting space. Bloody pennypinchers in Accounts keep squeezing more people in up here when what we really need is an extra floor.'

'That's all right. I was hoping we could talk at my place of work.'

She'd thought hard about what form of words to use. Rejected *Hammersmith police station* as unnecessarily officious.

He raised an eyebrow. 'You mean, the police station?'

'Yes.'

Now came the moment of truth. Literally. Did she tell him it was just an informal chat and risk him turning her down? Or did she step it up to a formal invitation to interview under caution? She recalled Jack's parting words as she pushed down on the handle of the meeting-room door. *Ffion, don't risk this blowing up in your face on a hunch.*

'It's just a chat,' she heard herself say.

'We could go for a coffee here,' he said, still smiling, head cocked to one side. 'It's a long way to Hammersmith and I'm a very busy man.'

So the friendly version of Ffion might have to take a back seat. She still had one more step she could take before going all out.

'I'm sure you are, Jonathan,' she said, going for a mollifying tone. 'But there are a couple of things I really would like your help with. You know, clarification. So, what I'd like to do is invite you to Hammersmith Police Station where I would like to interview you under caution. Now,' she added hurriedly, as he opened his mouth to speak, 'this would be entirely voluntary, but I do think it would be a good idea for you to come with me.'

He smiled at her. But she detected no warmth in it. She felt he was sizing her up. Like a snake might look at something small and furry. She felt the short hairs on the back of her neck erect. Didn't like it.

'What if I decide to decline your invitation?'

'That would be your right, of course. Although, I might then feel I had no option but to arrest you.'

'Arrest me? Why? You think I killed him, do you?'

'Did you?' The question slipped out before she had a chance to think.

'No. My wife did that,' he said, maintaining that same expression, a mixture of curiosity and amusement. 'As I think you might remember, given she was only just convicted of it.'

'Indeed. So, are you going to accept my invitation, Jonathan?'

She watched him. It was an odd sensation. He seemed unconcerned at the sideways glances coming from colleagues walking past them. No stroking the back of the neck or nail-biting, no tongue coming out to moisten suddenly dry lips.

He didn't look up at the ceiling. He just stared back at her.

Then he took a fast step towards her, making her stumble backwards. He pushed his face close to hers.

'Come on, then.'

* * *

Jonathan waived his right to legal representation almost before Ffion had finished explaining he was entitled to it.

'No need for lawyers, is there?' he said. 'It's not as if I did anything.'

Ffion had made sure to switch on the digital interview recorder before saying a word, so his refusal was there for posterity.

'Thank you for coming in, Jonathan,' she said. 'As I explained in the car, you are not under arrest and are attending this interview voluntarily. You do not have to say anything, but it may harm any future defence if you do not mention when questioned something you later rely on in court. Anything you do say may be given in evidence. Do you understand?'

'Well, it's hardly nuclear physics, is it?'

Ffion smiled. 'Is that a yes?'

Jonathan turned to the DIR. 'It's a yes. I did, just, manage to understand the caution supplied by DC Parry.' He turned back to her. 'That's a lovely accent you've got. South Wales?'

'That's right.'

'The Valleys?'

'Spot on.'

'Are your parents still there?'

'My mum is. My dad passed away in January.'

'My condolences,' he said, though he looked as if she'd just told him she'd sold her car not lost a parent. 'And how about you, Ffion?' He smiled at her. 'Are you a mum yourself?'

She opened her mouth to answer, then closed it again. Goosebumps had broken out on her forearms and the skin felt tender against her shirtsleeve.

'Perhaps we could begin?'

'Of course. What do you want to know?'

He leaned back, reached up to the ceiling and bunched his fists, then relaxed and folded his arms. No sweat patches in his armpits. Interesting.

'I know how painful this must be, and I apologise in advance, but can you tell me the story of that night, from when you went to bed, to when you called 999?'

Jonathan sighed.

'As I said at my wife's murder trial, I went to bed at about eleven. Sent a few emails. Read for a bit, then turned the light off and,' he shrugged, 'snuggled down on the old pillow and went to sleep.'

'What time do you think that was? Roughly.'

He shrugged. 'Midnight? Maybe a bit later?'

'And then what?'

He frowned. 'I remember waking up because I heard something. It sounded like splashing and my first thought was Melanie was having a bubble bath.'

'What did you do at this point?'

'I got out of bed, put a robe on. You see,' he leaned forwards and fixed her with that predatory gaze again, 'I sleep naked. And I went into the bathroom, where I found my wife drowning the baby. I grabbed her and pulled her away from the edge of the bath and got the baby out of the water but it was already dead. Then she fought with me and ended up falling into the bath and cracking her noggin against the bath taps. That knocked her out and gave me time to call the emergency services.'

'I see,' Ffion said, suddenly aware that she hadn't believed a single word of what she'd just heard. And the way he described his son as 'the baby' and 'it' was chilling. 'Tell me, Jonathan, what would you say if I told you we found your son's DNA on one side of the pillow from your bedroom and yours on the other side. He'd been sick, you see.'

Jonathan continued to look directly into Ffion's eyes. 'I would say I'm not surprised. I'd given him his bottle before putting him down and he vommed some of it back up,' he said. 'As for my DNA, well, it's my pillow, isn't it? I'd been sleeping on it for months. It would have been odd if there wasn't any of my DNA on it, don't you think?'

This was exactly the answer she'd been fearing, yet expecting. And she could imagine the CPS's response if she presented the evidence to them alongside Jonathan's explanation. Not pretty.

'How do you account for the absence of water in your son's lungs? Odd given that you say your wife drowned him.'

'It's not my job to account for it. I'm a banker not a pathologist, DC Parry. Anyway, what did that bloke at the trial call it? Post-immersion syndrome? Something about the kid's vocal cords closing off the throat when water gets in. Maybe he knew what he was talking about.'

'And the feather in his trachea? He must have inhaled it from your pillow.'

'If you say so. It doesn't prove much though, does it? He was lying on the pillow when I gave him his bottle.'

Ffion frowned. 'Not holding him?'

'Pardon?'

'You weren't holding him when you gave him his bottle?'

Jonathan's features seemed to ripple: a millpond after someone has chucked a stone into the middle. Then they smoothed out again.

'I guess not. It's easier just to plug it in when they're on their back, isn't it?'

'I always held my babies when I was feeding them.'

'Bottle? Or breast?'

She forced herself to smile. Then she lied. 'Bottle.'

'Ah, I see. What was it, problems latching on? Weak milk supply?' He glanced at her chest. 'Inverted nipples?'

Ffion felt it again. The rush of adrenaline. But not from the excitement of the chase. This was the fear of the chased. What was worse, she could feel the interview slipping away from her. She collected herself. Time to put Mr Master-of-the-Universe Jonathan Walker back in his box.

'Jonathan, did you kill Harry?'

'Who?'

'Your son!' Ffion said, not believing what she'd just heard.

'Yes, of course. Sorry. Stress of being given the third degree in the cop shop,' he said, rolling his eyes. 'No, of course I did not. I already told you this and swore under oath in a court of law. I did not kill him. My wife did.'

'I'm going to talk to Melanie. As a witness.' *Even though Jack advised against it.* 'She was very ill at the time of the murder. I think now she's recovered she might have a better recollection of the events of that night.'

He sneered. 'What, because she went on a magic mushroom trip with some maverick Californian shrink as her spirit guide? Good luck with that.'

There it was again, more visible this time. The sound of pure contempt for another human being. Surer now than ever of who, or rather what, she was dealing with, Ffion moved into her end-game.

'Do you want me to tell you why I'm taking this case so seriously, Jonathan?' she asked.

She could see it in his eyes: the answer he was dying to give. *'Not really.'*

'It seems you're about to, whether I want it or not.'

Ffion nodded. 'You're right. You see, when I was a little girl, my mum had another baby. But this time round she couldn't cope. Something happened inside her and she lost it for a while.' She swallowed, totally aware that her story was being recorded along with everything else in this airless little grey box. 'She killed my baby sister. Drowned her, just like you say your wife drowned Harry.'

He tipped his head to one side. 'Well, I don't "say" she drowned him. She *did* drown him. As the court found.'

Ffion fixed him with a long, searching look. 'Jonathan,

can you imagine how I felt, a little girl learning from her dad that her mum had killed her baby sister, the little girl she'd doted on, in the night? And now she was going to have to go away?'

She watched him, then. Observing the surface of his skin. The blood flow in the cheeks and lips. Looking for changes in the play of the intricate mesh of muscles around his eyes, nose and mouth. Watching his eye movements.

It was as if she'd just finished telling him about the administrative procedures surrounding charging someone with fraud.

'Totally,' he said, finally. 'That must have been awful. Like I felt when he died. Harry, I mean. When Harry died. I feel your pain,' he added.

'Thank you,' she said. 'One last thing, Jonathan, and then we're done here. Have you ever been in a fight?'

'What?'

'You know, a few too many beers in the pub and then you get into a ruck with someone afterwards,' she said, smiling, like it was a quite understandable lapse in someone like him. 'Maybe in one of those fancy watering holes near work I saw? Or on a work trip, perhaps? Letting your hair down a little too far?'

'Never.'

'Well, in that case, thank you for your time. If you'd like to come with me I'll have someone give you a lift back to Canary Wharf.'

He stood up, smiling and offered his hand to shake.

'Great. Glad to be of help. Do you think he'll use the old blues and twos?'

Ffion managed to creak her mouth upwards into a smile. 'You can only ask, can't you?'

Once she'd got rid of Jonathan, Ffion felt a wave a

nausea rush through her. She barely made it to the Ladies on the ground floor before throwing up into a toilet.

Dabbing cold water onto her eyes at the sinks, she stared into the mirror.

'Bloody hell,' she said to the tear-streaked woman facing her.

Ten minutes later, she was sitting with Russ in his office.

'He did it, guv.'

Russ smiled. 'Who did what?'

'Jonathan Walker. Killed his son. I've just finished interviewing him. He's guilty as sin.'

'Wait, you interviewed him?'

'Yes. I did. I had to.'

'Feef, what did I say about pursuing this case?'

'You said don't let it interfere with my other cases, which I haven't. And I think you said, follow your instincts and go after the bastard who murdered that little baby boy.'

'Yeah, well, that's about half right as I remember it. Jesus, Feef, did you even talk to the CPS?'

'I did, actually.'

'What did they say?'

'They said given the unusual circumstances of the case, it wouldn't be completely without precedent for me to invite Jonathan Walker to an interview under caution,' she said. 'Which is what I did.'

'Melanie Walker was convicted.'

'I know that, guv.'

'And she hasn't been acquitted.'

'Correct. I can see why you're sitting there, and I'm sitting here.'

He smiled, fleetingly. 'Look, we work well together. I

respect you, I hope you know that. And I think you could go all the way in this service. But not by cutting corners.'

'I get it. I do. And I'm sorry,' she said, meaning it. 'But he's a wrong 'un, guv. I can just feel it. It comes off him in waves. I know you know what I'm talking about. Remember Timothy Frayn?'

Who could forget Frayn? A mousey little man with sandy, mummy-brushed hair and a penchant for zip-up cardigans and beige slacks, Frayn had been convicted of the murders of five prostitutes, parts of whom had been found in an upright freezer in Frayn's semi-detached home. Russ had led the investigation and, after his first encounter with Frayn, had turned to Ffion and said, 'It's him.'

Frowning, no doubt at the memory of what the media dubbed 'Hell's Kitchen', Russ nodded. 'Let's just say, for the sake of argument, you're right about Walker. And,' he held up a hand, 'I'm not saying I believe you are. You still need to build a case against him. And at some point, there will have to be a formal appeal from Melanie Walker's legal team.'

'I know, guv. That's what I want to work on. But it would be a lot easier if you'd let me work on it officially. David's starting to wonder if I've got a secret boyfriend.'

Russ pushed a hand through his hair.

'Fine. Here's the deal. Carry on looking at Jonathan Walker. But I want regular updates. And I don't want any surprises, least of all financial, OK?'

'Yes, guv. And thanks.'

And she was out, home free. Given the green light not only to right a miscarriage of justice, but to put a psychopath away before he could hurt anyone else.

She looked at the time. It was late. If she left now she could make it home in time to have dinner with David. She'd go and see Melanie Walker in the morning.

30

Jonathan

I have to endure a certain amount of banter when I finally get back to the office. The traffic cop who chauffeured me was obliging, though. I persuaded him to turn on the lights for me and belt down the outside lane on Commercial Road. I told him I'd been dragged out of a crucial negotiation just to answer irrelevant questions from some ambitious Welsh DC with a broomstick up her arse. I could see he knew who I was talking about.

A couple of the guys go on about it just a shade too long. One of them, Fernando, his name is, transferred in from the Madrid branch a couple of months ago. I have to get right up in his face. I murmur a few words in his ear and he soon quietens down. It was only a joke, but he looks pale as he steps back.

I get away at seven. I wasn't lying about the negotiation. Well, I was lying in that I wasn't literally in the middle of the deal. But it is getting towards crunch time. And the bank, and therefore I, stand to benefit handsomely.

I park the Aston on the drive outside the front door. It would be safer in the garage, which I have had floored with these really beautiful industrial rubber tiles with diagonal ribs going in opposite directions to form a chevron pattern. But there is the obvious problem. If I put it in the garage, nobody else can see it. And I know it gives my neighbours, especially the men, a lot of pleasure to look at it.

I took delivery last month. I was getting bored with the Range Rover. And with nobody else living here to bother me, I had a lot of time to play around on the Aston Martin online configurator.

I chose Cosmos Orange for the body colour. Then I had to spend hours choosing every last detail, from the finish on the badging – I went for machined carbon fibre – to the colour of the contrast stitching on the perforated leather upholstery. Which took ages, by the way. Though I eventually reined in my creative impulses and went for the Cosmos again.

I stand on the doorstep for a minute or two, just to take in her beauty. I had an electrician in, the same guy who put in the security cameras, to fit a couple of concealed spots in the flower beds. They hit the car at just the right angle to set off the pearlescence in the paint. You get this really pretty silvery-yellow sparkle coming through.

Then I go inside. I really like having the place to myself. Not because I'm a slob, the sort of man who drops his jacket on the floor and kicks his shoes into a corner. If anyone was a slob it was her.

No, I like it because it's quiet. No screaming baby, no needy woman always asking for more money to buy crap with or what do I want for dinner, or where do I want to go at the weekend. How should I know? It's only Wednesday. I'll do whatever I feel like doing. At. The. Weekend.

So I go upstairs and into my dressing room. I take off my suit and hang it on the airing rack. You should never put a suit straight into the wardrobe: it encourages moths.

My Dunhill cufflinks – 18K gold with inset emeralds – go into the leather tray on my dressing table. My Patek Philippe Nautilus chronograph in rose gold joins its fellows in my watch box. Everything else goes into the laundry basket.

I had a walk-in shower installed and I use it now. I turn the head to a needle-jet pulse pattern. Ice cold for twenty seconds, scalding hot for another twenty, then something a little less bracing for five more minutes. I cleanse my hair and body. I've curated my toiletries after careful research and I use them now. Adam Grooming Atelier shampoo and conditioner. Dior Homme Shower Gel.

On my face, I use Tom Ford products exclusively. Exfoliating Energy Scrub first. Then, I apply Tom's Intensive Purifying Mud Mask. I leave it on for a few minutes after massaging it into my pores with small circular movements of my middle and ring fingers. Finally, I rinse.

I dry myself and wrap a fresh towel around my waist. I take a moment to check my abdominal muscles in the full-length mirror. I'm in excellent shape. The delineation is superb. It should be: I visit the gym five times a week before work.

I stand at the sink. Some of the guys at work are sloppy shavers. You can see it. The little nicks. The patches of bristles a fraction longer than the rest. Maybe some slight redness first thing. There's no excuse.

I apply Tom's Shave Cream with a genuine badger shaving brush. There's quite an interesting story attached to it. I shot the badger myself. I waited up all night for it at a friend's place in the Cotswolds. I took the pelt to Truefitt & Hill and had them make me a custom brush using the silvertip hairs. They're the finest, the rarest and the most expensive.

After I've finished, I massage in Tom's After Shave Balm, apply his Anti-Fatigue Eye Treatment and that's that. Finished.

I have a date tonight. A girl I met online. Emily, her name is. Or Chloe. I'll check before I go out. I select a midnight-blue silk shirt by Dolce & Gabbana and an Armani suit in teal. Black Gucci saddle-bit loafers, because despite what everyone says, you simply can't go wrong with the 'Big G'.

We're only meeting locally so there's no need to rush. I go into the sitting room and pour myself a drink. A generous measure of Bruichladdich 26 Year Old 1994. A snip at £285 a bottle and I like the fact they limit sales to one bottle per customer.

The whisky burns pleasantly. I know I should be enjoying this moment. I have a two-hundred-thousand-pound Aston on the drive, my walls groan with high-end art my dealer assures me will double or probably triple in value in the next five years, and I'm slowly turning a very expensive single malt into piss.

But it's not working.

I'm seething with rage. I'm gripping the cut-glass tumbler so tightly my knuckles crack and I have to make a conscious effort to relax my fingers. I've been working on grip strength at the gym recently, and I genuinely believe I could shatter it.

It's that Welsh cop-bitch and her insinuations. Her sing-song voice didn't fool me for a moment. She's got a sniff of something like a gun-dog with game in its nostrils, and she thinks it's coming from me.

Obviously it *is* coming from me. But I'm not going to let her snap a pair of cuffs on me. Maybe if she was a tart, I would. But then, that's what I have girls like Emily for. Or Chloe.

When I left the police station in the blue-and-yellow Vauxhall Insignia, sitting beside the overweight traffic cop with his bad skin and BO, I did think maybe I should kill Parry. She could hardly pursue her 'enquiries' if she were dead, now could she? But I came to my senses. They get a bit funny when one of their own is offed. It's all a bit tribal, but there you are.

I can't imagine we'd feel the same if another banker broke his neck on a ski trip or got pushed down the back stairs at the office. Or stabbed through the eye with a Namiki Emperor Dragon fountain pen, in black Urushi lacquer. Probably just calculate how much of his client list we could pick up.

No. No cop-killing. But she did point me in the right direction. Miss South Wales said she was going to talk to Mel.

I'll just have to beat her to it. She's staying with Disha and Gavin. They both work, so if I go round tomorrow during the day, I should have a clear run at her.

I'm calmer now. I pour some more of the whisky into my glass and smile at my reflection in the window as the sky darkens to a soft pink, edged with violet. I can see a tie in that colour. I take a quick photo with my phone. I'll send it to my tailor in the morning before I go to see Mel.

* * *

The next day I call the office and tell them I'll be in after lunch.

'Working from home,' I say.

They don't really care where I work, as long as I keep bringing in the money.

The traffic is apocalyptically bad. Some halfwit in one of those stupid electric cars has broken down on Uxbridge Road. Run out of battery, I suppose. Idiot.

When I reach the front of the queue I put the car into neutral and blip the throttle. The deliciously loud ripping noise from the exhaust makes the stranded driver look over at me, his face scrunched up and red. I buzz down the passenger window.

'Not so sustainable now, are you?' I say with a smile, before putting the Vantage into first and pulling away smoothly.

I watch him in the rearview mirror. He gives me the finger. So I signal and pull into a disabled parking spot. I get out and lock the Aston. Then I walk back to the stranded eco-warrior and his stupid battery-powered car.

He's standing with his back to me, phone clamped to his ear. I can't do anything about his insult here. Not really. The traffic is nose to tail and the pavement is full of people.

So I step up close behind him and take the phone off him. He turns round, fast, mouth open. Then he recognises me. A look flashes across his face. If I had to guess, I would say it was mostly fear and maybe a dash of curiosity. Like, *what is he doing standing here when he was in that amazing car a moment ago?*

'I'm going to find out where you live,' I say quietly, and smiling in case some nosey-parker in the street is watching. 'I'm going to come round and remove the finger you just showed me with a pair of very expensive Swiss-made secateurs. And I'm going to force you to eat it in front of your family.' I frown, like I've just thought of something. 'And if you call the police, I'll come back and cut your thumbs off, too.'

Then I give him his phone back and stroll back to my car.

I'm not going to do that. Obviously. How would I find out where he lives?

But what I do know is where Disha and Gavin Hart live. It's a very respectable Victorian villa on a long, tree-lined road in one of the more fashionable parts of Ealing. Stained-glass fanlight over the front door. Geometric tiles on the hall floor. Open-plan kitchen with an island. Nice garden. The usual bourgeois amenities.

Despite the house, Gavin Hart is one of those men who's always going on about there being 'more to life than money'. He's a science teacher, for God's sake. A science teacher in a state secondary school. I mean, Christ on a bike! Why not just be a road-sweeper? At least you wouldn't have to deal with all those out-of-control brats.

Disha's the brains in that marriage. The money, too. She's a GP, which means she's pulling in close to three hundred a year. Not bad for an immigrant. Did I say brains? I should also have said looks.

She is stunning. Dark, glossy hair which she wears long at dinners and parties and the like, but for work, she pins up, which is extremely sexy. Amazing dark eyes and lips you would just want to eat. Nice trim little body, which, thank Christ, she hasn't spoilt with pregnancy. You could bounce a ball off her stomach and her tits are like a twenty year old's.

I tried it on with her once. It was a New Year's Eve party at ours. Everyone had been drinking and I'd put out these little Japanese lacquer bowls of coke with sterling silver spoons I got from Asprey's. I found her in the spare bedroom. I think she'd had a bit too much of the champagne.

Anyway, she looked so sweet and vulnerable sitting there that I just thought, why not? But she pushed me away. I couldn't really understand it. Gavin was deep in conversation with some woman from Mel's agency, so he was hardly going to come looking for her. And it wouldn't have meant anything. I was horny, that's all.

But like I said, she rejected me. I left her to it. No sense in creating a scene. Though I sprinkled a little coke in her handbag. I thought it might be funny if one of her partners discovered it at work.

Where was I? Oh, yes. Lost my train of thought for a moment. It's a shame Disha will be at work. Otherwise I could pay her back for that rejection once I've dealt with Mel.

31

Mel

The sun is shining and Disha's taken the day off just to be with me. That's what she's like. She has people who rely on her for their health and she's still willing to put them to one side for me. You couldn't wish for a better friend.

'Was it awful in the hospital?' she asks me.

We've dodged the question of my mental health since Disha slammed the front door in the face of one final persistent journalist after that breakneck drive back from court. I suppose she just wanted to help me settle in. But now, with the house to ourselves, the moment has arrived.

'Honestly? For nearly the whole time I was in there I thought I was somewhere else.'

I explain how I imagined I was a practising psychotherapist. How I'd spent hours with poor catatonic April, asking her questions, nodding thoughtfully, while she 'answered'.

Disha reaches out her hand and gives mine a squeeze and I realise she's the only person who's touched me without also trying to restrain or hurt me since I was sectioned. My eyes prick with tears and I let them flow.

'Oh, Mel,' she says, and she rounds the table to kneel beside me and hold me.

I sob out all my sadness. Harry's death. My being sectioned. The trial. My conviction for infanticide. In the end Disha gets to her feet and says she needs her chair because her knees are killing her.

It's weird, but I start laughing then. It wasn't that funny, but I'm guffawing like I'm at a comedy club watching the world's funniest stand-up. I can't stop. I feel a wave of panic engulf me. It's not helped by Disha's expression. Her eyebrows draw together and her mouth looks tight.

'Hey, hey, come on,' she says in a sort of hushed, hurried voice. 'Hey! Take a breath.'

But I can't. I just laugh and laugh.

Then she slaps me.

It's not a hard blow. But it's enough. I stop, my mouth frozen open. I clap a hand across my lips.

A shudder runs through me and then I sneeze. Three times.

Am I going to start laughing hysterically again? No. Whatever it was, whatever emotional spasm that erupted so violently just a minute or so earlier has passed like a summer storm.

'Oh, my God, I'm so sorry,' I say before reaching into my jeans pocket for a tissue and giving my nose a good blow.

I must look a proper sight. My nose always goes as red as a beetroot when I've been crying.

'Don't be,' Disha says, with a small smile. 'I think your psychiatrist might describe that as cathartic.'

I smile back at her.

The doorbell rings. They've got a digital one with the speaker in the kitchen, which is how we hear it. The French doors are open because it's such a beautiful late-May day.

'Won't be a minute,' Disha says. 'It's probably a delivery. I think Gav's got some stuff coming from Amazon.'

She reaches across and squeezes my hand. I smile and nod as she gets up to answer the door.

While she's gone I close my eyes and just listen to the sounds of spring. Mostly what I hear is the drone of bees. The heat has brought them out in force and there's plenty of blossom for them to visit. Apple trees, especially. Disha and Gavin have this thing about obscure English varieties. I love their names. My favourite is Idared. Gavin pronounced it *Ida Red*. But I like to see it as *I dared*.

I hear footsteps and open my eyes. For a few seconds the colours have all gone wonky. The bright orange from the insides of my eyelids has been replaced with a ghostly underwater blue.

Disha's in the kitchen talking to someone and then pointing through the open French doors to where I'm standing. I can't make out the other person. It can't be the Amazon delivery guy. They don't come into the house, surely? I realise it's been a long time since I've lived anywhere where that would be a realistic question. But they don't, do they?

I blink and look again but it's just made the afterimages come back. Then my pulse jerks upwards and I feel panic engulf me. Because I recognise that silhouette.

32

Mel

I jerk to my feet, heart racing. It's the detective who arrested me. DC Parry. There's been a mistake. That's what she's come to tell me. The judge got his sentencing wrong. She's here to whisk me off to prison. *Do not pass go,* I think. *Do not collect £200.*

I stand up too fast and my head spins. I have to grip the edge of the table for support. As my vision clears, I see that the detective is smiling. Not a 'happy to see you' smile, but it looks genuine enough all the same.

Disha says, 'DC Parry wants to ask you some questions, Mel. That's all. There's nothing to worry about.'

Why is it when people say that, your immediate thought is, *who's died?* And also, by the way? When the police make unannounced calls, yes, there's always something to worry about.

'Would you like a cup of tea, DC Parry?' Disha asks. 'Or there's coffee? We have a pod machine.'

'I'd love a cappuccino. Thank you.'

'Of course,' Disha says and goes back into the kitchen.

I sit back down as DC Parry pulls out a chair from under the table for herself. She looks like she's lost some weight since the trial. I wonder, randomly, whether she's been hitting the gym.

She and I make small talk about the garden until Disha returns with a mug topped with foam and sprinkled with chocolate.

'Thank you,' DC Parry says. Then she looks at me. 'Can I call you Melanie?'

I nod. 'Although if we're going for first names, I prefer Mel. What should I call you, then?' I ask, unwilling to have an imbalance in our status.

'Ffion,' she says.

It's a lovely name. It was on my list if we'd had a girl. Jonathan said it was too provincial. Now we're on first-name terms, I relax, just a little. Surely if she was about to haul me away in a Black Maria it would be Mrs Walker? Or like they do on the telly – like she did when she arrested me: 'Melanie Walker'.

She looks at me and bites her lip. I suddenly realise she's nervous. But why?

'Mel, this is going to be hard to hear. But I think there might have been a miscarriage of justice in your case.'

All I pick up is the word 'miscarriage'. It sets off unpleasant associations. I imagine bloody sheets. Weeping women. Dead babies.

'Sorry, what do you mean?' Disha asks.

Ffion sighs. 'I mean, evidence has come to light that leads me to believe that you were not the person responsible for murdering Harry.'

She sounds cagey. Like she's hiding something. Even allowing for the stuffy cop-speak she's lapsed into.

'*Nobody* murdered him,' Disha interrupts. 'The charge they convicted Mel on was infanticide. Although, frankly, even that was a joke.'

Her kohl-rimmed eyes are flashing. She doesn't think I should ever have been charged with anything. In her opinion, it was a mental health crisis with a tragic and unintended consequence that required understanding and treatment. I tried to tell her that the judge agreed, which is why he sentenced me to probation not prison, but she won't be moved.

Ffion shakes her head. 'I think Jonathan did.'

'Jonathan who?' I ask stupidly. 'Not *my* Jonathan?'

She nods.

'You said you had new evidence,' Disha says. I am so glad she's here, because I'm not sure how well I'd have coped on my own. This conversation is starting to feel like the ones I had with April. 'What kind of evidence?'

'I'm afraid I can't say. But it points rather strongly at your husband, Mel.'

'But he found me,' I say. 'In the bathroom.'

'Is that what you remember? Because, and I'm sorry to put it in blunt terms, you were very unwell at the time. Mentally,' she adds, perhaps thinking I might have forgotten.

'Not exactly, but the details are the same, yes,' I say.

'What do you mean by "not exactly"?'

'It's like I said in court. My memory is patchy.'

She nods and smiles briefly. 'Tell me again.'

I suddenly feel short of breath, as if someone's sitting on my chest. I inhale deeply and close my eyes. And I find myself back at the hospital, coming round from my trip on the psilocybin. I can feel the freezing bathwater on my skin, the horrid pulling sensation of my clothes sticking to me. The weight of Harry's tiny body in my trembling arms. The smell of him. I feel tears start from my eyes.

'In my memory, I was sitting in the bath holding Harry to my chest. And he was alive. I was wearing jeans and a T-shirt.'

I open my eyes. Ffion is frowning, and consulting a notebook.

'You were sitting *in* the bath? Dressed?'

'Yes. I must've just lost it and got in with him in my arms and held his—'

I break down. It's several minutes before I can go on. Disha has pulled her chair round so she's sitting next to me. She's twisted awkwardly in her chair so she can put an arm around my shoulders.

'Do you want to stop?' Ffion asks. 'If this is too painful?'

I can see she doesn't want to. I realise that neither do I.

'It's fine,' I say, sniffing, then smiling at Disha as she offers me a fresh tissue. I blow my nose, and I cough as some snot goes down the back of my throat. 'Keep going.'

'At the trial, Jonathan testified that he found you kneeling *beside* the bath. The attending officer and paramedics confirmed they found you on the bathroom floor in your nightie.'

'So my memory got messed up,' I say. 'Like you said, I was suffering from psychosis.'

'Yes, but that means you can't confirm his version of events, doesn't it?' Ffion asks, eyes bright.

Disha sees why this matters before I do.

'So what you're saying is, leaving aside this evidence you've got connecting Jonathan to Harry's death, if Mel's got a different memory of what happened that night, we still haven't heard it?'

'That's exactly what I'm saying.'

Disha looks at me.

'We have to find a way to get to those memories,' she says. 'There's a hypnotherapist we refer patients to at the surgery. I could contact her.'

'Wait,' I say. Because although it's a good idea, this is just too much to take in. I turn to Ffion. 'Isn't there something you're not telling us?'

'What do you mean?'

'I just got found guilty of infanticide. Isn't there some law about two people not being convicted for the same crime?' I ask. 'Plus Jonathan's my husband. I'm not allowed to testify against him.'

She nods. 'You're half right. If I can gather enough evidence to take to the Crown Prosecution Service, then they will tell me that we have to get you legally acquitted before we can go any further. That would mean an Appeal Court hearing. But given that I wouldn't be going to them unless I had some pretty compelling evidence, I think an acquittal would be a formality.'

'What about the other bit?' I ask, looking at Disha, who smiles encouragingly.

'I know it's what everyone says,' Ffion begins, 'but it's a little bit more complicated than that. For a start, a spouse has *always* been able to give evidence against their partner – like your husband did – *voluntarily*.'

Where most English people would pronounce the word *VOLLENT-rilly*, in her mouth it comes out as *vol-len-TARE-i-ly*. Five syllables. Like she's singing.

'But in cases of assault on persons under sixteen, yes, a wife can be compelled to give evidence against her husband,' she says. 'I'm just hoping you'd not need to be compelled, Mel. Would I be right?'

I frown. I am struggling to stay afloat in the middle of

a conversation that has upended my world. A world that has already been stuck in a tumble-dryer at least three times this year.

'I suppose so,' I say. 'If you think Jonathan did it, I'd give evidence, of course I would. But you can see how dodgy my mind is. You'd think it would be burnt in like a brand, but I can't even get a detail like whether I was clothed or not right.'

'I know,' Ffion says. 'But maybe you and Disha could talk after I've gone. You know, about hypnosis. They can do all sorts of clever things these days.'

I have this sudden feeling she's patronising me and I shake my head.

'I know all about that,' I snap. 'I was on antipsychotics for the best part of three years. They even tried ECT. Do you know what that is?'

'Yes, I—'

I'm not willing to let her off that easily. 'They shave patches on your scalp and put these electrodes on you and then they run a bloody great electric current right through your brain!' I say, my heart hammering against my ribs. 'So, in E-C-T, that accounts for the "electro" and "therapy", but you know what the C stands for, right?'

She nods and says, quietly, 'convulsive.'

'Yes!' I say. 'Convulsive! They put this thick bit of rubber between your teeth so you can't bite your tongue off. They tell you to relax – hah! As if! – because apparently it's easier. But the first time I was so scared I was as stiff as a board. They sent the juice through me and the last thing I remember before blacking out was the sound of gunfire. It was the bones popping in my spine.'

The speech has left me breathless. But not tearful. In fact, I feel quite empowered. Free, somehow.

'Mel, I'm sorry for all the pain you've suffered,' Ffion

says. I believe her. Her face is open. Filled with sympathy. 'I'm sure your doctors were only doing what they thought was best.'

'Didn't stop me living in a fantasy world, did they?' I snap, then instantly regret it. 'Sorry. I know you're only doing your job.'

She stands and places her card on the tabletop. 'Talk to Disha. And call me at any time of the day or night if you want to. I promise I'll pick up.'

Disha shows her out and then comes back into the garden.

'You OK?' she asks. 'That was a lot to take in.'

I nod. Say, 'I'm fine,' mechanically. But inside I am about as far from fine as it's possible to get. Because if what Ffion said is true, then everything I thought I knew about my marriage, about my husband, is a lie.

33

Jonathan

Woodville Gardens is all resident's parking. That's literally what the sign says. The cretins at the council can't even get their punctuation correct. Unless they mean that the entire road is reserved for the use of a single resident. I pull into the first empty space I come to.

As I walk up the road to Disha's house, keeping to the opposite side of the street, I see a woman in a boring grey suit coming towards me. It's the Welsh cop. I turn smoothly and walk up the garden path of the house I'm passing. They have a tall hedge and once I'm through the gate it hides me from view.

I push my face up against the fragrant green leaves, being careful not to let any of the sharp little branches scratch my skin. I can see the cop. She's marching along like a little soldier. She stops at a car. A silver Ford Focus.

How very *average*. She pulls away and I withdraw from the hedge.

I hear the front door open behind me. I turn, smiling. An old lady stands there, frizzy white hair framing her suspicious face.

'Can I help you?' she asks.

I feel like answering, Yes, I'm about to kill my duplicitous bitch of a wife. I don't suppose you've got a carving knife you could lend me, have you?

Which, obviously, would be sub-optimal as a response.

I hold out my bank ID for a second.

'Police, Madam. We've had reports of a rapist targeting the elderly in this neighbourhood. Have you seen anyone acting suspiciously in the road recently?'

Her filmy grey eyes widen and her mouth drops open. Revealing possibly the world's worst-ever set of false teeth. She clutches the door frame with a knobbly claw.

'Oh, no, dear. Police, you say? But this is such a nice street. I've lived here my whole life. Twenty years since William died, and I've never…'

This is getting very boring, very fast.

'Look, don't worry, OK? He only goes for brunettes. You're completely safe. Take care now.'

It only takes me a few seconds to cross the road and walk up to Disha's front door. They have an ornate, pitch-roofed porch with a fretwork wooden border under the eaves. I step into its shade.

I give a good hard lean on the bell. Mel's probably still in bed. Lazing about as usual. Or has she gone back to her 'job'? Telling idiots in chainstore suits running crappy debt-laden companies that their ad is, in fact, wonderful, and no, they don't need to make their logo bigger.

I realise as I wait that I haven't given much thought to

how I'm going to kill her. Maybe I should have asked the old biddy for a knife after all.

I hear footsteps. Right. They said at my last appraisal I was good at thinking on my feet. 'Innovative,' was the word they used. I'll just have to innovate then, won't I?

Then the door opens and everything changes. Because it isn't Mel standing there, it's Disha.

She pulls her head back and blinks.

'Jonathan,' she says.

I smile. 'Hello, Disha. Is Mel here?'

She hesitates. Just for a split second. 'No.'

Lying bitch.

'Oh? I heard she was staying with you.'

'She was. She's gone.'

I keep the smile on my face. I check her out. She's wearing a tight white T-shirt which, firstly, really suits her skin tone and, secondly, clings to her tits like it's making love to them.

'I'm up here, Jonathan,' she says, coldly.

I look her in the eye. I can see myself reflected. A micro-me in a rectangle of sunlight behind the frame of the porch.

'I know you are, Dish,' I say. 'Where's she gone? Where is my wife?' I take a half step closer to her. 'Why don't I just come in and you can call her? Tell her I want to talk to her?'

She shakes her head. 'I don't think that's a good idea,' she says, moving towards me and pulling the door tight to her right hip.

I'm losing her. This mustn't happen.

'She is still my wife,' I say, struggling to keep my temper under control. 'Even after what she did. I have a right to see her.'

'No you don't,' she says. 'I want you to leave.'

223

Her chest is heaving. I imagine pulling that T-shirt up over her head and cutting her bra off her.

'What if I don't want to leave?' I ask, starting to enjoy myself. The temper is gone. Back into its box. 'I took the morning off to come over and see Mel. I just want to check she's all right.'

'You told her you wanted a divorce. By text!'

'I was angry, Disha, can't you see that? I was hurting,' I say. 'I was standing in my truth, but now I see I wasn't being the best version of myself.'

'Bollocks!' she says.

That's when it happens. It's not my fault. Any reasonable person would see that Disha made me.

I slap her, hard. Her head goes sideways and collides with the edge of the front door. *Clonk.* The whites show all the way around her irises. Her hand flies to her temple.

'Leave!' she shouts. 'Now! I'm calling the police.'

Before I can tell her what a very bad idea that would be, she slams the door shut in my face leaving me standing on her doorstep like a bloody Jehovah's Witness.

I shrug, turn, leave. Short of breaking in, there's not a lot I can do at this point. An old boy is glaring at me from the other side of the road. I stare him out. He turns away and carries on up the road, dragging this scruffy white dog behind him. It's trying to cock its leg while still hopping along on the other three. I burst out laughing. I've never seen anything so funny.

34

Mel

Disha comes back. There's nobody with her. Maybe it really was the Amazon delivery this time. Except her eyes are glistening and she's touching her right temple. There's a red handprint on her left cheek.

'Dish!' I say as I hurry over to her. 'What happened?'

'That was Jonathan,' she says. She sounds really shaky and I see her bottom lip is quivering. 'He just hit me.'

I lead her to a chair and she flops down into it.

'Where? Why?'

'I don't know. He said he wanted to see you and started spouting all this crap and I called him on it then he slapped me,' she says. 'Knocked my head into the edge of the door.'

'Here, let me see,' I say.

She leans towards me and gingerly I part her thick

black hair. There's no blood, thank God, but there's already a lump.

'Can you get my phone?' she asks me. 'I'm calling the police.'

'What? No! Please, don't do that.'

'Why?' she asks, eyes wide. 'Did you not hear what I just told you? Your husband just assaulted me. On my own doorstep.'

'I did. And I'm so sorry. He was looking for me and I brought him to your house,' I say. 'But please don't call the police. It'll only make it worse.'

'What are you afraid of?' she asks.

And then it hits me. As forcefully as my husband just hit my best friend.

'Him,' I say.

I know why he came to find me. He means to hurt me. *Like he hurt Harry*, an inner voice chimes in. This simple, ugly fact – that he tracked me to Disha's and hit her when she defended me – has done more to improve my reason than all the therapy.

'Then we *have* to call them,' Disha says.

I shake my head. 'I think that would put a target on your back.'

Her eyes widen further, her lips part and she touches the bump on her temple again, wincing as her fingers find the goose-egg my husband gave her.

'You're serious, aren't you? You think he'd try to kill me.'

'No, Dish,' I say. 'I think he *would* kill you.'

'But we can't just let him get away with it. He literally just attacked me.'

'OK. But not 999.'

I look at the tabletop. Ffion's card is still there. I pull out my phone and dial the mobile number.

'DC Parry,' she says.

'Ffion, it's Mel. Walker?' I add in case she's dealing with multiple Melanies.

'Yes, Mel. What's happened?'

How does she know? Of course! I'm an idiot. People don't call the cops unless something *has* happened.

'Jonathan was just here. He hit Disha.'

'What? Say again. You broke up there.'

I repeat myself.

'OK, stay there. Don't answer the door again. I'll call you from the doorstep when I'm there.'

It takes twenty minutes before my phone rings, making us both jump.

'It's Ffion,' she says.

I rush through the kitchen, almost tripping on the leg of a stool that's sticking too far out from the island. Down the hall to the front door. I stick out my hand towards the handle. I'm just starting to push it down when I freeze. My heart is already beating crazily. Now it seems to be pushing the blood right out of my ears, they're throbbing so loudly.

I stick my right eye up against the spy-hole. For one horrific second I imagine a screwdriver spearing through the little brass tube and impaling me. But all I see is Ffion standing there.

I let her in.

'We're in the garden,' I say and she follows me through the house.

'What happened?' she asks Disha.

While I was letting Ffion in, Disha got a tea towel and wetted it. She's pressing it to her head.

Disha explains and the story comes out exactly the way she told me, so I know it happened. I mean, of course it happened. It's just, I've been so bad at separating lies from fiction recently, I've even started to doubt my friend.

Ffion is taking notes as Disha talks. When Disha finishes – 'I told him to get lost and slammed the door in his face' – she closes the notebook.

'Have you got any security cameras at the front of the house?'

Disha nods, then winces again.

'Yes. One high up on the wall overlooking the road. Another one in the porch. It'll have caught him hitting me.'

'Can you show me?'

We follow Disha inside and upstairs to their home office. She sits at the PC and fiddles around with the mouse to get it to wake up.

She calls up the camera app and finds today's recording. She reverses through the last half hour at 24x, then stops, plays, fast-forwards at 2x, then slows it again.

There he is. Jonathan. Dressed in a blazer, dark polo shirt and pale chinos – his casual Friday look – striding up to the front door. His arm extends and goes out of shot at the bottom of the screen.

'He's ringing the doorbell,' I say unnecessarily, but I'm nervous. Fearful at what I'm about to see.

He starts talking. Disha isn't in shot. He waits, then says something else. Then he bares his teeth and his right hand sweeps up from his hip and swings from left-to-right across the screen.

And it's over. He steps back, pauses, then turns and walks back down the path. He stops at the gate and on the opposite side of the road an old man briefly comes into view. Then he shakes his head and walks on. A little white dog comes hopping along behind him. Then Jonathan turns to his right and disappears.

Ffion asks Disha to rerun the segment from where

Jonathan appears at half speed. It's agonising now, knowing what he's about to do. But as his hand arcs up, it passes across the screen and I realise what's wrong. Disha still isn't visible. That's what Ffion wanted when she asked her to replay it.

'Crap!' Ffion says.

'There's no proof he hit me, is there?' Disha asks, closing the app and swivelling round on the chair to look up at Ffion.

'I'm afraid not. We have your testimony, of course. But he could say, probably *would* say, he was swatting at a wasp or something,' she says. 'There's nothing there the CPS would even consider to be worth proceeding on.'

Disha stands. 'So, what you're saying is, this, this *psycho* comes to my house, assaults me on camera and, what? I just have to chalk it up to experience?'

Her eyes are ablaze, but I can see the fear behind the show of bravado. I've known Dish a long time. She's scared. Who wouldn't be? I need to leave as soon as I can. Get away from her and Gavin before Jonathan comes back.

'Listen,' Ffion says. 'It's not as bad as that. On the assault, I can't do a lot. But if – when – I can put together more evidence against him for Harry's murder, I can use this to support my case that he's a dangerous individual with a propensity to violence. It will work better in the context of other evidence.'

'Meanwhile Jonathan just gets to go off to work and do his mega-deals as if nothing happened?'

Ffion looks embarrassed. 'Sorry.'

Once Ffion has left for the second time, I tell Disha to come into the kitchen with me. I pour us a glass of wine each from a bottle in the fridge. I gulp some down.

'Listen, Dish, I think it's best if I find somewhere else to stay. I can't risk Jonathan coming back here. He might hurt you next time.' I cover my mouth with my hand for a second. 'I mean, obviously he just did, but, you know what I mean. *Really* hurt you,' I whisper.

I can't believe I'm saying this out loud. That I'm warning my friend I believe there is a very real chance my husband will come to her house, and inflict a great deal of pain on her. And, if he happens to be in at the time, on Gavin, too.

To my surprise, she nods.

'There's something not right about him, Mel,' she says. 'He was always an arrogant sod, but we all just put it down to his job, his politics, all that. But just now? I saw something that genuinely frightened me.'

'I need to get away. While Ffion's building the case against him. Somewhere he can't find me.'

She takes my hand in both of hers.

'Take the cottage.'

'What cottage?'

'Mine and Gav's,' she says, smiling for the first time since Jonathan came a-knocking. 'We bought it while you were,' she hesitates fractionally, 'poorly. It was supposed to be an Airbnb but we never got round to sorting out the paperwork, so we just use it ourselves. It's empty. You could go there today. The kitchen's stocked. You might need to go to the local Co-op and buy fresh stuff, but there's wine, cereal, crackers, and the freezer's groaning with ready meals.'

Her words are tumbling out like groceries from a spilled carrier bag. I can see she's simultaneously pleased to have thought of a solution to my problem and relieved to be seeing the back of hers. She loves me, I know that. But love can only stretch so far before it snaps. I don't know that I'd be half so accommodating if Gav turned out to be a nutcase and came to *my* door throwing punches.

'Where is it?' I ask. 'I don't care. I'm just wondering how I'm going to get there.'

'It's in Dorset. This lovely little village called Burton Bradstock. It's about twelve miles east of Dorchester. You're only a couple of hundred metres from the beach, too.'

I smile. 'It's OK, Dish,' I say. 'You can stop selling. I'll take it.'

And I throw my arms about her neck because, despite everything that's just happened, she's still thinking of me.

'Careful!' she yelps. 'You just hit my bump.'

'Sorry. Thank you so much,' I say when I've released her from the hug.

'How are you going to get there?' she asks. 'I'd lend you my car but I need it for work.'

'It's fine. I'll go back to ours and get mine. I've still got the keys.'

'No!' she says. 'What if Jonathan's there?'

'Tell me again what he said to you before he,' I pause, feel my cheeks heating up, 'you know, hit you.'

'He said something about taking the day off to come and see you, then he came out with all this garbage about living his truth or some rubbish like that. Then he hit me.'

'Think carefully, Dish,' I say. 'Did he actually say "I'm taking the day off"? Only, Jonathan hates taking time off work. He's paranoid. He thinks if he's not in the office someone will be stealing his clients.'

She frowns and looks upwards. Then back at me.

'What he actually said was, "I took the morning off to come over and see Mel."'

'You're sure?'

'Word for word. I promise.'

I nodded. 'Good. So he'll have gone home to change into a suit, then left for work. Let's be cautious and say forty-five minutes to drive home. Then half an hour to get changed, and—'

'Half an hour?' Disha looks incredulous. 'What does he do, lay out suits on the bed and stand there in his boxers deciding?'

'Yes.'

'Bloody hell, Mel. You're well out of it. For that alone.'

I laugh. It breaks the tension that's built up between us. Disha's laughing too. We start egging each other on with more and more ridiculous suggestions for how Jonathan gets ready for work.

'Irons his underpants!'

'Plucks his eyebrows!'

'Washes his shoelaces!'

'Twists his cufflinks so the emeralds show!'

'Folds his pocket square into an origami flower!'

I don't tell her he's done all of those things.

I bring us back to earth.

'Three quarters of an hour to get home. Half an hour to change. Then out the door. He left here, when?'

Disha checks her watch.

'About ten?'

'So he'll be clear of our place by eleven-fifteen.' I look at my phone. 'It's ten past eleven already. I can get the Tube to ours and by the time I arrive, he'll be long gone.'

Disha looks doubtful; two worry-lines have grooved their way down between her eyebrows.

'You're sure? I don't think this is such a good idea.

Maybe you *should* take my car. I can borrow Gav's or give him lifts to school till you're back. We've done it before, when mine was getting a new timing chain.'

'I'm sure,' I say. I'm not sure. I'm anything but sure. 'You've already done so much. I can't take your car, too!'

'OK, but take something with you. To protect yourself.'

I snort. 'What, like a knife?'

'No. Like a pepper spray.'

'Where am I going to get one of those? Do they sell them in Ealing Waitrose?'

She smiles.

'No. I've got one in the hall drawer.'

'What? But they're illegal, aren't they?'

'Technically.'

'What do you mean, "technically"? They either are or they aren't.'

She huffs. 'Fine. Yes, they're illegal. But they shouldn't be. Even in our lovely little corner of Ealing there are sexual assaults happening. It's got worse since you went into hospital, Mel. Much worse. I talked it over with Gav and he agreed. Not that I need the patriarchy to endorse my decisions about my personal safety,' she adds, with a wink. 'I'd rather get prosecuted for carrying an offensive weapon than raped. And I dare say I could get some decent support on social media. Crowdfund my defence. Might even lead to a change in the law.'

'Show me,' I say.

Nestling among purses, wallets, spare sets of car keys and all the odds and sods that collect in the nearest drawer to the front door, is a black cylinder about the size of a roll-on deodorant. It has a push-down button on the top and a red nozzle.

'Where did you get it?' I ask.

'On eBay. Fifteen quid.' She holds it out to me. 'Take it.'

I shake my head. 'No. You keep it. I'm on probation. If I got found with it on me I'd probably go to prison.'

Disha frowns and puts it back in the drawer. 'OK. But watch out for yourself, OK? I don't want you getting hurt.'

I smile. 'Don't worry about me. I'll be fine.'

35

Jonathan

I'm not sure when teachers stop for lunch. I'm assuming it's somewhere between noon and 2.00 p.m.

Personally, I don't take lunch. Eating in the middle of the day slows you down; it's a proven scientific fact. But I guess when you're droning on about atoms or the reproductive system of rabbits or whatever Gavin does all morning, slowing down really isn't that much of a hazard to your afternoon's work.

I parked up a few streets back a couple of hours ago. You don't want to be hanging around near a school these days. Some Nosy Parker will either come along and ask you what you're doing or call the police.

I haven't wasted the time. I've been on the phone constantly. In fact, I think I may have made a couple of hundred thousand for myself just by sitting here. By my calculations, Gavin would have to work for five years to make that much.

But now, according to my Panerai Luminor, it's five to twelve. Time to move.

I pull off Redwood Grove and through the gates of Ealing Academy. There's a sign for visitor parking. It directs me to a row of spaces in front of a low brick building with all the charm of a STI clinic. I reverse in, sliding the Aston over a white line so I've got half a space either side.

At the reception desk I put on my most charming smile.

'I'm a friend of Gavin Hart's,' I say to the woman behind the desk. 'I'm meeting him for lunch. Is he out of lessons yet?'

She eyes me as if I've just asked her if any of the children are available to be raped.

'I'll have to check. Name?'

'Jonathan,' I say, keeping my smile as wide as I can manage.

'Surname?'

'Smith.'

Without thanking me, she bends her head to her keyboard and tippy-taps for a few seconds.

'He's teaching Year Tens biology until twelve-thirty.'

'I see. Maybe I misread his text.' I point at my eyes. 'Need to get these tested. I might need specs. Yours are nice. Can I ask where you got them?'

She touches the edge of the frame of what must be the ugliest glasses I've ever seen. She smiles. 'SpecSavers on Ealing Broadway. They were ever so cheap.'

'I'll have to go and see them,' I say.

I leave her preening and go back out the double doors and return to the Aston.

Three boys – two black, one white – are gathered in front of it. They're taking photos on their phones.

'You like it?' I ask.

'Is this yours?' one of the black kids asks.

'Bought and paid for.'

'It's fire,' the other black kid says.

'You can come for a ride if you like. I'm waiting to see a friend for lunch. Mr Hart.'

They look at me through narrowed eyes.

'You a nonce, are you?' the white boy asks.

He strikes a defiant pose. Legs apart, hands in pockets.

I spread my own hands. 'Do I look like a nonce?'

The black kid who spoke first sucks his teeth. 'That's so lame, man. Like, exactly what a nonce *would* say.'

'If I met a nonce I'd cut his dick off and force him to eat it. They're scum.'

This gains a measure of respect from the Three Musketeers.

'For real?' the white kid asks.

I shrug. 'That or cut his eyes out. I can't see a blind nonce having much fun, can you?'

They look at each other. I can see the unspoken words flitting between them as if they were printed in the air.

What do you think?

He looks OK.

Yeah, but what if he's not?

I want a ride in that sweet motor.

Why don't you step up, then?

Why don't you?

'I'll go,' the taller of the two black kids says, eyeballing me. 'But I'm live-streaming it. You try anything, the whole internet's going to know you're a nonce, man.'

'Get in,' I say.

He gets his phone set up and then gets in like I tell him.

There aren't many places suitable for a car like mine around the school, but I find a couple of empty stretches where I come to a stop then use Launch Control to hit him with some serious acceleration. He whoops, all trace of the cool kid totally left behind.

As we're heading back towards the school, I think of a question.

'Do you know Mr Hart?'

'Science Hart or English Hart?'

'Science Hart.'

'Yeah. I've got him this afternoon for biology.'

'Any good?'

I catch a shrug in the corner of my eye. He makes a grunting noise.

'Got any dirt on him?' I ask.

The kid turns in his seat to look at me.

'I thought you said he was your friend.'

'More of an acquaintance,' I say. 'It might be fun to know something I can tease him about, though. You know, for the bantz.'

'Bantz? Really?'

He shakes his head and sucks his teeth again. It's weird. Even though I'm not remotely part of his 'community', the sound makes me feel stupid.

'Do you, though?'

'He perves on the girls in Year Twelve. Like, this girl, Jess? She told me he tried to touch her tit once. Like I said, a nonce. You want to be careful the company you keep.'

I nod my head. 'Noted.'

'How much do wheels like this cost you, then?' he asks after a while.

'Just south of two hundred thousand.'

He whistles. 'I wouldn't mind something like this when I pass my test.'

'You could. If you really wanted it. But if you'll let me give you some advice?'

'Speak.'

'Work your bollocks off at school,' I say. 'I know there'll be some kids who think it's cool to skip lessons or muck about in class, but – what's your name?'

'Marcus.'

'Marcus, you only get one chance at an education. I work for a French merchant bank, yeah? I make six hundred and fifty thousand a year basic salary and at least twice that in bonuses and commissions. You could, too. But there are no shortcuts, OK?'

'You really think I could make it in that world?'

'What, because you're black, you mean?'

'Yeah. Like, I don't know if you've noticed, but there's this little thing called systemic racism?'

'Let me tell you a secret, Marcus. In the world where I make my money, my very good money, there are racists, too. But they're idiots,' I say. 'They're underperformers. The people at the top? Do you think they care what colour your skin is? Or what god you pray to? Because they don't. All they care about is money. How much you make for the bank, for them, for the clients, for yourself. The more you make, the happier they are.'

'For real?'

'Listen, there are three directors in my team pulling in over a million a year. I'm white. Obviously,' I say and turn briefly to look at him. He smiles. 'Number two is a woman. Chinese. And number three is blacker than you. He's from Nigeria. Last year he made one-point three-seven-five. Nobody cares if Philip is black, brown, orange or completely fucking transparent.'

There's a pause. Not uncomfortable. I don't mind silence. I can hear the little cogs in his brain ticking round, meshing, driving gears, making connections. Good. What this country needs is more black bankers not more social workers or teachers or outreach workers. Get a kid like Marcus earning a million a year in banking and tooling around in a brand-new Ferrari he's just bought for cash he didn't make pushing coke – that's the kind of role model it's impossible to ignore.

We roll to a stop in the carpark and my informant gets out. 'Thanks,' he says.

His friends have disappeared. He leans down and sticks his head into the cabin. 'You got, like, a business card or something?'

I hand him one of my cards from my engraved sterling silver holder from Boodles.

'Nice one.'

'Take care, Marcus,' I call after him. 'And work your bollocks off!'

I check the time: 12.25 p.m.

At the reception desk my friend is still on duty. She looks up at my approach and this time favours me with a smile.

'Hello again,' I say.

'How was it?' she asks me.

'How was what? The drive?'

'SpecSavers.'

'Great. I booked an eye test for four this afternoon. And they have some really nice frames. They're fire,' I add.

She frowns. Then her face clears and she smiles. She's still plain, though. I'd have to be really desperate before I'd even consider it.

'You must have been earwigging on the children,' she says.

I smile and nod. 'So, is Gavin out of his lesson yet?'

'He should be. He might be going to the staffroom first.

They often leave stuff there while they're teaching.' She points over her shoulder to an open staircase that leads to a balcony running around the dining hall.

I turn away. 'I'll pop my head round the door and see.'

She shakes her head. 'You can't. You'd need to sign in so I can issue you with a visitor's pass. Why don't you just wait here for him to come down?'

I want to grab her by the hair and slam her stupid head into the desk. Why is she making my life so difficult?

'Good idea,' I say.

'Or you could call him,' she says.

Yes, I could. If I bothered to keep his number in my phone. But I leave – left – that kind of thing to Mel. I have a set of very strict criteria for people whose contact details I enter into my phone and I'm afraid Gavin doesn't make the cut. Nowhere near.

'Battery died,' I say, pulling the corners of my mouth down.

'Would you like me to?' she asks brightly.

'Well,' I peer at the name badge on her actually quite decent chest, 'Rosie, that would be extremely kind.'

She does some more of her secretarial stuff with the PC and then picks up the desk phone.

'Hi Gavin, it's Rosie on reception. I've got your friend Jonathan with me?'

Pause.

'For your lunch?'

Pause.

Frown.

She looks up at me.

'He says are you sure, because he hasn't got anything in his diary?'

'Perhaps I got the wrong day.' I roll my eyes like people do when they've made a mistake. 'Memory like a sieve.'

She winks. 'Leave it to me,' she murmurs.

'He says he was in the area. A spontaneous thing,' she embroiders.

She smiles and replaces the receiver.

'He'll be down in a couple of minutes.'

'Thanks, Rosie,' I say. 'You're a star.'

Five minutes pass before Gavin comes lolloping down the stairs. My Christ! What a mess. The man is actually wearing a hoodie. Beneath a cheap chainstore sports jacket. Why not just admit defeat and go to work in your pyjamas?

I paste a smile on my face and intercept him at the bottom of the stairs. I stick my hand out and he takes it reflexively.

'Hi, mate. The lovely Rosie was right,' I say, just loud enough for my voice to carry to her ears. I catch her touching her hair and smiling. 'I was meeting a client and I thought, why not see if I can lure Gav out from the horrors of school cuisine for a decent lunch somewhere? Local,' I add quickly, in case he only gets an hour or something.

Gavin smiles. 'Sure, why not? There's a decent Italian down the road. We'll probably get a table.'

'Excellent. I've got the car outside.'

Good. Disha hasn't called him to blab about making me slap her.

I had no idea restaurants like this existed anymore. Red and white checked tablecloths. Chianti bottles with straw bases. Little plastic packets of grissini on the table. And a mural running the full length of the restaurant that I imagine the artist mentally titled, 'A Tuscan Landscape'. Lots of cypresses, anyway.

We order and, while we're waiting, I smile at Gavin.

'How's your day been, mate?' I ask.

He rolls his eyes. 'Do you know, if some eminent psychologist went on the *Today* programme and said, "Yes, well, we've discovered that basically, fifteen year olds are psychopaths," I wouldn't be at all surprised.'

I laugh loudly. 'Too bloody right. I caught a couple of them about to key my car while I was waiting for you.'

He looks shocked. 'It's not damaged, is it? You could probably get it repaired on the school's insurance.'

'About to,' I repeat. Why doesn't he listen? 'Don't worry. They disappeared as soon as I turned up.'

Gavin shakes his head. 'That school used to be great, you know. But these last five years, something's happened. There's no work ethic with the kids anymore. They just want to be celebrities or influencers, for God's sake.'

I think back to Marcus.

'Some have ambition, I bet.'

He snorts. 'You've got more faith in them than I have.'

The food arrives. Gavin digs in like he's frightened someone might appear and snatch it away from him. I pick at mine. I ordered what they claim on the menu is seafood risotto. It looks like porridge with a few sad little frozen Norwegian farmed prawns who crawled in for warmth then died.

'How's Disha?' I ask.

He looks up at me and nods, wiping a splotch of red sauce off his chin.

'Yeah, good. Government cuts aren't making life any easier for frontline medics, but that's life, isn't it?'

I arrange my features into what I hope Gavin will interpret as worry mixed with sadness.

'Look, Gav, I don't know if Disha's said anything about me and Mel?'

He swallows. 'She did mention you guys were getting divorced. I didn't want to say anything in case it was, you know…'

'Too painful for me. Yeah, thanks, mate, I appreciate that. Truth is, it's just cutting me up inside,' I say. 'After what she did, you know, and then she just gets probation.'

He nods.

'Yeah, I guess so. It's such a mess. But—'

He stops. He doesn't know what to say next. Probably because his right-on attitude means he thinks he ought to be giving me the old 'yes, but mental health' line, but he also knows she's a child-killer. I save him the trouble.

'I need to talk to her, mate, but she's disappeared,' I say. 'I don't suppose you know where she is, do you?'

'I do. She's staying at ours.'

He smiles, obviously glad to be able to help.

But I ruin the moment for him. 'She's gone. I called in earlier. Disha said she's gone.'

Gavin pushes his lips out. 'Huh. She was there this morning when I left for work.'

'Well, she's not there now!'

He looks like I just slapped him.

'Hey!'

'Sorry, mate,' I say. 'That was wrong of me. I've just been under a lot of emotional stress recently. I wasn't being the best version of myself.'

He nods, like he understands me. Idiot.

'That's OK. I get it, Jon, I really do.'

'I was just wondering, do you have any idea where Mel might have gone? If she's not with you, I mean? I just want to share my truth with her.'

He opens his mouth and then his phone rings.

'Sorry,' he says. 'Better take this.'

He pulls it out and answers, looking at me and smiling. I refill his wine glass. I'm on sparkling water.

'Hey, babe, what's up?' he asks.

He smiles and nods. Mouths, 'Disha.'

Oops.

'Funnily enough he's sitting opposite me,' he says. 'We're in Il Barcaiolo. Jon's treating me to lunch.'

His face does this strange twitching motion. Like it can't decide what expression to make. Or like his features have had a falling out. His mouth goes in one direction and his nose goes in another. I have to fight the urge to laugh.

'OK. I will,' he says. Then he ends the call and puts the phone back in his pocket. No prizes for guessing what Disha just told him.

'Did you hit Disha?' he asks me, face white.

I put my fork down. I look at him. It's a very simple question. And the answer's pretty easy as well.

'What? Of course not!'

His forehead crinkles up.

'She just told me you did. She said you demanded she tell you where Mel was and when she wouldn't, you assaulted her.'

He's halfway out of his chair now. His face is still pale but there are two spots of colour high on his cheeks. They make him look like a doll. A couple having lunch at a nearby table look over. They look concerned. Like there's going to be trouble. Ridiculous. It wouldn't be much of a fight at all.

I jerk my chin in the direction of the couple two tables along.

'Sit down, Gav, you're frightening the elderlies.'

He sits. His chest is rising and falling. It's quite interesting really. I think of asking him, as a science teacher, if he knows what's happening to him. The adrenaline and suchlike. The fight or flight reflex. It's his limbic system – his lizard brain – going crazy. It thinks I'm a predator.

'Are you saying Disha's lying?' he asks me, breathing fast.

'No, of course not. I'm saying that she was emotional, and, very correctly, trying to do the right thing for her best friend,' I say. 'For some reason, my question triggered something in her and she lashed out at me. I tried to fend off the blow and, yes, I suppose our hands sort of crashed together in mid-air between us. But that's it, Gav. Really. No harm, no foul.'

Poor old Gav. He thought he was going to have to go into full caveman mode, protecting his woman, and now all that aggression's got nowhere to go. He is literally shaking.

'Jesus! I'm sorry, Jon. I thought…' He shrugs. 'I don't know what I thought.'

I smile my best reassuring smile. 'Hey, don't sweat it. It's nothing. I've had ten times worse playing rugby,' I say. 'Although, I tell you, if the doctoring doesn't work out, that wife of yours could have a great career as a bodyguard.'

He laughs and wipes sweat from his top lip.

'Fair enough. You know, she actually slapped *me* once,' he says.

'No! When?'

He scratches the back of his head. 'About a year ago. We were at a party. I was talking to one of my colleagues. She's new. Super-keen, you know? Hasn't had her optimism knocked out of her like the rest of us,' he says, rolling his eyes. 'Anyway, she's twenty-one and really pretty. I was pissed and I made this really clumsy pass at her. I didn't even mean anything. I was just drunk. Flirting, you know?'

I lean towards him. 'Oh my god! Gavin Hart, you're a player! What did you say to her?'

He leans towards me so we look like a couple of conspirators.

'I said, "Do you know, you look exactly like Jennifer Lawrence?"'

'What did she say?'

'"Thanks, I'll take that." And if I'd have left it there, it would all have been fine.'

'But you didn't, did you?'

He shakes his head.

'I said, and it makes me cringe even telling you, "In fact, if my wife wasn't here I'd make a pass at you".'

This is shaping up better than I'd hoped. I'm grinning.

'And?' I prompt him.

'And she said, "Oh, really? What would you say to me, then?" And I just blustered, you know? Because I realised as soon as she said it I was about to go through the thin ice I'd been walking on. I said something like I was sorry and I didn't mean anything. But she wouldn't let me go. She grabbed me by the arm and pulled me closer and she whispered in my ear, "Do you want me to bite your cheek?"'

I'm laughing now. I can't help it. 'So, Casanova, what did you say to that?'

He smiles ruefully. 'I say, "No thank you,", if you can believe it. So she says, "How about your lip?" And I say, "No thank you, I ought to go." But she's got one final one to land. She goes, "How about some strap-on action with no lube?"'

I'm laughing so loudly, the couple at the near table are looking over and smiling.

'Then what?' I say wiping my eyes.

'Then Disha arrived. She asked Ruby if, "my pissed

husband is bothering you?" And the bitch said I'd made an unwanted sexual advance. I mean, I *was* pissed *and* out of order, fine. But she just blew it out of all proportion.'

I've managed to stop laughing. 'Is that when Disha slapped you?'

He shakes his head. 'No. She put me in the car and drove me home. It was so embarrassing – it was only nine o'clock. She waited till we were inside, *then* she slapped me. Told me I was a sad, middle-aged perv, which is a bit rich given I'm not even forty.'

I compose my features into an expression I hope Gavin reads as concern.

'Listen, Gav. You know I said those two lads were about to key the Aston?'

'Yes,' he says, frowning. He's thinking, why are we talking about that again? I thought we were sharing my hilarious self-deprecating story about the battle of the sexes.

'I said I was meeting you for lunch and one of them sort of sneered and said why was I hanging round with – and this is his word, not mine – a nonce? Well, obviously I asked him what on earth he meant and he made this string of lurid accusations about you perving on teenaged girls at the school.'

His eyes have popped open like little flashbulbs. I can see the whites all the way round the irises.

'That's outrageous!'

'I agree,' I say. '*Totally* outrageous. The trouble is, Gavin, old friend, that kind of reputation follows a chap around, if you know what I mean? What if the *Ealing Times* were to get hold of it? Or the *Guardian*?'

'But there's nothing to get hold *of*,' he says. 'Anyway, how would they "get hold of it"?'

'Your wife catches you making inappropriate

comments to a young woman only just out of her teens,' I say, 'then you get a reputation at the school for being a nonce. After a while, people see the smoke and they start looking for the fire, don't they? It's human nature. You can't blame them.'

Gav looks as if he's about to vomit. I move my chair back a little. I'm wearing a very smart Ermenegildo Zegna stretch wool and silk-blend blazer and I'd hate to have to replace it. Then I see it on Gav's face. Realisation. To be honest I'm slightly sad it's taken him this long.

'What are you saying, Jon?'

'I'm saying *I'd* tell them. And can you please stop calling me Jon? My name's Jonathan. It's not that hard to pronounce.'

He shakes his head. His face has turned a very pale greyish-beige. Maybe it's the subcutaneous fat showing through. Or the veins. I should ask him; he is a science teacher, after all.

'Why would you do that? Is this about Mel? Look, Dish brought her home,' he says in this really whiny tone. 'We could hardly throw her out on the street, could we?'

'What, because *I* did, you mean? Look, *Gav*, just in case you've forgotten, my wife, whose mental health you seem so keen on preserving, murdered our baby boy.' I hold up a hand as his mouth opens. 'And if you say it was infanticide, you're going to be explaining to an A&E doctor how you got a fork stuck in your eye. I'm going to ask you one more time. Where. Is. Mel?'

He gets to his feet and points at me.

'You're still grieving for Harry. I get that. But you're out of order. I'm going. Thanks for lunch.'

He turns and half-staggers to the door, opens it and disappears into the sunshine.

I finish my water and signal for the bill, then look something up on Google Translate.

'How was your meal?' the old guy who runs the place asks in this ridiculous Italian accent.

I smile as I get up, fish a fifty out of my crocodile bill fold and drop it onto the table.

'Il mio risotto sapeva di pesce in decomposizione.'

While he's working out whether I really meant that my risotto tasted like rotting fish, I leave. I'd planned to use the day to deal with Mel but now I'm at a loose end. I could go into the office but I'm out of sorts. I decide to go home. I'll work from there for the rest of the day.

36

Mel

I emerge from Richmond tube station into bright sunlight. It bounces off the windscreen of a passing car and dazzles me. I stagger and bump into a young mum with a buggy. She tuts and mutters something about it being a bit early to be pissed. I want to stop and explain to her that I haven't been drinking and it was just a flash of reflected sunlight, but then I realise she probably doesn't care.

I put on the navy baseball cap Disha's lent me and pull it down low over my eyes. I stick my hands into the pockets of the bomber jacket that Disha has also given me.

On the walk to our house, which takes twenty minutes, I have this feeling I'm being followed. I can feel a pressure between my shoulder blades and I stop in front of a couple of shop windows and pretend to scrutinise the items inside, but really I'm trying to catch my pursuer's reflection in the glass. My pursuer! Who am I trying to kid? I mean Jonathan. I'm trying to catch sight of my husband.

But there's nobody there. Because I'm being paranoid. But then, what's the old joke? We used to tell it in the hospital when we were sane enough.

'Just because I'm paranoid, doesn't mean they're not out to get me.'

I force myself to smile as I climb Richmond Hill. Now that Jonathan's thrown me out, I see this neighbourhood through a visitor's eyes. My god, there's a lot of money tied up here in bricks and mortar.

A group of yummy-mummies are coming down the hill towards me. They're pushing these ridiculous buggies with cycle wheels. They're all wearing Lycra. Their bodies could be in a magazine article about Photoshopped celebrities. Only these are real. I should know – I used to have one. I used to be just *like* them. Taking Harry to yoga or music or whatever that week's must-attend class was. Christ! What was I thinking? He was just a baby.

They're passing me now and I have to step off the pavement. They look at me like I'm a beggar. Then a car honks its horn from behind me, startling me.

It's a Porsche. The driver, a man, naturally, buzzes down the window and shouts, 'Why don't you walk on the pavement? It's what they're there for.' Then he accelerates away with this horrendous raspy noise from his dick-replacement.

The women are laughing at me. I overhear one of them asking another, 'Wasn't that Mel Walker?' in a shocked tone.

And her friend says, 'I think so.'

And the first one says, 'Bitch.'

I run back to them and grab one by her bony shoulders

and shout, 'It wasn't my fault! I was ill,' into her smug, Botoxed little face.

Only I don't. I just hunch my shoulders, jam my hands deeper into my pockets and keep walking.

When I get to ours, the gates are closed across the drive. Jonathan's car isn't there, which is a relief. I'd been very clear with Disha that Jonathan would never willingly give up more time than he absolutely had to. But part of me, quite a big part, actually, thought he might have come home just to wait for me to make this exact move.

I stretch out a hand to the intercom box and my index finger hovers over the keypad.

Jonathan sneered when I suggested using half of each of our birthdays for the access code. Instead, he created a code using an online random number generator. He made me memorise it and for the first month after we had the gates installed, he tested me on it every night.

I punch in the code.

8 - 6 - 1 - 9 - 9 - 5

I wait for the mechanism to click and the gates to swing open on their silent hinges. Jonathan lubricated them every Sunday with a silicon product he used to buy off Amazon.

The lock doesn't click. The gates don't move. The LED that should have changed from red to green doesn't.

He's changed the code. I fight down another wave of panic. Because now I'm here, I want my car. I want Paolo.

Despite Jonathan's best efforts to persuade me to buy the 'right' car, I stuck to my guns. He wanted me to have a

Porsche 911 like the one that the dick on Richmond Hill was driving. To be specific, Jonathan wanted me to get a bright-green GT3 with these stupid spoilers all over it. I said I couldn't afford it and he said he'd pay for it. He just wanted to have another car he could play around in when he got bored of whatever supercar he was driving that month.

Anyway, I refused. He went into this massive sulk. I went into a car dealership in St John's Wood and emerged an hour later with an Alfa Romeo Spider in white with this gorgeous tan leather upholstery. I drove home with this ridiculous smile on my face. When Jonathan saw it he just pulled a face. All he said was, 'It'll turn into a pile of rust on the drive inside a year. Then we'll get you the GT3.'

But it didn't. And it hasn't. It's still there. It looks like Jonathan's been washing it, or at least having his mobile valeters keep it clean. Maybe he's been using it in the summer.

But it's on that side of the gates, and I'm on this side.

I stare at the keypad and frown, willing it to give up its secrets.

What has he changed it to? If it's another random code, I'm stuffed. I'll have to turn around and walk back down the hill and get the tube back to Disha's and ask to borrow her car and put myself even further into her debt. And I know she'll say yes, and she and Gav will find a way to make it work. But I don't want them to. I want *my* car.

I have two more chances. That's how this particular model works. Two more chances then not only do I get locked out for half an hour, but the box sends a text to the security firm's control room and then they call Jonathan. If he doesn't answer after three tries, they call the police.

What would Jonathan choose? I try to think myself into his mind. He's so obsessive about having the best of everything. About never buying anything until he's researched it to death. So what would my husband change the access code to?

What if he got lazy? What if, with me gone, he decided to make life a little simpler?

I enter the first six digits of his phone number. I'm just about to punch the green Enter button when I draw back. I clear the code and re-enter the last six, in reverse order.

$$1 - 9 - 4 - 3 - 8 - 2$$

Holding my breath, I press the Enter button. The little red LED shines on.

I have one more try. I mustn't waste it. In fact, what am I talking about? It's not a matter of wasting it. I have to get it right or leave empty-handed.

I close my eyes. *Please, grant me this small favour. Let me find a way to predict what Jonathan has chosen for the code.* My prayer is interrupted by his mocking voice when I made my suggestion about combining our birthdays.

'*I tell you what, Mel,*' he's saying. '*Why don't we just use your birthday? Hey!*' He slaps himself on the forehead. '*I know! Why don't we write it down on a Post-It and stick it to the box? That way we'll* never *forget it.*'

I open my eyes. Is it even possible?

I can't think of anything else.

I punch it in and without hesitating, press the Enter button for the third time.

Time seems to slow down. It's as if the box is thinking whether I've been clever enough to crack its code. I stare at the little red light, willing it to change to green.

The light stays red.

Which is great. Because now the stupid thing is sending out a little distress signal to the control room in Crawley.

Help! Help! it cries, like Penelope Pitstop. *I'm being tampered with! Call Jonathan! Call the POLICE!!*

37

Mel

Someone taps me on the shoulder.

'Mel, is that you?'

I whirl round, half-expecting Jonathan to have made it back from Canary Wharf in the few seconds since I failed at the third attempt. My heart's racing and I bring up my hands to protect myself, an unconscious movement that has nothing to do with my rational brain.

But it isn't Jonathan. It's Marcia, the woman who lives next door. Marcia's the CEO of her own pharmaceutical company. She founded it after doing her PhD. She and I always got on really well. Jonathan tried to interest her in using Lemaire et Monceau to sell the company, but when she rebuffed him he seemed to dismiss her from his life. Marcia drives a 911, a blue one. But she makes it look cool.

'Hi, Marcia,' I say, lowering my hands sheepishly. I

wonder if she's also going to sneer, or shout at me. Or call me a child-murdering bitch.

'How are you?' she asks.

'Oh. Fine, thanks. You?'

Instead of answering my reflexive, polite, Richmond Hill question, she puts her head on one side like a bird eyeing a worm, or possibly a snake.

'Really? Fine? After what you've been through, I'd have thought fine was the last thing you were feeling.'

I smile. 'You got me. No, I'm not fine. Not fine at all. You heard about the trial, I'm guessing?'

She nods. 'Hard to miss it. I just wanted you to know I understand.'

Her voice is steeped in compassion and for a second I wish she'd open her arms and pull me into a hug. But I must resist that thinking. I'm afraid if I let that happen I might never let her go. I'd be prised off her by paramedics, given a shot to calm me down and taken straight back to the hospital.

'Thank you,' I say.

She nods at my Alfa beyond the gate.

'Came back for Paolo, did you?'

'Yeah, but Jonathan's changed the code.'

'Have you rung the control room? You could explain you forgot it.'

I shake my head. 'I don't have the number.'

She points at the side of the box.

'It's right there, look, etched on the side,' she says. 'I have the same system. In fact I recommended the company to Jonathan.'

I follow the line of her outstretched finger and there it is, in faint but clear grey a few shades lighter than the rest of the brushed steel enclosure.

'Oh, my God, Marcia! You're a star. Thank you.'

'Listen,' she says, 'I have to go. Got a meeting. But next time you're back this way, call me. We'll go for a drink.'

'I will,' I say. 'Thanks, Marcia.'

She smiles and then she leans in and kisses me on both cheeks.

'Stay strong,' she murmurs into my left ear. 'He's an arse.'

I call the number etched onto the side of the box. It rings twice before I hear a couple of clicks. *Impressive service*, I have time to think before an efficient male voice with a trace of an Australian accent answers.

'Elite Security, Evan speaking. How can I help you?'

'Hello, this is Mrs Walker at 159 Richmond Hill,' I say. My voice has thickened since Marcia's parting embrace. I clear my throat. 'I'm afraid I've had a complete brain freeze and entered the wrong code three times. Could you give it to me, please?'

'Of course, Mrs Walker,' Evan says, and my heart, which so recently was sinking into the hot flagstones beneath my feet, rises again, like a phoenix, towards its rightful place. 'I just need to take you through security.'

'Great,' I say, trying to inject some enthusiasm into my voice to cover my fear that Jonathan will have changed our security questions, too. 'Fire away!'

'Let's just get these little fellows up on my screen here,' Evan says, and I hear a few clicks. 'Can you tell me your husband's mother's maiden name?'

Oh thank god! He hasn't changed them. He's been overconfident, or smug, or patronising or just forgetful. It doesn't matter. I'm home free.

'Garson,' I say.

'Excellent, thank you.' I hear satisfaction in Evan's voice. He knows he's dealing with the genuine article. 'Next up, what is the name of Mr Walker's first pet?'

Again, easy. I know, because Jonathan was always going on about this Labrador puppy his parents gave him on his sixth birthday. It died after only six months. Some sort of accident apparently, though he was never very forthcoming about the details. Too traumatic, he said, whenever I asked him.

'Captain,' I say.

'Thank you,' Evan says. 'Nearly there. Last question.'

My mouth is already half-open, in anticipation of a third easy question. Where did Jonathan go to school when he was eleven? Westminster. Where was Jonathan born? Guildford. What is Jonathan's favourite holiday destination? Mauritius.

'Who is the best winger that ever played for the English rugby union team?'

My mind clatters to a halt.

'Sorry, what? I missed that, Evan. Could you repeat it, please?'

'Sure. Who is the best winger to have ever played for the English rugby union team?'

Was this always number three? I can't remember. It's as if a mysterious force has sucked all the air out of Richmond. My mouth opens and closes like a fish on dry land. I can't think of a single rugby player, even though Jonathan used to drag me down to the Racing Page whenever the Six Nations was on. He'd always send me to the bar for more beers because he didn't want to miss a second of play.

I close my eyes and try to calm my whirling thoughts. Jonathan has an opinion on everything. And especially on rugby. I think of him holding forth at a dinner table, while the other guests' eyes glaze over or they studiously avoid making eye contact so they can continue their own covert conversations.

Jonathan's voice is loud, confident, aggressive, dominating the room as he gives his opinion on 'the lads'. I hear him now as if I'm sitting at that bottle-strewn table. *You only have to look at him. Jonny is probably the best fly-half that ever played for England. The man's a genius.*

I open my eyes and, smiling with relief, say, 'Jonny Wilkinson'.

'That's not what I have on my screen, Mrs Walker.'

My anxiety levels spike. I was so sure I was correct. But then I hear Jonathan's voice. He's still speaking. *Now, you might think, just because we share a first name, he's my man. But Jonny's got a problem. Those injuries. It's a weakness – a fatal weakness. You can't get behind someone with a weakness. No. There's only one man who deserves the accolade and that's...* He pauses dramatically, though nobody really cares. Then he gives the answer.

And so do I.

'Sorry, Evan, my mistake. It's Jeremy Guscott.'

'Excellent,' he says. 'You're through security. I'm going to give you the code now. Do you want to write it down?'

'I'll punch it straight in,' I say.

He reads out the six numbers – they're random, I'd never have guessed them – and I tap them into the keypad. I hit Enter, the red light flicks instantaneously to green, the lock clicks and the gates begin their torturously slow inward journey.

'I'm in,' I say. 'Thanks, Evan.'

'You're welcome. You'd be surprised how often it happens,' he says. 'Was there anything else I can do for you today, Mrs Walker?'

'No, thank you, Evan,' I say. Then, 'Actually, yes. Have you called my husband yet?'

'You beat me to it,' he says. 'I was just about to call him when you rang in.' He adopts a conspiratorial tone of voice. 'He'll never know! Your secret's safe with us. Have a good day.'

I slide between the gates as soon as the gap's wide enough and pocket my phone. Paolo's doors unlock when I squeeze the fob. Jonathan's not found a way to reprogramme the central locking, though I bet he tried.

I climb in, pull the door closed and thumb the button to lock all the doors. Now for the moment of truth. I twist the key in the ignition and, bless him, Paolo starts straight away.

I drive down the hill feeling that, for the first time since leaving court, I have a measure of independence back. As I reach the town centre, an unpleasant thought intrudes.

I'm not insured.

This is bad. If I get pulled over, the cop will have to arrest me for driving without insurance. And then I'll be in breach of my probation. I clench my jaw and straighten my arms. Well, I'd better not get stopped then.

I'll drive back to Ealing, arrange some insurance, get my stuff, head off to Dorset…and then, what?

I take the Kew Road off the big junction that offers an escape to the west if you turn left, or a return to Central London via Chiswick and Hammersmith if you go right. To my left are Kew Gardens. I glimpse the tops of trees over the high brick wall.

I look ahead, guiltily. It wouldn't do to cause an accident because I was staring at some exotic flowering tree when I should be keeping my eyes on the road. Especially since I am currently driving *sans* insurance. I just hope Jonathan's kept it taxed and MOTed.

And then my pulse stutters and fear washes through me. Coming in the other direction is an Aston Martin in a hideous shade of bright orange. There can't be two cars like it in London. It's Jonathan.

We pass each other. He turns his head and looks straight at me and it's as if he's somehow in the car with me. I can smell him. Those toiletries he uses. The aftershave. The *himness*.

I feel like I'm going to throw up.

38

Mel

I heave in a deep breath and then I drive on, feeling sweat breaking out on my neck and running down into my shirt. I was wrong about him going into the office. He must have been heading back to the house.

I check the rearview mirror. I can't see him. I relax. The road curves behind me and he's moved out of my sightline.

It was a horrible moment. He'll have seen that I've taken my car. I bet he thinks of Paolo as his now. And he'll also know I bypassed the security. He'll see it as me breaking in. I'd banked on having a few more hours' grace before he discovered it. But I'll be back at Disha's in twenty minutes or so. I'll still have time to pack, then I can be on my way, far out of Jonathan's reach.

I check the mirror again. A reflex action, nothing

more. And I see a fluorescent orange bonnet nosing out of a side road and pulling into the traffic behind me.

My pulse is racing. There are a few cars separating us, so he won't be able to see me. But there's nowhere to go. And I need to stay on this road to reach Ealing. The botanical gardens mean there are no turns to the left. And all the roads to the right just lead into a warren of residential streets. I have to keep going and hope the lights are green at the far end.

My eyes are flicking up to the mirror every few seconds. I hear an angry blast on powerful airhorns. Jonathan has swerved out onto the opposite carriageway and overtaken someone. They answer Jonathan with a weedy peep of their own.

We're approaching the lights. They're red. I slow down as the car in front of me brakes. They're being too cautious, rolling to a halt with fifty yards to go. Why can't they keep going? The lights will change before we get there and I can keep moving.

I glance at the mirror. I can't see Jonathan. There's a white van blocking the view. But at least he can't risk getting out and coming for me on foot. If the lights change, he'll have to run back or lose his precious car.

The lights turn to green. I tailgate the car in front and take the left-hand lane onto Kew Road. Past the red-and-sand brick Parish Church of St Anne with its verdigris cupolas. Past Kew Green, white slatted sight-screens rolled to the boundary of the cricket pitch. And then I'm onto Kew Bridge.

The car in front pulls into the outside lane and reveals the rear of a Ford Focus police car. The orange and yellow chevrons shimmer in the bright sunlight. POLICE it screams at me from the bumper: orange capitals on a bright-yellow strip.

I want to overtake. Open my window and scream at them that my violent husband is chasing me. That he wants to hurt me. But how can I? I'm on probation. A convicted child-killer in an uninsured car. They'd arrest me. Jonathan could cruise past and smile to himself knowing I was headed back to a cell.

So I tuck in as close as I dare behind that dazzling array of reflective plastic film. I check my mirror and my pulse, already racing, bumps in my throat. Jonathan has pulled round the white van into the outside lane. He's gaining on me. My stomach churns.

I grip the wheel. If he tries to ram me I'll just keep the doors locked and lean on the horn. The police in front will hear me and they'll have to stop. Or I could ram them. *That* would get their attention.

But Jonathan doesn't shunt me. Instead he pulls alongside and then slows to match my pace. I glance right. He's staring in at me. And he has a completely neutral expression. I thought he'd be baring his teeth or yelling noiselessly behind the glass. But he looks as though he's watching a not-very-interesting TV show.

Then he smiles and draws a finger slowly across his throat. And I feel my bladder start to let go. I clench my thighs and squeeze in my pelvic floor muscles like we learned at post-baby yoga.

We're almost at the north bank. I can see the Italianate tower of the Kew Bridge Steam Museum. It looks like it should be looking down on a Florentine piazza instead of a drab mixture of identikit apartment blocks and retail developments.

To reach Ealing, I need to turn right onto the Chiswick High Road. Up to the Chiswick Roundabout then left onto Gunnersbury Avenue. The police car signals left. I flick on my left indicator as well. He makes the turn and I tuck in behind him. I check my mirror and sigh with relief: Jonathan's in the wrong lane. He's blocked by a couple of cars.

But then I hear car horns again. I look up at the mirror. He's barged his way into a gap and is heading across two lanes of traffic into the filter lane that will bring him after me. My palms are slippery with sweat and I almost lose control as the steering wheel slithers through my hands.

Jonathan's nearly at the lights. Then they change. A young couple with a pram step off the curb. For a moment I imagine he's going to mow them down, killing their baby, just to get to me. But he doesn't; he's stopped.

I look ahead, just in time to avoid rear-ending the police car. I can see the driver checking me in his rearview mirror. I hold up a hand in apology and drop back a bit.

He pulls away and then I see my chance. Without signalling, I haul the wheel over and take a fast right turn into Green Dragon Lane. The Steam Museum is on my left but I'm not looking anywhere except straight ahead. The road is empty and I put my foot down.

There are white signs painted onto the road: 20 inside a circle. It's supposed to be a safe area for kids. I'm doing 40. Paolo bounces up and down on complaining suspension as I hit a speed-bump.

I'm looking ahead, straining to see round the gentle left-hand bend. But also glancing up at the mirror every few seconds to check whether Jonathan's seen me make the turn. I don't think he has. That car is impossible to miss and the road behind me is clear. I look over my left shoulder, just to be sure.

About halfway along, I realise I can't go back to Disha's. What if Jonathan abandons the chase and simply heads back to Ealing to ambush me there? I turn left into a little side road that leads to some low-rise blocks of flats. I turn right into a parking area shielded from Green Dragon Lane. There's a huge removals van occupying half of it so I slide round it and park in its colossal shadow. Now I'm invisible from the side road, too.

I turn off the engine.

And I wait.

My pulse is racing. My mouth is dry. Jonathan mustn't find me here. I need to get away. I'm a sitting target in the car. But I'm afraid to get out.

I see two burly guys in black polo shirts with the logo on the side of the van embroidered on the right side. They're walking back to the van. One's got a packet of cigarettes out and he's offering it to the other one.

I make a decision. I climb out and lock the car. I hurry over to the two men.

'Excuse me,' I say. 'Can you help me, please?'

They stop. 'What's up, love?' one says with a smile. He's nice-looking. Stubbly jaw. Kind eyes. 'You look like you've seen a ghost.'

'There's a man following me in a car,' I say. 'All the way from Kew Gardens. I need to hide from him. He's in a bright-orange Aston Martin. I'm going to go in there for a bit.' I point at a dark passageway that leads to a stairwell. 'If you see him and he asks if you've seen me, can you tell him you saw my car going up Green Dragon Lane?'

'Of course,' he says. He turns to his friend. 'We'll send him on his way, won't we, Loz?'

The other guy, younger, also unshaven, though in a more designer-y way nods.

'No problem,' he says to me. 'If he gets any ideas, we'll put him straight. Tell you what. You go and make yourself scarce. Maybe ten minutes?' I nod. 'Then we'll beep the hooter three times to let you know the coast's clear.'

'You're a star,' I say. 'Thanks.'

Then I run off. I literally run. I take stairs two at a time and walk down a landing until it turns a corner. I come face to face with a little boy playing with some toys cars on the landing outside a front door. His, I assume.

He looks up at me.

'Hello.'

'Hello,' I say, smiling.

He holds up the cars for my inspection. One yellow, one black. 'These are my cars. This one is the goodie and this one is the baddie.'

I squat down beside him.

'Is the baddie chasing the goodie?'

He laughs. 'No, silly! They are going to destroy the dinosaurs.'

This takes me off guard. Then I notice a couple of plastic dinosaurs between two of the railings. One has a long neck and tail, the other's more of a predator-type.

'I see. Is that one a T-Rex?' I ask, pointing at the toothy one.

His eyes, a soft hazel, widen and he grins. 'Nooo! It's a Velociraptor, and it's going to eat the Diplodocus. That's why the cars have to be friends. So they can kill it.'

We stay like this, him talking, me asking what he clearly finds staggeringly but entertainingly ignorant questions. The front door behind us opens. A skinny young woman comes out. She looks down and her eyes narrow.

'Who are you?' she asks. Her tone makes it sound like, *Why are you molesting my child?*

I get to my feet.

'My name's Mel,' I say. 'I'm running away from my

abusive husband. He chased me in his car and I needed a place to hide.'

I don't even think about the words as they tumble from my mouth. I just want someone to take me in and protect me.

She smiles and she opens her mouth to welcome me. To say how she understands my problem and aren't men bastards and we women have to stick together. Then a different kind of light goes on behind her eyes. I see it. The recognition. From the photos in the papers, and on social media. The reports on every TV channel for days.

'Jordan, get inside,' she says.

'But, Mummy.'

'Now!' she snaps.

The little boy gathers up his cars and his plastic dinosaurs and scoots round the backs of his mother's knees and into the flat.

She jabs a finger into my chest, baring sharp little teeth. I've never seen such hatred before.

'Piss off right now before I call the police.'

I turn to go. There's no point trying to explain.

She hisses a terrible word that makes me flinch.

Tears start from my eyes as I take the walkway back the way I came. I dash them away with the backs of my fingers. Then I hear three sharp blasts of a car horn. Lorry horn, I correct myself.

I hurry back down the stairs and over to the car. I sniff, and paste on a smile that feels as real as Jordan's plastic dinosaurs.

'Thank you,' I say.

The older guy shrugs. 'It's nothing. Listen, I know this'll probably sound weird, or like defensive or something, but we're not all arseholes. It's a shame what you have to put up with. I'm sorry.'

I want to hug him. But I think it'll probably embarrass him and produce more tears from me, so I nod, and thank him again. I climb into Paolo and moments later I'm driving, at just below twenty, along Green Dragon Lane until it turns into Burford Road. I turn right into Ealing Lane and then head north. Only I'm not going back to Ealing.

At the roundabout beneath the Chiswick Flyover, I turn left onto the Great West Road. Fifty minutes later, I'm pulling into a parking space at Fleet Services on the M3 – about thirty miles southwest of London. I have no memory of the drive.

I call Disha.

'Where are you? I've been worried sick,' she says. 'I thought Jonathan had, well, done something to you. He had lunch with Gav. Gav said he was acting really weird.'

That doesn't surprise me, but it does scare me. Again.

'I'm fine, Dish. Really. I got the car but I met him coming the other way. He chased me.'

'Seriously?'

'Yeah, seriously. But I lost him.' I want to giggle. I sound like an actor in a terrible thriller on Netflix. I bite my lip until it hurts. 'Has he been back to yours?'

'No,' she says. 'And I don't think he will. If I even *think* it's him at the door, I'm calling the police. But when are *you* coming back?'

'I'm not,' I say. 'I'm at Fleet Services on the M3. I'm going to go straight to the cottage if that's OK?'

'But you haven't got the keys! I was going to give you my set when you got back here,' she says.

My stomach flips at the thought of having to drive back into London. I imagine running into Jonathan again and this time he catches me. Starts hurting me. But Disha's speaking again. 'No, it's all right. Our neighbours there have a spare set. Their place is called Curlews. I'll call and let them know you'll be knocking for the keys.'

'Thanks, mate. I really owe you'

'It's fine, really. But what about your stuff? You've only got what you're wearing.'

'I'll manage. I'll find somewhere local to buy the basics. Can you text me the address?'

'Sure, hold on,' she says. Then, 'What about your meetings with the probation officer?'

'They call themselves offender managers now,' I say, trying to keep it light when I still feel like I might look up and see that orange sports car nosing along the rows of parked cars like a shark looking for a feed. 'I'll call her and explain I needed to get away but I'll come back into London for our meeting. I'll call Dr Silverman, too. I just need to get my head straight.'

My phone pings while we're talking. I take it away from my ear. It's Disha's text.

'Take care, Mel,' Disha says. 'And call me if you need anything. Or if you just want to talk. Any time of the day or night. Yes?'

'Yes,' I say. 'Ma'am.'

She laughs. 'Listen, I have to go. You're sure you're OK?'

'I'm sure.'

'Sure, sure?'

'Sure, sure.'

'Call me. I mean it. Bye, lovely.'

'Bye, Dish. I love you.'

'I love you, too.'

Alone in the car park, alone in Hampshire, alone full stop, I realise I have no plans beyond simply escaping London. But that's all right. I need some headspace.

Like I told Disha, I can still come back for the meetings

with my offender manager. But in the cottage, I'll be alone, in a place where nobody knows me. I'll change my appearance so nobody recognises me. And, maybe, just maybe, I will find the time and the space to do the one thing I haven't been able to so far.

I will mourn Harry.

PART IV

ACTIONS AND CONSEQUENCES

39

Ffion

Ffion spent all morning reading the evidence she'd gathered on Jonathan Walker. He'd beaten two Emiratis half to death over some trivial incident outside a nightclub. Thus proving he was capable of extreme violence. His HR files, which, thanks to Amélie Aubert, Ffion had had access to, revealed other occasions when he'd been cautioned over his aggressive behaviour towards colleagues.

And she had the fact that, apart from Jonathan, the only person who was present who could corroborate or refute his testimony was his wife. A woman who, quite frankly, was out of her mind at the time and unable to remember a single detail, like whether she was dressed or not.

Had that been all of it, Ffion wouldn't have pursued the case at all. She'd have listened to Russ's advice and let it go. Yes, Walker might be a nasty piece of work and quite possibly a psychopath. But, if you believed what you read in the Sunday papers, half the CEOs in the country were as well, so it was hardly surprising in a merchant banker.

But that wasn't all of it, was it? She paged through the forensics from the night of Harry's murder. Because that was how she thought of the crime now. No way was this infanticide, or in the judge's dry legalese, *maternal filicide*. Jonathan Walker had smothered his baby son with a pillow – the *actus reus* or voluntary bodily movement. And he'd done it intending to cause death – the *mens rea* or guilty mind.

Harry hadn't drowned. Yes, there was the medical explanation for the absence of water in his lungs – so-called post-immersion syndrome – but that was a statistical long shot. She had a pillow with Jonathan's DNA on one side and Harry's on the other. She had a feather in Harry's trachea that matched those inside the pillow.

The QC for the prosecution had done a brilliant job of destroying the defence pathologist. At the time, Ffion had been delighted as Ms Toombs took Dr Begu's academic record and professional credentials and dissolved them in alcohol. Now, she felt sorry for her. If only she'd had duck down in her pillows.

But wait. What exactly had the bedding company salesman said in his affidavit? She spent a few minutes trawling through the evidence until she found it. Hungarian goose.

Under Alfie Weir's patient questioning, Mike Buckman had revealed that the feathers found in Harry's throat and Jonathan's own pillow were also Hungarian. The daft-sounding Hungarian Frizzle Feathered goose.

She frowned. Was there more than one type of Hungarian goose? Was it a species? A breed? She didn't know. But she had to find out.

Then she smiled. Mam had a cousin who was a poultry farmer. Ffion picked up the phone.

'Hi, Mam,' she said.

'Oh, Ffion! How lovely to hear your voice. You haven't been in touch for ages.'

'Don't be daft, I called you last month.'

'Like I said, ages.'

'Well, I'm calling you now, aren't I?'

'Sorry, love, of course you are. Now, how are the girls?'

'They're fine. So's David. And I am, too, but this is a work call. I'm sorry.'

'Oh, that's all right. The wheels of justice must keep turning, eh? Rich man and poor, equal before the law, that's what your da used to say. Do you remember?'

'Course I do. I was thinking about that cousin of yours. Ralph, the one with the poultry farm. Is he still in business?'

'Of course he's still in business!' Mam sounded shocked. 'He had a mini-stroke last year, well it didn't stop him for long. A month later he was on that quad bike of his, racing about the farm like he was a teenager!'

'Could you give me his phone number?'

'It's in my address book. Hold on, love, I'll go and get it.' Ffion heard Mam bustling about the farmhouse, opening drawers, rummaging around. She was only sixty but recently Ffion had caught one or two disturbing little signs that her memory wasn't all it might be. Was sixty too young for dementia? No. Everybody'd heard of early-onset Alzheimer's.

Mam came back on the line.

'Right. Yes, here we are. Ralph Griffiths, Pen Dewi Farm, St Lythans. Got a pen, love?'

'Yes, Mam.'

Ffion transcribed the number. 'Thanks. Look, I've got to go.'

'I'm fine, Ffion, thanks for asking.'

'What? Oh, sorry, Mam. How's your knee?'

'Oh, it's healed up nicely. Dr Banerjee said I'll be good as new in a month or so.'

'Great. I'll call you soon. Promise. Love you.'

'Bye, love. Kiss the girls for me.'

Ffion dialled the number Mam had given her.

A man answered. 'Pen Dewi Farm.'

'Is that Ralph Griffiths?'

'Speaking. Who's this?'

'It's Ffion Parry, Mr Griffiths. I'm Wendy Price's girl. I think we're second cousins. Or first, once removed. Related, anyway.'

He sounded happy to hear her voice.

'Ffion! My goodness. Last time I spoke to you, you were a little girl chasing the ducks round the farmyard. And none of that Mr Griffiths nonsense! Call me Ralph. How is the world of crime, then?'

'You know I'm a copper?'

'Know? Your mam's like a tap that's got stuck on when she starts talking about her amazing daughter in the Metropolitan Police,' he said, with a smile in his voice. 'According to Wendy, you're busy clearing up every murder in London single-handed.'

'I'm a lowly DC in Hammersmith, but I do my bit, yes.'

'Good for you, Ffion. Now, is this a social call or do you need me to help the police with their enquiries?' He adopted a comically deep tone for the last bit.

'Do you still farm geese, Ralph?' she asked him.

'And ducks, turkeys, quail and guinea fowl.'

'I'm working on a case that involves goose-down. Do you know anything about Hungarian geese?'

'Know about them? I got hundreds of them. There's a lovely couple a few miles away who came out from Liverpool to start this boutique' – Ralph put special emphasis on the word so it came out as *be-yoo-teek* – 'bedding company. All hand-stitched. I supply them with the down, you see. Hungarians produce the best quality. No question.'

'Have you heard of the Hungarian Frizzle Feathered goose?'

'I got a flock of them in my top pasture.'

'Are there other kinds, or is Hungarian goose just shorthand for that breed?'

'It's the same, really. Some birds have the frizzle gene. It makes their feathers curly. But no, to answer your question, it's just the one breed. They're a cross between the Pomeranian and the Emden, if you're interested.'

Ffion thanked her cousin, promised to call in next time she was visiting home and hung up.

'Bollocks!' she said loudly.

Rob looked up. 'Problem?'

'Lead just petered out.'

'You back on the Harry Walker case?'

'Yup. Russ greenlighted it. I thought if I could prove that the goose feathers from the pathologist's pillow came from a different breed to the ones Jonathan Walker had in his pillows, we could tie it back to him.'

'But you can't.'

'Nope.'

'Hard luck. Onwards…'

She smiled. 'And upwards. Coffee?'

'Nice one.'

She made two coffees and then settled at her desk

again. So the Hungarian angle was a bust. But it couldn't be! She needed to eliminate Dr Begu as a source of the feather.

She called up the affidavit and then rang the company. The woman in the sales department she reached said yes, Trevor Gough was still the sales manager, yes, Trevor was in the office today and, yes, she'd be happy to put Ffion through to him.

Ffion thought she detected a degree of malicious delight in the young woman's voice at the thought her boss might be interviewed by the police. Interesting. She filed it away.

'Trevor Gough. How can I help you?'

The voice was jovial, professional, slick.

'Mr Gough, I'm DC Ffion Parry with the Metropolitan Police. I'd like to come and see you in connection with the Harry Walker case. Will you be in for the rest of the day?'

'I have a meeting in five minutes for half an hour, but it's onsite. Other than that, I'm free. Come when you like, DC Parry.'

An hour later, Ffion was showing her warrant card to the receptionist at Northwood Beds. Five minutes after that, she was being shown into the sales department by the young woman she'd spoken to on the phone.

40

Ffion

'Is the Octopus in trouble, then?' the young woman asked.

'Octopus?' Ffion echoed.

The woman mimed a pair of hands wandering over her body.

'Trevor thinks MeToo is a request.'

'You should report him to HR.'

The woman rolled her eyes. 'Like that would change anything. He's far too valuable to the company. They'd never do anything.'

Just like Jonathan Walker, Ffion thought.

The young woman showed her into Gough's office then withdrew, but not before shooting Ffion a look all too easy to read.

Watch yourself.

The middle-aged man whose office it was rounded the desk to shake her hand. He offered her a hot drink, which she declined. The desk was crowded with paper files, and samples of fluffy white down in clear plastic bags.

Seated again, Gough leaned back in his chair, hands interlaced across a corpulent belly that spoke of too many business lunches and too few laps of his local park. More than a couple of Ffion's colleagues had the same look.

'What can I do for yourself, DC Parry?' he asked.

She retrieved a copy of his affidavit from her briefcase and showed it to him.

'Is this the affidavit you signed that was used in the trial of Melanie Walker?'

He took it from her and pulled a pair of reading glasses from an inside pocket. Perched them on the end of his nose and then peered at the document.

'Well, it's got my autograph scrawled across the bottom so I'd have to say guilty as charged, officer!'

He handed it back. As he leaned forward, he looked at her chest. The young saleswoman's evident pleasure at her boss's imminent interview with a detective came back into focus.

She offered a tepid smile. What a creep.

'I have a couple of questions about the goose-down your company uses in its bedding, Mr Gough,' she began. At this, his mouth twitched. 'It says there the pillows you supplied to Dr Begu were filled with Hungarian goose-down.' Another twitch. Bigger this time. Odd. 'So, I wanted to ask you if—'

She got no further. Something seemed to crumple inside his face. Trevor Gough's cheeks flushed pink. His eyes, until recently locked onto her bust, now flicked left and right as if unable to rest in one place. He clasped his hands until the knuckles paled.

'We were having problems with our regular supplier,'

he blurted. 'He was in trouble with the Budapest mafia, if you can believe it?'

'OK,' she said. Where the hell was this going?

'Yes. So we were left with a hole in our supply chain, d'you see? Orders needed filling, as did duvets,' he said, then the blush deepened and he carried on without waiting for a smile. 'Anyway, there was a brief period, and this is not something I'm proud of, but needs must when the Devil, or the Budapest mafia, drives, that's what they say, isn't it?'

His eyes were wide and he'd begun almost panting, so short were his breaths.

'Trevor, what exactly are you trying to tell me?' she asked, although an idea was dawning that, if he confirmed it, would take the case forward in a single massive jump.

'It wasn't Hungarian goose-down in that bedding set,' he said.

'But that's what it says on your affidavit. Are you saying you lied?'

He was on the verge of tears. His eyes shone.

'I had to! We have a reputation to protect. Not just in Guildford. We've an online shop,' he said. 'Customers all over the world. They trust Northwood Beds not just for the quality of our bedding but —'

It was Ffion's turn to interrupt. 'Trevor, I don't really have time for the sales pitch just now. If it wasn't goose-down, what was it?'

He shook his head. 'No. You've got it wrong. It *was* goose-down. But from China, not Hungary.'

'Are they the same breed?'

'No, that's the point! Totally different. Hungarian goose-down is the best in the world, OK? Plus, you've got the animal welfare to think of. Humane harvesting, everything,' he said, his words colliding in his mouth as he gabbled them out. 'Chinese geese, they're not in the same league at all. At all,' he repeated, as if she might be about to disagree with him. 'Am I in trouble?'

'Yes, you're in trouble!' she said. 'You submitted a false affidavit to a lawyer prosecuting a murder trial. A woman was convicted of infanticide partly as a result of your evidence.'

He actually was crying now. 'What's going to happen to me?'

'Right now? Nothing. But I'm going to submit a report to my boss and to the Crown Prosecution Service. There's every chance they'll want to charge you with perverting the course of justice,' she said. 'In that case, you'll be arrested.'

'But I can't be arrested. The business depends on me. I'll be ruined.'

Ffion stood. She had no time for sob stories. 'As it stands, Trevor, the only person who's been ruined is Melanie Walker. And if I may offer you a word of advice?'

'Yes, anything,' he said looking up at her with reddened eyes.

'Keep your hands to yourself from now on. Or we might be adding a charge of sexual assault to the sheet.'

And then, feeling the buzz of a case going her way, she left.

As soon as she got back to Hammersmith nick, Ffion went to see Mike Buckman and got the number of the ornithologist at the Zoological Society of London.

Ffion's question, after she'd been put through to the scientist, and introduced herself, was simple.

'How different are Chinese and Hungarian geese?'

'Generally or genetically?'

'Genetically.'

'They have some points in common, but only in the

way a long-legged buzzard would with a rough-legged buzzard, if you see what I mean?'

Ffion smiled. Scientists all had this touching faith that mere mortals would see the world the way they did.

'I might be sending you another feather to take a look at. If I did, would you be able to fast-track it for me?'

'Is this in connection with that terrible murder case?'

'The same, yes.'

'Of course. And no charge. Just send it over.'

Ffion thanked him and hung up. Next, she called Dr Begu and arranged to visit her after work.

At 7.05 p.m. that evening, Ffion drove over to Brook Green, a gentrified neighbourhood of a few dozen streets centred on the park for which the area was known. She parked outside Dr Begu's house, a neat Victorian terrace with scarlet geraniums in terracotta window boxes.

The woman who opened the door looked happier by far than the cowed figure who'd eventually been released from the witness box at the trial.

'DC Parry, come in,' she said. 'Drink?'

Ffion was just about to ask for a beer when she remembered the doctor's courtroom confession.

'A cup of tea would be great, thanks.'

Dr Begu smiled. It transformed her. 'You can ask for wine, if you want. It's all right. I won't weaken.'

Ffion smiled back. 'Actually, tea would really hit the spot. Plus, I'm driving.'

When they were seated on a small paved patio at the rear of the house, Dr Begu touched her hair and smiled nervously at Ffion. Her lips performed a complex series of small movements as if she wanted to speak but didn't know – or had forgotten – how.

'It was embarrassing. In court,' she said, finally. 'I did

make a mistake. One. But I'm never allowed to forget it for long. Is that why you're here?'

'Not exactly. I mean, no. Nothing to do with that. And, by the way? I thought you were extremely,' Ffion searched for the right word, 'dignified. Ms Toombs had a job to do and she did it. It can't have been pleasant.'

'It wasn't. So what do you need from me?'

'I wanted to ask if I could take a sample feather or two from your pillows and duvet. The ones filled with goose-down you bought from Northwood Beds.'

Dr Begu's eyes widened. 'Of course. But what for? I thought the case was over.'

Ffion sketched in the background to the reopened investigation into Harry Walker's death.

'So you think it might not have come from me after all?'

'That's what I want to establish.'

'Oh my god. I really hope you can. I've hardly been sleeping since the trial. It really knocked me back, being exposed like that. I started wondering whether I actually had contaminated the body.'

Ffion finished her tea and Dr Begu led her through the house and into the master bedroom.

Wearing purple nitrile gloves, and using tweezers she'd borrowed from Mike Buckman, Ffion extracted two feathers each from all four of the pillows and the duvet. She placed them in separate evidence bags, which she sealed with red tape, then labelled.

The next morning, Ffion drove the five miles to London Zoo and asked to speak to Dr Isaac Williams in the ornithology department. He came to meet her and she

288

handed over the five evidence bags, asking him to ensure he didn't cross-contaminate the feathers and to reseal and relabel the bags every time he opened them.

He nodded.

'I've done chain-of-evidence work before. I know the drill,' he said with a smile. 'Give me a couple of days, OK?'

'You said fast-track.'

'This *is* fast-track.'

She pulled a face.

'I don't suppose you could manage it in *one* day, could you?'

He looked at the feathers. Back at Ffion.

'Lunchtime tomorrow. It's the best I can manage. Honest,' he added.

She thanked him. There were plenty of other cases clamouring for her attention. She could wait.

41

Ffion

Just after 1.30 p.m. the following day, Ffion accepted a padded envelope from a courier.

At her desk, she slit the envelope. She fished out the evidence bags, each meticulously resealed, signed and dated by the scientist at the ZSL. He'd included a printout from the DNA lab.

Two lines jumped out at her in ten-foot tall, flashing blue letters:

Breed: Chinese goose
Likelihood: 99.999%

'Yes!' she shouted. 'Yes!'

She went to see Russ.

'Guv, I've nailed him. Walker, I mean. He did it. I can prove it.'

'Sit, slow down, breathe, explain,' Russ said with a smile.

'The feather in Harry's trachea couldn't have come from Dr Begu. It's the wrong breed. The salesman at the bedding company swore a false affidavit, which I think we should charge him with, by the way,' she said, trying and failing to comply with Russ's second order, 'but anyway, that's the major plank kicked out from under Jonathan Walker.'

Russ steepled his fingers under his nose.

'What else have you got on him?'

'He committed an extremely violent assault in Dubai a few years back that lost one victim an eye. He's got a history of aggressive behaviour at work. He's absolutely unemotional, even under stress. He's a psychopath, guv. And he murdered Harry. I know it!'

She watched Russ's face, trying to deduce his intentions, though Russ had a stone-cold poker face. It was like trying to read a statue. Her heart was racing.

He lowered his hands. 'Give him a tug.'

* * *

Ffion stood facing Jonathan in the centre of the bank's trading floor.

'Jonathan Walker, I am arresting you on suspicion of the murder of Harry Walker.'

As she recited the caution, she made sure her voice carried beyond the sharp-dressed man facing her and into the ears of his colleagues, who'd all stopped what they were doing to stare at the action.

She had time to wonder whether this was the first time

one of the bank's employees had been arrested on site. If it wasn't, the charges would have related to financial crime, surely.

'You're making a big mistake, DC Parry,' he murmured.

'We'll see about that, won't we? Did you understand the official caution I just gave you?'

'Yes. It was no harder to decode than the last time you delivered it.'

Ffion turned to the uniformed PC next to her. His name was Eric Latu and he was Tongan. Everybody at Hammersmith called him Jonah, on account of his resemblance to the famed New Zealand rugby player, Jonah Lomu. Facially, they were miles apart. The resemblance was entirely physical: Eric weighed seventeen stone ten pounds and topped six foot four.

'Cuff him,' she said.

'Turn around, please,' Eric said in his resonant baritone voice.

As mild as a lamb, Jonathan spun round and positioned his hands behind his back where Eric could reach them. The clicking of the ratchets as he tightened the cuffs on Jonathan's wrists broke the silence in the open-plan office.

Ffion let Eric lead Jonathan in front of her. She spotted the guy who'd made the crack about Welsh virgins.

'Afternoon,' she called cheerily.

42

Jonathan

They tried to hustle me into a quick interview as soon as they got me back to the cop shop, but they hadn't reckoned with Jonathan Walker's superior skills. When they offered me a free lawyer, I thanked them kindly and said I'd prefer to use my own. She wasn't available until today, which meant I had to spend a night in the cells.

So, Jonathan Walker, one, Hammersmith cops, one.

We sit facing them now. My lawyer's first name is Charity. It's hilarious. I'd no sooner *give* to charity than I'd wear an off-the-peg suit, but I don't mind *paying* for it. She works for PTF Robinson, one of the firms we use at the bank. I look sideways. The material of her white shirt has curved out between two of the buttons and I can see the lace edging of her bra cup.

Charity smells lovely. L'Eau D'Issey. I, on the other hand, do not smell lovely. I haven't been able to shower or shave. My face feels grimy, my eyes gritty. As for my suit, it'll need to go straight to the dry cleaner.

Facing us are two detectives. The Welsh one, Ffion. And an older male, who introduced himself as Detective Inspector Russell Palfreyman.

Ffion's talking. I sit straighter.

'Jonathan, you gave one account of the night Harry died in Melanie's trial,' she says. It's cute the way she calls me 'Jonathan'. It's my name, obviously, but I think they must be taught to do it. To get the prisoner to lower their defences, I suspect. She'll have to do a lot better than that. 'Is there anything you want to change in that account now?'

'No.'

'What would you say if I told you that I had conclusive proof that the feather the pathologist found in Harry's trachea came from your pillow?'

'I thought it came from the pathologist's pillow.'

She shakes her head. She's wearing her hair up. Her earlobes are pierced by gold studs. One each side, though, I can see two further pairs of holes beside them and another in the cartilage at the top. Was she a wild child in her youth?

'It didn't.'

'Well then, I'd say, as I did during my wife's murder trial, that it's no mystery. I gave Harry his bottle on that very same pillow, that very same night.'

'Yes, I remember,' she says. 'And apparently, during this presumably gentle activity, he inhaled with such force that he managed to suck a feather all the way down his windpipe to just before the…' She consults her notes again, though I suspect it's for show. Christ knows why, it's not as if anyone in this room buys it. '…tracheal bifurcation.'

I shrug. 'I suppose he must have.'

'You're a violent man, aren't you, Jonathan?'

It's a surprising question. I purse my lips as I consider how best to answer it.

'I wouldn't say that.'

'No? You've never assaulted anyone? Hit them? Wounded them so severely they needed hospital treatment?'

'I might have given someone a Chinese burn at my public school. It was quite primitive,' I say with an easy-going smile.

She nods. 'I see. So, you didn't assault two men outside the Boudoir nightclub in Dubai on January fifth, 2018?'

Charity leans over slightly. I bend my head so her lips are almost brushing my ear. It gives me a chance to explore the landscape of her cleavage, discreet and well-hidden though it is.

'No comment,' she murmurs. I feel her warm breath swirl into my ear. My cock twitches.

I could easily counter this accusation, but I'm paying for Charity's time so I might as well follow her advice.

'No comment.'

'Jonathan, I have testimony from witnesses confirming that you did indeed assault two men so severely that one man sustained a broken cheekbone and three broken teeth and the other lost an eye. That's true, isn't it?'

'No comment.'

'Bit cowardly, wasn't it? Going mental like that in a totally unprovoked attack?'

'It wasn't unprovoked!' I shout.

She raises one eyebrow and cocks her head on one side. She's smiling. Just a little. Ffion tricked me into losing my temper. The little Welsh cunt is cleverer than I gave her credit for.

'What was it, then?'

I can hear Charity's breathing beside me. She's disappointed. Tough. We'll do it my way.

'They insulted me.'

'Oh dear. What did they say to upset you?' she asks in that stupid la-la-la accent of hers.

'It doesn't matter.'

'No, go on. I'm dying to hear this. I mean,' she turns to the male detective, 'it must've been something *terrible* to cause you to lose your temper like that.'

'If you must know, one of them called me a paedophile.'

'Oh well, I can totally understand why that would have caused you to beat two men senseless,' she says. 'Are you a paedo, then? Is that why you lost it? Because you're a nonce?'

'Of course I'm not! The club does employ young hostesses, but they're all above the age of consent.'

'I'm sure they are,' she says, sarcastically.

I run a hand over my hair and smile at her. At this point, I'm thinking seriously about launching myself across the table and killing her. I could get my hands over her head and then choke her out with the cuffs. They might try and Taser me, but the uniformed giant standing to attention at the back isn't carrying one and I'm sure the two detectives aren't. By the time they hit the panic button, she'll be dead meat.

'Do you have a question for my client?' the fragrant Charity asks.

Her voice is upper class and husky. Like the Scandi woman who's on that late-night culture show. Not that I have much time for telly. My cock stirs again. I fantasise about taking her doggy style in my cell, with her kneeling on the bench. It calms me.

'Must've been hard not getting a decent night's sleep after Harry was born?'

'I managed.'

'Really? You work long hours, from what I've been able to find out. In at 6.30 a.m., not leaving before 9.00 p.m. most nights. Can't have been easy. What were you getting? Three hours a night? Four?'

'I managed. Like I said.'

'Did it make you angry the way Harry wouldn't sleep through the night?'

'No. It was my wife's job to deal with it.'

She frowns. I realise I've made a mistake.

'It?' she repeats. 'Not Harry?'

Charity leans over again and murmurs in my ear.

'By "it", I meant the waking up, not my son.'

'Right. So even though he kept waking up and crying, and screaming, and being put down then waking up again and crying, and crying and *crying*…you were totally calm and you never once thought about killing him?'

'Correct.'

'You told your boss you wanted to kill him, though, didn't you?'

'I did no such thing!'

'Have you forgotten what Ms Aubert said at Melanie's trial, Jonathan? I can remind you if you like.' She pulls out a sheet of paper from her file. 'She testified that you said, "I'd like to strangle the little fucker" to her.'

'A figure of speech, nothing more.'

'Quite a violent figure of speech to use about a six-month-old baby?'

I shrug. 'He couldn't hear me.'

'No. Of course he couldn't. Good point. So you still deny murdering him?'

'I do.'

'Let's move on.'

'Yes, let's,' I say.

Charity nudges my leg under the table. I think she means for me to stop being rude to Ffion, but it's such fun. And I like the sensation of her thigh touching mine.

'How well do you sleep, Jonathan? I mean, if you were rating yourself on a scale from one to ten, where one is a rubbish sleeper and ten is Olympic gold medal, where would you put yourself?'

'Ten. I can sleep for England.'

'Really? You're not one of those men who wake up if a bird tweets outside their window or a car alarm goes off nine streets away? You look the type.'

Charity gives me another warning leg-bump. I shake my head. Now she's just irritating me. This is child's play. I wish I'd saved myself her fee.

'Listen, Ffion,' I say, smiling, though inside I'm seething. How dare she? 'I work *incredibly* hard, OK? Probably the hardest of anyone in this room. Probably in this entire police station. When I'm on it, I am one hundred and fifty percent *on it*. But when I'm off it, I need to recharge. It's how I perform to the level I do. My head hits the pillow and that's it. I'm out. A car alarm could go off in my bedroom and I'd sleep through it.'

'Sorry, Jonathan, my mistake,' she says.

She looks down, devastated. Silly bitch. Why they let a mere detective constable loose in the adult world escapes me. I suppose they think it's a good learning opportunity.

'So there you are, having your Olympic-level bye-byes, dead to the world. How did you hear Melanie,' she consults her notes again, 'taking a bubble bath?'

I look at her. There's that supercilious little smile again. I sigh.

'The bathroom door was open. My bedroom door was open. The sound must have just caught me wrong.'

She looks down at her files again. 'Actually, Jonathan, you testified in court that both doors were closed.'

'No. They were open.'

Charity leans over.

I can't stop myself. It just comes out. 'Right, you're fired!' Her stupid lipsticked mouth drops open. 'Get out. I'll deal with this myself.'

She gathers her things and leaves, her heels clicking on the hard floor. I watch her arse until the door closes behind her. Then I turn back to Ffion.

'For the DIR, the suspect has just instructed his legal representative to leave,' Ffion says, looking straight at me. 'Which she has just done. So, Jonathan, the bathroom door was open, was it?'

'Yes.'

'So you admit to perjuring yourself?'

'What?'

'In court you said the door was closed. You just said, under caution, that it was open. So you lied in court,' she says. 'That's perjury. A very serious criminal offence. You might not know this, Jonathan, but under the Perjury Act 1911, perjury carries a maximum sentence of two years' prison. Or seven years' penal servitude. Ever been to Australia?'

I push my chair back. I need to give myself room to manoeuvre. I measure the distance from my new position to Ffion. It's a little over a metre and a half. I'm one-point-eight-five. I stretch, like my arms are tight and raise my cuffed wrists over my head.

And then she does something that does, genuinely, surprise me.

She brings her left hand up from under the table. It's

holding a bright-yellow device. She depresses a switch on the grip and a blinding, blue-white arc crackles loudly between the two copper contact points on the side facing me.

'Armed police!' she shouts, straightening her arms and pointing the Taser at my chest. 'Put your hands down and sit still. Jonah, secure the prisoner, please.'

He pushes himself off from the wall and he's behind me incredibly quickly. I don't have time to move. Not that I would. Every predator knows when they meet a bigger one.

He yanks my arms down and in a couple of seconds he's unlocked my handcuffs and re-cuffed my right wrist to the tubular steel frame of the chair. A second set of cuffs goes on to my left wrist and now I'm well and truly secured. Just as Ffion wanted. Clever girl. She's been provoking me all along. She wanted me to attack her. Well, not today. But who knows, maybe another.

During all of this, the male detective hasn't moved. And he doesn't look surprised, as far as I can tell. They must have discussed it between them in advance. He's looking at me like I'm some sort of interesting specimen, which I suppose, in a way, I am.

She lowers the Taser. Puts it on the table. Still within easy reach, though.

'Now, where were we?'

'You'd just accused me of perjury,' I say. 'But now I think about it, I was right the first time. The bathroom door was closed.'

'Closed,' she repeats, making a note. She looks up at me. 'Then I'll ask you again, Jonathan. How did you, a world-beating heavy sleeper, get woken up by your wife having a bubble bath through two closed doors?'

'She was drowning our son.'

'You didn't know that at the time, though, did you, Jonathan?'

I really wish she'd stop using my name like that. It's like someone poking me in the middle of the forehead.

'Look, I woke up. I must have, I don't know, sensed it somehow. I went into the bathroom and there she was.'

She shakes her head. 'No. That's not what happened at all. What really happened was you fetched your crying baby son, Harry, took him into the spare bedroom and smothered him with the pillow you'd just been sleeping on,' she says. 'Then you put him in the bath, went and got your wife, who, unlike you, was deeply asleep under the influence of powerful sleeping medication, and set up a scene in the bathroom to make it look like she drowned Harry. You called 999 and the rest we know.'

It's amazing. She's absolutely nailed it. Every little detail. I'm impressed.

'No,' I say. 'That is not what happened at all. What happened was what I said happened at the trial. At which Melanie, the boy's mother, was convicted of killing him.'

'I'm going to talk to her again. Jonathan,' she says. 'All she needs to do is remember one detail that contradicts your story and you'll be charged with Harry's murder.'

'In case you've forgotten, she is, still, my wife,' I say, glad I haven't bothered doing anything about the divorce. 'You can't make her give evidence against me.'

She smiles at me. 'That's where you're wrong, Jonathan. Under Section 80 of the Police and Criminal Evidence Act 1984, a wife can be compelled to testify against her husband where he committed violence either against her or a child under sixteen.'

'I didn't know that,' I say, with a shrug. 'But as I didn't do either of those things, I don't really care.'

'Jonathan, if you confess now, a judge will look

favourably on that as evidence of your cooperation. Show remorse and that will add another weight in the pan on your side of the scales,' she says. 'With the sort of legal talent you can no doubt afford, you'd probably be sent to a secure psychiatric hospital rather than prison.' She pauses. For effect, I think. 'You killed Harry, didn't you?'

It's then that I see it. In all its glory. That wasn't a pause for effect. It was the hesitation of a poor poker player betting on a card-dead hand. That's why she wants me to confess. It's as if someone has painted it in huge capital letters on the wall behind her head.

SHE'S GOT NOTHING

I look at her. I form my mouth into a downwards-turned curve. Sad face. I open my mouth and lean as far towards her as the two pairs of handcuffs allow.

She leans in towards me. Beside her, the male is copying her movements, his avid eyes glinting.

'No,' I say. 'My wife killed Harry.'

She sits back with a look on her face like she's tasted bad sushi.

'Interview suspended at 11.17 a.m.'

She gets up and leaves, the male bringing up the rear and shooting me a look over his shoulder.

I look up at my XXXL gaoler.

'You can probably unlock me now,' I say.

43

Ffion

Ffion followed Russ into his office, closed the door behind her, then slumped into a chair.

'You did your best, Feef,' Russ said.

'Can you extend custody, guv?'

'For what? Is there a realistic prospect of finding more evidence in the next twelve hours?'

She shrugged. 'I might get lucky.'

'Seems to me, your luck just ran out. Without a confession, all we've got is circumstantial evidence. Don't get me wrong,' Russ said, as Ffion opened her mouth to argue. 'It's *high-quality* circumstantial, but that's all it is.'

'But we can't just let him go.'

'I don't think we have a choice,' Russ said. 'Look, take it to the CPS, see what they say, OK? Best offer. If they're happy we hold him for longer, great. I'll authorise extended custody.'

Ffion levered herself out of the chair, suddenly feeling very tired, and left her guvnor's office.

At her desk she called Jack at the CPS and explained the situation. His answer was depressing.

'I'm sorry, but you're nowhere near meeting the threshold for charging him with murder. Plus you've also got the small problem of his wife being found guilty. We can't authorise a charge until Melanie Walker's been formally acquitted,' he said. 'The best I can advise is you release him under investigation.'

Back she trudged to Russ's office.

'No go. CPS won't play ball.'

Russ scratched his right temple. 'You've got to let him go, Feef. I'm sorry. Put it on the back burner. If something turns up, great, you can have another go at it.'

'But what about Melanie? I'm worried he'll try to get to her,' Ffion said, aware even as she spoke how desperate she sounded. 'She's our last remaining hope of a conviction: the only other person who was present in that bathroom when Harry died. Can I at least put Jonathan under round-the-clock surveillance?'

Russ's eyes popped wide open.

'Are you having a laugh? It costs forty grand *a day* for twenty-four-seven surveillance. I haven't got that sort of cash floating about.'

'Then you're signing her death warrant.'

'You're being melodramatic. If you're worried, go and see her. Tell her to take precautions,' he said. 'Give her a rape alarm. Your personal number. Whatever you like. Just don't spend money I don't have.'

'But, guv…'

'That's it, Feef. Go and release him.'

'Yes, guv.'

Ten minutes later, having managed to shuck off the

feeling she was a teenaged girl being grounded by her da – again – Ffion made her way down to the custody suite.

She had a word with the sergeant first, then waited while he sent a custody officer to fetch Jonathan Walker.

With Jonathan standing in the little booth in front of him, the sergeant handed over a brown A4 envelope containing his personal effects. Jonathan made a great show of buckling on his watch, threading his belt into his trousers and re-lacing his shoes. When he was finally ready, he turned to face the custody sergeant.

'Jonathan Walker, you are hereby released under investigation. You are on bail for twenty-eight days,' the sergeant said. 'During that time you must not travel outside the UK and you must return to this police station within twenty-four hours to surrender your passport. Furthermore, you must not make contact with or visit your wife, Melanie Walker. If you breach these conditions, you will be re-arrested and taken back into custody. Do you understand?'

'Perfectly. May I go now?'

'Yes.'

Jonathan turned to Ffion and smiled in a way that brought the short hairs on the back of her neck to attention.

'Watch yourself, Ffion,' he murmured. 'It's a jungle out there.'

Then he turned away from her, strutting towards the exit as if he was going up to collect an award.

She blew out her cheeks.

'We just let a murderer out, Joe,' she said.

The sergeant shrugged. 'On the bright side, I've got a spare cell for Friday night.'

Arriving back in CID five minutes later, Ffion picked up her bag and headed out.

'Where are you off to?' Rob asked.

'I need to speak to Melanie Walker.'

* * *

Ffion reached Ealing at 6.20 p.m. She rang the doorbell and stood back, hoping Mel was in. Disha opened the door.

'Oh, it's you.'

Nice to see you again, too.

'Is Mel in, please? There's something I need to talk to her about.'

Disha folded her arms across her chest. 'She's not here.'

'When will she be back?'

'I mean she's not here anymore.'

'Where is she?'

'Somewhere safe.'

Ffion took a moment to compose herself. Clearly Disha's former politeness had been for her friend's benefit.

'Look, Disha, I don't know if it's the police in general you have a problem with, or just me in particular, but I've got some information that Mel really needs to hear. It concerns her husband.'

That did the trick. The suspicion left Disha's face. 'Oh,' she said. She peered past Ffion then held the front door open. 'Come in.'

Ffion took a seat at the glass-topped kitchen table. Its polished surface bore not a single fingerprint or greasy streak. Not a single drop of tomato ketchup or dried-up coffee spill. A million miles from the much-scratched, dented and paint-stained pine number in Ffion's own kitchen.

'What is this information?' Disha asked.

'I'd rather tell Mel in person.'

'Fine, but I want to listen. Is that OK, or is it breaking some law or other?'

It had been a long, and trying day, during the course of which Ffion had levelled a Taser at a man she was convinced was a violent psychopath and who, she'd been equally sure, had been about to attack her.

'No, it's not breaking *some law*, as you put it,' she said, feeling her temper mounting and unable to do anything about it. 'I don't know what axe you've got to grind about the police, but spare me the student protester act, OK? The respect for my job I can manage without, but I am *trying* to protect your best friend, so please do me the honour of treating me with basic courtesy.'

Disha blinked. Swallowed. 'I'm sorry. I was completely out of order. I'm just worried about Mel,' she said. 'Look, would you like a cup of tea?'

'Have you got any wine?'

'Yes. Of course. Red or white?'

'Red, please. Just a small glass.'

Disha fetched two glasses that looked as if they belonged in an advert for a new dishwasher tablet – *No clouding. No scratches.* While Disha opened the wine, Ffion looked around the kitchen. A huge, double-doored fridge dominated one wall. Its front and sides were devoid of artwork. There were no certificates on the walls. No mini-blackboard covered in multicoloured chalk scribbles: 'Mia art project' or 'Elspeth piano 4.30!!!'.

Disha handed her a glass half-filled with a deep purplish-red wine that, when she raised it to her mouth released an aroma of blackberries. She took a sip.

'Wow! That didn't come from Tesco Metro, did it?'

Disha smiled and then drank from her own glass. She was very attractive when she smiled. Large dark-brown eyes beneath thick eyebrows. A perfect heart-shaped face with a pointed chin that made her look like a pixie.

'We bought it on holiday ten years ago. There are only a few bottles left. It's nice, isn't it?'

'Nice? It's *lush!*'

Disha laughed. 'I'm glad you like it.' Then her face turned serious again. 'I'll call Mel, then you can speak to her.'

Ffion nodded and watched as Disha tapped her phone. She noticed that the other woman kept the screen tilted towards her so Ffion couldn't see what she was doing.

'Hi lovely… Yeah, I'm fine. Listen, I've got Ffion here with me. She wants to have a word. I'm handing you over, OK? I'm going to put you on speaker.'

She tapped the screen again and then laid the iPhone on the table between her and Ffion.

'Hi, Mel. How are you?' Ffion asked.

'I'm fine. What's this all about?'

'We arrested Jonathan for Harry's murder two days ago. But today I had to release him. We didn't have enough evidence to hold him.'

'Oh my god! He'll be furious. With me. He'll think I had something to do with it.'

'Which is why I wanted to speak to you. Where are you at the moment?'

'I'd rather not say.'

'It would be safer if you confided in me, Mel.'

'I don't think it would.'

'I want to advise you to take precautions. Have you got a rape alarm?' The line went silent for a few seconds. 'Mel? Did you hear me?'

'Yes. And no, I don't have a rape alarm.'

'It might be a good idea to get one. And maybe avoid going out on your own?'

'Great,' Mel said, the line breaking up into staticky buzzing. 'So my murderous husband is on the loose, you think he's coming for me and your advice is buy a rape alarm and don't go out. For how long?'

'We're trying to find more evidence so we can bring him back in for further questioning. That's all I can tell you right now. I'll going to give my personal mobile number and my home number to Disha,' Ffion said. 'She can text them to you after I've gone. Call me. Any time of the day or night, Mel. I don't care if it's three o'clock in the morning. Call me if you're in the slightest bit worried. I promise I'll take you seriously.'

'Thanks but no thanks. I'll look after myself.'

The line clicked.

Disha pulled the phone back to her side of the table.

'Write your numbers down for me. I'll make sure she gets them.'

'Thank you.'

She pushed her half-finished glass away, thanked Disha and left her to her spotless, child-free home. Back at the station she went to find Russ.

'I've just been to see Mel.'

'How did it go?' he asked.

'She wasn't there. I gave her the standard advice about taking precautions, but she more or less told me to shove it.'

Russ shrugged. 'You did your best, Feef. But before you go, just record in your policy book that you advised the witness to take precautions and she refused to accept the advice. You might not be able to save her life, but you can save your own bacon.'

* * *

Ffion pushed through the front door half an hour later. She'd texted David before leaving and suggested they have dinner together unless he was too hungry. His reply came back instantly.

Great! I finished Elspeth's fish fingers so I won't starve xx

'Hiya!' she called out. 'Mummy's home.'

'Mummee!' Mia and Elspeth chorused, clattering down the stairs from the room they shared and throwing themselves at Ffion.

Ffion shot out a hand to steady herself against the hall wall as her daughters squeezed her legs and almost toppled her over.

'Wow! What a welcome,' she said, laughing. 'How are my two big girls?'

'My tooth came out at school, look!' Mia said, baring her teeth to reveal a gap in her lower incisors. 'Watch this.'

She pushed her tongue against the teeth, extruding a little pink bud.

'Eww! Gross!' Elspeth said, twisting her face up into a comical expression of disgust.

'How about you, Else? Anything good happened to *you* today?'

'Miss Root gave me another green apple on the learning tree. I've got the most in the class now. Even more than Sophie Kerry-Monks.'

'She's a poo-head,' Mia said.

'Mia Charlotte Parry!' Ffion said, stifling another laugh. 'What do we say about calling people names?'

Mia looked upwards, her pink cheeks already dimpling with a mischievous grin.

'We say, calling people names is…' She paused, causing Ffion to admire her younger daughter's sense of timing, '…very funny and also clever and grownup. And I should get a star on my sticker chart and a bar of chocolate also.'

Both girls dissolved into peals of giggling.

Ffion disengaged herself from their hugs, put her case down under the coat rack and went into the kitchen.

David was standing at a work surface, chopping an onion. He was wearing an apron featuring a cross-eyed woman holding a large glass of wine. Beneath it, in curly script, the legend read:

> I like cooking with wine.
> Sometimes I even add it to food.

He put the knife down and came over to meet her. He kissed her on the lips, taking his time. He'd always been an excellent kisser. Ever since their first sixth-form disco, she'd known she'd marry him one day.

'Ugh! That's disgusting!'

Ffion turned to see Mia standing in the doorway, her arms folded.

'No it isn't! It's lovely. I like kissing Daddy.'

'And I,' David said, before mashing his lips against Ffion's and waggling his head all over the place, 'like kissing your mum,' he finished, his voice muffled.

Mia screamed and ran off. 'Elspeth! Elspeth! Mum and Dad are sexing. They're going to have a baby!'

David's hand crept up to Ffion's breast. 'Mm. It's nice to have you home early,' he murmured into her hair.

Gently, because she was actually enjoying it, she disengaged his hand. 'Yes, well, Mr Parry, play your cards right and maybe later I'll remind you what you've been missing while I've been banging my head against a brick wall for the last couple of weeks.'

'OK,' he said. 'Then I'd better get back to my oyster delight.'

'Sounds lovely,' she deadpanned. 'What's for pudding?'

'Viagra ice cream.'

She burst out laughing. God, she'd missed this. Her and David bantering and mucking about while one of them cooked. She realised she'd let the case take over her life. It wasn't healthy. Everyone knew at least one copper who'd either retired early through stress or gone to an early grave because they couldn't leave the job – often one unsolved case – behind. She had no intention of swelling their ranks.

'What is it, really?'

David scraped a mound of chopped garlic and onions into a frying pan in which a slab of butter was melting. They began to sizzle immediately, releasing a delicious aroma that promised wonderful things to come.

'My special: spaghetti vongolé. And for dessert, something I whipped up earlier. A New York-style baked rum and raisin cheesecake.'

'Are you *trying* to make me fat?'

'No, but Sainsbury's is.' He grinned. 'Anyway, you're not fat. You're cuddly. I don't want a girl without any flesh on her bones. It'd be like cuddling a xylophone.'

'David Parry, you are a sexist pig!' she said, mouth open in mock outrage. 'I don't know if you'd heard, but the seventies finished some time ago. It's not all about what *you* like, you know? You're supposed to value me for my brains and my professional skills, not just my tits and arse.'

'Sorry, love. I take it back. You *are* fat. And I *don't* fancy you. But I find your massive brain very,' his eyes flicked up to the ceiling, 'empowering.'

'Pour me some wine, poo-head.'

* * *

Later, after making love twice, once urgently, during which David finished too early, apologising even as he came; and then again, slower, leaving Ffion gasping and clutching her husband to her, she slipped out of bed and tiptoed downstairs. She made herself a cup of instant decaf and got the files out of her briefcase.

There had to be something she'd missed.

44

Mel

The morning after I arrive in Burton Bradstock, I call an independent hairdresser in Dorchester and ask for an appointment with their creative director.

The receptionist says they're fully booked with no availability for the rest of the week. I ask her, please, to let me speak to the manager. I say I'm not complaining but it's very, very important I get my hair cut sooner than that.

The woman who comes on the phone is friendly but initially gives me the same line as the receptionist. So I tell her an edited version of my story.

'I've run away from my husband,' I say. 'He's been controlling and abusing me and I desperately need to change my appearance.'

The manager's all business now. She tells me to come over the next morning at 8.00 – 'before we're officially open' – and she'll look after me personally.

When I arrive, she lets me in herself. Her name is Jayne. She's about ten years older than me and has a look behind her eyes that says she's heard many stories at least as bad as mine. She asks me what my hairstyle was like before. What kind of thing I want now. I ask her for something manageable but really different from the blunt, jaw-length bob I used to have.

'And I'd like to change the colour, too,' I add. 'It used to be a silvery platinum-blonde.'

She smiles. 'What about a forward graduation, one-length cut, keeping it shoulder length? Long enough, just, if you wanted to wear it in a pony tail again. Short, but not too short. Say three or four inches longer than your classic bob?'

'It sounds great,' I say. 'But can you leave the front a bit longer? So I can sweep it forwards if I need to.'

She looks at me, then; not suspicious, but like she can read my mind.

'A little bit of extra camouflage?' she asks.

I nod, mutely.

Three hours later, she whisks the cape off and holds up a mirror to the back of my head.

'What do you think?'

'It's fantastic!' I say, meaning it. The woman looking back at me bears no semblance to the drab who walked in here three hours earlier. I imagine a pair of oversized sunnies and my baseball cap. I tug some hair forward experimentally and drape it over my right eye.

'Very Goth,' she says. I laugh. And then I cry.

'Hey, hey,' she says, coming round the chair to squat beside me.

She offers me a tissue from a box printed with lilies of the valley and I blot the tears, then blow my nose.

'Thanks,' I say. 'You're a life-saver.'

I realise in that moment that I mean that literally.

I buy some groceries and some clothes on the way back to the car. Undies from Marks & Spencer, and a bunch of everyday stuff – jeans, T-shirts, tops, sweatshirts – from whichever shops have things in my size.

When I get back to the cottage and put my shopping away, the next thing I have to do is call my offender manager. By some miracle, Val is totally understanding about my fears. I get the feeling she's had an abusive relationship in the past. Either that or she's simply worked with women who have. I'm beginning to learn there are a lot of us.

She says it's, 'outside offender management protocols' but that she'll come to me for our meetings. I think she's secretly pleased to be able to get out of London for a few hours once a week.

That was three weeks ago. Apart from my meetings with Val, and my calls with Disha, my connections to my old life, my London life, have been severed. I try not to think about Jonathan, telling myself I need to look forward, not back.

* * *

Little by little, I am learning to find small moments of peace in my new life down here. Like yesterday. I bought some mackerel, so fresh it smelled of the sea. Its skin was this lustrous silver, shot through with blue-green, those charcoal grey chevrons like the evening sky. I asked the fishmonger to clean it for me, though I intend to learn how to do it myself, and grilled it with butter and lemon juice. I ate alone, at my kitchen table, listening to the radio. And I felt … calm.

After dinner, I washed up and put everything back in

the cupboard, wiped down the work surface and took the tinfoil I used to protect the grill out to the dustbin so the cottage wouldn't smell of fish for a week.

I walked down to the beach and took my shoes off, digging my bare toes into the damp sand. The setting tinted the sea a coppery red. Nobody else had chosen that moment to visit the sea: I had the beach to myself. Not ready to go back inside yet, feeling safe for the first time in a long time, I set off along the sand, swinging my shoes from a finger, revelling in the shock each time an icy wavelet bathed my feet.

By the time I got home, it was dark. For the last half-mile I'd been looking over my shoulder from time to time: I couldn't help it. But of course there was nobody there. Smiling to myself, I tried to carry a little of my upbeat mood back inside with me, giving the door a good slam but fighting down the urge to lock and bolt it. It's not as if Jonathan was going to suddenly appear and batter his way in with a sledgehammer, now was it?

The cottage is starting to feel like home, too, even though it's probably only a quarter of the size of the house in Richmond. I can tell Disha organised the décor; Gav has no sense of colour. Each room has a feature wall painted a shade of teal or the grey-brown of beach pebbles. Plenty of ornaments, too, mostly in variations of a deep, dark red I'd call crimson.

Bookshelves in every room, groaning with high-end fiction by the sorts of authors who win literary prizes. Rushdie, Atwood, Evaristo, McEwan. And the gorgeous fireplace in the sitting room, in front of which I sit every night. It's not really cold enough for a fire but I light one anyway. I like the way the firelight flickers on the heavy brocade curtains, making their patterns of twining creepers and tropical flowers seem to move in the half-darkness.

* * *

When Val visits me, we go for long walks along the coastal path or if it's raining, just sit here by the stone-flagged hearth, drinking coffee and eating my home-made biscuits. If I've lit a fire, I might lean forwards, retrieve a poker from one of the wrought-iron firedogs and stir the blazing logs.

She asks me a set of questions that don't change from week to week, entering my answers onto a form on her laptop.

'It's a box-ticking exercise more than anything else,' she says to me one day. 'How's the treatment going?'

'Good,' I say easily. 'Yes, Dr Silverman is really pleased with my progress.'

Which is broadly true. In fact when I spoke to Dr Silverman for the first time after that initial meeting with Val, he told me that long walks, decent sleep, and the distance I had put between myself and my old life was the best treatment I could get anyway.

I asked him about drugs and he told me in no uncertain terms that he was firmly against the idea of prescribing any further medication. Which suited me fine. If I never have to hear the words clozapine, citalopram or trazodone again, it will be too soon.

We agreed I would call him once a week to discuss my mental state and any worries I might have. Now I'm not in the hospital, I am to call him Nate, which I find very hard. 'Nate' sounds like an old friend, a tennis coach, or possibly a work colleague. Not the man who once sat making notes while the ECT lit my brain up like Blackpool illuminations.

'Have you thought about getting a job?' Val asks.

'I haven't, to be honest. I've been living off my savings.' She makes a note.

'It mightn't be a bad idea. Nothing too stressful. Maybe a few shifts in a pub, or in a shop?'

I know it's wrong of me, but those two suggestions make me mourn for the life I used to lead. I used to have a 'proper' job. A well-paid, demanding, glamorous job. I promise Val I'll think about it. What I really want to do is ask her about Jonathan. About the case, whether she's heard anything. I tried before, but she closed me down. She said she couldn't discuss it. She wasn't unfriendly about it; it was against the rules.

I wave after her when she drives away down The Barrow, negotiating the narrow bits where my temporary neighbours have parked their 4x4s tight up against the fronts of their cottages.

I turn and there's a middle-aged man striding towards me from the other direction. He looks odd, somehow. His eyes are fixed on mine and he's scowling. He's wearing black gloves with holes punched out over the knuckles.

My pulse goes into this fluttery rhythm and I look around for something I can pick up and wave at him. *Keep away!* I want to scream. *Stay back!*

His fists clench and his knuckles, furred with black hair, bulge obscenely through the holes in the leather.

I go to slam the door but he shouts at me, and at first, because I'm panicking, I don't hear him. It sounds like he just yelled, 'You accused me!' For an insane fraction of a second, with my fingers already curling around the door handle, I think he must be talking about a trial. *My* trial.

Then I see that his eyebrows have jumped up towards his hairline and his thin lips are sketching an approximation of a smile. Not 'You accuse me,' but 'Excuse me?'

I stop.

'Yes?'

He arrives at the front gate and I can see he's out of breath.

'We're trying to find Friary Road,' he says. 'This is Burton Bradstock, isn't it?' I think of telling him that his satnav would tell him that when his smile changes into one of apology. 'Bloody satnav just died, didn't it?'

I manage to find an expression that feels like a smile, although from his face, I'm guessing I'm close but not within reach of the cigar box.

'Where are you parked?' I ask.

He turns and points.

'Back up on the main road. I'm sorry if I startled you but we're late – I mean *really* late – for a family celebration.'

I give him directions and then he's off, showering me with effusive thanks before turning and literally running back the way he came.

I go indoors again. And I lock the door.

45

Mel

Three months have passed. Yes, I am finding some peace and some relief at just being on my own down here. But it's not a pure coastal idyll.

Most nights, I dream about the trial. Sometimes it's just a fragment: Ms Toombs sneering at me or Alfie, doing his best to defend me until he turns into a schoolboy in shorts, fishing around in his satchel for the right document. Other times it's a full-on horror show: a tidal wave of water rushing through the doors at the back of the courtroom and sweeping the jurors from their seats to crash into the dock, fish-eyed with terror as they suck the water down into their lungs.

How could I? That's the question that haunts me in my waking hours, once the dreams have left me panting on the side of the bed and soaking in my own sweat. How could I have drowned my own child? Part of me still denies it happened. I know I was severely ill, but I did, still, love him. I loved him so much, I would have done anything for him.

Anything.

I try to remember what it was like to be a mum, but the memories are all jumbled up in my mind. It's like a photo album where someone's been through it and removed most of the pictures, so there are informative captions – 'Mummy and Harry at the Park" – but no image to bring them to life.

Harry is a there-but-not-there presence in my waking and sleeping hours. Defined not by what he is but by what he isn't. I cry a lot, and the tears and the pain feel genuine. Yet I still can't *attach* them to him. It is grief, but it's unanchored.

I try writing poems. They're dreadful. The sort of thing the copywriters at my old agency would have sneered at and called 'therapy writing', like that was the worst thing in the world. I burn them.

In the end I decide to let my feelings take care of themselves. It sounds like the sort of thing Nate might say. When I tell him, he agrees with me.

'You never really bonded with him, Mel,' he says to me on one of our calls, making me cry, but silently, so that he doesn't ask me if I'm all right. 'That's why your memories feel piecemeal.'

The people in the village are welcoming, but reserved. On the rare occasions I go to the pub, they don't all fall silent and eye me like I've brought the plague, but nor do they invite me to their houses for coffee or to join their book groups or darts teams. Which is fine. I want to stay hidden.

I've changed my name, too. I had the idea in the bath just after I'd fallen asleep and dropped my paperback into the water, then jerked awake convinced I was drowning. Not legally. But down here, I'm Emma. No surname. I pay for everything in cash so nobody sees my real name on my credit cards.

I wear a baseball cap whenever I go out. I've even changed my walk, because I read somewhere that you can be recognised by your gait long before anyone can get close enough to see your face. I always used to wear heels for work, so now I wear trainers and affect a sort of rolling style.

I've tried to look after my hair, too. I haven't been back to Jayne. But there's a local woman who's a freelance hairdresser. Jackie works from home and keeps it looking good. Jonathan, who I still think about every day, will be looking for the old me. The blonde, classic-bob-wearing me.

On confident days, I imagine walking straight past him in the centre of Dorchester and him not recognising me. On anxious days, I imagine him turning, snarling, choking me in the middle of the street and shoving my body to the ground.

A week after the conversation with Val about getting a job, I realise I will have to start thinking about making some money. My savings are still mostly intact; I'm so glad I decided not to spend them all on an expensive lawyer. Alfie did a brilliant job, and although an acquittal would have been the best outcome, all things considered, I think he did the best he could with what he had to work with.

I kick around all sorts of ideas: dog-walking, gardening, even selling hand-made greetings cards on Etsy. But they're all crap. Poorly paid or unlikely to ever happen.

I am talking to Disha about it one night, each of us halfway down a bottle of red.

'I need something well paid, that I can do from here,

and that doesn't involve me going anywhere Jonathan could find me,' I say.

'Why don't you do your old job?'

'How can I? Agencies want their account teams to meet clients, wine and dine them, attend awards ceremonies,' I complain. 'Not to mention be available in the bloody office all hours of the day and night.'

'No, dafty, that's not what I meant. Not the account manager bit, the copywriting bit,' she says. 'You were always telling me you had to rewrite stuff so the clients would approve it.'

It's typical Disha. Seeing a problem from just a little bit of a different angle to everyone else. It's a genius idea.

I spend the next week setting myself up as a freelance copywriter. By 11.00 p.m. on the Friday I've put a basic website together using a free platform. I call myself 'Coast Copywriting'. I write the copy carefully, avoiding giving any clues as to my location or my name anywhere on the site. Obviously I'll have to sign off when I'm emailing clients but I'll stick to Mel and never use my surname.

The hardest thing is contacting everyone in my old network. I need the work, but I'm fearful of their reactions. I've had enough of people spitting in my face or screaming death threats as the G4S guards hustled me into court without adding in the subtler forms of rejection I might encounter from my ex-clients and colleagues.

But I have no choice. It's that or starve.

To be fair, most people are decent about it. I get fifty-one rejections before I land my first job. Robyn was an account manager at a rival firm when I went into hospital. She's now heading her own agency. She says one of their writers has just gone on maternity leave and they need someone to produce everything for a new campaign, from website and brochures to social media posts and press releases. I bite her hand off at the elbow and promise I won't let her down.

The truth is, I love it. I rediscover the joy in writing I had at uni when I read English; the headlines and hooks just seem to fall from my fingers onto the screen.

After a few rounds of editing, Robyn sends the copy off to the client. Then there's just radio silence for almost a week. I try not to think the worst, but I keep imagining Robyn will email me saying the client is horrified at how bad the copy is and how they aren't going to pay.

Eventually, she emails me. The subject line is ominous.

Your copy…

My stomach clenches with nerves and I can hardly bear to open the email. My eyes skitter over it, unable to process a word. I breathe in and out then focus on the line right at the top.

…is amazing!!!

With a mile-wide grin on my face, I start to read the rest of her message.

OMG the client LOVED what you wrote for them! They're literally ecstatic. They want you to write all their stuff from now on. Pleeez say you can do it?

What's a girl to do? Naturally, I say yes. Over the next month, Robyn sends a steady stream of jobs my way, and after a while I get sniffs of interest from a couple of other agencies. Bless her, Robyn must have put the word out, which is so kind. I remember when we found someone good we used to try and keep them all to ourselves.

Then a local company gets in touch. Nothing major, just a little engineering outfit on an industrial estate a few miles from where I live. But their MD found my website and he liked what he read. I write a press release for him and when it gets picked up by the local paper and BBC Radio Solent, he comes back and asks if I'll 'tart up' their website.

I tell Val what I've achieved and she looks genuinely pleased for me. She says it means she can tick the boxes for 'economically active' *and* 'embracing societal norms'.

I still have my weekly calls with Nate, too, but I get the increasing sense these are pretty much box-ticking exercises for him as well. He also approves of my working and wants to know basic stuff, like

Are you sleeping?

'For England.'

Not too tired to get up in the morning, though?

'Nope, up with the lark, full of energy.'

How's your mood?

'Yeah, fine.'

Still weepy?

'Sometimes. But it feels OK, not like it might never stop.'

In touch with friends?

'I text with Disha, but mainly I'm just happy to get to know myself again.'

Any news on the divorce?

'Nothing. I think Jonathan might have put it on the back burner. Making money was always his passion.'

Plans to return to London?

'None. I like it here. I could see myself living here permanently. Getting a dog, maybe.'

It's true. I could. Can. Not in the cottage. I'd have to find somewhere to rent initially. Buying would be the dream, but that would mean sorting out my finances. Which would mean contacting Jonathan.

That particular thought fills me with dread. I'd have to do it all through lawyers, which would mean money. Possibly a lot of money. Jonathan would get nasty, I know he would. Christ, he came to Disha's looking for me! I'm fairly sure from what Ffion told me it wasn't for a frank and no-fault chat about the future. So I can just imagine his response if a solicitor sent him a letter.

For now, I'm happy just being here: it's been six months and I've never felt so content. Somehow, I've managed to reinvent myself. I have my own, admittedly tiny, business, and a steady income.

Last time we spoke, Disha said they were happy for me to stay on at least until next summer. That's ages away. She said it makes them comfortable knowing someone's here to make sure nothing happens. I suppose she means a fire, or kids graffiti-ing the front door. But she's just a worrier. I've never lived anywhere this calm.

I don't want to say it, in case I jinx my luck, but I feel my life has finally turned a corner.

PART V

CRIME AND PUNISHMENT

46

Jonathan

It takes me six months to find Mel.

I realise she's going to need money. Her savings aren't enough to keep her in the style she grew accustomed to being married to me. She'll have to get a job. Now, what sort of work do people look for after an extended break? Anyone? No?

I'll tell you. The same work they were doing before. Which in my dear wife's case means advertising.

I set up a Google Alert on my phone.

If anyone, anywhere in the world, loads a web page or a social media post containing the words 'Melanie Walker' or even just 'Melanie' or 'Mel' plus 'advertising' or 'copywriting' or 'marketing', I'll get to hear of it. And once I get to hear of it, I can start narrowing my focus down.

Like I say, nothing happens for half a year.

Then, while I'm working on a bid document late at

night, my phone coos to me. 'Ohh, Jon-a-than.' The voice is that of a girl I slept with just after Mel pissed off to the hospital.

I use it for all my alerts now.

I tap the link. And I nod to myself with satisfaction. It's a web page. A testimonial.

The social media advertising copy Mel wrote for my nutrition business was amazing! So much better than I could have done myself.
Analiese Mitchie, Mitchie Nutrition & Holistic Wellness

The site belongs to a marketing agency called Coast Copywriting. I make a note.

Now, for all I know, there are hundreds of women called Mel peddling copywriting to 'nutrition and holistic wellness' companies. But what if there aren't? What if there's just one? *My* one?

I check the *Contact us* page, but there's only a mobile number and a form. No address or email. I note down the number. Then I call a girl I know.

Katerina is Russian. Actually, no, she isn't. She's from Billericay in Essex. And her name is Katy. But she does a very good Russian accent. She works for an escort agency the bank uses when we're entertaining clients from the Gulf. She can do other accents, too. Including the one I'm hearing in my head. A polished upper-middle class voice from somewhere in the Home Counties.

'All right, Jonno?' she says in her normal voice, all white stilettos, bleached hair and knockoff Louis Vuitton handbags.

'I've got a job for you.'

She's all business now. Slips into that delectable St Petersburg accent.

'What is gentleman's name?'

'It's a lady, not a gentleman.'

'Is double for girls,' she says, still in character.

I laugh. 'I just need you to make a call for me.'

'What kind of call you are needing?'

I explain what I want and that I want her to do it at my house. We agree a fee and she comes over the next night.

I hand her the sheet of paper with the number on it and a little script I've prepared. She scrutinises it then looks up at me.

'Is that all?' she asks, back now in Billericay.

'That's all,' I reply, smiling.

She calls the number and puts the phone on speaker.

'Coast Copywriting. How can I help you?'

It's Mel. *My* Mel. I nod at Katy.

'Oh, yah, hi,' she says, looking down at my notes. 'My name's Davinia Macaulay. My husband Jimmy and I have just opened a *rather* special little B&B in Dorchester and we're looking for a copywriter to do our website.'

'Oh, well, you've come to the right place. And you're practically on my doorstep.'

'Really? That's fantastic! You see, Jimmy and I, we feel it would be best for the copywriter we hire to come and spend a complimentary weekend with us. You know, really get the feel of the place so they can write it up properly.'

Katy's improvising now. Brilliantly. Like she does everything else.

'That sounds amazing. It's a very generous offer. And at least you wouldn't have to fork out for rail tickets or anything.'

'So, where are you based?' Katy asks, winking at me.

This is it. The money shot. I look at the phone, breathing easily, wondering if Mel will swallow the bait.

'Burton Bradstock. I'm only fifteen miles from you.'

'Fantastic!' Katy gushes. 'I'll pop our address into this little form here and then we can sort out a date and a rather lovely room for you to enjoy. *Ciao* for now!'

She taps the red button and holds her hand out.

'Fancy doubling your money?' I ask her. I glance at the ceiling.

Katy grins. 'Charmer.'

47

Mel

The young man smiles as he walks towards me out of the sun. It's too bright to look at his face: the fierce yellow light is blazing around his outline. He appears to be floating in a cloud of golden dust. Pollen, I suppose.

'Hi, Mum,' he says, in a beautiful resonant voice that sounds musical, as if he's a singer.

I open my mouth to greet him, but I can't remember his name.

I smile instead and hold my arms wide.

He enfolds me in his arms and I place my ear to his chest.

I listen for his heartbeat. That steady thrum that tells us everything is OK, everything is good and pure, and we're going to be fine for another day.

I can't hear anything.

I jerk away from him, panicking. He's no longer

smiling. He is opening his mouth, but now he's the one struggling to speak. I see why. He has a feather caught between his lips.

I pinch its soft white barbs between my thumb and forefinger and pluck it free.

Then he opens his mouth.

It's full of feathers. They come tumbling out in a white cloud. I open my mouth to scream and suck them in. They block my mouth, then my nose. I feel my throat packed tight with them. I'm choking.

I'm choking, I'm choking imchokingimchokingim-chokigimchoingim…

* * *

It's 4.55 a.m.

My chest is heaving, my face is wet with tears and the sheets are soaked in sweat. The dark tendrils of the nightmare still have their needle-like roots pushed into the crevices in my brain. I clutch my fist to my sternum, which aches as if someone has punched me there.

I rush downstairs and check the front door. It's locked and the bolt is across. I go to the dining room and open my laptop and set up a new document. While the nightmare is fresh – horribly fresh – in my mind, I write as much of it down as I can remember.

I know it's pointless trying to go back to sleep. I don't want to, anyway. I put the kettle on and while it's boiling I go upstairs to dress.

I want to know what the dream meant. I want to know what happened to Harry. To *remember*.

And I think I know how.

48

Mel

I manage to wait until 9.00 a.m. before I call Nate.

'Hi, Mel,' he says. 'Have I got my dates mixed up? Is this our regular call?'

'No, Nate,' I say, thinking it still feels weird calling my psychiatrist by his Christian name. 'But there's something I want to ask you.'

'Go on then. I'll do my best. A long as it's not about football. Bit of an ignoramus in that particular field. No pun intended.'

I laugh, for the sake of politeness.

'Have you got Flick Barber's number?'

It clearly isn't the question he was expecting.

'What?'

'I wondered if you had Flick Barber's number?'

'Do you mind telling me why you want to speak to her?'

For a second, I have this totally ridiculous notion that he's having an affair with her. I dismiss it. But there's something behind his question. A tone I don't like. I decide on the spur of the moment to lie.

'I'm thinking of writing a book. About my experiences. I wanted to interview her.'

'I don't think that's a good idea,' he says.

'Why?'

'It could just stir up a lot of trauma you very successfully assimilated.'

It sounds, even to my untrained ear, like psychological BS. I try again.

'But as a psychiatrist with her specialist knowledge, she could provide some valuable insights.'

'She's not practising anymore,' he says, which I think is a bit of *a non sequitur*. 'She left UCLA.'

'Where did she go?'

He sighs. 'Look, Mel, I really don't think Flick's the right person to talk to about all this. If you want to talk to someone other than me about postpartum psychosis, I can recommend a colleague. He's very good.'

I don't want to talk to one of Nate's colleagues, I want to talk to Dr Barber. And now I'm even more sure I don't want to tell Nate the reason. I wonder why he's being so difficult. Maybe I need to push back a little. Lean in.

'Should I Google her? Is that what you're saying?'

Another sigh, deeper this time.

'No. Look, as your psychiatrist, I have to advise against this course of action, but if you're really set on talking to her, she teaches at the Maudsley.'

'The hospital?' I ask, not believing my luck. 'In London?'

'Yes.'

I thank him and end the call. Something was very off

about his behaviour though. Maybe they *are* involved emotionally. Nate's still married as far as I know, so that would explain it.

I thought she'd be back in Los Angeles. Now I know she's in the UK, I don't have to wait until late afternoon before calling her. I dial the number for the Maudsley's switchboard and the receptionist puts me straight through.

'Hi, this is Flick.'

On hearing her drawling Californian accent, I can see her as if she were here with me. Her tousled blonde mane and those sea-blue eyes.

'Dr Barber, it's Mel Walker. Melanie. You treated me—'

'—in Hammersmith Hospital, and got savaged by that wolverine in a wig in court for my troubles! Hey, Mel, how are you?'

'I'm good. Look, I wanted to talk to you about something.'

'You caught me just about to go into a meeting. Can I call you later this morning?'

'Of course!'

I give her my number.

She calls back two hours later. I'm trying to edit a blog post for a local nutritionist, but the words won't play ball. I jump when my phone – a cheapo pay-as-you-go from a shop in Dorchester – rings.

'Hello?'

'Mel, it's Flick. And before we go any further, drop the Doctor Barber bit, OK? You make me feel like my mom.'

'Sorry, Flick,' I say, finding it much easier than when Dr Silverman reminds me to call him Nate.

'So, what's going on in your world that you need help from a blonde bimbo who the *NEJM* thinks is one step up from a snake oil saleswoman?'

343

I think she's joking. I laugh dutifully. My nerves are getting in the way of my ability to judge humour. I used to be much better at reading people. In preparation for this call I've written out my speech; I quickly pull it up on screen.

'I dreamed about Harry. He had a mouthful of feathers. I've also been trying to remember what happened the night he died, but I can't: there's nothing there. And I wondered…' – *deep breath, read the rest of it: this is why I wrote it out, after all* – 'whether you'd agree to help me recover my memories.'

The words come out in a rush and I have to clamp my lips together to stop myself retreating behind a *but of course if you can't, I'd totally understand.*

She doesn't say anything for maybe five seconds. I can feel my pulse throbbing in my fingertips. Which are also tingling. An odd sensation.

'You know what? I would love to help you. On one condition.'

'Name it.'

'Careful, you don't know what it is yet. I might ask for your soul.'

'Careful, I might agree.'

'Touché. Where are you living these days?'

'Dorset. On the coast.'

'Nice. Are you free this weekend? Fancy entertaining a visitor from the colonies? I've never visited Dorset.'

'I'm always free at the weekends. And in the evenings. And during the day, apart from work. There's a spare bedroom, too, so you could stay. I mean, not that you have to stay here, that was a bit forward of me, or,' I'm gabbling and I can't stop, 'there's a nice pub with bedrooms down the road about a mile or so or you could drive back. Unless you want to drink. Sorry, do you drink?

Not that it's any of my business, that was rude of me, I just meant—'

'Whoah! Rein those horses in, girl, they're going to run away with you.'

She laughs and I picture her eyes crinkling with good, healthy humour.

'Sorry. I'm more nervous than I thought I was.'

'Relax.' *Relaaax.* 'How about I come down on Friday after work and we just take it as it comes?'

'Perfect.'

I'm trying so hard not to start babbling again, I've become terse.

'Sooo?'

'So, what?'

'Your address, honey? I'm brilliant, but I'm not psychic.'

* * *

The next two days pass quickly. I've a lot of writing to do for clients. I am so past the time when I cried because that cow strung me along about her bloody B&B and then ghosted me.

I manage to get the blog post edited and off to the nutritionist, who says she's delighted. I get another little job from Robyn that takes me until 6.00 p.m. on Friday night. Then I shut down the laptop, close the lid and go into the kitchen to pour myself a glass of wine.

I take it into the garden and sit at the wooden table and listen to the birds singing their little hearts out.

The doorbell rings at 8.15 p.m.

Flick stands there holding a bottle wrapped in white tissue paper, twisted round at the neck to form a little flower.

If anything, she looks even more glamorous than when I saw her last. Her hair is still the first thing I notice, but she's softened her look. Her tan has faded in the English light and she's wearing less makeup.

I welcome her inside, trying to find a happy middle ground between over-effusive and taciturn. I put the wine, red, by the Aga to come up to room temperature, and offer her a glass of white from the fridge.

I take her out to the garden and we sit at the table facing towards the sea, which lies a few hundred metres away over a low grassy rise. The waves are just audible.

'Cheers, guvnah!' she says in a cod-Cockney accent about as good as Dick Van Dyke's in *Mary Poppins*.

'Cheers,' I say and we clink rims, then drink.

'You look good, Mel,' she says. 'I love what you've done with your hair.'

I touch it reflexively. It feels silky. 'Thanks.'

'So, what's going on?'

And here we are. At the point I've been working up to since waking before dawn three days ago.

'I wondered whether you'd agree to treat me with psilocybin again.'

She frowns.

'Since that business with Silverman, I've got no access to psilocybin. It's kind of a touchy subject.'

Silverman? Not 'Nate'? Or 'Doctor Silverman'? Clearly whatever's going on between them, it's not an affair.

'What business?'

'He lied to me. To us both, actually.'

'About what?'

'When I treated you, he didn't have a Home Office licence for the psilocybin.'

'What?'

346

'Oh, he applied for it. But the paper-pushers in Whitehall Street, or wherever your civil servants do their bureaucratic voodoo, were dragging their heels.'

'So he went ahead without it?'

'Yup.'

'But is that illegal? He's still treating me!'

'It's kinda murky. They granted the licence eventually, but I'd already given a lecture about the treatment.' She raises a hand palm outwards, though I have no intention of interrupting her. 'It came to the attention of the authorities and there was practically a diplomatic incident.'

'What happened?'

'Long story, short, your man got off with a disciplinary warning from the Royal College of Psychiatrists and a demotion. I got a "Dear John" letter from UCLA. I mean, not exactly. I had tenure, but the dean made it pretty clear to me I was *persona non grata*,' she says, curling her lip. 'I could have stayed, held my head high and ignored the bastard, but I thought, screw 'em, I'll try my luck in good old London Town.'

'Bloody hell!'

She drains her glass and refills it, and mine. 'Tell me about it.'

'So does this mean you can't treat me?'

She shakes her head.

'No. It means we have two ways to go,' she says. 'One, we use a hypnosis technique called M-RAR, which before you ask stands for Memory Regression and Retrieval, which I am qualified to use in a therapeutic setting...'

'And two?'

'We use M-RAR plus a natural source of psilocybin, which would be ten times more effective.'

'You mean magic mushrooms?' I whisper.

She nods. 'You're deep in the boonies down here.

There must be a local purveyor of life's little extras. Maybe operating out of that jolly old pub down the road?'

I shake my head. 'I hardly go in there. I wouldn't know where to begin.'

She smiles at me. 'Looks like this reformed San Diego punk needs to give you a little lesson in how it works on the other side of the looking glass.'

I offer to cook us something while she explains, and we move into the kitchen. Flick clues me in about identifying the local drug dealer while I rustle up a basic spag bol.

The doorbell rings. I've had a bit too much wine already and I'm a little unsteady on my feet. I check the spy-hole before I open the door, but it's fine. Another helpless-looking middle-aged bloke. Probably a lost tourist. They're always driving up the Barrow trying to reach the sea then knocking or ringing and asking for directions.

Smiling and hopefully not reeking too strongly of Rioja, I open the door.

'Hi!' I say, brightly. 'Lost the beach?' Bloody hell, I do sound pissed. I try again. 'Hi.' Better.

He smiles. He's soft-looking, with a bit of a paunch and one of those chunky-knit cardigans with wooden toggles.

'Hello,' he says. 'I'm sorry for dragging you away from your dinner.' Christ! He *can* smell the wine on me. 'I was looking for Malcolm and Flo Neville. But I can see I have completely the wrong house.'

I frown. 'Yes, I think you have. But there's nobody on The Barrow by those names. Are you sure you have the right street?'

There's a bit of befuddlement on both sides as we try and work out where he's gone wrong, then he sort of shrugs and apologises – again – and leaves.

'Who was that?' Flick asks when I rejoin her in the kitchen.

'Clueless tourist. We get them all the time.'

* * *

Saturday is drugs-buy day. Through Becky, who pulls pints behind the bar in the King's Head, I reach her ex-brother-in-law Matt. Through Matt, I find my way to a cottage, well, more of an outbuilding, on a nearby farm. And there, wreathed in cannabis smoke and wearing a lazy smile, listening to sitar music like a sixties hippie, I find Ed.

He peers at me through eyes the colour of boiled prawns.

'Yeah, I got shrooms,' he says. 'Twenty gets you five grammes. That's enough for a decent trip.'

I hand over two twenties.

Ed goes to a back room and I listen to him rustling for a few minutes. He comes back with a little plastic bag. It contains what looks exactly like the dried wild mushroom mix I used to buy from the Italian deli on Hill Street in Richmond. Little wizened brown and cream things that resemble bits of wood rather than edible fungus.

I thank Ed and then, feeling guiltier than I ever did in court, step out into the sunshine, blinking after the gloom.

All the way on the drive back to the cottage, I keep checking the rearview mirror. I'm convinced a cop car is going to pull me over and find the bag of mushrooms. But it doesn't. In fact, I only see one other car on the drive back, and that's someone I know vaguely from the village. We wave and pass and then I'm alone until I sit down at the kitchen table with Flick, after having locked the door and closed all the curtains.

49

Jonathan

Closing out the search is child's play. I've hired an ex-cop who does some investigative work for the bank from time to time. And I send him down to Burton Bradstock with a picture of Mel. The brief is simple. An address.

It doesn't take him long.

He calls me one Friday evening.

'Found her,' he says.

I reach for my notebook.

'Go on.'

'Turning Tide, The Barrow, Burton Bradstock, DT8 9GG.'

'You're sure?'

'She's had her hair done, but yes, it's her.'

'Bill me.'

'Already have.'

I thank him. Refill my glass. And I smile at the thought that very soon all my problems will be behind me.

Best of all, there's no hurry. I can pick my time. She thinks she's safe tucked away in her twee little cottage on the coast.

Good for her.

I think I'll go down tomorrow.

50

Mel

I watch, fascinated, as Flick goes to work with the magic mushrooms. Along the way, she delivers an impromptu lecture on the legal, moral, scientific, countercultural and ritual aspects of consumption of *Psilocybe cubensis*. It all boils down – literally, if you like your shrooms as a tea – to this. They give you psychedelic trips, like LSD.

On a good one, you get hallucinations, heightened sensations and everything can seem hysterically funny. On a bad one, acute anxiety, paranoia, demonic visions and, just to mix things up a little, projectile vomiting.

Flick explains how, at the cutting-edge of psychotherapeutic use, the role of the psychiatrist is like that of the shaman in a tribal ceremony. The doctor helps the user into the trip, sometimes using physical touch to reassure them, then can add verbal stimuli to shape the transcendental experience before leading the user back to reality at journey's end.

First, she grinds the dried mushrooms into fine powder, using the NutriBullet on the kitchen counter. I believe this is almost certainly the first time it's been used to process a Class-A drug.

Next, Flick asks me to hand her two lemons from the fruit bowl and a squeezer. I can't find one, but there's an olivewood reamer in the drawer. I hand it to her.

'This process is called Lemon Tek,' she says. 'The citric acid breaks down the psilocybin. It intensifies the hit, basically, which is what we need for therapeutic use.'

She juices the lemons and pours the cloudy liquid into a tumbler. In goes the little heap of beige powder. She stirs it vigorously with a teaspoon, then hands it to me.

'In one,' she says.

I smile, though my stomach is turning somersaults, and knock it back.

The lemon juice is so strong I flinch. Then I swallow. I can't taste anything else bar the citric hit.

Flick smiles at me.

'Well done. OK, let's get you into the sitting room.'

She leads me by the hand and points at the sofa.

I know what to do. We did it like this in Dr Silverman's office. Only there, it was a functional grey couch. Here, I have the luxury of a deep, squashy sofa upholstered in soft sage-green cotton. I sink into it and close my eyes.

Flick pulls over an armchair and takes my hand. Her hand is slender and her grip is firm, warm and dry. I smile and try to regulate my breathing.

'Don't force it,' she says. 'Let it come naturally.'

So I just let go of everything. Except Flick's hand. Which seems to grow in mine until I wonder how I can still be holding it. It's pretty funny, really. It feels like an inflatable hand or like one of those giant foam ones they wave about at football matches…

…and she has the nicest voice i have ever heard

i mean not just her accent which makes me think of sun-kissed girls on sandy beaches and surfers and palm trees and boys on roller

blades and convertible ford mustangs and jangly electric guitars and a

million billion trillion

movies but its got something else too a kindness and a wisdom like

she knows all there is to know about me and about everything and shes asking me to count down in

threes from eighty seven which is stupid

because who can do that and also picture

my first pet who was called sophie and was the best cat in the world

and listen to the music shes put on and I love this is it vivaldi or no its the rolling stones or maybe blondie anyway it is so cool and I wish

'It's the night Harry died,' Flick says from inside my head.

That's weird. Where did the music go? Where's the beach?

Flick's voice is still there, sort of droning on, but I'm not really listening.

And I'm at home. *My* home. My *marital* home. The home I live in with Jonathan, and my miraculous little baby, Harry.

I should feel exhausted, I know that. We did a campaign for Amnesty International once. Pro bono, to burnish the agency's right-on credentials. I had to read all these reports on torture around the world.

One of the most effective methods, used by everybody from the CIA to the Syrians, is sleep deprivation. You don't need a generator. Or those awful surgeon's tables covered in stainless-steel implements like they have in movies. A 100w lightbulb, a bloody great speaker and a CD-player and you're all set.

No CD-player? No problem. Just smash a metal tray against the bars every thirty minutes or so.

No metal tray? How about a newborn baby with an undiagnosable and apparently untreatable case of not needing more than an hour's continuous sleep at a time?

That's what we've got. I love Harry more than life itself, if that doesn't sound like too much of a cliché, but oh, how I wish he would sleep through the night. Just once.

I *should* feel exhausted. I *should* feel like the sandman ordered a ton more than he needed and dumped the whole lot under my eyelids.

But I feel awake, alert and aware of everything around me. I sit up in bed. Jonathan's down the hall, sleeping in the spare bedroom.

We have a flatscreen TV in here, mounted on the wall opposite the bed. Jonathan insisted. He likes us to watch porn on it. He says it's empowering.

But tonight it's showing…me.

I'm wearing jeans and a shirt of Jonathan's. I go into Harry's bedroom. I lift him out of his cot. I cuddle him to my chest then take him into the bathroom.

I must have run the bath already. It's brimming.

I climb over the side holding Harry carefully.

When I sit down, water slops over the side and soaks into the bathmat, turning it from tangerine to a dark brick-red.

Then, smiling at my baby, I lower him into the water until it closes over his head. I lift him up again and smile at him. Peekaboo! Then Jonathan comes in and takes Harry from me.

A huge caption flashes onto the TV screen.

FAKE NEWS!

And I remember. This *did* happen. But not the night he died. It was a month earlier. I freaked out and got in with Harry, but he was never in any danger. As soon as his feet touched the cold water he started screaming and I snapped out of my trance or whatever it was. Even if Jonathan hadn't found me, I would have jumped straight out and got Harry warm and changed.

The movie, or show, or whatever it is runs backwards fast. Jonathan hands Harry to me. I dunk him in the water then yank him up again, jump out of the bath and speedwalk backwards out of the bathroom and into the nursery. I plop Harry down into his cot then reverse out, back to my bedroom.

It starts again.

This time, I kneel beside the bath. I'm wearing my nightie. I put Harry into the water and hold him under. No smiling. No peekaboo! as I lift him clear. Jonathan comes in. Pulls Harry out of the bath and lays him on the bathmat. Then he drags me to my feet and we tussle. I fall into the bath and knock myself out on the taps.

This is the story Jonathan told in court. The one I *can't* remember.

The caption is back. Twice as big as before.

FAKE NEWS!

And now I get it. The shrooms are showing me both versions of that night. The one I *thought* was real. And the one Jonathan *told* me was real. The one he told the police. The one he told the court.

What really happened, Mel? Flick asks from somewhere inside my head. And I answer.

'I gave him the idea.'

The TV screen snaps to black with a terrifyingly loud click. I get out of bed. I'm wearing my favourite Boden nightie. Pale-blue cotton with little pink roses.

I can hear something. Jonathan's voice. A repetitive sound. It sounds like a mantra. Is he meditating? I creep down the hall. It's definitely Jonathan's voice. It's coming from behind the spare door.

I push my ear against the door. This close to the wood, I can smell the beeswax our cleaner applied a couple of weeks ago.

'Shut up, shut up, shut up, shut up,' Jonathan is saying. Then, one final time, 'Just shut up, you little fucker.'

I imagine he's making a call to Japan. It's the time difference. Whoever it is they must have really pissed him off. It can't be a client. It must be one of the bankers in the Tokyo office.

I open the door quietly. I think maybe I can rub the back of his neck, get him to calm down before he says something he'll regret.

He hears the soft creak of the hinges and spins round. Sees me looking at him.

'What are you doing?' I ask.

Because he's not on the phone. He's leaning on a pillow, which is humped between his fists.

'It's not a good time, Mel,' he says.

'What *is* that?' I point at the hump. 'What have you got under there?'

I see a flash of powder-blue. For an absurd moment I think he's trying to iron one of his shirts by flattening it under the pillow.

He stands and comes towards me. I look past his right hip. At the humped pillow.

'It's not a good time,' he says again.

The blue fabric isn't the tip of a shirt tail. Not unless Jonathan has taken to wearing ones made of fleecy brushed cotton. It's a soft, curving shape only as big as my thumb. There's another one beside it. Two little thumbs. No. Two little...

...feet. They're feet!

It's a babygro. I lunge forward and snatch up the pillow.

Harry is lying there. On his back. He's got a little sick on his cheek.

I pick him up and hug him to me. He's floppy and his skin is cool to the touch.

'I said it's not a good time,' Jonathan says.

I say his name over and over again.

'Harry? Harry! Harryharryharryharry!'

Then Jonathan slaps me, hard across the side of the face.

'It's dead. It can't hear you. So shut the fuck up, why don't you?'

Then he spins me round by my shoulders and pushes me into the bathroom. 'Sit there,' he says, pointing at the loo. I collapse onto the seat, still holding Harry to me.

Jonathan pushes the plug down and turns on the cold tap.

I do nothing while the bath is filling. I just watch. I feel numb inside.

He turns the taps off and then he takes Harry from me. He puts him on the bathmat then heaves me to my feet.

'In we go,' he says, and then he throws me sideways into the bath.

I crack my head on the taps and the world is filled with stars and bright-white pain.

Jonathan hands Harry to me and I open my arms to clasp my baby to me.

Then he yanks me out of the bath and throws me down onto the tiles. He puts Harry next to me. He pulls out his phone.

I hear a woman screaming. It must be one of the neighbours. Only the house is detached, miles from the next one. My throat is hurting. I realise the screamer is me.

I roll over and look at my baby. He looks so peaceful. Then I hear a sort of rushing noise and everything bleaches out like a photo with an Instagram vintage filter, and I can't move.

I hear Jonathan speaking calmly into his phone.

'Police please. And ambulance. My wife has just murdered our baby.'

51

Mel

'Ten, nine, eight...'

Is Flick going to launch a space rocket?

'seven, six, five, four...'

'three,'

'two,'

'one.'

My eyes flutter open. I stare up at her. She has an unreadable expression on her face. Is she angry with me?

There's a little vein, like a blue worm, wriggling under the thin, tanned skin at her left temple. It swells and sags once a second. I imagine the blood pulsing along that fine tube, distending the walls with its pressure.

'Elvis is back in the building,' she says. 'Drink this.'

She hands me a glass of water with a straw in it. I lever myself up onto my elbows and twist awkwardly until I free a hand to take the glass. The water tastes amazing. Like drinking pure light. I finish the glass and hand it back onto her.

'Thanks.'

I swivel round until the sofa is supporting my back.

'How are you feeling?' she asks, leaning forwards with her forearms resting on her knees and her hands clasped between them.

'I feel…'

This is harder to answer than I expected. I know what happened. To me. And to Harry. But I don't feel sadness. I don't want – or need – to cry. I feel light inside. Calm. Like there's a spaciousness in my mind, or maybe my heart, that has never been there before.

I try to complete the sentence.

'I feel…clear.'

'Go on,' she says, with an encouraging smile.

'It's like I've been living with a…a bandanna tied across my nose and mouth,' I say, struggling to find a metaphor that will show her what I'm experiencing. 'You know? So I can suck in enough air, but only by concentrating on every breath.'

'And now?'

'And now I don't have to think about it. I don't have to worry I'll suffocate.'

'What happened?'

'Don't you know? I thought you were there?'

She smiles.

'I was here, honey, holding your hand. I asked you questions and guided you to the places you need to visit, but whatever you saw, heard or experienced, for now it's still inside your head.'

So I tell her. About the TV set. About Jonathan smothering Harry. About how he staged everything so it looked like I did it. About how calm he seemed when I asked him what he was doing.

All the time I'm talking, I think, now the tears will come, but they don't.

'Why can't I cry, Flick?'

She shrugs. 'I think you've done your crying. What you haven't done is grieving.'

I feel it, then. A heat in my chest. I wonder if it's heartburn from the Lemon Tek. But it's not. It doesn't have that acidic grip on my oesophagus. It's growing stronger. Rising into my throat and face, pulsing behind my eyes and then lighting up my brain like a volcano erupting, spewing boiling lava. A white-hot fountain of pure hatred.

'He murdered Harry,' I grind out between clamped jaws. 'He murdered my baby.' I lunge forward and grab Flick by her upper arms and stare into her face from a few inches away.

'He has to pay!'

I scrabble for my phone. It's wedged into my hip pocket and in the end I pull so hard I rip the stitching so the pocket tears.

My hand is shaking and it takes me three tries before I can call up Ffion Parry's mobile number.

'Mel? Is that you?'

'Yes. It's me. Ffion, I remembered.'

'What do you remember?' she asks and even though we haven't spoken for six months, I can hear the excitement in her voice.

I give Flick what I'm sure must look like a demonic smile.

'Everything.'

'And by everything…?'

'Jonathan murdered Harry. He smothered him with a

pillow and then he took me into the bathroom with him and he made it look like I drowned Harry. He threw me into the bath and I smacked the back of my head against the taps.'

She's all business.

'Right. Where are you? At Disha's?'

'No. Well, yes. But not in Ealing. I'm at their cottage in Dorset.'

I give her the address.

'Stay there,' she orders. 'Don't answer the door to anyone until I get there. I'll text you from the front door.'

The line goes dead.

Flick raises an inquisitorial eyebrow.

'She'll be here in three hours or so,' I say. 'Less if she puts her blue lights on. Call it two and a half.'

'You OK?'

I nod. Then, out of nowhere, I voice it. The thought that's been inhabiting my head for some time now.

'There's something wrong with Jonathan.'

'No shit.'

'I saw him doing it, Flick. Not a dream. Not a hallucination. It was my actual memory,' I say. 'Like I was back there that night only all the drugs that the doctors were pumping through my system, all the brain fog caused by the psychosis: they were all gone.'

She nods. 'Whatever altered state we're in caused by drugs or disturbed mental function, we are still present at every moment of our lives, Mel,' she says, taking my hand again. 'What happened on the trip was that you reconnected with that part of yourself that was always in there, somewhere, just unable to make its voice heard.'

A couple of months ago, I might have dismissed Flick's explanation as just Californian psychobabble. But she's right. She's absolutely right. What I saw was what happened. I'm sure of it.

'What is it?' I ask.

'What is what?'

'The thing that's wrong with Jonathan?'

She breathes in and exhales like a yoga breath. *Haaa*.

'It's extremely unprofessional to volunteer a diagnosis before one has conducted a thorough psychiatric assessment.'

'Oh, of course. Sorry.'

'But,' she says, holding up a finger like a lightning conductor, 'in his case I am going to make an exception. I watched him in court,' she says, 'giving his evidence and afterwards. Putting that together with what you just told me, I think he's a classic psychopath. He's cunning, manipulative, willing to take huge risks, highly goal-driven and absolutely unbothered about the idea that other people have feelings or desires of their own.'

'I thought psychopaths were all deranged serial killers,' I say. 'You know, cutting up bodies and eating them.'

She smiles but it's a weary kind of expression.

'You've been watching too many movies,' she says.

We talk some more and everything falls into place. All the lies, including the ones I've been telling myself, crumble.

Men like Jonathan make damn sure you never see their real faces until it's far too late. What really got in the way was my inability to believe that I could be lured, tricked, coerced into an abusive relationship in the first place.

Somewhere, I don't know where, I'd formed the impression, no, more of a belief, really, that women like me didn't get caught in those men's webs. We were too smart, too confident, too bloody *empowered* for it ever to happen to us. It was something that happened to other women. Poor women. Uneducated women. Women who were too blind to see what was right under their noses.

But men like Jonathan, they know that it *does* happen to women like us. It happens to any women they decide it's going to happen to. *Because they're psychopaths.*

They just use your own mentality against you. If you're fearful, they dominate you from the off, threatening, blustering, bullying. But if you're confident, they bide their time. They lull you, just insidiously worming their way into your mind.

It's like that old story or proverb or whatever it is about the frog getting slowly boiled alive by being placed into a saucepan of cold water and then having the gas turned up underneath it.

By the time you notice the pain, and the trap you're in, it's way too late to think of climbing out.

I go and check the front door. And the back. Both are locked. Flick says she'll stay with me until Ffion gets here. Then we'll take it as it comes.

Maybe Ffion will want me to go back to London with her. I hope she's going to arrange protective custody. Is that what they call it? Or is that being locked up? A safe house, then. Shit! I'd settle for a couple of burly cops with Tasers and truncheons as bodyguards.

52

Mel

I must have checked my watch a hundred times since I called Ffion. She has to be almost here. For the last half hour my bladder has been sending me increasingly assertive messages. I've ignored them: I really want to be right here, ready to let her in. But it's making it clear to me that unless I give in, it's going to let go.

I hurry upstairs to use the loo. I bolt the door out of habit. It's not as if Flick is going to burst in waving a carving knife or something.

As I sit there, I realise that this is almost over. Ffion's going to take me back to London. She'll keep me safe from Jonathan until they arrest him. There's no way they'll let him out on bail. Then there'll be a trial. He'll go down for it, I'm sure.

The doorbell rings. It can't be Ffion. I'm clutching my

phone like it is a magic amulet and it hasn't so much as trembled. It's probably a neighbour wanting to borrow a pint of milk.

I wash my hands and dry them on one of Disha's super-soft jade-coloured towels. And I head downstairs. The bell rings for a second time. I ignore it.

Flick's in the hall. She's walking to the front door. Her hand is outstretched.

'Flick!' I shout. 'No!'

She turns and smiles. 'Relax, honey. The cavalry's here.'

She must have seen Ffion coming up the path through the front window. Odd she didn't text. Or is she about to? But then, why ring the doorbell?

Flick's fingers are closing on the handle.

She's pushing it down.

And then the latch clicks and the door flies inwards, knocking her off her feet. Flick cries out as she hits the floor. I hear a crack. Broken bone, I think.

And my husband – Jonathan – is standing there. No, not standing, barging into the house.

He looks up the stairs at me and smiles.

'Hello, Mel.'

He steps over Flick's supine form, making for the stairs. I freeze. I know I shouldn't. I know I should run. But somebody forgot to tell my leg muscles.

'You bastard!' Flick shrieks.

She scissors a kick up towards his groin. Her foot catches him right at the top of his thigh. It's not bad, but it's not *on target*. He grunts with the pain and finishes his step in a half-jump. Then he turns and kicks her hard in the temple. Her head thumps against the skirting board and flops to the ground with a hollow sound, like when you hit a coconut shy at the fair.

'Bitch!' he mutters. Then he turns towards me.

Finally, my legs regain their power. I run back up the stairs and race down the short hallway and into the master bedroom. I glance at the bathroom on the way past, with its locking door. But my mind flashes on that scene in *The Shining* when Jack Nicholson is coming for Shelley Duvall and he hacks through the bathroom door with an axe. *'Heeeere's Johnny!'*

I slam the bedroom door closed behind me and look wildly round the room for something I can use as a weapon. But there's nothing. Not so much as a golf club under the bed Gav might keep in case of burglars.

The chest of drawers, then. I run to it and put my back against it. If I can just shove it over a few feet I can block the door off and call Ffion. She'll have to call for backup. Or is that just on TV? Christ! How should I know?

The chest of drawers is oak. Disha told me when she gave me the rundown of what was where. Oak. And it's full of clothes. It won't move.

The door handle twists. Jonathan walks into the bedroom as if he owns it.

'Hi, darling,' he says.

Then he closes it behind him.

My heart is jittering in my chest. I can see sparks round the edge of my vision.

I put my hands out.

'Jonathan, don't. Please.'

He cocks his head. 'Don't what?' he asks.

Then he takes a step towards me.

'Don't hurt me,' I stammer.

I hate myself for it. I know he hates what he sees as weakness.

'But I have to. I came all this way. You're going to talk

to the police, aren't you? You're going to tell them it was me. That you remember everything.'

'How did you know?'

'Oh, so you *have* remembered!' he says. 'I knew that Welsh cop was all for getting you to testify against me. But I was hoping your poor little brain was still fried by all the drugs and two-forty volts AC Dr Silverman pumped through you.'

This is bad. But it's not too bad. If I can just keep him talking, maybe Ffion will arrive before he loses it.

'How did you find me?' I ask, retreating until my back hits the wall.

He takes another step closer.

'With great difficulty. To cut a long story short, a combination of cutting-edge online research and old-fashioned shoe leather. Not mine, I hasten to add. A very accomplished and discreet ex-cop called Steve Batt.' He smiles. 'The main thing is, darling, I'm here now.'

Another step.

I realise he's not going to let me keep him talking. He came here to kill me. He glances over at the double bed. Inadvertently, I follow his gaze.

As I look back at him I see his fist swinging in. It connects with my cheekbone with a smack I feel rather than hear. The pain arrives a split-second later. An explosion of fire and red-and-yellow light between my ears.

I stagger and he helps me on my way, grabbing me by the shoulders and hurling me sideways. I fly across the bed and land diagonally on my back. A muscle tears in my side – a searing pain from hip to ribcage.

He's on top of me. Straddling me. I look into his eyes and there is absolutely nothing, and nobody, there. It's like looking into a void where a human being should be. He's so calm as he drags over a pillow and grips it at the sides in his fists. Then he plunges the soft mass down over my face.

Just as it hits me I turn my face to the side and this saves me, I think, from instant suffocation. But he's slammed his bodyweight down onto it and my nose is so compressed I can hardly get a whisper of air into my lungs.

No! This is not going to be how my life ends. His knees are each side of my chest, but my hands are free. I flail a fist upwards and feel it connect with something soft. His nose? There's a gratifying shout of pain.

He releases the pressure on the pillow momentarily and knocks my hand aside. I just have time to twist my head and gasp in a huge *whoop* of fresh air into my burning lungs.

Then the pillow is crowding my nose and mouth again. That last breath is trapped inside me. It's all I have. Unless I can get free. I grab Jonathan's wrists, but it's like pulling at fence posts that have been concreted down into soft earth.

I picture Flick kicking upwards, aiming for his balls.

My legs are a million miles away. My vision's dimming. I don't have much time. I let go of his wrists and thrust my right arm down and across my chest. I find his groin, disgustingly hot against my belly. I twist my hand over, dig my nails in and squeeze his balls with every last rage-fuelled ounce of strength I have left.

He screams this time and the pressure on my face vanishes. I know I've found that sweet spot that can reduce any man to a weeping baby. I twist hard, and buck my hips at the same time, lifting the left higher than the right. It works, I tip him off me. He bounces on the bed and then topples sideways onto the floor in the narrow space between the bed and the wall.

This is my chance. I am up and off the bed and out the door before Jonathan can get to his feet.

'Come here, Mel!' he roars.

I reach the hallway and almost lose my footing as I take the stairs in a skittering rush. Flick's eyes are still closed. I pray she isn't dead. But I have no time to check for a pulse because Jonathan is at the top of the stairs.

'I'm going to kill you!' he screams, all trace of that sardonic grin completely and utterly erased from his snarling face.

If the man I married is in there somewhere, there is no visible trace of his presence. Just a monster, white teeth bared, eyes bloodshot.

I run for the kitchen. There are plenty of things I can use to defend myself in there. I reach the door and see the knife block. Perfect.

Then my head snaps back. Jonathan has caught me with an outshot arm and a fistful of hair, which has grown out from the cut Jayne gave me so many months ago.

He yanks me towards him and I yelp from the pain: it feels like a chunk of my scalp has come away. Then I'm staggering backwards and he spins me round and slams me up against the wall facing the fireplace in the sitting room.

His face is inches from mine. His mouth is like a wild animal's. Canines seem magnified into fangs. Strings of spittle between upper and lower jaws. I can smell his breath. Mint. He always keeps them in the car.

'You sad, mad cunt,' he hisses. 'You thought you could get away with it. Escaping me. Leaving me to face a trial because you forced me to shut him up.'

His hands are on my shoulders, pushing me flat against the wall.

'I didn't force you to do it! You're insane, Jonathan. You're a psychopath. Flick told me.'

'"Flick told me",' he mimics in a high-pitched whiny voice. 'Yes, you did force me, Mel. You had him, then you couldn't keep him quiet. How was I supposed to make money on four hours' sleep a night? You left me no choice. Now I'm going to get you out of my life, too.'

He moves his hands from my shoulders to my throat.

Why did I never see it? Too late. Far, far too late.

53

Mel

I can feel my eyes bulging. They feel like they might burst from the pressure. I hear a voice telling me to go for *his* eyes. Is it mine?

I drive my clawed fingers into his eye sockets. I feel my nails sink into the soft tissue.

Jonathan screams. He pulls away from me, catches his heel in the rug between the two sofas, and stumbles. I lunge forwards, arms outstretched and shove him right over his breastbone.

He tries to right himself, arms windmilling, but he's falling backwards.

The back of his head hits one of the firedogs with a sickening crunch like stamping on bubble wrap. His eyes roll upwards in their sockets. Then they close.

I stagger over to where he's lying. He looks like Christ on the cross, arms outflung, one ankle crossed over the other. Only the head looks wrong. It's propped up instead of lolling to one side. I look at the other firedog: the one not embedded in the back of my husband's head. It is capped with a pointed fleur-de-lis finial.

Panting and suddenly shaking all over, I retreat to the kitchen. I scrabble a mug out of the cupboard and fill it at the tap then drink it down, cold water splashing out the sides and running over my neck and onto my front.

I drink a second mugful. I heave in a breath and blow it out again. I need to check on Flick. I hear her stirring. A groan. Oddly masculine.

I turn. And I scream.

Jonathan is pushing himself up onto his elbows. Something bad has happened to his face. The left side is drooping. His mouth hangs open on that side, exposing his lower teeth. His left eye stares off to one side. But the other, blood-red, is fixed on me.

'Mel,' he groans. 'You… I…kill…you.'

Something happens to me, then. It's like when Flick hypnotised me. I feel calm. No, not calm. Calm would be like relaxing with a glass of wine and a book, feet curled up on a sofa and maybe a nice dog beside me to keep me comfortable. I feel…

…purposeful.

It's time Jonathan was gone. For good. Not arrested. Not charged. Not remanded in custody, tried, sentenced and imprisoned. Because that route has too many turn-offs before the destination. Talented defence lawyers. Unimpressive witnesses. Sympathetic juries. Time off for good behaviour. And then he's out and looking for me.

I go to the block holding the cook's knives and I select one with a nine-inch blade. The handle is cool to the touch. I grip it tightly in my fist and go back into the sitting room.

Jonathan is standing, just. He's pulled the firedog free; blood is coursing down from the back of his head and soaking into his shirt. He is leaning drunkenly to his left side, his hand waving around by his hip as if it's looking for something to hold onto to support the body it's attached to.

I march up to him.

And I stab him.

I stab him as hard as I can, on the left side, high up, where I imagine what passes for his heart sits.

The knife handle twists in my hand as the blade hits a rib, and then the force of my blow drives it deep into his chest. I yank it free and it makes a horrific screeching sound as it scrapes past the bone.

Then I hit him again.

And I pull the knife free.

Dark blood wells out of the chest wound. He stands as still as a pillar, eyes revolving wildly as if someone gave a doll's head a whack. Then, in slow motion, he collapses sideways, hits the sofa and crumples to the floor.

I stand above him, the knife gripped tightly in my fist, waiting to see if he's going to come back for a third try. But he just lies there, bleeding onto Disha's cream-and-caramel cow skin rug.

Very deliberately, I skirt his body and sit on the other sofa.

I look down at the knife in my hand. It's shaking. The silvery blade is streaked with blood. Jonathan's blood.

It's over.

But then an unwelcome thought intrudes into my brain.

Are you sure?

He was unarmed. He was incapacitated. As I look at him now, I can see the red crater in the back of his head where the firedog shattered the bone.

Will the police be able to tell that I stabbed him, not in self-defence, but because I wanted him dead and gone forever? That I didn't trust the justice system to protect me?

I need to make it look believable. As if, at the moment I stabbed him, he was determined to kill me, just as he had been right up to the moment he was impaled on a sharp-pointed piece of artisanal ironwork.

Then I recall something I saw on a TV show once. A pathologist was talking to a detective.

The pathologist held up a floppy hand and showed the detective the palm.

'See? No defensive wounds.'

That's what *I* need. Defensive wounds. So it looks like Jonathan was attacking *me* with the knife.

I pull up my sleeves.

Then I lay my left arm on my knee, hand turned out to expose the soft, pale skin on the inner surface. And I place the knife across that tender expanse. Slowly, teeth clenched, I draw it from left to right. The blood wells up behind the blade and I feel fierce white heat. Tears flood over my lower lids and I whimper from the agony of what I'm doing to myself.

Gasping, I do it again. Harder this time. I don't want to hit a vein, but it has to look real.

Finally, I put the knife in my left palm and close my fingers over the back of the blade. I squeeze, clamping my jaws so as not to scream. Blood wells up between my knuckles.

I look down at the bloody handle and I realise it needs to have Jonathan's fingerprints on it as well as mine. It's the first thing they'll look for. I squat down beside him and, my guts suddenly churning, fold his limp fingers around the handle and squeeze them.

Then I just drop the knife in the middle of the carpet.

'Mel?'

I yelp in shock. Whirling round, I see Flick in the doorway. She looks like she's got the world's worst hangover.

'Oh my god, Flick! Are you all right?'

'Yeah, I think so,' she says, slumping into the sofa I just vacated. 'I just came round. It was so quiet, I thought he must have taken you somewhere. Either that or killed you and then left.' She looks down at Jonathan and nods. 'I guess he didn't leave.'

She must be in shock. But at least she didn't see me stabbing him.

'Let's get you into the kitchen,' I say. 'You had a really nasty fall.'

She shakes her head, then winces.

'If anyone needs medical attention, it's you, honey. Have you seen your arm?'

I look down. The cuts on my arm and across my palm are bleeding freely. The whole place looks like a slaughterhouse.

'Come on,' she says. 'They must have a first-aid kit somewhere around here.'

Flick finds a big green plastic box with a white cross on it and is soon bandaging my arm and hand as if her speciality is emergency medicine, not psychiatry.

'What happened?' she asks me, nodding in the direction of the sitting room.

I open my mouth, figuring out the right way to tell the story.

Then my phone vibrates, making me jump.

I pull it free with my good hand. It's a text from Ffion.

I'm outside

Flick lets her in and warns her about the scene she's about to enter.

I meet her in the sitting room. She glances down at Jonathan, then at me. Her eyes go to my bandages. Now it's her turn.

'What happened?'

Flick puts her hand on my arm.

'She's in shock,' she says. 'He attacked me then he chased Mel all over the house. I was groggy because my head hit the wall. He cornered her in the sitting room. He had a knife.' She points to the butcher knife on the bloodstained rug. 'He tried to kill her but she fought back. He lost his grip on the knife. Mel got it off him and stabbed him.'

Ffion nods as she listens, looking at Flick, then me, then Jonathan then back to Flick. I sink down onto the sofa, mute.

Ffion gets her phone out and starts issuing instructions. I'm not really listening. Because although I wasn't in shock before, I am now.

54

Mel

I go with Ffion voluntarily to be interviewed under caution at Hammersmith police station. The experience is somewhat different to my previous visit. I feel like this time they believe I am on the side of the angels. Ffion asks me to tell her what happened from the moment Jonathan entered the house until she arrived. So I do.

I tell her how he kicked Flick in the head. How he tried to smother me with a pillow, then strangle me. How he grabbed me and hit me. How I fought back, in fear of my life. And how, when he came for me with the kitchen knife, I managed to get it off him.

'How?' she asks. 'He was strong and fit.'

'I grabbed it by the blade as he tried to stab me,' I say, showing her my bandaged hand. 'And I kneed him in the balls. They'll probably be bruised.'

'Then what?'

'Then I stabbed him.'

'In self-defence.'

I notice she frames it as a statement I can agree with, rather than a question. Ms Toombs would probably say she's leading the witness.

I nod. 'In self-defence. He was going to kill me. He said so.'

Ffion points to my left arm.

'Under the bandages?'

'More defensive wounds,' I say.

She looks at me steadily for a few seconds. I feel calm, though. I know she doesn't want to arrest me for his murder. Then she nods, as if she's reached a decision.

'We'll get the police surgeon to have a look at you, but I'm sure that's what he'll conclude.'

I sign a statement and then she tells me I'm free to go. Suggests it would probably be for the best if I stayed within a few hours' drive of London. I tell her that suits me fine.

Outside the police station, I call Disha.

'Hi, lovely, what's up? Everything OK? Where are you?'

'Everything's fine. I'm in London. Can I stay at yours tonight?'

'Of course. But why are you in London?'

'I'll explain when I see you.'

* * *

Over the next few days, I begin, slowly, to rebuild my life. I can't bear to return to the house, and now the threat from Jonathan has passed, Disha and Gav are happy for me to stay with them, just while I sort things out.

I talk to our solicitor and discover that as Jonathan died without making a will, everything passes to me.

I call Flick, who was also interviewed under caution, and we meet for a coffee round the corner from the Maudsley.

When we're sitting at a quiet corner table, I ask her the question that's been spinning round and round in my head ever since she spoke to Ffion down at the cottage.

'Why?' I ask her in a low whisper.

She sips her coffee. She knows what I mean. She doesn't ask me to clarify.

'Honey, the first thing they teach you at med school is *primum non nocere*.' Her Californian drawl makes the Latin phrase sound cool. '"First, do no harm". Trouble is, what if doing no harm means causing *more* harm down the road?'

'You're saying you think what I did was morally right?'

She smiles. 'I'm a psychiatrist, not an ethicist. What I will say is, it was necessary. People like Jonathan never reform. They can't. He'd have served his sentence, bided his time, probably acted like a model prisoner. Then he would've got out and come after you. And he *would* have killed you.'

Weeks pass. Ffion calls me. She's discussed the case with her boss and with the CPS. They're not bringing charges. Flick's account plus my testimony and the forensic evidence tell their own eloquent story. I acted in self-defence. In fear for my life and in the heat of the moment, I used reasonable force to protect myself, possibly also saving Flick's life.

Months pass. My legal team mounts a successful appeal to have me acquitted of the original charge of infanticide. Ffion speaks to the media from the steps of the Court of Appeal and explains, in her beautifully precise, carrying voice, that there is now conclusive evidence that it was

Jonathan who murdered Harry and that I was the victim of a miscarriage of justice.

I go back to see Dr Silverman; I tell him I can't call him Nate anymore. I explain that I'm done with therapy. I tell him, also, that although it was wrong of him to treat me with the psilocybin without a Home Office licence, I will be forever grateful to him for that. He nods silently. He looks on the verge of tears.

A year passes. I sell the house in Richmond and liquidate all of Jonathan's assets, which were considerable. I make a series of large, anonymous donations to charities for abused women and I also provide some funding for Flick to resume her research into the therapeutic uses of psilocybin.

I move back to Dorset and buy a cottage. Not in Burton Bradstock. But somewhere with the same peaceful atmosphere and short walk to the beach through sand dunes pierced with marram grass and sea holly. My business thrives and now I don't have to hide my true identity.

Once a month, I drive up to London and park a few hundred yards away from the tree-lined entrance to Richmond cemetery on Lower Grove Road.

His grave is well-tended. I replace the flowers. And I kneel by his headstone. I place my left hand, with the long white scar across the palm, on the cool, grey granite.

'I love you, Harry,' I say. 'You're always with me. In here.'

Then I place my left hand over my heart so that the wounds touch.

IF YOU ENJOYED THIS BOOK ...

Read on for an extract from *Hit and Run*, the first book in the popular DI Stella Cole series.

HIT AND RUN

THE BABY'S CRYING grew louder. It had taken on a frantic edge. Richard Drinkwater knew the translation off by heart.

Feed me! Feeed meee!

But he couldn't.

Not till he got her home, anyway.

He didn't have the equipment, as he liked to joke to his wife. But she'd gone back to work with the Metropolitan Police, leaving precisely measured-out bottles of her milk in the fridge each morning.

Now Lola was hungry and she wouldn't stop screaming.

The traffic was murder. It was rush hour. And there'd been an accident somewhere to the north of them. It would have been quicker to unbuckle Lola from the car seat and walk her home. The lights up ahead seemed stuck on red. Even when they did turn green, one car, at most, managed to squeeze through.

"Come on, Lola," he crooned. "Soon be home. Then you can fill up on Mummy Ultimate. Kristina will be there too, so you can snuggle up with her."

Sometimes he thought his daughter loved her nanny more than either of her hard-working parents. Either her or the giant teddy bear they'd christened, for no reason they could fathom, Mister Jenkins. When squeezed, the bear emitted a random sequence of squeaks, bleats and catlike mewing sounds that seemed to amuse Lola.

The baby paused in her efforts to burst either her lungs or her father's eardrums. Drinkwater's shoulders dropped a little, and his stomach began to unclench. He checked the rear-view mirror, sitting up straight in his seat so he could catch sight of his three-month-old daughter. Her face was red and streaked with tears and snot. As he watched, she drew in a mighty breath and then let it out again in a scream so high-pitched it made him flinch. He caught a whisper of milky breath in his nostrils that made him smile despite the industrial noise issuing from his daughter's tiny mouth.

A car behind him sounded its horn. Twice. One of those twin-tone numbers precisely calibrated to emit the most horrible discord possible. He angled the mirror so he could see the make. Bastard! It was a Porsche. Some rich git working in a bank and earning more in a week than he did in a year. *Well, darling,* his mother's voice sounded deep inside his head, *perhaps you should have become a criminal barrister instead of all that human rights nonsense. Then you'd be earning a proper living instead of scraping along the bottom looking after your so-called clients.*

His own car was a silver 1974 Fiat Mirafiori he liked to claim to friends was a classic. He slammed it into first and lurched forward, closing the gap between him and the car in front, a big, shiny, royal-blue BMW.

388

Lola's screaming had settled into a steady, metallic screech now. In for five, hold for a beat, let it out in a shriek until her throat caught and she coughed, choking and wailing to silence. Repeat till Daddy had an aneurysm.

Then, a miracle. The traffic lights ahead turned green again, and instead of merely sitting there as they cycled through amber, red, red-and-amber, green, as had been happening for the last five minutes, the traffic moved off smoothly.

"Yes!" he shouted, slamming both open palms onto the steering wheel and bringing forth an even more desperate scream from the baby. "Oh, sorry, darling. But look, Daddy's on the move again. We'll soon be home, and everything will be all right."

As he approached the front of the queue, Lola screamed again. *Will we have to wait through another red?* he thought. *No. We're going.* He put his foot down and surged towards the traffic light, smiling as he began to catch the car in front. He craned his head to snatch another look at his baby daughter in the mirror.

The baby burbled out a couple of random sounds, "da ba". Then she smiled, a wide, gummy expression of pure joy.

His eyes popped wide open. "What, Lola? Did you say 'Dada'? Oh, my God, your first word. In a traffic jam too. Mummy's going to have a fit."

He accelerated across the box junction, heart full at the sound of his name on his daughter's lips.

The light was on amber now, but that was just a 'hurry up' signal in this part of London.

The lights changed to red just as Richard Drinkwater reached the white line indicating where stopping traffic should wait. Oblivious to anything but his daughter's renewed screams, he flew across the junction to a chorus of angry blasts of motorcycle and truck horns. He drove on for another mile or two, through gradually thinning traffic, until he reached Putney. Turning off the High Street, he heaved a sigh. The road was empty ahead and behind, as if somebody had barred anyone else from entering this little part of residential London.

Sticking the indicator on and singing to Lola, whose screams had subsided to a steady, muted keening, he turned into the street that led towards Oxford Road, and their house, and sped away from the junction.

Then it was his turn to scream.

Approaching on his side of the road was a car. It was being driven at speed. He swerved to avoid it.

But it was too little, too late.

The bang as the oncoming car smashed his offside rear wing with its own front end was loud enough to rattle windows in the houses on each side of the street. He, himself, heard nothing. His slewing, bouncing progress across the street was terminated by a cast-iron pillar box, manufactured during the reign of King George VI, and as solid now as it was then.

The Fiat hit the kerb and left the ground. Richard Drinkwater's last coherent thought was that Lola had stopped screaming. Then the top of the pillar box punched in the side window and met his head coming in the opposite direction at thirty miles per hour.

As people began to emerge from their houses and run towards the car, intent on rescue, Drinkwater's corpse was catapulted back against his seat, his skull smashed like an egg.

Detective Inspector Stella Cole was sitting at her desk on the Specialist Crime and Operations Division's Homicide and Major Crime Command floor at Paddington Green

Police Station. She was joking with a colleague about a recent case they'd closed.

"No way, Jake," she said, laughing. "He's as sane as I am. If that brief tries to plead insanity, she's going to get My Lady Justice Miranda Jeffery's patent leather stiletto right up her Cambridge-educated arse."

The paunchy, balding detective sergeant perching on a desk beside her spread his hands wide, revealing an expansive belly that stretched his grey shirt tight.

"You say that, Stel, but you weren't there when we nicked him. I'm not saying he had his old mum's corpse in a rocking chair, but it wasn't far off." He raised his head and called across to another DS. "Oi, Frankie. Tell her. Wayne Stebbings's flat. It was in a right state, wasn't it?"

The female DS ambled over, hitching up her black polyester trousers, which had slipped down over her hips.

"He's right, boss," she said. "Stebbings had all these dildos and whatnot lined up on shelves."

The male DS, Jacob "Jake" Tanner, grinned. "Go on, Frankie. Tell her the best bit."

Frances "Frankie" O'Meara blushed. "There was one of those sex dolls, boss."

"What, a blow-up one, you mean?"

"No. Like a real woman. Jointed and everything, looked like a sort of shop-window dummy." The blush spread, deepening from a pale pink to a furious coral. "She … it, well it was all done up in underwear, boss. Like a tart's, I mean. You know, stockings and suspenders, corset, the works."

"Unbelievable," Jake said. "And as for his porn stash, well, let's not even go there, because…"

Frankie shushed him, her eyes signalling a warning. "Shut up, Jake."

From the door leading to the rest of the station,

Detective Chief Superintendent Adam Collier was signalling to Stella. His handsome face was stern, lips set in a straight line.

"Stella, could I have a word in private, please? My office?"

He turned on his heel and left.

"Wonder what that's all about," Jake said. "Is it true you're going to confess to being the phantom KitKat stealer?"

"Fuck off, Jake," Stella said, rising from her chair.

She reached DCS Collier's office three minutes later, knocked once, then entered, as was station protocol when summoned by a senior officer for a private chat. Usually it meant either a promotion board was coming up, or you were in the shit. But Stella hadn't heard of any vacancies for a DCI, and Collier hadn't called her "DI Cole" either, so a bollocking wasn't on the cards.

Collier was immaculate in his charcoal-grey suit. He always was. They called him "The Model" behind his back because he looked like he'd been recruited from an agency to promote a healthy and clean image of the force. His white shirt gleamed in the light from the fluorescent tube above his head, and the knot on his bright pink tie was a perfect equilateral triangle. He glanced up, found Stella's eyes and held her gaze. His smooth-shaven cheeks looked tight, and there were creases around his eyes that brought his upper lids down to darken their irises.

"Have a seat, Stella," he said in a soft voice.

"Thank you, sir," she said, frowning. "Everything okay? You heard my lot just nicked Wayne Stebbings for the Mannequin Murders?"

"Yes, yes I did. Excellent work. We can close Operation Palermo today. Really, very, I mean, yes, a great result." He looked down at his fingers. "Look, I'm afraid I have some bad news. Normally we'd have a family liaison officer here, and someone close to you, as well, but we go back, so…"

Stella's pulse suddenly began bumping in her throat, and a surge of adrenaline flushed through her body.

Oh, no. Please, God. Not Lola. Please not Lola.

"It's the worst, I'm afraid."

No. Anything but that. My house burnt down. I'm being kicked off the force.

"There was a fatal traffic accident. Richard–"

That's funny. Who turned the sound down? I can see your lips moving but I can't hear what you're saying. Why call me in about a FATACC anyway?

Stella sat very still in her chair watching as The Model's mouth opened and closed. She could hear surf roaring in her ears, waves crashing in over shingle, then *shushing* back out to sea again. Her hands gripped the hard, plastic arms until her knuckles turned the colour of bone. Slowly, oh so slowly, she let her head fall back on her neck until she was staring at the ceiling. One of the tiles had a crack in it that looked like a duck. Or maybe it was a rowing boat. Or Portugal. She drew in a deep breath. And groaned it out again. It wasn't a scream. Not as such. More like the sound of an animal in pain. Her mouth hung open, and she let the deep, wounded cry sail out from between her stretched lips.

Collier leapt to his feet and came round the desk to comfort her. He knelt in front of her and pulled her unresisting body towards him and hugged her tight. The moaning went on, even when her head flopped forward like a rag doll's, and she buried her still-open mouth in his shoulder. Frankie O'Meara appeared at the door.

"Sir?" she asked, green eyes open wide at the incongruous sight that greeted her.

"Can you help me up, please, DS O'Meara? I've just had to give Stella some bad news. The worst. And maybe take care of her? I've got an FLO coming up to talk to her but, you know, a friendly face…"

As his words tailed off, Frankie came forward. She prised Stella away from Collier and hugged her shaking body to her chest.

"Come on, Stella. Let's get you somewhere quiet where you can sit down. Then I'll run you home."

22 JULY 2009

INHABITING HER OWN body like a spirit, Stella sat on the hard, wooden bench outside the courtroom. Beside her, holding her hand in a soft grip, was her FLO, a plump, sweet-natured cockney WPC called Jaswinder Gill. It was 11.30 in the morning, and Stella's first pill of the day, washed down with a tooth mug full of white wine, was smearing her grief into something harder to get hold of and therefore less painful to bear. She'd not been able to attend any of the trial, but under Jaswinder's urging had agreed to come for the verdict.

A clerk emerged from the polished double doors.

He looked down at the two police officers.

"They're coming back."

"Come on, Stella," Jaswinder said. "Let's go."

Stella stood up, clutching Jaswinder's hand tighter.

"What if–?"

"We'll cross that bridge if we have to, OK?"

They pulled a door each and made their way to the seats reserved for friends and family of the victim. To Stella's right sat Jason Drinkwater, Richard's younger brother. His face was a mask of stone, scarred by childhood acne, betraying no emotion. He sat straight on the bench, staring ahead. As Stella slid in next to him, he unclasped his hands from his lap and held one, palm uppermost, out to his side. Gratefully, she took it. Her parents were dead, both of cancer within a year of each other. Heavy smokers. Richard's parents sat on the other side of Jason. His father, Harry, offered her a small, tight-lipped smile, leaning around his wife. She, Annette, offered no sign that she'd even noticed Stella. Her lips were pressed together, accentuating the creases around them and the vivid pink of her lipstick.

Stella looked around the courtroom. The public benches were full. The usual mixture of pensioners who fancied somewhere warm to sit for the day, the trial junkies taking notes in grubby notebooks, and, she supposed, some ordinary citizens who simply wanted to see what happened when justice was enacted in their name. Also in attendance were a fair number of journalists, including a court artist, her bony hands twitching over the paper with coloured pastels.

The whole scene felt unreal. The barristers in their grey-white wigs and black gowns like crows; the judge in her red robe and longer version of the lawyers' wig. And there, in the dock, hateful, verminous, smiling – *Why?* – was the man who'd snuffed out her husband's life: Edwin Deacon. Cheap suit in shiny blue material. Blond hair cut short and greased into shape like a sixties barber's model. He was cleaning under his fingernails with one canine tooth and then inspecting his handiwork.

With a *huff*, a door opened against a damped closer, and the jury members trooped back in to take their seats. Stella watched closely to see whether any of them would look at her, or at Deacon. A young woman, third from the front, maybe twenty-three or twenty-four, looked at Stella from under a fringe of blonde hair. Her expression was impossible to read. A sad smile that could mean, 'we've brought you closure', or 'we've let you down'. When they were seated and the hubbub that accompanied any personnel change in court had subsided, aided by a sharp word from the judge, he turned to face the jury foreman. He spoke, in a crisp, upper-class voice.

"Have you reached a verdict upon which at least ten of you agree?"

The foreman cleared his throat, then he, too, looked at Stella.

"Yes, My Lord."

"What is your verdict? Please answer only guilty or not guilty."

The silence was total. Jaswinder squeezed Stella's hand. Jason's hand was sweating against her other palm. It tightened. *I wonder what he's going to say*, Stella thought. Then, *What will I tell Lola when she's old enough?*

The stocky foreman opened his mouth. He seemed to have moved into slow motion. Stella could see the jerks between the frames as the movie played out in front of her. She watched his chest inflating inside his suit jacket and shirt as he prepared to speak. Then, with an audible *click* inside her brain, reality snapped back into focus.

"Guilty."

Sighs and gasps hissed out around her. She could hear pens scratching at the reporters' notebooks and the oily scuffing of the sketch artist's pastels on the paper. Her mother-in-law was weeping, and a wisp of her perfume – Chanel No. 5 – curled away from her and enveloped Stella. The judge spoke again.

"Is that the verdict of you all or by majority?"

"Of us all, My Lord."

"Thank you all. You have discharged your duty, which, as I said at the beginning of this trial, is one of the most sacred duties a citizen can perform. It is right and proper that you should feel proud of your contribution."

The foreman smiled at the praise, turned and nodded to the others, and sat.

The judge looked down at Deacon, who looked, if anything, bored by the proceedings that were about to engulf him. Stella's focus was slipping again, and the judge's words were overlaid with a crackle of static. She closed her eyes, but that made the feeling of floating worse.

"Edwin James Deacon, you have ... guilty of causing death by careless driving. By your thoughtless actions, you ... on this family ... remorse ... three years ... and also banned from driving ..."

Stella was breathing fast, too fast, she knew. Her heart was stuttering in her chest. She heard Jaswinder from miles away asking her if she was OK. She nodded, but that made her head swim. Across the courtroom, she saw Deacon being led from the dock. As he stepped down, he looked directly at her. His face was clear and sharp against the darkening background. He smirked. Then his lips moved. What was he saying? It looked like, "You've been bad."

Then, mercifully, the curtains swung shut, and all was black.

The months that followed passed in a haze of tranquillisers and thin-stemmed glasses of white wine. During her waking hours, one thought more than any other circled around and around inside Stella's head: *three years*. Three! People got more than that for aggravated assault. With good behaviour, Deacon could be out in two. That wasn't fair. That wasn't justice.

Somehow, she knew she was going to get herself back to work. She was going to dig into the case files and she was going to find the evidence that would see Deacon retried for murder and put away properly. Just, not yet. A pill and a glass of the old Pinot Grigio first.

To continue reading *Hit and Run*, order from Amazon here.

Published by Tyton Press, an imprint of Sunfish Ltd, PO Box 2107, Salisbury SP2 2BW: 0844 502 2061

Cover illustration copyright © Nick Castle

Author photograph © Kin Ho

Edited by Nicola Lovick

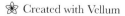 Created with Vellum

ACKNOWLEDGMENTS

I want to thank you for buying this book. I hope you enjoyed it. As an author is only part of the team of people who make a book the best it can be, this is my chance to thank the people on *my* team.

For their kindness, generosity, knowledge, and willingness to support me, thank you to:

Dr Daniel Meron, who helped me understand a little about psychiatry, and to whom I also dedicate this book.

Chris Saunby and Jen Gibbons for their insights into police procedure and the realities of 'The Job'.

Charlie Woodhouse, for briefing me on legal matters and the sights, sounds and smells of a real courtroom.

Jayne Prigent, for designing Mel's new hairstyle, and whose name I also borrowed for her fictional counterpart.

Sarah Hunt and Jo Maslen, for being my first readers.

Nicola Lovick and Liz Ward, for their brilliant copy-editing and proofreading.

The members of my Facebook Group, The Wolfe Pack, who are an incredibly supportive and also helpful bunch of people.

Nick Castle, my cover designer.

And for being a daily inspiration and source of love and laughter, and making it all worthwhile, my family: Jo, Rory and Jacob.

The responsibility for any and all mistakes in this book remains mine. I assure you, they were unintentional.

Andy Maslen
Salisbury, 2022

ABOUT THE AUTHOR

Photo © 2020 Kin Ho

Andy Maslen was born in Nottingham, England. After leaving university with a degree in psychology, he worked in business for thirty years as a copywriter. In his spare time, he plays guitar. He lives in Wiltshire.

Printed in Great Britain
by Amazon